NICOLAS MATHIEU

Nicolas Mathieu was born in 1978 in Épinal, a small town in north-eastern France. After studying history and cinema, he moved to Paris, where he worked variously as a scriptwriter, a news editor, a private tutor, and a temp at City Hall. His first novel, *Of Fangs and Talons*, won the Erckmann-Chatrian prize, the Transfuge prize and the critics' award at the Prix Mystère. His second novel, *And Their Children After Them*, was published to universal acclaim in 2018 and won various prizes including the most coveted prize in France, the Prix Goncourt. He lives in Nancy.

'I couldn't put the book down'
Thomas Chatterton Williams, *New York Times*

'A deeply felt novel, filled with characters that demand
the empathy of the reader . . . There are no villains in
the book, but there is a deep sense of humanity in all
its flaws. It's easy to see why *And Their Children After
Them* won so many awards in its native France.'
John Boyne, *Irish Times*

'*And Their Children After Them* invites comparison with the great
naturalist and realist writers of the French nineteenth century.'
Times Literary Supplement

'*And Their Children After Them* . . . finds space too for beauty,
for tenderness, for hope . . . you might think of a Ken
Loach movie with a soundtrack by Bruce Springsteen'
Boyd Tonkin, *Financial Times*

'The plot, involving drug dealing and simmering
violence . . . keeps you turning the pages'
Sunday Times

'Mathieu won France's prestigious Goncourt prize for
this absorbing Nineties narrative set in a French valley
community left stranded by the decline of industry . . .
a multi-viewpoint panorama of thwarted aspirations,
spiced with breathy sex scenes and nostalgic detail'
Mail on Sunday

and their children after them

NICOLAS MATHIEU

TRANSLATED FROM THE FRENCH
BY WILLIAM RODARMOR

SCEPTRE

Originally published in French in 2018 by
Actes Sud, Arles, France as *Leurs enfants après eux*
First published in Great Britain in 2020 by Sceptre
An Imprint of Hodder & Stoughton
An Hachette UK company

This paperback edition published in 2021

1

This book is supported by the Institut Français
(Royaume-Uni) as part of the Burgess programme.

A CIP catalogue record for this title is available from the British Library

Paperback ISBN 9781529303865
eBook ISBN 9781529303841

Printed and bound in Great Britain by Clays Ltd, Elcograf S.p.A.

Hodder & Stoughton policy is to use papers that are natural, renewable
and recyclable products and made from wood grown in sustainable
forests. The logging and manufacturing processes are expected to
conform to the environmental regulations of the country of origin.

Hodder & Stoughton Ltd
Carmelite House
50 Victoria Embankment
London EC4Y 0DZ

www.sceptrebooks.co.uk

N. M. For Oscar

W. R. For Toby

There are others who are not remembered,

as if they had never lived,

who died and were forgotten,

they, and their children after them.

SIRACH 44:9

1

Anthony stood on the shore and stared.

With the sun directly overhead, the lake's water looked as dense as oil. Every so often, the passage of a carp or a pike broke its velvety surface. The boy sniffed. The air was heavy with the smell of mud, of leaden, baked earth. July had scattered freckles across his already broad back. He was just wearing football shorts and a pair of fake Ray-Bans. It was hot as hell, but that didn't explain everything.

Anthony had just turned fourteen. He could devour an entire baguette with Vache qui Rit cheese as a snack. At night, wearing headphones, he sometimes wrote songs. His parents were idiots. When school started, he would be in year 10.

Lying next to him, his cousin was taking it easy. He was half asleep, stretched out on the nice towel they'd bought at the Calvi market the year they went to summer camp. Even lying down, he looked tall. Everyone thought he was at least twenty-two or -three. He used that assumption to get into places he shouldn't. Bars, nightclubs, girls.

Anthony took a cigarette from the pack he'd slipped into his shorts and asked his cousin if he didn't agree that they were bored out of their skulls.

3

His cousin didn't stir. You could make out the exact outline of the muscles under his skin. From time to time a fly landed near the fold of his armpit. Then he would twitch, like a horse bothered by a horsefly. Anthony would've liked to be like that, slim, with well-defined abs. But he wasn't the type. Despite doing press-ups and sit-ups in his bedroom every night, he remained square and massive, like a slab of beef. At school, one of the monitors once gave him some shit about a burst football. Anthony told him to meet him after class. The guy never showed up. Also, his cousin's Ray-Bans were real.

Anthony lit his cigarette and sighed. The cousin knew perfectly well what he wanted. For days now, Anthony had been pestering him to go over to the 'bare-arse' beach. They'd dubbed it that in an excess of optimism because you might see girls topless there, at the very least. Anyway, Anthony was completely obsessed.

'C'mon, let's go there.'

'Nah,' muttered his cousin.

'C'mon. Please.'

'Not now. Just go for a swim.'

'Yeah, sure...'

Anthony looked out at the water with his crooked eye. His right eyelid drooped lazily, and it threw his face off, making him look perpetually grumpy. One of those things that was out of whack. Like the heat enveloping him, like his taut, off-kilter body, his size ten feet, and the spots sprouting all over his face. Go for a swim, the cousin had said. What a laugh. Anthony spat between his teeth.

A year earlier, a boy called Colin had drowned on 14 July – Bastille Day, easy to remember. That night a crowd of people from the surrounding area had gathered on the lakeshore and in the woods to watch the fireworks. People lit campfires and barbecues. As usual, a fight broke out shortly after midnight. Guys on leave from the barracks went after the Arabs from the estates, and the Hennicourt inbreds waded in. Then the regular campers got involved, most of them young, but a few fathers, too, Belgians with big bellies and sunburn. Dawn revealed greasy paper, bloody sticks, broken bottles, even one of the sailing club's Optimists stuck in a tree; not something you saw every day. The boy called Colin, on the other hand, was nowhere to be found.

He'd definitely spent the evening at the lakeshore, though. That was confirmed because he went with his mates, who all testified later. Ordinary kids with names like Arnaud, Alexandre and Sébastien, who'd just passed their baccalaureate exam and didn't even have driving licences. They'd come to watch the usual fights without intending to get personally involved, except at one point they got caught up in the melee. After that, everything was kind of vague. Several witnesses said they'd seen a boy who'd seemed hurt. People mentioned a T-shirt covered with blood, and also a cut on his throat, like a mouth revealing dark, liquid depths. In the confusion, nobody stepped forward to help him. Come morning, the boy's bed was empty.

The prefect ordered a search of the neighbouring woods over the following days, while divers dragged the lake. For hours, onlookers watched as the firefighters' orange Zodiac came and went. The divers tumbled backwards out of it with a distant splash, and then you had to wait, in dead silence.

They said that the boy's mother was in the hospital, on sedatives. Others that she'd hanged herself. Or that she'd been seen wandering the streets in her nightgown. The boy's father was a town cop, and he was also a hunter. Everyone naturally thought the Arabs had done the deed, so people kind of hoped for a settling of scores. He was the stocky guy who stayed aboard the firefighters' boat, bareheaded in the blazing sun. People watched him from shore, watched his immobility, his unbearable calm and his slowly ripening scalp. They found his patience disgusting, somehow. They would've liked him to do something, move at least, put on a cap.

What really upset people was the picture published in the newspaper later. In the photo, the boy called Colin had a nice face, graceless and pale; a good face for a victim, actually. His hair was curly on the sides, his eyes were brown, and he was wearing a red T-shirt. The article said he had passed his baccalaureate exam with top honours. If you knew his family, that was quite an accomplishment. Just goes to show, said Anthony's father.

In the end, the body was never found, and Colin's father went back to work without making a fuss. His wife hadn't hanged herself or anything. She just took pills.

Anyway, Anthony had no desire to go swimming. His cigarette hit the water's surface with a little hiss. He looked up at the sky, then frowned, dazzled. For a fraction of a second, his eyelids were in balance. The sun was high; it must have been three o'clock. The cigarette left an unpleasant taste on his tongue. Time was dragging by, but at the same time the start of classes was approaching at top speed.

'Oh, fuck it,' said the cousin, standing up. 'You're such a drag.'

'We're bored, like big time. Nothing to do, every day.'

'All right, then.'

His cousin draped his towel around his shoulders and climbed onto his mountain bike, ready to take off.

'C'mon, move your arse. We're going over there.'

'Where?'

'Move it, I said.'

Anthony jammed his towel into his old Chevignon backpack, retrieved his watch from a trainer, and quickly got dressed. He'd barely got his BMX upright before his cousin disappeared down the road around the lake.

'Wait for me, for fuck's sake!'

Ever since they were kids, Anthony had followed his cousin everywhere. Their mothers had been close as well, when they were younger. The Mougel girls, people called them. They'd been picking up the cutest boys at the canton's dances for a long time before they eventually settled down with Mr Right. Hélène, Anthony's mother, chose one of the Casati sons. Irène did even worse. The Mougel girls, their men, cousins and in-laws were all part of the same world, anyway. To see it in action, you could just check out the weddings, the funerals and the Christmas festivities. The men said little and died young. The women dyed their hair and looked at life with gradually fading optimism. When they got old, they retained the memory of their men, beaten down on the job, at bars

6

or sick with silicosis, and their sons dead in car crashes, not counting the ones who packed up and left.

His cousin's mother, Irène, also belonged to that category of abandoned wives, so he grew up fast. At sixteen, he knew how to mow the lawn, drive without a licence, and cook. He was even allowed to smoke in his bedroom. He was bold and self-confident. Anthony would have followed him into hell. He, on the other hand, felt increasingly alienated from his family's ways. He found them awfully small in their stature, their jobs, their hopes, even their misfortunes, which were common and predictable. Among those people you got fired, divorced, cheated on or cancer. In other words, you were normal, and everything beyond that was seen as relatively unacceptable. Families grew that way, on great slabs of anger over depths of accumulated pain that, lubricated by pastis, could suddenly erupt in the middle of a party. More and more, Anthony thought himself above all that. He dreamed of getting the fuck out.

When they reached the old railway line, the cousin ditched his bike in the bushes. Crouching down on the tracks, he studied the Léo-Lagrange recreation centre, which lay below the railway embankment. The boathouse was wide open, and there wasn't a soul in sight. Anthony left his BMX and joined him.

'No one's around,' said his cousin. 'We're gonna grab a canoe and go.'

'You sure?'

'Well, we sure aren't gonna swim there.'

His cousin sprinted down the bank, pushing through the brambles and weeds. Anthony followed. He was scared; it felt great.

Once in the boathouse it took them a few moments to get used to the darkness. There were dinghies, a 420 and some canoes hanging from a metal rack. Life jackets on hangers gave off a strong mouldy smell. The wide-open doors were like a movie screen cut in the damp shadows, showing the beach and the sparkling lake in the flat land beyond.

'C'mon, we'll take this one.'

Moving in tandem, they unhooked the canoe the cousin had chosen and grabbed some paddles. They paused a moment before leaving the coolness of the boathouse. It felt good. A windsurfer cut a clear wake on the lake's surface in the distance. No one was coming. Anthony could feel the heady dizziness that comes before doing something stupid. It was like when he shoplifted at the Prisu or pulled risky stunts on a motorbike.

'Okay. Let's go,' said his cousin.

With the canoe on their shoulders and paddles in hand, they took off running.

The Léo-Lagrange centre mostly hosted well-behaved kids whose parents parked them there while waiting for school to start. That way, instead of getting into trouble in town, the kids could go horse riding and ride pedal boats. There was a party at the end, and everyone would hide away to kiss and drink on the sly. The cooler boys were sometimes even able to score with a counsellor. But the group always included a few weirdos, tough kids from the countryside who'd been raised on horse-whippings. If those guys got hold of you, things could get ugly. Anthony tried not to think about that too much. The canoe was heavy. He had to make it as far as the shore, thirty metres away, tops. The boat's gunwale was cutting into his shoulder. He gritted his teeth. But just then his cousin tripped on a root, and the canoe nose-dived. Stumbling behind him, Anthony felt his hand snag on something sharp, a splinter or something sticking out inside. He knelt down and looked at his open palm. It was bleeding. His cousin was already back on his feet.

'C'mon, we don't have time.'

'Just a second. I hurt myself.'

He put the wound to his lips. The taste of blood filled his mouth.

'Hurry!'

Voices were approaching. The boys jogged on, awkwardly lugging the boat, watching their feet. Carried by their momentum, they went into the water up to their waists. Anthony thought of his cigarettes and the Walkman in his backpack.

'Get in!' said his cousin, pushing the canoe away from shore.

'Hey there!' yelled someone behind them.

The voice was sharp and male. Other shouts followed, getting closer. 'Hey, you! Come back here!'

Anthony hauled himself into the canoe as best he could. His cousin gave one last shove and climbed aboard in turn. On the lakeshore behind them, two counsellors and a girl in a swimming costume were yelling.

'Paddle! We're on our way now. Let's go!'

After some hesitation, the boys found their rhythm, with Anthony paddling on the port side, and the cousin to starboard. A crowd of yelling, excited kids gathered on the beach. Counsellors ran into the boathouse and came out carrying three canoes.

Fortunately, the cousins' boat was cutting across the lake's surface with reassuring smoothness. They could feel the water's resistance in their shoulders and a heady sensation of speed under their feet. Anthony noticed a streak of blood snaking down his forearm. He put his paddle down for a moment.

'You okay?' asked his cousin.

'It's nothing.'

'You sure?'

'Yeah.'

Red drops falling between Anthony's feet made an outline of a Mickey Mouse head. A thin, open cut ran across his palm. He brought it to his mouth.

'Paddle!' shouted his cousin.

The boats pursuing them carried two or three people apiece, including grown-ups. They weren't that far behind, and Anthony began paddling harder than ever. The sun beat down on the dark lake waters, making a million white flashes. He could feel sweat running down his forehead and along his ribs. On his back, his T-shirt stuck to him like a second skin. He was worried. Maybe they had called the police.

'What are we going to do?'

'They won't follow us.'

'You sure?'

'Paddle, for fuck's sake!'

9

After a while the cousin changed direction, now hugging the shore. He hoped to quickly reach Le Pointu, the thin spit of land that divided the lake in two. Once they rounded that point, they would be out of sight for a few minutes.

'Look,' he said.

On the neighbouring beaches, bathers had stood up to see better and were whistling or shouting encouragement. Anthony and his cousin were in the habit of always going to the same place, a fairly accessible beach called the Déchetterie – the dump. It was said to be near a sewer outlet, which was why there were so few people there, even in mid-season. The lake had other beaches. The Léo-Lagrange one was behind them. The campground beach was over there. Further on was the American beach, where the inbreds hung out. On the far side of the Pointu spit, the sailing club had the prettiest beach of all, with pine trees, almost golden sand, huts and a bar, like at the seaside.

'We're getting there,' said his cousin.

A hundred metres ahead on the right, an old, tumbledown forest service cabin marked the beginning of the Pointu. The boys turned round to see how far behind their pursuers were. They didn't seem to be catching up, and the counsellors appeared to be having a big discussion. Even from a distance, the boys could tell they were irritated and arguing. At one moment someone stood up to make a point, and someone else made them sit back down. They finally turned back towards the recreation centre. The cousins grinned at each other and Anthony allowed himself to give them the finger, now that their backs were turned.

'So what do we do now?'

'What do you think?'

'They're going to call the police for sure.'

'So what? Paddle!'

They continued on their way through the reeds, staying close to shore. It was past four, and the light wasn't as blinding. The sound of croaking rose from the mass of leaves and branches tangling the bank. Hoping to see frogs, Anthony kept his eye on the water's surface.

'Your hand okay?'

'Yeah. Are we going to be there soon?'

'Ten minutes.'

'Fuck! This was really far!'

'I told you. Just think about the bare arses.'

Anthony could already imagine the place, as sort of like the porn section at the video store. He would sometimes slip in there, his belly tense with fear, looking at as much as he could before some adult came to kick him out. The urge to see girls' bodies was overwhelming and constant. He kept magazines and videotapes in his drawers and under his bed, not to mention tissues. His pals at school were all the same way, totally obsessed. It was making them crazy. That explained most of the fights, now that he thought of it. One wrong look in a hallway would set them off, and suddenly they were at it, struggling with each other, rolling around on the tiles and yelling every name in the book. Some of the guys managed to go out with girls. Anthony had kissed a girl once, in the back of the bus. But she wouldn't let him touch her breasts, so he dropped her. He was sorry now. Her name was Sandra; she had blue eyes and a nice arse in her C17 jeans.

He was drawn from his ruminations by exhaust noises coming from behind the trees. He and his cousin immediately froze. People were coming their way. Anthony easily recognised the recreation centre's Piwi 50s, cranky little motocross trikes. The centre had long offered motorbike activities, which had made it successful, much more than paddleball and orienteering courses.

'They're driving around the lake on the road.'

'Looking for us, for sure.'

'They shouldn't be able to see us, though.'

Just the same, the cousins weren't taking any chances. Hearts pounding, they crouched down in their canoe and listened.

'Get rid of your T-shirt,' muttered the cousin.

'What?'

'Your T-shirt. You can spot it a mile away.'

Anthony pulled his Chicago Bulls top over his head and slipped it under his bum. The sharp chatter of the motorbikes hovered above their heads like a bird of prey. The boys kept quiet, impatient and motionless. A sweetish smell rose from the rotting vegetation on the water's surface. Mingling with their sweat, it made them itch. Anthony shuddered at the thought of all the things crawling in the swampy water.

'We're gonna get there too late,' he said.

'Shut up.'

The motorbikes eventually drove away, leaving a vague quavering echo. Stealthily, the boys paddled onwards. When they rounded the Pointu spit, the horizon widened to reveal the other half of the lake. The famous bare-arse beach was finally in sight off to starboard. It was grey and enclosed, inaccessible from the road – and nearly deserted. A motorboat was at anchor some thirty metres offshore.

It had been a complete waste of time.

'Fuck, there's no one here,' moaned Anthony.

They actually spied two girls, but they were wearing bikinis, even the tops. From a distance it was hard to tell if they were pretty or not.

'So what do we do?'

'As long as we're here...'

They got closer, and the girls began to stir restlessly. The boys could now see that they were very young, and nervous; worried, mainly. The smaller one stood up to call to the motorboat. Standing in the water, she whistled between her teeth very loudly, but without success. She ran back to her beach towel and sat close to her friend.

'They're scared,' said Anthony.

'And you're not?'

The cousins landed, pulled the canoe onshore, and sat down near the water's edge. They couldn't think of what else to do, so they lit cigarettes. They hadn't exchanged a glance with the other people there. Mostly they were aware of their presence behind them, their dull, impenetrable hostility. Anthony now sort of felt like leaving. But at the same time, it would be a pity, after all the trouble they'd taken. They should've known how to go about it better.

After a few minutes the girls gathered up their things at the other end of the beach. They were really pretty, actually, with ponytails and girls' legs, bums, tits – the works. They started calling to the motorboat again. Anthony shot little glances their way. He felt bad to be bothering them like this.

'That's the Durupt girl,' whispered his cousin.

'Which one?'

'The smaller one, in the white.'

'What about the other girl?'

His cousin didn't know that one, but you couldn't miss her. A neat, heavy figure from her neck to her ankles. Her hair, which was tied very high, tumbled down with a terrific impression of weight. Her bikini was laced across her hips. It probably left distinct lines on her skin when it was untied. Her arse especially, was incredible.

'Yeah...' agreed his cousin, who could sometimes read minds.

Eventually, the people in the boat responded. They turned out to be a couple, an athletic-looking guy and a woman so blonde it almost hurt your eyes. They quickly pulled themselves together, and the guy yanked hard on the starter cord. The boat swung round with a long whine like a food blender and reached the beach in no time. The guy asked the girls if they were okay, and they said yes. Meanwhile, the blonde was staring at the cousins as if they'd just ridden through her bedroom on a moped. Anthony noticed that the guy was wearing brand-new Nike Airs and hadn't even bothered to take them off before jumping into the water. He was now striding towards them, followed by the girls. You could tell he was determined to lay down the law. The cousin stood up to face him, then Anthony did, too.

'What the hell are you doing here?'

'Nothing.'

'So what do you want?'

This was a slippery slope. The guy wasn't as tall as the cousin, but he looked tough and confident. He wasn't about to drop things just like that. Anthony had already clenched his fists. But his cousin defused the situation with a word.

'Do you have any rolling papers?' he asked.

Nobody had an answer for that. Anthony was standing with his head cocked at an angle, a habit he'd picked up to hide his lazy eye. His cousin pulled out a wet package of rolling papers.

'I dropped mine in the water.'

'You have something to smoke?' asked the guy in surprise.

Anthony's cousin took a Kodak film canister from his pocket and rattled the little ball of hash inside. Abruptly, everyone relaxed, especially the man. Without even noticing, they began to mingle. The guy had rolling papers. Now he was all excited.

'Where did you score that? There's nothing available right now.'

'I have some weed, too,' said the cousin. 'You interested?'

Clearly, yes. Two weeks earlier the local police had been messed around by the kids in the ZUP housing estate. As payback, they launched a raid after a tip-off on some apartments in the Degas tower. Word was that half the Meryem family was more or less in jail, and you couldn't make a single score in the whole town. In the middle of the summer, that was seriously shit.

Other networks were thrown together, fast. The inbreds were making round trips to Maastricht, and the cousin had set up a thing with some Belgians in the campground – two brothers with piercings who spent their time doing E while listening to techno music. As luck would have it, they were spending two weeks in Heillange on a family holiday. Thanks to them, a shuttle from Mons brought Dutch skunk and something like Moroccan Red that made you feel like dunking biscuits in warm milk and watching Meg Ryan movies. The cousin was selling it around the Grappe housing development at twice the normal price, a hundred francs a gram. The consumers bitched a little but preferred to pay up rather than stay straight.

When Anthony took a last ride around the neighbourhood on his bicycle in the evening, he could catch the smell of that special dope filtering out through half-open skylights. Up in the attic, kids barely older than him were getting bombed while playing *Street Fighter*. On the ground floor, their father was watching *Intervilles* with a beer in his hand.

The cousin lit a three-sheet blunt and handed it to the guy, whose name was Alex and who was becoming more and more friendly. Then it was Anthony's turn. He took a few hits and passed it on. He knew the Durupt girl by name. Her father was a doctor and she had a reputation of being fairly brazen. It was said she'd even wrecked her old man's BMW one Saturday evening, which was pretty remarkable for someone who didn't even have a learner's permit. She put out, too. Looking at her, Anthony imagined doing things.

By contrast, the other girl had appeared out of nowhere. She'd plopped down right next to him, which is how he noticed her freckles, the fuzz on her thighs, and the drop of sweat sliding from her navel down to the waistband of her bikini bottoms.

Right away, his cousin rolled another blunt, and Alex bought two hundred francs' worth of skunk from him. Everybody was nice and relaxed now, laughing easily, their mouths dry. The girls, who had brought bottles of Vittel water, handed them around.

'We mainly came here to see topless girls.'

'What you heard was bullshit. Nobody ever gets naked here.'

'Maybe they used to.'

'Maybe you want us to strip?'

Anthony turned to his neighbour, the girl who had asked the question. She was full of surprises. At first glance she gave an impression of passivity, of almost animal indifference. Seeing her like that, lazy and vague, you'd imagine her sitting on a station platform waiting for a train. But she was also a smart-arse, funny and determined to have a good time. She'd pretty much dozed off after the first joint. She smelled really good, too.

'Hey, listen to that!'

In the distance you could hear the whine of 50cc engines, the same ones as before, with their high notes and deep backfires.

'They're looking for us.'

'Who?'

'The guys from the recreation centre.'

'Wow, they're hotheads this year!'

'What do you mean?'

'The fires, that was them.'

'No, it wasn't. That was the inbreds.'

'So what are they after?'

'The canoe. We swiped it from the centre.'

'No shit, you really did that?'

They laughed for a good long time, feeling sheltered, stoned and relaxed. The heat had dropped and something soft, a smell of charcoal, woods and parched pine trees, rose to their nostrils. The setting sun had quietened the insects, leaving only the lapping of the lake, the distant hum of the motorway, and bursts of two-stroke engines occasionally ripping the air. The girls had put on T-shirts and removed their bikini tops. You could see their breasts moving under the fabric. They didn't care, and the boys pretended not to care either. Anthony eventually took off his sunglasses. At one point he caught his neighbour trying to make sense of his off-kilter face. Then, a little after six o'clock, the girls began to get impatient and restless. It was probably time to go home. When the girl sitting on the ground close to Anthony got up, her knee brushed his. A girl feels really soft; it's something you never really get used to.

This one was called Stéphanie Chaussoy.

That was the summer Anthony turned fourteen. It all had to start somewhere.

2

Having hidden the canoe, the two boys rode their bikes home through the Petit-Fougeray woods. As usual, Anthony played at slaloming between the dashes on the centre line, a habit that gave his cousin fits. While climbing the hill near the warehouses a few days earlier, Anthony found himself facing an oncoming VW bus. The driver had had to swerve aside. When his cousin asked if that wasn't a little stupid, Anthony said he had the right of way.

'What right of way? You were in the middle of the road!'

At times, Anthony drove him crazy. It made you wonder if he was really all there.

But the road was empty now and the boys pedalled fast, facing the sun, followed by their shadows. After the afternoon heat, the surrounding woods seemed to sigh and relax. The declining day felt like a countdown, because Alex had invited them somewhere. A friend was throwing a big party at his parents' place, and Anthony and his cousin were welcome to drop by, provided they brought their dope, of course. The festivities were supposed to take place in a big house with a pool. There would be booze, girls, music and a midnight swim. Anthony and his cousin said okay, they would see what they could do. Being cool seemed to require a lot of concentration.

Problem was, the party in question would be in Drimblois, a forty-kilometre round trip, and by bike. That is, unless they borrowed Anthony's father's Yamaha YZ. The motorbike had been languishing under a tarpaulin in the back of their garage for years. But it wasn't even worth considering. Anthony didn't mind facing an oncoming VW bus, but dealing with his old man was no joke.

'Who cares? He won't even notice,' argued his cousin.

'No, it's too risky,' said Anthony. 'We'll just have to do it by bike.'

'C'mon, it's already seven o'clock, it'll be a lost cause.'

'I can't! I mean it. He'd kill me if I took his motorbike. You don't know him.'

In fact, his cousin knew Patrick Casati pretty well. He wasn't a bad guy, but sometimes just a finger smudge on the TV screen could put him in a mood that was painful to watch. The worst part came later, when he realised what he had done. Embarrassed, paralysed with guilt, unable to apologise, he would try to win forgiveness by talking quietly and offering to dry the dishes. Anthony's mother, Hélène, had packed her bags and gone to stay with her sister several times. When she came back, life resumed as if nothing had happened. Still, a kind of heaviness hung between them, something that didn't give you much of a taste for family life.

'Your sweetie will be there,' the cousin insisted. 'We gotta go.'

'Who do you mean?'

'Oh, come off it. You know very well.'

'Yeah...'

Stéphanie was already like one of those jingles that get stuck in your head and drive you crazy. Anthony's life had been turned upside down. Nothing had moved, but nothing was where it used to be. He was suffering; it felt good.

'That girl is something else, no kidding.'

'Yeah, sure is.'

His cousin chuckled. He recognised the look on Anthony's face. It was the same as when he was thirteen and had a crush on Natasha Glassman, a girl with different-coloured eyes who wore Kickers. Stung, Anthony stood up on his bike, needing to burn off all his extra energy. Pedalling out of the saddle, he sped off – in the middle of the road, of course.

The cousin lived with his mother and sister in a narrow, two-storey terraced house with a peeling stucco facade and geraniums in the windows. When they got there, the boys ditched their bikes in the gravel and ran inside. In the living room, his cousin's mother was watching *Santa Barbara*. She had a habit of raising the TV's volume to the max, so Cruz Castillo's voice took on a somewhat unexpected prophetic dimension. Hearing them race up the stairs, she yelled:

'Take your shoes off before going up there!'

Because there was carpeting upstairs, of course. Reaching the landing, Anthony glanced into his cousin Carine's room. The door was ajar and he could see someone in short shorts sitting on the floor with her legs extended: Vanessa. The insults started flying right away: you virgin, little weirdo, wanker. Carine was eighteen and hung out with Vanessa, who was only sixteen. The two friends spent all their time together, bad-mouthing people, doing nothing and imagining sad love stories for themselves. In summertime they combined these activities with tanning their bare breasts in the Léonards' garden. Vanessa's father would pop by unannounced from time to time. The girls laughed it off, but Vanessa thought it was kind of creepy. What they didn't know was that Anthony, who lived in the same housing development, sometimes spied on them through the hedge. They were a pair of real snakes, and he was careful to keep his distance. He now beat a retreat before they came after him physically. It had happened before. They were pretty tough.

Once in his cousin's room, he flopped down on the bed. The place was right under the roof and hot as hell, despite the fan. The walls had shelves of VHS tapes, some *Baywatch* photos, and a poster of Bruce Lee, looking very relaxed for once. Plus a big TV in a fake wood case, a four-track video player, and an empty aquarium that a neurasthenic python had once briefly occupied. Strewn in the corners were dirty socks, motorbike magazines, empty beer cans and a baseball bat. His cousin was already rolling a two-sheet joint.

'This is so lame.'

'Yeah.'

'So what do we do?'

'I dunno.'

They stayed like that for a while, taking turns toking, not doing anything except thinking, while the fan dispersed the smoke. They looked at each other, sweaty and on edge.

'For once we have a thing to do.'

'Yeah, but my dad'll tear me a new one if I touch his ride.'

'That girl is something else, though.'

'I just can't do it, I'm telling you.'

Anthony was feeling upset. His cousin knew how to get to him.

'What's the worst that could happen to you? Nine times out of ten, he'll never even notice. He doesn't give a shit about that bike any more.'

That was partly true. Anthony's father didn't want to hear about the motorbike. It brought back too many memories, things he'd given up, things that felt like his freedom. Not that this changed the prohibition; quite the contrary. Absent-mindedly, Anthony touched his right eyelid. He'd got some smoke in his eye.

'What do you really want?' asked his cousin.

'What are you talking about?'

'You've never gone out with a girl.'

'Sure I have!'

'Oh, your story about the back of the bus, give me a break. And the Glassman girl, you bored us with her for two years, and in the end: diddly squat.'

Anthony felt his throat tighten. He'd thought about that girl constantly from year five till the end of year eight. In class he always tried to sit closest to her. During gym, he gazed at her with the eyes of a beaten dog. He made mixtapes from the radio dedicated to her: Scorpions, Daniel Balavoine, Johnny Hallyday. He'd gone so far as to ride his bike around her neighbourhood. But in the end, he hadn't even dared ask if she wanted to go out with him. Cyril Medranet, the maths teacher's son, eventually scored with her. Anthony wanted to smash his face in but had to settle for swiping his backpack and tossing it into the Henne. He'd got over her. She was a bitch, anyway.

'Well, I guess that's that.'

His cousin took a last drag and stubbed out the joint, then turned on the Mega Drive. It was all over. Anthony could've wept.

'Oh, fuck it all!'

He jumped off the bed, ran out of the room, and sprinted down the stairs. He'd rather risk a beating than face yet another evening getting wasted and playing *Sonic* while girls were drinking, being picked up, and letting other tongues play with theirs. Having made up his mind, he raced towards home on his BMX. But at the end of the street he saw Carine and Vanessa coming back from Derch with shopping bags full of beer. They were in his way, so Anthony slowed, then put a foot down.

'Where are you off to?'

'What's your hurry?'

'Hey, look at me when I'm talking to you.'

Vanessa lifted his chin. She and Carine both wore their hair long, with one strand held back with a barrette. They were wearing vest tops, short shorts and flip-flops, and they smelled of coconut oil. A gold chain glittered at Vanessa's ankle. Anthony noticed that his cousin Carine wasn't wearing a bra. She was a good size 36C, which he knew from snooping in her bedroom when she wasn't there.

'So where are you going?' repeated Vanessa, trapping the BMX's front wheel between her legs to keep him from leaving.

'Home.'

'So soon?'

'What're you gonna do?'

'What are you looking at?'

'Nothing...'

Anthony felt himself blushing. He lowered his eyes again.

'You little perv! You want to see if I have a tan line?'

Vanessa showed him the lighter skin on her hip. Anthony backed away to free his wheel.

'I have to get going.'

'Come on, don't do your little queer number.'

Carine, who had already started drinking one of the beers, stood behind him, giggling. But she came to his rescue anyway.

'It's okay. Leave him alone.'

She took another swig of beer, and some of the liquid glistened on her chin. Anthony tried to free himself again but Vanessa wouldn't let him go.

'Oh, Anthony,' she simpered, touching his cheek with her palm. Her hand felt surprisingly cool, especially the fingertips. It made him feel all strange. She smiled at him, then burst out laughing.

'All right, get out of here.'

He turned tail and fled.

Anthony could feel their eyes on his back for a moment, and went through the stop sign before turning onto rue Clément-Hader. It was completely empty at this time of night and ran steeply downtown. On the horizon, the sky had taken on exaggerated colours. Feeling exalted, he let go of the handlebars and spread his arms. The speed whipped the sides of his T-shirt. He closed his eyes for a moment, the wind whistling in his ears. Through this half-dead, strangely beaten-up town, built on a hillside and underneath a bridge, Anthony picked up speed, feeling the thrill of the moment, his very youth pulsing through his veins.

3

Anthony immediately recognised old man Grandemange's laugh. The neighbours were probably having a drink with his parents on the patio. He walked around the house to join them. The Casati house was one storey high with nothing around it except a dying lawn, where the boy's footsteps made a sound like crunching paper. Fed up with weeding and maintaining it, Patrick Casati had doused everything with Roundup. Ever since, he'd been free to watch Grand Prix racing on Sundays in peace. Along with Clint Eastwood films and *The Guns of Navarone*, that was pretty much all that could soothe his heart. Anthony didn't have much in common with his dad, but at least they had that: television, motorsports and war films. Sitting in the darkened living room, each in his own corner, was the most intimacy they allowed themselves.

Anthony's parents had had just one ambition their whole lives: to ultimately have their own house. And for better or worse, they had succeeded. Only twenty years of mortgage payments remained before they really owned it. The walls were plasterboard, and the roof was sloped, like any place where it rains half the time. In the winter, electric heating produced a little warmth and phenomenal bills. Aside from that, they had two bedrooms, a kitchen diner, a leather sofa and a sideboard with embroidered linens. Anthony felt at home there, most of the time.

'Hey, it's the handsomest of them all!'

Évelyne Grandemange spotted him first. She'd known Anthony since he was little. He had even taken his first steps in their driveway.

'To think that he took his first steps in our driveway,' she said now.

Her husband confirmed this with a nod. The Grappe housing development was more than fifteen years old now. It was sort of like living in a village. Anthony's father looked at his watch.

'Where were you?'

He said he'd spent the afternoon with his cousin.

'I stopped by the Schmidts' this morning,' said his father.

'I finished everything before I left.'

'Yes, but you forgot your gloves. Come and sit down.'

The grown-ups were sitting on folding chairs around a plastic garden table. They were nursing Picon-bières, except for Évelyne, who was drinking port.

'You smell like mud,' remarked Anthony's mother.

'We went swimming.'

'I thought you said it was disgusting there, with all that sewer water. You're going to get spots.'

'It won't kill him,' said Patrick.

'Go on, get yourself a chair,' said Hélène.

As a joke, Luc Grandemange waved Anthony over to sit on his lap, slapping his thigh.

'Give it a try, it can take it.'

The man was a good six feet tall, with hands hard as wood that were missing three fingertips. To hunt, he used a special rifle with a trigger he could pull with his ring finger. He was a compulsive joker who wasn't especially funny. Anthony knew a lot of guys like that, who told jokes more to be sociable than anything else.

'Thanks, but I'm not staying.'

'Where are you off to?'

Anthony turned to his father, whose face had stiffened. When that happened, the skin tightened and looked like rather handsome suede.

'Tomorrow is Saturday,' answered Anthony.

Luc intervened: 'Leave him alone, he's on holiday.'

Anthony's father sighed. Back in the day, Patrick Casati and Luc Grandemange had worked at the Rexel warehouse, shortly after the blast furnaces shut down. They were part of a group of men who retired voluntarily and took the training programme to become forklift operators. At the time, it seemed like a good opportunity; driving forklifts all day long almost felt like playing a game. But since then, Patrick had had problems. He lost his job and his driving licence the same day, and for the same reason. He was able to get his licence back after six months of administrative hassles and a spell in rehab with the Croix Bleue. But work was scarce in the valley, and he finally decided to start his own business. He bought an Iveco dumper truck, a mower, tools, and some overalls with his name embroidered on the front. Nowadays he did small jobs here and there, mainly paid under the table. In good months he could bring in four or five thousand francs. With Hélène's salary, they mostly made ends meet. Summer was the busy season, and he'd pressed Anthony into service mowing lawns and cleaning swimming pools. The help was especially useful when he had a hangover. Anthony had had to trim the shrubs at Dr Schmidt's place that morning.

His father finally took a beer from the cooler at his feet, opened it, and held it out to him.

'All he thinks about is going out.'

'It's his age,' said Luc philosophically.

Grandemange's T-shirt revealed some of his belly, a pale, fairly revolting mass. He was already getting up to give Anthony his chair.

'Here, sit for a second. Talk to us.'

'He's got even taller, hasn't he?' said Évelyne.

Hélène insisted in turn that Anthony stay for a while. The house wasn't a hotel, she reminded him. With every second that passed, he was missing a little of the Drimblois party.

'Whatever did you do to your hand?'

'It's nothing.'

'Did you disinfect it?'

'I told you, it's nothing.'

'Go and get yourself a chair,' said his father.

Anthony looked at him. Thinking about the motorbike, he obeyed. His mother followed him into the kitchen. He would have to endure a swab with rubbing alcohol and a bandage.

'Don't bother, it's nothing.'

'I have a cousin who lost a finger that way.'

His mother was always coming out with edifying anecdotes like that: carelessness turned tragic, bright futures cut short by leukaemia. Over time, it had practically become a philosophy of life.

'Here, let me see.'

He displayed his bandaged hand; it was perfect. They could go back onto the patio.

There, they drank a toast, and Évelyne started asking him questions. She wanted to know how things were at school, and how he was spending his holiday. Anthony answered evasively, and she listened with a benevolent, nicotine-stained smile. She'd brought two packs of Gauloises for the evening. Whenever there was a pause in the conversation you could hear her breathing, a hoarse, familiar whistle. Then she would light a fresh cigarette. At one point Anthony's father wanted to drive a big wasp away that was buzzing around the Apéricube wrappers. When it wouldn't leave, he fetched an electric fly zapper. This produced a *bzzt!* sound, a burnt smell and a wasp on its back.

'That's really disgusting,' said Hélène.

Patrick's only response was to down his Picon and take another beer from the cooler. They started to talk about the accident that had just happened in Furiani with the neighbour. Grandemange said he didn't find the carnage especially surprising. He'd seen what Corsicans were like on building sites, he said with a laugh. As they often did, they talked about football, Corsicans and wogs. Évelyne moved away; she didn't like it when her husband got started with that kind of talk. It must be said that the police's recent misadventures had rattled the development. The ZUP housing estate wasn't that far away. People could already imagine Arabs in hoodies setting cars on fire, like in Vaulx-en-Vélin. Luc and Patrick couldn't help pointing out the increasing danger, with themselves as the last line of defence.

'You're the one who ought to go over there,' said the big man, gesturing to Anthony with his chin.

'We have problems with those people all the time,' said his father.

'When I was a volunteer with the fire department, we had calls to the ZUP. Little niggers no taller than this would try to swipe the keys to our truck.'

'So what then?'

'Then nothing; we put out the fire. What could you do?'

'That was your mistake.'

They laughed, but not Anthony, who had stood up so he could slip away.

'Where are you going?'

This time it was Hélène, his mother, who stopped him.

'I've gotta go.'

'Who with?'

'My cousin.'

'Did you see Irène?'

The sisters hardly saw each other any more. Some business over a mortgage on the house Irène occupied that the sisters had inherited. Money problems, as usual.

'Yeah.'

'So how is she?'

'I don't know, fine.'

'Meaning what?'

'I told you, fine.'

'Oh, all right. Go on then, if you're going to be unpleasant.'

His father didn't stir. He and Luc were already pouring themselves fresh glasses of Picon. At nightfall, their anger was fraternal, and they fed it by staying close, complicit and fierce.

Anthony took advantage of this to go to his bedroom, which was much less cool than his cousin's. His father had found him a bunk bed plastered with Panini stickers, pictures of French and Argentinian football players, and one of Chris Waddle wearing an OM Marseilles jersey. Anthony used a board on trestles as a desk. He didn't even have his own chair, which made doing homework hard. Plus, there were always people in the house: an uncle, friends, or a neighbour over for a drink. He started searching his wardrobe for something to wear. He couldn't find anything better than black jeans and a white polo shirt. It was size L, with 'Agrigel' on the pocket. If he hadn't spent all his money at the county fair and at the Metro, he might be able to afford some decent clothes. Truth be told, he'd never much worried about his clothes up to now. But he'd recently noticed conversations at school taking an unusual turn. Guys now lusted after Torsion running shoes or a Waikiki T-shirt. As Anthony contemplated his pathetic reflection in the mirror, he vowed to start saving money.

The motorbike was in its usual place at the back of the garage, wedged behind an old ping-pong table. After carefully folding the tarpaulin covering it, Anthony inhaled the pleasant smell of petrol and ran his hand over the studded tyres. It was a red-and-white 1982 Yamaha YZ, bearing the number 16. His father had done some racing, once. When he was in a good mood, he let Anthony drive it around the neighbourhood. Hélène didn't like it. Motorbike riders all wound up crumpled on ambulance trolleys; you didn't need to be a statistician to know that. But Anthony had motorcycling in his blood; even his father said so. When he went through the gears or leaned into turns, he was in his element. He was sure to have his own bike some day. In his head, this obsession was mixed up with images of the seaside, sunsets, girls in bikinis and Aerosmith songs.

Anthony rolled the Yamaha through the darkness, taking care not to bump into his mother's Opel. As he cautiously opened the garage door, a voice brushed the back of his neck.

'I was pretty sure I heard some noise in here.'

His mother was outside, smoking a cigarette. He could see her framed in the door against the dark blue of the evening sky. She had a sweater draped across her shoulders, her arms crossed. She was staring into space.

His hands on the handlebars, Anthony didn't say anything. He thought of Stéphanie and felt a little like weeping.

His mother dropped her cigarette and crushed the butt under her leather clog.

'Did you think of the scene your father would cause over this?'

Hélène had stepped closer and Anthony could smell her: a mix of cold tobacco, lime shampoo, sweat and the alcohol she had drunk. He promised to be careful. He was begging her.

'You know, sweetheart…'

She was standing very close now, swaying. The light from the overhead fixture fell on her thighs, tracing a single bright line in the darkness along her leg and shin. She moistened her thumb and rubbed something off Anthony's cheek. He pulled away.

'What?'

She seemed to be elsewhere.

'I was your age when we lost Mum,' she continued.

She put her forearms on her son's shoulders and clasped her hands behind his neck.

'Life isn' always fun, you know.'

Anthony kept quiet. He hated this kind of conversation, when his mother looked for excuses, for allies.

'Mum, please…'

'What?'

After a moment of indecision, she kissed him on the cheek, while almost falling down. She seemed wobbly, and just barely caught herself on the wall. This made her laugh. A kid's laugh, high and brief.

'I think I overdid it a lil' bit. Hurt myself, too.'

She brought the finger she'd scraped on the cement to her mouth. She sucked the blood, inspected the finger, then put it back in her mouth, smiling.

'This is about a girl, isn't it?'

Anthony didn't answer. She smiled again, then turned on her heel to head back to the patio, walking straight at last. She was tall and very slender. In the development, they called her the slut.

When Anthony was a safe distance away, he kick-started the YZ. High-pitched firing exploded in the darkness, and he raced off into the shattered evening. He rode fast, without a helmet, the wind bellying his oversized polo shirt. The weather was still fine. Very quickly he stopped thinking about anything and just rode.

4

Anthony's cousin climbed on behind him, and they headed for motorway D953. He revved the engine, putting his leg out in the turns and speeding up in the straight sections. The speed drew tears from their eyes and filled their chests with pride. They were racing across a land in darkness, bareheaded, incapable of accidents, too fast, too young, insufficiently mortal. Just the same, Anthony's cousin asked him to slow down at one point.

Drimblois was a little model village, with a church, a few farms along the motorway, some newer houses, and an old dental building with a wrought-iron grille. It only took them twenty minutes to get there. When they arrived, they rode around for a while before identifying the house where the famous party was taking place. It was a handsome modern building with a lot of glass. Lights were on in all the rooms, the lawn was as smooth as a golf course, and the swimming pool at the back glowed a bright turquoise. After a brief hesitation, the YZ came to a stop next to the other bikes. Anthony put his foot down.

'Here we are.'

'Yep,' said his cousin.

The air was fragrant with the smell of woodsmoke, grilled meat and newly-mown grass. Music was playing: reggae, maybe 'Natural Mystic'.

'Looks cool.'

'I forgot the bike lock,' said Anthony.

His cousin had got off the bike and was looking the place over.

'There's no risk, anyway,' he said. 'Just stash it over there.'

He was pointing to a long farm building with closed shutters. Logs of wood were stacked nearby, awaiting winter. Anthony hid the motorbike behind them, but he felt uneasy about it.

His cousin pulled a small bottle of rum from his jacket and took a long swig before handing it Anthony. Then he took a can of beer out of his backpack and did the same. They drank like that, taking turns, then threw the empty can onto the freshly cut lawn. That made them laugh, and they headed in.

On the patio on the other side, a crowd of young people was milling around a big table set with salad, crisps, bread and bottles of wine. There was also quite a bit of booze, with bottles stuck into a tub of ice. Tall, sharply dressed guys were manning the barbecue while drinking Sol beer. They belonged to the swimming club, as you could tell from their shoulders, their self-satisfied air and, especially, the names on their T-shirts. These were the coolest guys in the valley: athletes, wannabe surfers. They got all the girls, and nobody could stand them. A whiny rock 'n' roll piece that sounded like R.E.M. had replaced the reggae.

'Do you know anyone here?'

'Not a soul,' answered the cousin.

At that, he rolled a joint.

The guests all seemed happy to be there, in any case. Anthony spotted a couple of girls he could fall in love with on the spot. Tall girls with ponytails and little, light-coloured tops. They had white teeth, clear foreheads and tiny little arses. Boys were chatting with them as if it were no big deal. It was going so smoothly, Anthony could hardly stand it. Off in a corner, two guys in old deckchairs were sharing a box of rosé. Their T-shirts and long hair suggested they were serious Iron Maiden fans.

'C'mon, let's leave,' said Anthony.

'Now that we're here? You've got to be kidding!'

They found beers in the kitchen and started to drink while strolling around the place. Nobody knew them, so people stared a bit, but without any particular animosity. The house really was beautiful. There was even a foosball table on the mezzanine. The two cousins made regular trips to the fridge to resupply. Gradually, faces began to look familiar, and as the alcohol took hold they became friendlier with lots of people.

'Hey, there you are!'

Alex had grabbed them in a friendly way.

'It's cool that you came.'

'Yeah,' said the cousin.

'It's not bad here, is it?'

'Whose place is it?'

'Thomas's. His father is a radiologist.'

The boys received this news casually. Alex turned to the cousin and asked:

'Do you have a few minutes?'

'Sure thing.'

Anthony found himself all alone. Stéphanie and her friend Clémence hadn't arrived yet, so he got another beer to pass the time. It was his fifth, and his head was starting to spin quite a bit. He needed to piss, too. Rather than go looking for the bathroom, he walked down to the swimming pool and found a quiet spot nearby. Very high above him, the unthinking moon was shining. Anthony was feeling good, and free. There wasn't any school tomorrow, or for weeks to come. He filled his lungs, breathing in the night. Life wasn't so bad, when you got right down to it.

'Hi there!'

Anthony barely had time to button his flies. Steph and Clémence were walking straight towards him.

'Have you seen Alex, by any chance?' asked Clem.

'Yeah. He's with my cousin.'

Steph was wearing tight jeans, leather Grecian sandals and a white top. Clémence was dressed the same way, in a different assortment of colours, with gold bangles on her right wrist. The two of them were really gorgeous together, even better than separately. Still, there was something special about Steph. Anthony tried to think of something to say. All he could come up with was:

'Want to smoke a joint?'

'Cool,' said Steph.

Anthony took out his rolling papers. He was about to crouch down to roll the joints, but Clémence stopped him.

'Wait! We're not gonna sit there. It's where you just peed.'

Anthony blushed, but it was too dark for the girls to notice. They walked a little closer to the pool and sat in a circle, quickly smoking a joint of Moroccan without saying anything. The music was pounding now. Anthony was concerned about the neighbours. If this went on, they might well call the police. He pointed this out to the girls, who didn't seem especially worried. They were preoccupied by more serious problems. Someone who was supposed to be there apparently hadn't shown up yet. This was a problem, especially for Steph.

'Do you go to Fourrier?' asked Anthony.

They turned to him, seeming almost surprised to find him still there.

'Yeah.'

'What about you?'

Stéphanie had asked the question.

'I'll be at Clément-Hader when school starts,' he said.

That was a lie. Anthony had barely squeaked into year ten. He didn't quite know what to say, so he spat between his teeth. The girls exchanged a knowing look, and Anthony wished he could dig a hole to hide in. They soon ditched him and headed for the patio. He watched them walking away, with their narrow shoulders, bums moulded by their jeans, slender ankles, and those bouncing ponytails, graceful and haughty. He was very drunk now and starting to feel bad. Dizziness and melancholy had replaced his earlier exaltation. As he stood up in turn, thinking maybe he would go sit on a chair for a while, his cousin ran over, grinning broadly.

'Where were you?' he asked.

'Nowhere. I was smoking with the girls.'

'They're here?'

'Yeah.'

'So?'

'So nothing.'

Anthony's cousin studied him for a moment.

'When we go home, I'm gonna drive.'

'What did the guy want?'

'It's crazy. Everybody inside wants something to smoke. I sold them bars of hash for six hundred francs.'

'Seriously?'

The cousin showed him the money, and Anthony immediately cheered up. To the point of feeling thirsty again.

'Just the same, take it easy,' said his cousin.

Two beers later, Anthony decided to brave the living room. It was full of couples draped on sofas and slouched on the floor, kissing and making out. The girls put up no resistance, and hands were roaming under their T-shirts. Tangles of arms and legs could be seen, along with bare skin and pale jeans. Nail varnish added splashes of colour.

Steph and Clémence were there too, in the back, leaning against the French windows, with three boys that Anthony didn't recognise. They were on the floor close together, knees touching, looking mellow. The tallest of the three was even lying down. But the boy next to him was the one who caught your eye: leather jacket, dirty hair, really cool, an over-the-top Bob Dylan type, both laid-back and pretentious. Plus, 'Let It Be' was playing – depression city. Anthony took a few steps in their direction. He would have loved to join the little group, but of course that was impossible.

Then Leather Jacket pulled a little vial from his pocket and unplugged it. He raised it to his nose and took a big sniff, then handed it to Steph. They took turns snorting, which was followed by long peals of sick laughter. The effect seemed almost instantaneous, but it dissipated within a minute, and they quickly lapsed back into the same languorous torpor. Steph and the cool guy were exchanging glances, discreetly hooking up. It must have been thirty degrees in the room. How could that little jerk wear a leather jacket in this heat? When the vial was about to go round a second time, Anthony made his move.

'Hi there,' he said.

Five pairs of eyes turned to him.

'Who's that?' asked the tallest boy, the one lying down.

Steph and Clémence clearly no longer had the slightest idea. The tall guy sat up and snapped his fingers. Even when seated, you could tell he was really buff. With his pastel T-shirt and bare feet in Vans, he looked like a dumb California surfer.

'Hey, you there. What do you want?'

Clémence had just taken a hit and was giggling nervously as she fiddled with her ponytail. Steph took a turn and inhaled deeply.

'Wow! It feels like having Mr Freeze in my head.'

The others found that an excellent comparison, exactly spot on. When the vial got back to the guy in leather, he asked Anthony:

'Want to try it?'

Looking blearily at Anthony, they all waited to see what would happen next.

'What is it?'

'Try it, you'll see.'

Without knowing quite why, Anthony thought they all looked like a family. It wasn't anything special, just details in their clothing, their attitude, their general ease. He couldn't say exactly why, but it made an odd impression of lacking, inadequacy and smallness. He wanted to put on a good show. He took the vial.

'Go ahead,' urged Leather Jacket, miming a sniff in the air.

'Leave him alone, Simon,' said Clémence.

The Californian joined in: 'Hey, you okay? Think you can handle it?'

He said this with his right eye closed, imitating Anthony's asymmetrical face. Anthony clenched his fists, which was the stupidest thing he'd done so far.

'Cut it out, you're being stupid!' said Clémence, prodding the imitator with her foot.

Irritated now, she turned to Anthony: 'So what do you want? Hurry up!'

But Anthony could no longer make a move. Gripped by a kind of vertigo, he started at the big hunk. Steph, who was watching all this with bovine indifference, decided it was time for a change of scene.

'Okay, then...'

She had got to her feet and was stretching like a big cat. The California hunk stood as well; he was easily a head taller than Anthony.

'C'mon, we're just playing around,' said the third boy.

'Besides, he can hardly stand up.'

'You gonna puke?'

'He's definitely gonna puke.'

'He's all white.'

'Hey!'

Anthony didn't know where he was any more. He put the vial to his nostril and took a big sniff, more to have something to do than anything else. His brain immediately felt like it was caught in a draught, and he started to laugh. Leather Jacket retrieved his vial. The others took off, leaving Anthony alone, cross-legged, head down, completely out of it.

When he got his wits back, he was lying on some steps, outside. His hair was wet and his cousin was trying to get him to drink some water. Clémence was there, too.

'What happened?'

'You passed out.'

Anthony lay there for a moment, not understanding. He heard music and the voices of the others and struggled to keep his eyes open. Clémence left, and he again asked what had happened.

'You were drinking like a fish. You fell down, that's all.'

'I snorted something, too.'

'Yeah, Clem told me.'

'Oh yeah?'

'She's the one who came to get me when you collapsed.'

'She's not bad, either.'

'Yeah, definitely.'

His cousin explained about the two guys, Hunk and Leather Jacket. Anthony recognised their names. They were the Rotier brothers, a pair of spoiled troublemakers who thought they were the lords of the valley. Their uncle had been the mayor for thirty years before pancreatic cancer made him step aside. Even when he was very sick, he was often seen walking around Heillange, his town, scowling, a swollen belly under his very high belt. His yellowish face was especially striking. It looked sucked in on itself, with the hooded eye of a bird of prey rolling around. He died without ever resigning, a town councillor to the grave. The other Rotiers pretty much all made their mark as politicians, pharmacists, engineers, successful businessmen and doctors. You could find them as far away as Paris and Toulouse. They held responsible positions in training and management both here and there and practised necessary, licensed professions. Which didn't prevent some of their offspring from having difficult adolescences. This was clearly the case with Simon and his brother.

'I don't know what I snorted,' said Anthony.

'TCE or poppers. Those guys are nuts, they'll take anything.'

'Your girlfriend did some too.'

'I know.'

'Did you have a lot to talk about?'

'A bit.'

When Anthony got his bearings, they walked around the house twice. He was feeling really wasted and wanted to go home.

'Let's go now, okay? I'm beat.'

'It isn't even midnight yet.'

'I'm feeling crap. I want my bed.'

'There's lots of bedrooms upstairs. Just go and lie down for an hour or two.'

Anthony didn't have a chance to argue. As they were walking towards the patio, the guests' cheerful racket abruptly stopped, leaving only the voice of Cyndi Lauper singing 'Girls Just Want to Have Fun'. In the sudden silence, it seemed completely incongruous.

The cousins went to see what was going on. Everybody was standing in a circle around two intruders. They wore tracksuit jackets, hair shaved on the sides and their arses flat in their trousers. They were looking both vindictive and lost, so it was hard to tell if they were about to attack or had just been jumped. The smaller of the pair had a signet ring and a gold chain over the collar of his Tacchini jacket. The other one's name was Hacine Bouali.

Anthony knew that kid, at least; they went to the same school. Hacine spent most of his education zoned out under the scooter shelter, spitting on the ground. When you passed him in the hallway, you usually looked down. He had a reputation of being dangerous, crashing parties so he could drink for free, steal stuff and cause chaos. Then he would split at the last minute, just before the police arrived. He obviously wasn't welcome here: fifty people's silence was making that clear. Finally, a very small guy stepped out of the crowd to resolve the crisis. He was so well proportioned, so cute with his bowl haircut, you could mistake him for a Playmobil figure.

'We don't want any trouble,' he said. 'You can't stay here.'

'You can go fuck yourself,' said Hacine.

'We came peaceful like,' added his pal. 'Why are you giving us shit?'

'You weren't invited,' explained Playmobil. 'So you can't stay.'

'Come on, we don't want any trouble,' said one of the swimmers.

He had pulled up his sweatshirt hood and was advancing, palms raised.

'Now get out of here,' he added.

'Don't be so cheap,' began Hacine's pal. 'We'll just have a quick brew, and then we'll split.'

The swimmer took another step towards them, spreading his arms as a sign of peace. He was wearing flip-flops, which kind of argued in favour of his goodwill.

'Come on, you guys. Grab a beer and make tracks. We don't want any hassle.'

After a momentary silence, Hacine spread his arms in turn.

'I fuck all your mothers,' he announced.

In the silence, fat hissed as it dripped onto the barbecue coals. The impassive stars shone steadily. No one dared contradict him.

'C'mon, guys, this isn't worth getting into a fight over. Let's drop it.'

'You're starting to get on my nerves, man,' said Hacine.

His acolyte chimed in again:

'Hey there, it's all good. We're not doing anything wrong. We just want to have a drink, quiet like.'

But Playmobil was having none of it. When you have people crashing your party who have no business being there, at some point you have to put a stop to it. Besides, his parents were coming back the next day, so it just wouldn't do. Then Hacine muttered something about 'racists'. The swimmer snapped his fingers under his nose, twice.

'Hey, you, wake up! You aren't welcome here, so get lost. This has gone on long enough.'

'Look, arsehole—'

Hacine didn't have time to say more. A red-headed girl in a flowered dress had appeared at a first-floor window and shouted:

'I just called the police. I'm warning you, I just phoned them. They're on their way.'

She held up a cordless phone to show that she wasn't bullshitting them.

'So get out of here,' said an emboldened Playmobil. 'Now.'

The two scroungers weren't much to look at, actually, with their shifty posture, sparse moustaches and oversized Nikes at the end of their skinny legs. But it still required fifty people, one swimmer and the police to deal with them.

Hacine began to retreat while trying not to lose face, which mainly consisted of swaggering like some guy from the Bronx. When he got as far as the barbecue, he gave it a big kick, tipping it over onto the grass. It hit the ground hard, shooting hot coals as far as the patio. A girl standing nearby suddenly began to utter high-pitched shrieks.

'You guys are complete arseholes!' cried her girlfriend.

'C'mon, get the fuck out of here!'

'She's been burned!'

Now the intruders really had to leave quickly. To be on the safe side, people followed them out into the street. They took their time crossing the village, turning round from time to time to shout insults and give people the finger. They gradually disappeared from view, and the whine of a scooter was eventually heard fading away in the distance.

Ten minutes later, the party was resuming, in waves. People gathered in little scandalised groups, laughing as they described what had happened, hardly believing it. The girl who'd been burned was still whimpering a bit but was all right. Sweatshirt Hoodie just had to act modest while gathering his laurels. Only Playmobil was still agitated. While waiting for the police, he ran around picking up joint butts and yelling that this was the last time he would put up with this.

A police cruiser actually did show up later, and people told the cops what had happened. They didn't seem too surprised, or very interested, for that matter. They left the way they'd come.

The first splashes could be heard at the back of the garden, and Anthony made his way down to the pool, which looked like a blue screen between the branches. A dozen swimmers were drinking beer and ducking underwater. A couple was kissing by the edge, their mouths locked. At one point a girl climbed out of the water completely naked and danced for the onlookers' amusement. Anthony could hardly believe his eyes; these people would try anything. She was even applauded. Her pussy was waxed and she had tiny boobs. It was really beautiful. At the same time it felt very distant.

'Aren't you going swimming?'

Steph was standing under a willow tree a few steps behind him. She seemed a little confused, her expression vague. Her jeans had a grease stain on the left thigh. Anthony didn't answer, so she said it again:

'You going swimming, or what?'

'Uh, I don't know.'

She had started unstrapping her sandals and was soon barefoot in the grass.

'Isn't your pal here?'

'He's my cousin.'

'Right, your cousin. This party's too weird. It feels like it's been going on for two days.'

'Yeah,' said Anthony, not understanding what she meant.

'It'll be morning soon.'

He checked his watch.

'It's only three o'clock.'

'Damn, I'm cold,' said Steph, fumbling with her belt buckle.

She unzipped her jeans and tried to slide them down her thighs, but the fabric caught, stuck to her skin. Then she pulled her top over her head. She was wearing a pale swimming costume, less sexy than the one from that afternoon.

'Okay, I'm going for a dip.'

Anthony watched as she headed for the water, her bum bouncing and her thighs pumping. Just before the edge, she gathered herself and dived, arms outstretched. Her body slid into the water with exquisite ease. When she surfaced, her mouth was wide open, she was laughing and her ponytail made wet circles in the air. The swimmers sitting on the steps started to shout. Anthony couldn't hear what they were saying. He took off his shoes in turn and unbuttoned his jeans, but realised he was wearing pants with colourful umbrellas on them. This gave him pause. He was shivering a little. It was true, it was cold as hell. On the patio, the sound was suddenly cranked up and everybody listened.

It was a song being constantly played on the M6 channel. It usually made you want to smash a guitar or set fire to your school, but here it made everybody thoughtful. It was still almost new, a title from a similar depressed American city, a shithole town very far away, where little white punks in plaid shirts drank cheap beer. The song was spreading like a virus wherever you found loser working-class kids, pimply teens, fucked-over crisis victims, teen mums, morons on motorbikes, stoners and school dropouts. A wall had fallen in Berlin and peace was already starting to look like a terrifying steamroller. In every town across this deindustrialised, one-dimensional world and in every blighted village, kids without dreams were now listening to a group from Seattle named Nirvana. They were letting their hair grow and turning their sadness into anger, their depression into decibels. Paradise was good and lost, the revolution would not take place; the only thing left was to make noise. Anthony bobbed his head in time, along with thirty other people like him. He shivered as the song ended, and then it was over. Everybody could go home.

Around five in the morning he was awakened by the cold settling on the garden. Without realising it, he'd fallen asleep on a chaise longue. He was under a tree. He sneezed a few times and went looking for his cousin.

On the ground floor of the house, a little group was still chatting, hoarse and intimate, their hair wet. Girls wrapped in big towels huddled against their boyfriends. A faint smell of chlorine hung in the air. Dawn would come soon, and Anthony thought of the sadness that would follow, that little twinge of pale sunrises. Besides, his mother was going to kill him.

Upstairs, he looked in the bathroom, opened bedroom doors. The beds were full of sleeping shapes, three or four to a bed. The two heavy-metal guys had found a trapdoor and climbed up onto the roof. They were drinking wine under the stars. Anthony asked if they'd seen his cousin.

'Who's that?'

'My cousin. The tall guy.'

The metalheads offered him a drink. Anthony refused.

'So you haven't seen him?'

'No.'

'Did you look in the bedrooms?'

'I just did, all of them.'

'Sit down, then. See how beautiful it is.'

The nearest metalhead pointed to a spot on the horizon where a thin ochre sliver was rising from the earth, filling the sky with light. The night gradually turned blue.

'Did you try the shed in the garden?' asked the other one, who had his hands behind his neck and was gazing at the sky. Tufts of fair, almost red hair stuck out of the sleeves of his T-shirt.

Anthony went through the house again. Seeing the now-empty living room felt a little like visiting a crime scene. Beer cans, cigarette butts, a record spinning in the empty air, speakers making that little crackly hiccup at the end of a record. The sky had already lightened. He went through the garden. Oddly enough, the swimming pool was perfectly clean, a toilet-bowl blue, glowing and artificial. He stood on the edge for a moment, rocked by the tiny wavelets and fighting an urge to dive in. He could see bikini bottoms in the depths, or maybe they were knickers. He thought of Steph, whom he hadn't seen since the swim. Anyway, he didn't care. He spat in the water. He was just exhausted.

'Hey there!'

He turned to find his cousin waving at him from the patio. He was wearing a T-shirt that didn't belong to him. Anthony joined him, dragging his feet. They took the path out to the front gate.

'It's almost dawn. Where were you?'

'Nowhere,' said his cousin.

'Did you see Steph again?'

'No.'

'What's that T-shirt?'

'It's nothing.'

Anthony had a headache. A rooster crowed. They reached the stacks of wood where they had left the bike a few hours earlier. In another life, practically.

The YZ wasn't there. Anthony fell to his knees.

5

A little later that morning, Hacine had an appointment at Heillange City Hall, in a shabby ground-floor office. He'd hardly slept, and he was cold. The mayoralty was housed in a former primary school, which explained its endless hallways, echoing stairwells and fortress-like chill. In fact, everyone who worked there was careful to always bring a sweater. Hacine hadn't taken that precaution, and he was freezing his balls off. This of course put him on edge, especially since he'd rather be almost anywhere else.

Facing him, a young woman with bulging eyes and novelty earrings was studying his CV. She made a comment from time to time, or asked a question. On her earrings, you could make out a little elephant or a cat; it was hard to tell. Without looking up, she asked him:

'Here, for example, what did you mean by that?'

She was pointing at an entry under the heading 'Interests'. Hacine leaned over to look.

'Boxing,' he said simply.

'I see.'

After getting her bachelor's degree, the young woman had specialised in employment law, a discipline that benefited from the healthy employment figures of the 1960s. It was a fast track to management positions in human resources, a sector that had steadily grown during the previous thirty years despite the notable job losses that characterised the same period. Once she had her diploma (baccalaureate + five years), it took her less than two months to get a job. As a result, she tended to view unemployment as one of those abstract threats that mainly appeared on the evening news, like malaria, tsunamis and volcanic eruptions. At the moment, she was introducing Hacine to the finer points of putting one's skills in the best light. The boy was being only moderately cooperative. The young woman tried again. She was intrigued by this boxing business.

'And what do you call it?'

'Muay Thai. It's Thai boxing.'

'Do you think it's a good idea to put that down?'

'It's a sport,' answered Hacine.

'Yeah, but with your profile, see ...'

Hacine frowned. In his case, this meant looking disdainful while pursing his lips into a duck face. Given the shadow of moustache decorating his upper lip, the resulting look was pretty unusual.

The young woman smiled.

'Do you see what I mean?'

'Yes.'

'Good. And here, under information technology skills, can you be more specific?'

'Well, computer stuff.'

'Do you have a computer at home?'

'Yeah.'

The boy had hooked his feet around the legs of his chair. It squeaked on the tiled floor each time he moved, so he tried to keep still. How much longer was this bullshit going to last?

'Give me some examples. What do you know? Word? Excel?'

'A little of everything.'

'It's important to be specific. You're listing real-world skills, see? That's what you're selling. Can you run Office software, for example?

'Yeah. I do some coding, too. JavaScript. Stuff like that.'

'That's good. In fact it's really good.'

The compliment hurt Hacine's feelings. What did this cunt think, that he just knew how to press the power button? At that, he shut down. Too bad. She would certainly have liked the edifying story of a kid who went to Microfun every Saturday morning. Located at the foot of the ZUP developments hill, the little shop salvaged old computer equipment and passed it on to schools or to the poor, or resold it by weight. An Amstrad 6128 cost more than three thousand francs, and neither Hacine nor any of his pals could afford gear like that, so they went to Microfun instead. They spent hours dismantling obsolete IBM towers, swapping processors and advice. His year–nine tech teacher even helped him solder some of the parts. He wound up building a pretty decent tower, powerful enough to play *Double Dragon*, anyway. But since then, Hacine had more or less quit doing that stuff. As he thought about it, he realised he'd pretty much quit everything recently.

'And you've been to Frankfurt?'

He nodded.

'London. And Bangkok.'

'Yes.'

'You've done a lot of travelling for someone your age.'

She was looking at him with a friendly smile while fiddling with an earring. Or maybe the smile was mocking. She must think he was a bullshitter. He'd actually never been to Frankfurt – what the hell would he do in Frankfurt? – but that didn't give this bitch the right to doubt him.

'Do you speak English?'

He moved his head in a way that might mean yes.

'Okay. Anyway, everybody puts that down,' she said, suddenly perking up.

Just then, the woman's phone began to ring. Her hand hovered indecisively over the phone for two or three rings. Hacine felt more and more tense. Was it some sort of test?

'Hello…Good morning…Yes…Of course…'

Her 'yeses' were drawling and motherly. In fact, she gave the impression she was talking to an idiot. This made Hacine feel somewhat better. Apparently, she talked to everybody that way.

'Of course, sir. Call us back when classes start. Yes, all right...'

She was mimicking the exchange, while taking Hacine as her witness. People asked such questions! After advising her caller to check with the national employment service, she hung up.

'It's like that all day long.'

There were more questions. Hacine's CV did have quite a few dubious entries. It's true that everybody fudged a bit, but it was important to keep it modest. Depending on the situation, transatlantic voyages, fluent English, internships with ministries and a passion for philanthropy could arouse suspicions. What mainly bothered her was the Thai boxing business.

'See what I mean? Especially given where you come from.'

'But what about the job?' said Hacine. 'Do you have something or not?'

'What do you mean?'

'I don't know, my dad told me to come to City Hall. He said you had jobs.'

'Oh no, not at all. Your father came to the mayor's office, but I don't know what they told him. We just do orientation here. We help people get back into the workforce.'

'So there's no job, actually.'

'There must have been a misunderstanding. Our role is to help people put themselves across well, regain their self-confidence. We help them write their CVs and get training. We can also do coaching. Besides, you aren't eighteen yet, are you?'

Hacine confirmed this. He was suddenly sorely tempted to ask her what the fuck he was doing there.

'You're a minor, too, so there won't be anything. And in summer, forget it.'

As Hacine was leaving, she insisted on going with him because she wanted to have a smoke. That way, he was sure not to get lost. The place was practically deserted, and in the empty hallways the young woman's high heels made a somewhat intimidating managerial clicking. By contrast, her attitude had become decidedly friendly, almost familiar. After all, she was young and open-minded; they could get along. Once out on the pavement she shook his hand with obvious pleasure. And then, without warning, her face fell.

'I forgot to ask. Do you give high fives?'

At first, Hacine didn't understand.

'You know,' she said. 'This sort of thing.'

She was holding her palm out, so he was forced to slap it.

'Because I met some employers the other day, they were super put off by that. They have young people who high-five people at work, with everybody. It just doesn't look good, see?'

Hacine wondered if she was making fun of him. Apparently not.

'I gotta get going.'

'Yes, of course.'

He could've taken the bus over the road; the number 11 went straight to his place. But he was afraid she might want to keep him company while he waited. He'd rather walk home. He could sense her looking at his back, until the moment he turned the corner. It was lucky he had pockets; he could put his hands in them.

On the way, he stopped at a bakery to buy a Coke and two croissants and ate his breakfast as he climbed the hill to the ZUP estate. It was already hot, and the coldness of the Coke was almost incredible. He soon spotted Eliott hanging out in the courtyard. As they did every year, the fairground people had set up a bumper-car carousel and a little stand where they sold waffles. Hacine and his pals hung out there all day long. When Eliott saw him, he waved, and Hacine ambled over to join him.

'What's with this piece of shit?' he asked, kicking the wheel of Eliott's wheelchair.

'Battery's dead. The motor's shot anyway, so I took the old one.'

'That sucks.'

'No shit.'

49

'What'd you do to get downstairs?'

'I manage, don't sweat it.'

It was a point of honour with Eliott not to let his handicap be a nuisance for people. In fact, it had become something of an advantage. The police once showed up in the Manet tower lobby for an ID check, when Eliott was loaded like a mule. Not only did the police not search him, but they even carried him up to the mezzanine so he could take the lift. Eliott pointed out that you really had to be stupid to stick a stairway right in front of a lift. The cops agreed, feeling embarrassed, as if they'd drawn up the plans themselves.

'Any news?'

'Nothing new. Dead as a doornail. If we don't score tomorrow, I won't have anything left.'

With the Meryems sidelined, the problem of hash resupply had reached a critical level. Hacine had even tried to call his brother, who lived in Paris.

'What about your brother?' prompted Eliott.

Hacine shrugged. They were silent for a moment, then Eliott continued:

'D'you go into town?'

'Yeah.'

'What for?'

'Nothing special.'

Eliott didn't pursue it, and Hacine went to sit on a low wall nearby.

'Hot as hell already.'

'Yeah.'

Hacine began contemplating the decorations on the bumper-car carousel: Michael Jackson, werewolves, a mummy, Frankenstein. It was gaudy and beautiful, with coloured lights that were switched on at nightfall. In the last few years, the other carnival attractions hadn't bothered to come. Hacine was very fond of candyfloss.

The temperature gradually rose, and the two boys moved into the shadow of the boules court shelter. From there, they could see customers coming. Except that for the last two days, they'd all gone away empty-handed. The buildings around them rose indifferent and cube-like. Dust motes floated in the sunlight.

After lunchtime the others began to show up. The gang usually consisted of maybe ten guys. There was Djamel, Seb, Mouss, Saïd, Steve, Abdel, Raduane and little Kader. They all lived in the neighbourhood. They got up late and came on foot or by scooter. They stayed for a while, went off to take care of stuff, then came back. This way, there was a continuous stream of familiar faces, a rotation of friends that broke up the monotony of dealing. Whatever the case, by the afternoon there were almost always five or six boys endlessly waiting under the shelter, leaning against the fence or perched on a low wall, spitting on the ground and smoking joints. Sometimes older guys came by for a chat. A handshake, a hand on the heart, a few quick words: How's the family, how're things, doin' okay? Most of them had settled down. They were now doing temp work or had little short-term contracts with Carglass or Darty. Sami had just opened his kebab stand near the station. People asked him how business was. Even when he put a good face on it, you could sense the anxiety, the constant fear of bankruptcy. To think he had once been the biggest wholesaler in the valley. Now he drove a little Peugeot 205. Feeling ill at ease, the boys promised to stop by later, and Sami went off to work, his love handles stuffed into an OM Marseille T-shirt, with his two kids and his credit card debt. Then the little kids rode back from the swimming pool on their bikes. There was some teasing back and forth, but overall there wasn't much to do while waiting for the bumper-car stand to open. Often, heat and boredom would go to people's heads like alcohol. Guys would even start fighting, just to relieve the boredom and idleness. Then calm would fall again, like a hammer.

Soon little Kader showed up on his scooter. He wasn't wearing a helmet and rode in flip-flops. He did a wheelie, for show. Seb was there too, with his 49ers hat shoved down to his ears.

'So what are we doing?'

'What do you mean?'

'I don't know. We move.'

'So, go ahead and move.'

'I mean tonight, man. It's Friday. What're we doing? For real.'

'Let's get a six-pack of beer.'

'Yeah.'

'You guys give me a pain. Swigging beer outside, like bums.'

Hacine had spoken, so there was nothing more to be said. He'd been in a foul mood since the start of the holidays. It was understandable. His scooter had died in June and since then he'd had to walk everywhere, like a drudge. It started with the ignition, then all of a sudden the cylinders, pistons, rings and spark plugs all went to hell. With the shortage of hash on top of everything, it was getting really hard to lead a normal life. Hacine spat between his front teeth. Nobody stirred. Eliott took it on himself to roll a blunt.

By a little after three, time had become like a paste, greasy and infinitely stretchable. It was the same thing every day. By the afternoon, a diffuse numbness took hold of the estate. From the open windows you no longer heard the sounds of children or TV sets. The towers themselves seemed ready to collapse, swaying in the waves of heat. Every so often, the howl of a pimped out motorbike would slash through the silence. The boys blinked and wiped away the sweat staining their hats. Their nerves simmered inside. The boys felt sluggish and hateful, an acrid taste of tobacco on their tongues. They felt they should be somewhere else, have a job, in an air-conditioned office, maybe. Or be at the seaside.

For his part, Hacine was seriously worried. He'd not even seen ten customers since the morning. New sources of supply must have sprung up. Supply and demand obeyed the laws of magnetism and had probably been drawn to each other elsewhere, like rejected lovers. If the shortage lasted much longer, he and his friends would be screwed; they would lose everything. He let it be known that his brother might bail them out, but he didn't really believe it. That son of a bitch was doing business for real, with guys from Bobigny. He was living outside Paris and hadn't been to Heillange for at least three years. He wasn't answering phone calls. Couldn't be counted on. If this went on, they would have to turn to the inbreds. Those guys always had contacts and connections. But Hacine didn't like the idea at all. Doing business with those guys was really risky.

They were capable of anything. Besides, they fucked each other, the degenerates. Hacine felt sick just thinking of it.

He was turning all this over in his head when Fred showed up. He was a true druggie, always easy, always affable. Hacine couldn't stand him. Especially because the piece of shit acted all buddy-buddy, on the grounds that he had once known the Bouali cousins, the guys who first set up hash distribution in Heillange in the eighties.

'Greetings, brother,' said Fred.

'We got nothing. Get lost.'

Everything happened the way it usually did. Fred would pretend not to hear, and Hacine became more and more monosyllabic. Then Fred began to beg: a hit, man, just one little hit. Insults started to fly. Eventually they became threats, and Fred agreed to leave, albeit slowly and miserably. His greatest fear was being sober. He hadn't managed to do anything with his life: no job, no wife, no crime. Living with his mother, he endured in poverty. Fortunately, his mum required a whole pharmacy of medications, so Fred would console himself there when he had nothing to smoke. The local doctors were accommodating. The whole valley was in palliative care, somewhere.

'Seems he's got the virus, too,' said Eliott, watching Fred slink away.

'That's bullshit.'

'He's dying; you can tell.'

'Well, let the son of a bitch die.'

Around five, the bumper-car lady showed up with her mother, who ran the waffle stand. The two spent their time glued to their chairs, stuffing themselves with churros and sweets. Oddly enough, the mother was as skinny as her daughter was fat. When they started the generator, the track lit up. Mum turned on her waffle irons and started the candyfloss. The smell of caramel spread through the courtyard. There was music.

For their part, the boys had gone home and now returned with shiny hair and smelling of body wash. Some had gone a little overboard on the deodorant. They tried to look bored and blasé, but mainly they seemed excited. Finally, the girls arrived, two by two or in little groups. Eyes lowered, laughing to themselves, long dark hair, sidelong glances. They settled on the other side of the track, sitting on benches or leaning against the safety barrier. They came from other Heillange neighbourhoods, or from Lameck or Étange; some even took the bus from Mondevaux. They were allowed to come because it was holiday time, and provided they didn't get home too late. ZUP boys didn't pick up girls in the neighbourhood because they inevitably wound up being someone's sister or daughter. But these visitors were fair game. Because of this tiny piece of county fair, they showed up every day. An opportunity not to be missed.

Hacine was the first to make his way to the cash register. He bought ten tokens for twenty francs. Behind the glass, the woman was already sweating. She recognised the song coming out of the loudspeakers and turned up the volume. It was a sappy Bryan Adams number, and her mother rolled her eyes. She had just started her first waffles and was fanning herself with a classified-ads newspaper. The other boys were already lined up to get tokens. They were off and running.

When he'd spent his first ten tokens, Hacine bought ten more. He drove in circles for nearly two hours. His pals bumped into him, and vice versa. And during that time, all he did was think about the girl standing off to the side with a pair of friends, the one with hoop earrings and a French manicure. She watched him, but each time he looked in her direction, she turned her head away. Every day, they hoped something would happen. It never did. He didn't know her name, or anything. He hadn't mentioned her to anyone. She left a little before eight o'clock. She never stayed very long.

Feeling disgusted, Hacine left the track and went back to the low wall where he spent his life. Eliott asked him what the problem was.

'Nothing. Just leave me the fuck alone.'

Plus, Saïd and Steve had managed to get girls into their bumper cars. Those losers. Hacine spat between his teeth. Little Kader looked over at him. That was exactly the wrong, stupid thing to do.

'What?'

'Nothing.'

'What are you looking at?'

'I told you, nothing.'

'Stop looking at me like that, you little prick.'

This went on for a while, and Kader eventually had to look down. Overhead, the sky was caught in the jaws outlined by the towers. The windows cut into their facades looked like narrow eyes and sick mouths. The sweet smell of waffles hung in the air and Freddy Mercury sang 'I Want to Break Free'. After a while, Hacine left. Little Kader was pissed off. He'd been bawled out for no reason at all.

'Man, I don't know what's up with him,' he said. 'We were at a party yesterday, and he was already acting crazy.'

'How so?'

'I dunno, he kicked over a barbecue, called everybody sons of bitches.'

'Well, he's right. They *are* sons of bitches.'

'Yeah, no shit.'

They laughed. Still, you had to wonder sometimes whether he wasn't a little nuts.

Hacine roared down the ZUP hill flat out, leaning forward on the Yamaha. He raced through downtown in third gear. The trick was to never hit the brakes. You just had to anticipate the turns and rev her up coming out of the curves. The little motor snarled angrily in the narrow streets. As he passed, people saw only a thin figure with two skinny arms sticking out of an extra-large T-shirt. When people saw him, they immediately fell uncomfortable, and draw their own political conclusions. Inside Hacine's chest, a seventeen-year-old heart was trapped in barbed wire. No way was he stopping for red lights. He couldn't stand it any more. At times, death seemed like an enviable fate.

He soon found himself on the motorway that ran all the way to Spain, and decided to stop near a field with enormous rolls of hay. He left the motorbike and walked across the dry stubble. He strode quickly, his lip moist, bare arms swinging along his body. His tongue tasted like a copper coin. He made a dry rustling as he went, leaving a flattened furrow in his wake. He walked until he got tired then sat down in the shade of a hay roll. He took his Zippo lighter from his pocket and started to play with it, snapping it open with his thumb and lighting it on his jeans. The sun had faded and now shed a soft, enveloping light on the countryside. It was an old bronze-coloured lighter, like they had in Vietnam. He'd taken it from some kid during the middle-school final exams. Year-ten students from Hurlevent, a private school downtown, came to Louis-Armand to sit for the test every year. In their Benneton sweaters, the kids were quite a sight. Their parents would drop them off while glancing around nervously at the grey public buildings. It was like a train platform after a draft call-up. This republican tradition of holding the exam away from one's local school had been going on for a while. The very first sessions produced a variety of plunder and other compensatory vexations. But this low-grade class struggle no longer yielded much. The rich Hurlevent kids spread the word and now left their First Communion watches at home. The ZUP kids weren't about to steal their Tann's satchels. Last time, Hacine went after a grungy group of guys in rock 'n' roll T-shirts, which is how he acquired two guitar capos and the Zippo.

Its blue flame smelled pleasantly of lighter fluid, and he lit a piece of straw at his feet. It caught fire immediately. Despite the temptation, Hacine stamped it out with his heel. The copper-coin taste spread through his mouth. He felt acid in his chest and his mouth filled with saliva. He lit his lighter again. The hay roll caught fire in a great crackling of heat and a sigh of smoke. The flames rose, sharp and voluptuous. It smelled wonderful. He took a few steps backwards, to see better. Already the fire was spreading along the ground, seeking more to feed on. Hacine breathed deeply. He was starting to feel the amazing calm that came over him every time. He could finally go home. When he took off on the motorbike, you'd think the whole valley behind him was in flames.

'Have you been smoking again?' asked the old man.

Unable to find his keys, Hacine had had to ring the bell to get his father to open the door. The man stood there with his bare feet in slippers, dressed all in denim, his collar buttoned. The eyes in his wrinkled face were unreadable. His razor had missed a clump of white whiskers under his nose. He was less and less able to see that spot.

'No, I haven't,' said Hacine. 'Okay? Can I come in?'

'You smell of smoke. Are you smoking?'

'I told you, no!'

Frowning, the old man leaned over to sniff his son's T-shirt. He grumbled, but stepped back to let him through. Once inside, Hacine took off his Nikes. The hissing of a pressure cooker came from the kitchen. It smelled of potatoes.

'Some people, they saw your brother,' said his father seriously.

His rough voice was low and beautiful. Words washed around in it like stones in a sieve.

'They're dreaming.'

'They say they saw him.'

The boy turned to his father, whose pupils had taken an uncertain edge and opalescent colour that normally indicated old age, though he was only fifty-nine.

'Why would they say that if they did not see him?'

'I don't know. They got mixed up.'

'They told me he was there.'

'It's nonsense, stop it,' moaned Hacine.

The man seemed dubious. He hadn't seen his older son for a long time now. Hacine's heart sank. He and his father were squeezed together in the narrow hallway. The wall had mirrors, old photos, things from over there. Their shoes were lined up on the floor.

'What are we eating?' asked Hacine.

'The usual. Come on.'

The father went back to his stove. He fried two hamburgers and turned up the volume on the radio, which covered the sizzling of the meat. Then he cut the flame under the pressure cooker, and they sat down at the table. The father drank water; the son poured himself a glass of grenadine. It wasn't night yet, but the temperature was already more bearable. You could smell coffee that had been kept hot all day. They ate with an elbow on the table, not speaking. Then the phone rang, and Hacine ran to the living room to answer it. It was his mother. She was calling from over there. She said it was hot. She said she was happy she would see him soon. She asked if he was being good. Then his father took the receiver and talked with his wife for a few minutes in Arabic. Hacine shut himself in his bedroom so as not to bother them.

Later, his father came to get him.

'Did you go to City Hall?'

'Yeah.'

'There was work?'

Though he'd lived here for nearly thirty-five years, Hacine's father still spoke this approximate French, even while acquiring the valley's thick accent. Every time he opened his mouth, Hacine felt like hiding.

'Of course not. There wasn't any job.'

'No job? She told me it was good.'

The old man entered his bedroom, to make sure.

'No,' said Hacine. 'You didn't understand. She's just there to help people who're looking for work. But they don't have anything. They're useless.'

'How so?'

'She helped me with my CV, that's all. She's useless, I tell you.'

'Oh, really?'

The father's brows contracted in a frown, and he muttered something inaudible in Arabic. Under his moustache, the narrow movements of his brown lips were hard to see. Hacine asked him to repeat it.

'You have to work,' his father declared, with sudden solemnity.

'Yeah, but there has to be a job, too.'

'You find. If you want, you find,' said his father, totally convinced.

'Right. By the way, I'll go shopping on Monday morning. There's nothing left in the fridge.'

'Yes, that is good.'

It was all very well for the old man to lecture him, but when Hacine filled the fridge, the sermons stopped. The boy stood up, saying he was going out.

'To go where?'

'I don't know. Nowhere.'

'What do you mean, nowhere?'

'I won't be home late.'

'You always come home late.'

Hacine had already left the room. In the hallway, he quickly put on his shoes and jacket but was unable to avoid a final word of advice.

'If you do stupid things, watch out.'

Hacine promised, and went off to join his mates in the courtyard. Kader was in a grumpy mood, and Hacine teased him just enough to make it up to him. Then they went back to hanging out, watching the bumper-car ballet. Eliott, who had practically nothing left, rolled a needle joint. With six guys, it was pretty tight. And instead of relaxing them, it out everybody on edge.

'So what do we do?' asked Saïd.

It was the normal question, the same one asked ten times a day.

'I don't know.'

'Let's move.'

'Move where?'

'Just move, we'll see.'

'C'mon there, don't go to sleep on us.'

Each of them tried to drag on the joint as hard as possible. Mouss was the unlucky last one. He just stubbed out the tiny butt in the dirt.

Soon the carnival women switched the electricity off, and the last customers disappeared into the darkness. Then the two women left in turn with the cash box, waving goodbye to the boys. The buildings now composed a landscape of straight lines spangled with glowing points of blue light. The estate's age dissolved in the night. All that was left were masses, edges, illuminated windows and more boredom.

'Fuck, it's depressing.'

'Bollocks, what do we do?'

'C'mon, who cares? We'll do something.'

'Roll another joint, at least.'

'No can do, I'm almost out.'

'It's okay, you'll score tomorrow.'

'Then we'll see tomorrow.'

'Don't be a dick, it's no big deal.'

'Tomorrow, that's all.'

The day was ending. On Monday Hacine would see about selling the motorbike. He knew a scrap dealer. He was sure to get at least five hundred francs for it.

6

It was already well into the morning by the time the cousins reached Anthony's house. They were dirty and defeated. Patrick Casati was behind the wheel of his truck, waiting for them. Luc Grandemange was there, too, in shorts and Birkenstocks, holding a steaming mug of coffee. He burst out laughing when he saw the boys coming, but it was more to lighten the mood than anything else. On the truck radio, a nasal voice was repeating the name of the call-in show, *Stop ou encore*.

'Where have you two clowns been?' asked Anthony's father.

Through his Vuarnets, he was looking above their heads, as if telling time by the course of the sun. The boys stopped a safe distance away, their arms hanging down.

'Pair of fine feathered friends you have there,' said Grandemange.

Patrick cleared his throat and grabbed the bottle of water near him on the seat. He swallowed about half of it before putting it down. He wasn't in that great shape either, apparently. He cleared his throat again and coughed.

'I've been waiting for you for hours. Where've you been?'

'It's Saturday,' said Anthony.

'So what? Does that make it okay for you to stay out all night?'

The boys had walked a long way back from Drimblois, sticking a thumb out each time a car passed. They hadn't said a hundred words to each other during the whole trip. Anthony was starting to feel sick to his stomach.

'They're just kids,' said Grandemange genially. 'It's no big deal.'

'Yeah. But I think I'll take care of my own business, if you don't mind.'

Grandemange got the message.

Anthony's father jumped down from the Iveco cabin. He was wearing steel-toe boots, denim Bermuda shorts, and a vest that showed his bare arms. As he rummaged in his pockets for his cigarettes, the boys could see the knotty delts and tendons under his tanned skin.

'I guess I'll be going,' said Grandemange.

Patrick pretended not to hear. After lighting a cigarette, he turned back to Anthony.

'So? Do you have an explanation?'

'Okay, I'll leave you to it,' said Grandemange again, trying to keep smiling. He raised his hand with the missing fingers to wave goodbye.

'All right, say hello to Évelyne for me,' said Patrick.

He'd be sure to do that, he promised. He walked off, dragging his feet. The size of his calves was shocking. He'd once had a blood test and learned that his cholesterol level was off the charts. That kept him awake for three nights worrying, but didn't make him cut back on the charcuterie. He thought we've all got to die, anyway. Anthony's father picked a shred of tobacco from his tongue. Anthony could see himself in his sunglasses, looking deformed and none too sharp.

'Well?'

'We were with some friends and got a little drunk, so we thought we'd better sleep there.'

Anthony's father's lips curled in an ambiguous smile. To the cousin he said:

'I think they're expecting you at home.'

The two boys quickly high-fived each other, and the cousin took off in turn. Anthony found himself alone with his hangover, under the sun and his father's eyes.

62

'What was that crap? You guys shake hands like niggers now?'

Anthony didn't say a word. He was thinking of the empty space at the back of the garage.

'Come on, get in,' said his father. 'There's work to do.'

'Can I take a shower first?'

'Get in, I said.'

He obeyed. His father took the wheel. The truck started up and Anthony leaned by the window to get some air.

'Put your seat belt on. I don't want to get another damn ticket.'

Leaving the development, Patrick was already in fourth gear and doing nearly eighty kilometres an hour. He hardly took his foot off the accelerator going over the speed bumps before the primary school next to the fire station. Anthony could feel his stomach churning and thought he was going to puke. They would have to stop for a minute at least, to get some fresh air. He turned to his father, but Patrick was staring at the motorway, his square hands locked on the steering wheel, a cigarette between his index and middle fingers. The sky drifted endlessly across his sunglasses. They left the town behind, and it took Anthony another ten minutes to screw up his courage to speak.

'You gotta stop.'

His father looked at him.

'Not feeling well?'

'No.'

In fact, the boy was white as a sheet. With a hydraulic groan, the truck came to a stop on the shoulder. Anthony jumped out of the cabin and hadn't taken three steps before heaving up everything in his stomach. When he straightened, he was drenched with sweat. He wiped his face and mouth with his polo shirt. The bandage on his right hand was filthy. In front of him, the motorway to Étange, Lameck, Thionille and eventually Luxembourg stretched out of sight. A Fiat Panda roared by, followed by a little old man on a motorbike towing a trailer. The nasal *putt-putt* rose, and the man passed them with his eyes on the horizon and an open-face helmet on his head, looking imperial. As Anthony's gaze followed him, it lit on the truck's rear-view mirror. In it he could see his father's jaw, his heavily muscled shoulder, and the first greying hairs on the back of his neck. Anthony spat, to get rid of the bitter taste in his mouth, and climbed back into the truck.

'Feeling better?'

'Yeah.'

'Here.'

Anthony accepted the water bottle and took a long drink. The truck started up again. Heat was already raising blurry reflections on the asphalt. Oddly enough, they never saw the little old man on his motorbike again. It was as if he had completely evaporated.

On the radio, the announcer was wishing a nice break to the people holidaying, in August, and good luck to the July people who would be back at work on Monday. Then the first notes of 'J'aime regarder les filles' could be heard in the cabin.

'You don't happen to know what your mother's up to, do you?'

'What do you mean?'

Patrick took off his glasses and rubbed his face and the back of his neck. Then he briefly let go of the steering wheel to stretch. The truck was now speeding through meadows and fields of rapeseed that no longer displayed their harsh pre-harvest yellow. High-tension lines periodically scratched across the gently rolling landscape.

'She started in on it again this morning. On you, too, Mr Shitstorm, for not coming home last night.'

'So what happened?'

'Nothing,' said his father tersely. Then after a silence he added:

'Anyway, if she wants to leave, I won't be the one to stop her.'

They continued on their way. At home, fights could break out over anything – a man's glance, the TV programme, the wrong word. Hélène knew which buttons to push. His father didn't have the words. Anthony told himself that if he ever raised his hand to her, he would kill him. He was almost strong enough now. He felt like a wet rag, and a little like crying. And the motorbike, fuck.

———

Forty minutes later, they pulled up in front of a big house in a hamlet called La Grange. You had to wonder what it was doing out in the middle of nowhere, with its symmetrical facade, slate roof, sundial and ring of white gravel paths. Around about there were just long, mostly abandoned farm buildings, woods, vestiges of little businesses and dumped agricultural vehicles.

'Whose place is this?' asked Anthony.

'I don't know. A property company called me. We have to mow the lawn, trim the hedges, make everything ship-shape. They're going to sell it.'

The sign hanging on the fence contradicted him; it read 'Sold'. For some time now, little deserted settlements near the border had been coming back to life. This was thanks to Luxembourg, which had long suffered from a shortage of manpower and naturally turned to its neighbours to attract the arms and heads it lacked. Lots of people were now hitting the road every day to go to foreign jobs. Over there, the pay was good but social services meagre, so people's lives straddled the frontier, working on one side while living on the other. As a result, these transborder infusions were reviving moribund areas. A school would be saved; a bakery would open next to a shuttered church; houses would suddenly pop up in the countryside like mushrooms. An entire world was rising from the earth, as if by magic. And every morning and evening, throngs of commuting workers with bags under their eyes would crowd the trains and jam the motorways, seeking the means of their subsistence abroad. Underground, the economy had found new ways to develop.

Anthony mowed the lawn while his father trimmed the hedges. Lulled by the drone of the mower, he forgot his worries. When the sun was high enough, he took off his polo shirt and shoes. Blades of grass stuck to his sweaty chest and face. They itched, but if he started to scratch, he would never be able to stop. He pushed and pulled the heavy, whirring machine, circling the trees without thinking of anything. Glancing at his bare feet in the dry grass from time to time, it occurred to him how easily he could stumble. After all, it was hot and he was tired; that's how accidents happened. His feet would slip right under the blade, which would go on turning at three thousand rpm without slowing. Strangely enough, that cheered him up. Blood often struck him as a means of escape.

Around three o'clock, his father called him to eat. Anthony was almost finished, and he walked up to the terrace with a pleasant feeling of accomplishment, sweaty and covered with bits of grass. His father came over, gestured for him to wait, then said:

'Follow me.'

They walked around the house to the garage, where his father screwed a garden hose to a tap on the wall. After a few hiccups, the water spurted onto the ground in a strong, steady stream.

'Get undressed,' he said.

'What are you talking about?'

'Get undressed, I said. You're not going to eat like that.'

'I'm not getting naked.'

'Don't argue. Just pretend I'm not here.'

The boy took off his jeans and pants, covering his crotch with his hands.

'You think I give a fuck about your little thingy?'

Anthony's father started to hose him off. He put his thumb on the hose fitting to increase the pressure, and the water shot out, stinging and alive. At first it was unpleasant and even kind of humiliating, but then Anthony gradually got used to it, and the cool water did its work. His father sprayed the back of his neck and his head, to help clear his thinking.

'So?'

'What?'

'Feels good, doesn't it?'

'Yes.'

His father turned off the water and rolled up the hose.

'All right. We'll have a quick bite, and then you can help me finish the hedges.'

They walked back to the terrace, where his dad handed him a butter and sausage sandwich. The cooler he'd brought was half full of beers.

'Want something to drink?'

'Sure.'

His father handed him a can and they sat down on the lawn in the shade of a cherry tree. The smell of cut grass was delicious. The sunlight played through the branches above their heads. They drank their beers, exchanging a few words. Patrick drank a second one before eating his lunch. He was happy with the way the work was going.

'Nothing beats a lazy man once he puts his mind to it.'

Anthony smiled. All in all, he was pretty pleased with himself. He was enjoying the calm of the countryside. The food was good and so was his fatigue. He liked working in the open air and he liked it when his father was satisfied. It didn't happen that often.

'I shouldn't have told you what I said earlier.'

His dad was sitting right there, very calm. He touched his unshaven cheek and it made a good male sound, reassuring and gentle. He talked about his problems with Hélène. He must've really fucked up, and was already feeling bad about it.

'It'll all work out, anyway.'

He cleared his throat and started searching for his cigarettes. That would be it for today. Then he stood up, grabbed his gloves and stuck a cigarette between his lips.

'All right. When you gotta do it...'

Anthony watched as he went back to work, wearing his gloves and smoke coming from his nostrils. At times like this, he almost forgot what his father was capable of.

It took them another three solid hours to finish the hedges. Before leaving, they took the time to smoke a last cigarette and contemplate the result of their efforts. It was good work: the house was clean; everything was neat and tidy. Anthony would have been happy to stay there, enjoying the silence and his father's quiet presence. But they still had a way to go to get home. They packed up their gear and locked the fence. Anthony had almost forgotten the whole business earlier. The Drimblois party seemed very far in the past. Funny, how easily you forget things when you're busy. The drama had been diluted by work and sweat. He almost didn't feel guilty any more. Then he thought of his mother. She'd had all day to brood about this. He couldn't imagine what state she must be in.

Anthony fell asleep on the journey home, his head against the gently vibrating window. When he awoke, they were almost there. His father decided to clear the air while they were still alone.

'So what did you get up to last night?'

'I told you, we were at a party.'

'So?'

'So nothing. It was just a party.'

'Where was it?'

Drimblois was too far away. If he told the truth, his father would want to know how they'd got there and who had brought them back.

'In town,' said Anthony.

'At whose house?'

'I'm not really sure, some rich kids' place.'

'How do you know them?'

'Through my cousin.'

After a silence, his father asked if there had been girls there.

'Yeah.'

Nearly a minute passed before his father spoke again.

'Anyway, this is the last time you're staying out like that. Your mother was half crazy this morning. If you ever pull another stunt like this, I'll kick your backside.'

Anthony looked at his dad. He had the face of a tired man who drank too much and slept badly. It was as changeable as the tides. A face he loved.

They found Hélène sitting in the kitchen under the neon light fixture, leafing through the television listings and smoking a cigarette.

'Smells good,' said Patrick, pulling up a chair to sit down. 'What are we eating?'

Hélène tapped her cigarette's ash, then stubbed it out. She was smoking Winstons. There must've been like twenty-five butts in the ashtray. Anthony didn't even dare look at her. She was wearing her reading glasses, never a good sign.

'Potatoes,' she said. 'With eggs and a salad.'

'Perfect,' said his father. Then, turning to Anthony: 'Isn't there something you need to say?'

'I'm sorry,' he said.

His father continued.

'He puked on the drive there, you know that?'

'In any case, you aren't going out any more,' said his mother. She had wanted to say this crisply, but her voice broke halfway through. Patrick asked if she was all right.

'Sure. I'm tired.'

'You see?' he said, gesturing to his son.

'I'm bushed, too,' said Anthony. 'I'm going to bed.'

'You're going to eat first,' said his father. 'When you work, you gotta eat.'

There was no answering that. Anthony sat down at the table and his mother served them. The potatoes were mushy; the eggs viscous and too salty. Anthony gobbled the food at top speed. For his part, his father seemed in an excellent mood, as was often the case at day's end. Or else he had something to feel guilty about that he preferred to forget. He began to talk about upcoming jobs. It was looking pretty good for the summer. A little more, and it would be full-time work. He caught himself almost thinking his business was booming. He asked his wife if there was still something left to drink. She served him a big glass of wine directly from the box.

'Is this still the stuff from the barbecue?'

'Yes.'

'It's good, we should get some more.'

'I'm not sure it's worth buying five litres of wine at a time.'

The father took a big swallow and sighed with pleasure. Anthony had finished his plate, and stood up.

'Wait a moment,' said his father.

Anthony froze. His mother was already putting the leftover potatoes into a Tupperware bowl. Even from the back, just looking at her moves, you could tell she was worried.

'There's a good film on TV tonight.'

Picking up the television guide to make sure, he added:

'*Kelly's Heroes*. Got a 3.7.'

'No, I'm dead,' said Anthony. 'I'm off to bed.'

'Ah, these kids…'

Once in his room, Anthony undressed quickly and got into bed without even taking a shower. He was hoping he'd fall asleep soon and forget everything. He switched off the light and closed his eyes. From the end of the hallway he could hear his parents talking as they did the dishes. His old man must've drunk another glass; you could tell from the way he was talking, fast and a little whiny. His mother answered only with a yes or no. At one point, she must have told him off. Anthony heard, 'Oh, not that shit again!' and nothing further. Then someone turned on the TV in the living room. Almost immediately he recognised his mother's footsteps in the hallway. She came in without knocking.

'So what's all this about? What happened?'

She was speaking very quietly. Anthony lay still without reacting, so she closed the door and came to sit on his bed.

'What did you do with the motorbike?'

She shook him.

'Anthony…'

'I don't know.'

'What do you mean?'

It was too long and too complicated, he told her. He just wanted to sleep.

That's when she slapped him. She brought her palm down flat and hit her son's face with all her might. In the small bedroom with the shutters closed, the slap sounded like a firecracker. Anthony sat up and grabbed his mother's wrist before he got slapped again. His ear was ringing.

'Hey! You're completely nuts!'

'Don't you get it?' she said. 'Don't you even realise?'

Her voice was barely audible. She was talking to herself. Or maybe to God.

'It wasn't my fault,' he moaned. 'When we came out, it wasn't there any more.'

'But how could that happen? What are we going to do?'

They heard a sharp crack in the house, like a beam or a footstep. Hélène stiffened, jerking her head towards the door.

'Mum…'

He had to call out a second time to pull her from her daze. When she turned back to him, her eyes were large and moist, looking lost; her hands were shaking.

'I'm so sorry, Mum.'

She quickly wiped her cheeks, sniffed and yanked the hem of her T-shirt down. She got to her feet.

'What are we going to do?' asked Anthony.

'I don't know. We're going to find it. We don't have any choice.'

And before leaving the bedroom, she said one last thing:

'Otherwise, this family is done for.'

7

Anthony had been counting on his cousin to help him out. That was a mistake.

He tried to call him all day Sunday, even stopped by his house, without success. On Monday, same thing. He was nowhere to be found.

But thinking about it, this was nothing new. His cousin wasn't very reliable. But he was running out of time and he knew he couldn't manage the situation by himself. Every time he went into the garage he looked at the empty space under the tarpaulin and stood there, wondering whether he should run away or shoot himself.

Fortunately, his mother had come across an old box of Xanax, which she took before going to bed. She would be in a stupor until noon the next day. At breakfast on Sunday morning, she stood in front of an open cupboard for five minutes, unable to decide whether she wanted bread or crackers. And on Monday she went off to work without her glasses, and even without her high heels. Patrick had noticed her semi-comatose state, but he had long since settled the issue of Hélène's moods: she was complicated.

His cousin finally surfaced on Tuesday. Anthony found him in the bathroom at his place, bare-chested and in his underwear. He had just stepped out of the shower and was putting gel on his hair.

'Where were you? I've been looking for you for three days.'

'I was busy.'

Anthony couldn't believe it. How could you possibly not give a fuck to that degree? His cousin calmly went about getting dressed. He brushed his teeth, put on a T-shirt. Finally they went upstairs. The bedroom seemed unusually neat. His cousin put on some music, as usual. It wasn't noon yet, too soon to smoke anything. Anthony didn't trust himself to sit down, so he waited, hands in his pockets.

'Stop being so moody,' said his cousin. 'Sit down.'

'I'm in such deep shit, I don't know what to do.'

His cousin stood at the open window, clipping his nails. Birds were singing, very close by. The weather guy had announced record heat, but a little breeze stirred the curtains, and the temperature was still quite bearable. Anthony collapsed onto the bed and stared at the ceiling.

'Your bike's never going to turn up,' said his cousin after a moment.

'What do you mean?'

'By now, it's long gone.'

'Gone where?'

With an elliptical wave, his cousin suggested distant countries. There were routes that went through Marseille to Algeria and even beyond. He had seen that on a *Le Droit de savoir* programme. Guys could dismantle your Peugeot in seconds flat, and the spare parts would show up as far away as Bamako. Anthony was willing to believe that was true, but it had nothing to do with his father's Yamaha.

'So what do you want to do about it?'

'I don't know. We'll just have to go see Le Grand.'

His cousin blew the little pile of nail parings off the windowsill then turned to face Anthony. He hadn't looked him in the eye once since he'd come over.

'It won't do any good. You just have to tell your old man, that's all.'

For Anthony, that was unimaginable.

Once, when his father was passing a truck on the motorway, he was honked at by a big black German car coming up behind him. The guy must've been doing two hundred kilometres per hour and had flashed his headlights from very far away to get Patrick to pull over. Hélène and the boy had turned round to see. It was a prodigious, purring black car, sleek as an artillery shell. Probably a Mercedes; Anthony couldn't remember. But instead of pulling over, his father had eased up on the accelerator so as to stay even with the truck. Not a muscle in his face moved. He kept it up for at least five minutes, which is a long time in a Lancia with a V-6 sitting on your arse.

'Patrick, stop it,' his mother had said.

'Shut up.'

The tension in the car got so high, they had to crack the windows to defog them. The episode ruined the start of their holiday. On the way home, the family took an alternative route.

Anthony now started nagging his cousin, insisting that it was their only chance. At last, he finally gave in. They would go see Le Grand.

Around two that afternoon the boys found themselves in front of L'Usine. The wind had died and the valley was as hot as a frying pan. The air seemed thick, the asphalt like glue. Everything felt sticky. Just before they got to the bar, the cousin laid down the law.

'I'm letting you know now: we're gonna be in and out, fast. I don't want to spend all day there.'

'Okay.'

'We go into the bar, then we leave.'

'Agreed.'

'And I do the talking.'

L'Usine stood right across from H4, the blast furnace that had survived the longest. It was on a very straight two-way street leading to the cemetery. His cousin went in first. Inside, the temperature was around thirty-five degrees, and the guys at the bar seem to have melted into the decor. There were five of them. Anthony knew all their first names. The door closed behind them, as if snuffing out a candle.

'Hi kids,' said Cathy, the owner.

The boys returned her greeting as their eyes adjusted to the darkness. With a soporific whirring, three fans stirred the air. The regulars were perched on stools drinking beer, except for Rudi, who preferred the faux-leather banquette in the back – an odd choice, considering he was wearing shorts.

The boys walked over to the bar, feeling a bit intimidated. Heavy-lidded eyes turned towards them. Someone sniffed. Others tried to wave, to be polite. The overall ambience was that of a wax museum.

'So what's new?' Cathy asked.

'Nothing special.'

The cousin put his elbow on the bar and leaned over to give her a kiss. Anthony was a step behind him. He felt ill at ease, and eventually realised that Rudi was staring at him from his banquette. The man was breathing fast, his mouth half open, looking dazed, as usual. A cowlick rising from his skull accentuated his look of dullness. On this day Rudi was wearing a brand-new magnetic blue Castorama T-shirt.

'It's hot!' he suddenly shouted.

'Hey!' said Cathy sharply.

Startled, Rudi took a sip of his beer. He was now staring off into space, still panting. It was said he'd had meningitis when he was little.

'Pay no attention to him,' she advised.

Turning to Anthony, she asked him if he was being stand-offish. No, no, the boy answered, before coming over to kiss her in turn.

'And how's your father? We don't see him around any more.'

'He's pretty busy.'

'Say hello to him for me.'

'Sure.'

'Tell him we'd enjoy seeing him again.'

Considering the unpaid tab Patrick had left behind, that wasn't likely to happen.

'All right, gents, what can I serve you?'

'We just came to see Le Grand. Is he here?'

'Manu? He's probably in the back shooting pool.'

She shouted 'Manu!' With her accent, it sounded like 'Manoo!' Cathy was from Schiltigheim originally. The customers didn't react. They just took another sip of beer and returned to their few sluggish thoughts.

After a second shout, Le Grand finally appeared, holding a pool cue.

'You've got visitors,' said the owner.

But Manu had already spotted the boys and hurried forward to shake hands.

'Hey, what do you know?' he said, revealing a row of shiny-white teeth, all fake. 'So it's you!'

'Yeah,' said his cousin.

'I thought you were dead. What're you up to these days?'

'Nothing special. It's holiday time, that's all.'

'Oh, really?'

After trading a few more barbed remarks with hidden undertones, Le Grand ordered three beers. He and his cousin had done a lot of dealing for a while, but things had gradually become strained. His cousin, especially, began to keep his distance, because Manu was bizarre. He was dangerous and possessive, and almost always high on coke. You sensed they'd had a series of complicated interactions. When Manu was done teasing him, he turned to Anthony and asked about his father.

'He's okay. Taking it easy.'

'Has he found work?'

'He went into business.'

'What kind of business?'

'He's a landscape gardener now.'

Manu was glad to hear the news. Cathy set three opened Kronenbourgs on the counter. Drops glinted on the cans, as if they were in full sunshine. Anthony could feel his mouth watering. Le Grand paid and passed the beers around. They drank to Patrick's success. The chill of the beer went right through them. It was alive, fresh; you'd think it was springtime.

'Nothing better,' said Manu.

His can was almost empty already.

'We wanted to talk to you,' said the cousin.

'Oh, really?'

Le Grand started to chuckle in that funny way he had. You would've thought he was yelping, with his perfect teeth in his sweaty face.

'Can we step outside?' asked the cousin.

'We're fine right here.'

Manu had long ago made L'Usine his home base. He lived nearby and spent his life here, playing pool and throwing darts, sitting on his arse, drinking and hanging out with friends. He felt so at home that he'd offered to help Cathy fix up the place. She turned him down, even though the joint had been stewing in its juices for nearly a decade without fresh paint or air conditioning, or even much housekeeping.

The place was historic. The regulars called it L'Usine; other people stayed away. People drank in silence until five o'clock, and more energetically afterwards. Depending on their temperament, they were then sick, funny or mean. Cathy ran her world with a firm hand. The police didn't bother coming by, because she knew how to deal with drunks. From time to time when she was in the mood, she would put on a CD of Joe Dassin songs, and you could glimpse, under her layers of make-up, the young girl she'd once been.

'I'd still rather we stepped outside,' insisted the cousin.

'Oh, all right.'

They finished their beers before leaving.

'See you later,' said Manu.

Rudi, who hadn't missed anything of the scene, grew suddenly agitated, tugging at his collar and waving his hands.

'Where you going?'

As before, he spoke too loudly, and Cathy suggested he calm down, otherwise he would have to do his drinking somewhere else.

'Nowhere,' answered Manu. 'We'll be right back.'

'Can I come?' asked Rudi worriedly.

'Don't budge. We'll be back, like I said.'

'Wait...'

Rudi had begun extracting himself from the banquette, which was no easy task.

'I told you to stay put,' said Le Grand. 'I'll be back, there's no reason to panic.'

The regulars enjoyed the spectacle, but without hoping for much from it. Manu was standing near the door. He did look sort of odd, with his tight jeans and his Doc Martens. His tattered Jack Daniel's T-shirt was darker at the armpits. But what was most unusual was his football player haircut: long on the back of his neck, and almost nothing at the temples. It would be hard to guess his age.

Cathy promised to keep an eye on Rudi, who had settled down.

Outside, Manu and the boys were dazzled by the sunlight. Le Grand squinted so hard, you couldn't see his eyes.

'So what's this little secret of yours?'

The cousin was about to blurt it out, but Le Grand raised his hand. 'You hear that?'

The empty street in front of them was lined with unremarkable brick houses. The few windows were whitewashed. On the other side, the echoing carcass of the blast furnace rose in the shimmering heat. All around it lay a rusty jungle, a tangle of piping, bricks, bolting and steel mesh, a mass of stairs and railings, pipes and ladders, empty warehouses and sheds.

'Hear that?' Le Grand repeated.

In the distance, you could hear a clatter of dings and clangs.

'What is it?'

'Kids playing with slingshots. Completely out of their minds. They shoot ball bearings at each other. The walls are spotted with holes. It'll all come crashing down one of these days.'

'Can't anybody stop them?' asked the cousin.

'Why bother?'

For a century, the Heillange blast furnaces had sucked the life out of the region, gulping down people, time and raw materials all at once. On one side, carts on tracks trundled in fuel and mineral ores. On the other, metal ingots left by train before taking rivers and streams to slowly make their way across Europe.

Located at the crossroads, the mill's insatiable body had lasted as long as it could, fed by roads and exhaustion, nourished by a whole network of channels, which, once everything was deposited and sold by weight, had cruelly bled parts of the town dry. Those ghostly absences stirred memories, as did the overgrown train tracks, fading billboards and bullet-riddled street signs.

Anthony knew this story well. He'd been told it his whole childhood. From the firebox stoking hatch, ore turned to cast iron at fifteen hundred degrees, in a burst of heat whose tenders caused pride and sometimes even death. The mill had hissed, moaned and roared for six generations, even at night. Since interrupting it would cost a fortune, it was better to tear men from their beds and their wives. And in the end, all that was left were reddish shapes behind a fence with a small padlock. Someone held an art opening there last year. A legislative candidate suggested turning it into a theme park. Now kids were destroying it with slingshots.

'The fire department came round the other day,' said Le Grand. 'They found a kid who was half dead. He'd been hit in the temple.'

'Oh yeah?'

'Yeah.'

'So what happened?'

'I don't know, I don't read the paper.'

'Who was it?'

'One of those weird kids from Hennicourt. Seems he was bleeding like a stuck pig when they found him.'

'You can't kill those people. He probably pulled through.'

The sarcasm, which was usual when talking about the inbreds, didn't get a laugh out of Manu. His father had worked at Metalor from middle school until his accident. His uncles had spent their lives in there as well. His grandfather, too. It was the same with the Casatis and half the people in the valley.

'All right, guys,' Manu continued in his monotone. 'What is it you want?'

'It's about the Boualis.'

'So?'

'You know them, right? You're tight with everybody.'

'I don't know anything. I never see those people. What's this problem of yours?'

In a few words, the cousin explained. The party and Hacine showing up. The motorbike disappearing. Their suspicions. When he heard about the bike, Le Grand whistled admiringly.

'Man, when your dad hears about this...'

'You sure you can't talk to them?'

'To say what? You don't even know if it was them.'

Put that way, the whole approach looked completely ridiculous, of course. The cousin went on chatting, for appearances' sake, and then the conversation dried up. The low ping of ball bearings ricocheting in the mill resumed. Shading his eyes, Le Grand tried to see inside, then gave up.

'C'mon, I'll get you a drink. It'll be something, at least.'

The boys thought he was going to treat them to another beer at L'Usine, but instead of that, he invited them to his place. He lived just down the street towards the cemetery. The boys didn't dare refuse.

On the way, Anthony thought about the half-crazy kids who were shooting up the steel mill. They lived in tiny settlements strung along empty motorways with run-down farms, abandoned post offices, and walls bearing Monsavon advertising posters. No one knew why, but all the people living there looked more or less the same, with oversized heads shaved bald as cue balls, and ears that stuck out. You hardly ever saw them in winter, but when spring came they drove into town in their patched-up cars. When you encountered them downtown, they hugged the walls, but in their element, they weren't so constrained. People said they ate dogs and hedgehogs. Anthony had been in primary school with a few of them:

Jérémy Huguenot, Lucie Kreper and Fred Carton. They weren't especially mean, but they were already tough and proud, quick to throw a punch. You didn't see them after year six. They probably clustered in technical schools until they were of age. After that, they lived marginal lives on benefits and petty theft, incestuous families that got into fights and once in a while gave birth to a force of nature that scared the hell out of the whole country.

Manu's apartment was up under the roof, and it was even hotter than in the bar.

'Have a seat,' he said, pointing to the sofa bed.

He threw the windows open. The boys were already drenched with sweat.

A little dog was asleep in a basket on the floor, panting. On the visible beams were stacked paperback books and pieces of decorative African art; a dreamcatcher hung in a corner. Aside from that, there wasn't much, a big orange armchair and a *Subway* poster on the wall. A drawing pin had popped out, and the poster's upper-right corner curled down.

Manu emerged from the open kitchen with a six-pack of beer he'd bought at Aldi. It was Labatt 50 – cheap stuff – but it came straight from the fridge. He took one, left the others on the coffee table and dropped into his armchair.

'Drink up while it's still cold,' he said.

The boys did so. The beer was icy, a treat.

After setting his beer down, Manu swung his chair around so he could scratch the head of the little dog, which was still sleeping in its basket. It was a small black-and-tan mutt with a pointed muzzle. The dog sighed at being stroked, and Manu poured some beer into its bowl.

'Want a little drink?'

He moved the bowl closer to the dog, which opened a dubious eye before lapping it up. Then it lowered its head back in the basket.

'Poor animal. In this heat, he sleeps all day long.'

After that, he switched on the hi-fi. A guy started singing 'Je peux très bien me passer de toi'. It was a good song, and Manu turned the volume up a little.

'You've got a nice place,' said the cousin. 'I didn't know you did any travelling.'

'Are you kidding? Three-quarters of the stuff here comes from the Saint-Ouen flea market. Back in the day I used to go there all the time. Guys were always giving me crap like that.'

He took a long pull on his beer and set the can down, carefully putting it on the ring it had left on the coffee table.

'Anyway, I'm comfortable here. I have a room for my daughter. It's not too far from downtown. I'm easy. Except for the summer; that's a killer.'

The cousins were in agony sitting on the sofa bed, which was as hard as wood. Le Grand sipped his beer and watched them, clearly pleased to see how uncomfortable they were.

'You guys okay?'

'Yeah.'

Suddenly serious, he leaned towards them and said:

'You know, the Bouali family, I mainly knew the cousins when I was working at L'Escale. Saïd and I were locked up at the same time. But I'd be amazed if I talked to him twice in my life. And as for the kids, nothing. I keep my head down now.'

As he talked, Manu rummaged under the coffee table. There was all sorts of junk down there: video tapes, magazines, food wrappers, a baby bottle with curdled milk. The cousins exchanged a glance. They were starting to regret having come.

'Aha, here it is.'

Manu had found what he was looking for, a little metal patch kit. Opening it, he shook two grams of cocaine out onto the coffee table. It was lumpy and slightly pink. Anthony had never seen coke before, and his mouth immediately went dry. Manu was now busy making three neat symmetrical lines, using a playing card, an eight of diamonds.

'Hey, Manu, we aren't doing any coke,' ventured the cousin. 'It's totally cool, but we're gonna head home now.'

The dog opened its jaws and yawned. Seeing what its master was doing, it hopped up and gaily shook itself. Anthony felt a stab of dismay. The little dog had only three legs; the fourth was just a blackened stump. He watched as it hopped over to its master. Manu wet his finger, took a little coke, and offered it to the dog, which barked and happily licked it. Manu chuckled, showing him off to the cousins.

'He's funny, isn't he?'

'Yeah,' said Anthony.

'But seriously, Manu,' the cousin tried again, 'we're going to head off. There's this thing I gotta do.'

'You're gonna have a taste first. Even the dog does it.'

Le Grand rolled a Post-it note and inhaled a line of coke all at once. It must have been four inches long.

'Okay, your turn.'

He handed the Post-it to Anthony, who was literally dripping with sweat.

'Wait,' said the cousin, 'we—'

'Don't give me a hard time.'

Meanwhile, the dog was growling and spinning around in its basket at top speed, trying to catch its tail.

'What a little wretch,' said Manu, laughing.

The dog was spinning, hopped up and determined. The boys could hardly believe their eyes.

'Okay, calm down now,' said Le Grand. 'Hey!'

He slapped the little dog on the rump, and it groaned and lay down.

'It's the same old routine, every time. He wants a taste, and then he goes half crazy.'

Manu turned back to his guests, sniffed a couple of times and smiled, displaying his synthetic teeth again. Anthony realised that his face reminded him of someone. Oh yeah: the old Inca in *The Seven Crystal Balls*.

'Damn, but it's hot!' said Manu, yanking off his T-shirt. Underneath, he was lean as a rake. Even when he was seated, his stomach didn't bulge. He turned back to Anthony, doggedly.

'Okay, here we go. Time's up, pal. Go ahead. You take a big snort, and bingo!'

Anthony knelt in front of the coffee table. His forehead was sweaty and his chest was so tight he thought he might faint.

'You'll see. It'll do you good.'

Anthony put the straw in his right nostril and inhaled hard. When he stood up, his fear was gone. He'd done it. He was feeling kind of proud of himself.

'Ha ha!' Le Grand laughed. 'So?'

Anthony was blinking. Aside from the irritation in his sinus, nothing happened. He sniffed. He pinched his nose with his thumb and index finger. He smiled. He ran his tongue over his lips.

'Holy shit!'

Le Grand burst out laughing.

'See what I mean?!'

Anthony wouldn't have been able to describe the sensation. It was nothing like drinking or smoking weed. He felt completely in control, sharp as a scalpel. He could pass the baccalaureate as an independent candidate. And Steph suddenly seemed incredibly approachable.

His cousin followed suit, and when he raised his head, he was smiling, too. The two boys had met on the other side, safely home, all things considered. And it felt damn good.

At that point, the afternoon started to race by at an alarming speed.

Manu cut another three lines. Then he found a bottle of pastis and poured them big glasses on the rocks. Anthony was talking-talking-talking at top speed about the meaning of life, about coke and he was thanking Manu, he was so happy to be there, no shit it was so cool, he dare say he'd like to try it again. As he talked, he revelled in his precision, his exactly calibrated elocution, the unbelievable speed of his thoughts. Talking felt like being in a speed-skating race; the feeling of speed in the turns was phenomenal.

Soon, he took off his T-shirt. His cousin was grinding his teeth, then got bare-chested as well. Manu wanted them to listen to something on the hi-fi. He spent a long time pressing Fast Forward and Play on the tape player. He was looking for a Janis Joplin song where she prays to God to give her a Mercedes-Benz, but it must've been on another cassette, and he finally gave up. Glancing at his watch, Anthony was surprised to see that it was only a little past three. He had the impression he'd been there for hours. The dog had gone back to sleep. Anthony asked what had happened to its paw.

Manu returned to his armchair, suddenly in a bad mood. With his cigarette, he started singeing the few curly hairs growing below his belly button. An unpleasant charred smell filled the room.

'It was an accident.'

'Car crash?'

'No. An arsehole at a party. The dog was asleep on the sofa. This moron sat down on him.'

'Oh, shit.'

'He broke his paw in four places. Nobody told me. By the time I found out what had happened, it was too late. They had to cut it off.'

'No...'

'He whimpered for hours, poor thing. And not one fucking person got off his arse to help.'

Manu drew so hard on his cigarette, you could hear the tobacco crackle. The story had pretty much killed the mood, as if from then on, the little dog's presence kept them from having a good time. Anthony's head felt heavy. He saw his cousin putting his T-shirt on.

'D'you really want to get your bike back?' asked Manu.

'What?'

He took his time before answering, to keep them in suspense. He took another long drag, his cheeks sunken, eyes wide and rolling – a crow.

'Your bike. Because if Hacine swiped it, there's only one way to get it back, pal.'

He stood up and went into the kitchen. The boys could hear him fumbling for something under the sink. When he staggered back, his shoulder bumping along the wall, he was carrying a bundle. He tossed it to them but misjudged the throw, and the thing hit the floor with a thump.

'Go ahead. Take a look.'

'What is it?' asked the cousin.

'What do you think?'

The shape of the bundle didn't actually leave much doubt about what it contained.

'Go ahead.'

Anthony picked up the gun and peeled away the old *L'Équipe* newspaper pages. The pistol was wrapped in a cloth. It was a MAC 50. He took it in both hands and gazed at it. It was super beautiful.

'It's loaded,' said Manu.

What made it really impressive was its density, the big screws in the grip, the feeling of solidity and, really its extremely rudimentary character. Anthony ran his thumb along the grooves in the extractor. His cousin came over to take a look. He, too, touched it.

'Let me see.'

Regretfully, Anthony handed it to him.

'It's heavy.'

Le Grand was back sitting in his armchair, smoking yet another cigarette. He looked as if he was about to be sick. He attempted a smile and, with a disdainful gesture, tapped his ash in mid-air.

'It's clean. I'm giving it to you.'

The cousin laid the gun on the coffee table. Anthony was sorry that he hadn't gripped it; he was itching to, now. He would like to hold it and see how it felt, having that possibility at the end of his arm.

'We're gonna take off now,' said his cousin.

'Oh yeah? And just where d'you think you're going?'

'It's all good, Manu.'

A tiny vein was throbbing under Le Grand's eye. Casually, he flicked his cigarette butt across the room.

'You've got a lot of nerve, you little shit.'

The cousin gestured for Anthony to follow him to the door.

'You come to my place, you drink my beer, you snort my coke for free. Just where the fuck d'you think you are?'

'Listen, it was cool,' said the cousin, his hands raised in an appeasing gesture. 'We're just gonna go now.'

'You aren't going anywhere.'

Then Le Grand gagged on something. It hit his sternum and burned his whole oesophagus. He struggled briefly, chin on his chest, eyes closed. When he opened them, his pupils were so dilated they were like a bottomless lake, black and impassive. Anthony shivered. The gun still lay between them on the coffee table. Le Grand leaned over and grabbed it.

'Now get the fuck out of here.'

He was holding the gun with strange indifference. It dangled from his bent wrist between his open thighs.

'Are you gonna be okay?' asked the cousin.

Manu looked pale, and drops of sweat began to run down his temples. He sniffed.

'I said beat it.'

As Anthony walked by him, Le Grand's long, thin paw grabbed his biceps. It was burning hot, and there was something disgusting about the contact. Anthony thought about AIDS. He knew very well you couldn't catch it from skin contact; they said that on TV often enough. But the thought occurred to him anyway. He felt a chill on the back of his neck as he pulled free.

'Go on, you little fucker…'

The two cousins ran out, slamming the door behind them. On the landing, the air felt cool. They stumbled down the stairs at top speed. Anthony wondered what happened to the guy who sat on the little dog.

8

The two boys walked home by way of downtown and Blonds-Champs. What remained of their high made the distance disappear and they were hardly aware of it. But it was still very hot and you could feel the weight of the town, its smell of melted tar and dry dust, its slow descent into evening.

Anthony was walking in silence, lagging a little behind. He was feeling torn. On the one hand, he was glad he'd snorted coke at Manu's. That was a hell of a milestone and he wished he could shout it from the rooftops. On the other hand, the mess he was in wasn't resolved. Also, his cousin was striding along ahead of him, not saying a word. What could he be thinking? Was he in a bad mood? Other people's inner lives were certainly pitiful.

'Hey, what did I do?' he asked. 'Are you pissed off, or what?'

The cousin's only response was to pick up his pace, to the point where Anthony had to start jogging so as not to be left behind. Here he was, someone who'd got as buzzed as one of the Rolling Stones and this was bringing him down.

'Wait up, for fuck's sake! Wait for me!'

Just as they were about to head up rue Clément-Hader, Anthony's mood changed. He was suddenly overcome by the old malaise, of being sick of it all. It would never end, this feeling of being under people's thumb, being young and having to account for himself. At times he felt so bad he started getting desperate ideas. In films, people had symmetrical faces, clothes that fitted, and means of transport, usually. Whereas he lived by default, failing exams, getting around on foot, hopeless with girls and he couldn't even keep it together.

When they got to his cousin's house, Anthony at least had the satisfaction of finding his BMX against the wall where he'd left it. The two boys stood for a moment without speaking. It was between three and five, when the day gets a second wind.

His cousin didn't ask him in. Anthony couldn't bring himself to leave.

'So what's your problem?' he asked.

'You just have to tell your old man. That's it, end of story.'

'I can't do that.'

'How many times are you going to say that? What do you wanna do, go after it with a gun?'

His cousin said that in a nasty, sarcastic way. Never had the gap between their ages seemed so wide.

'Bye, man,' he said and went inside.

Anthony stood there alone for moment. Around him, the block remained cruelly unchanged, with its cheap houses, dried-out trees and head-high fences. Kids had written their names on the pavement in chalk. Letter boxes overflowed with flyers.

After a moment, he climbed the three steps to the front door and went into the little house. His cousin hadn't got very far, because his mother intercepted him as he was crossing the hall. As usual, the sound from the television filled the whole place. Anthony went in, and when Irène saw him framed by the living-room door, she deigned to lower the volume a little and said:

'Well, you sure look like hell.'

She was lying on the sofa, TV remote in hand. On-screen, an American detective was driving on the Santa Monica Freeway. With its shutters closed, the little living room glowed with California light.

'What's the matter? Did you two have a fight?'

The boys didn't respond. With Irène, it was usually best not to bring grist to her mill, since her mood depended too much on whatever pills she happened to be taking. She started blurting out whatever crossed her mind. Where was her daughter, for starters? She was supposed to come and dye her hair. The cousin didn't know. Then it was her bills, her problems with the neighbours, her job, her colonoscopy, the laundry, the ironing, the television, everything. From time to time Irène circled back to the great story of her life, 'my depression'. She said this in the tone she might use to say 'my daughter' or 'my dog'. This illness, which she had endured for years, had become a kind of companion, a presence. Her old boss was giving her grief. She'd been off work for a year and now the bastard wanted to fire her. But she actually wasn't too worried; the doctor had reassured her. If worse came to worst, she could always contact the labour inspectors. She understood her boss, though. He had to keep the business going. But hell, those bastards were making enough money off the backs of people like her, so she wasn't about to start pitying them.

At that point, something happened on the TV screen, so Irène turned up the sound and forgot them. It was over. The cousin took advantage of this to go upstairs and Anthony followed.

It was funny when you remembered what Anthony's aunt used to be like. When he was little, Irène worked as an accountant for a shipping company that specialised in refrigerated products. Whenever she visited, she would bring them crates of yogurt and creamy Danette and Liégeois desserts that were just past their sell-by dates. She was seeing a truck driver then, a bearded guy named Bruno. Anthony's mother would often invite them and the two cousins and when they came over, it was party time. The dinners would last until well past midnight, and Anthony always ended up falling asleep on the sofa, lulled by the grown-ups' talk. His father would bring out the liqueurs with the words 'Prune' and 'Plum' written in blue ink on schoolboy notebook labels. The smell of Gauloises, the men picking tobacco from the tips of their tongues. The knock-knock jokes. The women chatting in the kitchen. The coffee maker burbling at one o'clock in the morning. His father's arms as he carried him to bed.

Once, when the boys were in Anthony's bedroom, his cousin pulled out a strange little catalogue labelled René Château that was full of pictures of completely naked women. They looked at it in hiding with the door closed, but Carine had demanded to see, too, otherwise she would tell the grown-ups everything. Anthony was ten; his cousin, twelve. As they paged through the book, they pretended not to be especially surprised, but the business of that hair between the women's legs puzzled them. Carine showed them hers. She didn't have any hair, just a neat little crack in the middle that seemed intriguing. Anthony had pulled his trousers down, too. That was all a long time ago.

The boys – silent, hostile and uncomfortable – hadn't been in the cousin's bedroom for ten minutes when someone rang the doorbell downstairs. That was unusual. The Mougels didn't get a lot of company besides Anthony and Vanessa, and they didn't bother ringing. The cousin leaned out the window and told the visitors to come upstairs.

'Who is it?' asked Anthony.

Footsteps could already be heard on the stairs. Looking annoyed, the cousin made a few moves to straighten up his bedroom a bit. Anthony asked the question again:

'So who is it?'

'You can't stay here,' his cousin said with a sigh. 'You've got to leave.'

Clémence appeared in the doorway then, with Steph right behind her. Without thinking, Anthony put two fingers to his drooping eye. What the fuck was going on?

'Hi,' said Clémence.

Her hair was in a chignon, and she was wearing eyeliner. A sweet scent like candyfloss trailed in her wake. For her part, Steph looked very annoyed. With all four of them there, the bedroom now seemed tiny, and especially ugly. The cousin, who noticed, fluffed up the pillow and hid some of the wires on the floor. Clémence walked over to him and they kissed lightly on the lips. Anthony was blown away. A pop kiss. He looked at Steph.

'So, what of it?' she asked.

So, nothing. The lovebirds went to perch on the windowsill, sharply silhouetted against the bright outside light. They were young and gorgeous.

The next five minutes were pretty painful. Steph didn't make the slightest effort, Anthony didn't dare, and the other two would have preferred to be alone. This diplomatic imbroglio was expressed by tense silence, avoidance and Steph's sighing. Finally the cousin took Clémence's hand to lead her out of the room.

'Where are you going?' grumbled Steph.

'We'll be back.'

'You're kidding, right?'

'We'll be back in a minute. Just roll yourself a joint.'

The couple disappeared, and Anthony found himself alone with Steph. This was mind-blowing, unhoped-for, magnificent. He again touched his fingers to his right eye.

For her part, Steph started examining the VHS tapes along the walls. Head bent, she read the titles, from time to time raising an eyebrow in dismay. The very short sleeves of her white T-shirt revealed a vaccination scar on her left shoulder. Anthony could have just reached over and touched it. She looked a bit like a kid with her dungaree-shorts, round calves, the crease of her neck and the curls on the back of her head. She picked up a magazine and started to fan herself with it. The room was like a furnace and her skin took on a damp sheen. She was sloppy and heavy. The kind who ate with her fingers, licking them clean afterwards. She flopped onto the bed and leaned on her elbows, crossing her legs. As her right foot waved in the air, her trainer came loose. Anthony noticed that when her thighs pressed on the quilt, they changed shape and acquired a touching orange-peel texture.

'Hey there!' she snapped, when she caught him staring.

Anthony turned bright red and scratched his head. He announced he was going to roll a joint.

'What about his mother?' she asked.

'Nah, it's no problem. She never comes upstairs.'

'You sure?'

'Not a chance, I promise.'

This answer didn't completely reassure her. Anthony found rolling papers and hash in the little desk and started assembling them. What he would've liked to do was to talk about his little visit to Manu. That was sure to show her he was a real man. But Steph had other preoccupations.

'What about his mother, though? Doesn't she work?'

Anthony didn't know how to answer that, so he said:

'She has health problems.'

'Like what?'

'Her heart.'

That was pretty universal and it satisfied Steph. Anthony finished rolling the joint and held it out to her.

'Here.'

'Nah, I'm good.'

Steph was actually wondering how Clémence could possibly have dragged her here. This house was disgusting. How many people could live in here? It smelled of dog and the carpet was vile. She was especially thinking about the crazy lady downstairs who'd let them in. She'd asked if they were of age and then bummed a cigarette from them. That was certainly a new one.

Right from the first hit, Anthony felt his mouth becoming dry and pasty, and he was sorry he'd suggested rolling a joint. On the other hand, the odds of him sharing a kiss with Steph in the next hour seemed pretty remote. From lots of little details – her bracelet, the way she held herself, her perfect hair, the smoothness of her skin – he sensed that she came from an exclusive, chic world. Feeling envious, he confusedly imagined summer houses, family photos, an open book on a deckchair, a big dog under a cherry tree – the kind of clean happiness he saw in magazines in the dentist's office. This girl was definitely out of his league.

'Do you know if they've been seeing each other for a long time?'

'No,' said Steph. 'Anyway, I don't care.'

He held the joint out to her again.

'I told you, no. It's too hot. That's disgusting.'

Seeing the effect of her words, she was almost sorry she'd been so curt. This kid with his closed eye was sort of funny. He was a change from Simon. Just thinking about Simon made her sick. She jumped at the chance to resume being a girl unlucky in love, wallowing in her heartache. Really, she would've liked to think about nothing else all day long. Which was more or less what she was doing when Anthony interrupted her:

'What the hell are they up to?'

'What do you think?'

'I don't understand why he didn't tell me anything.'

'Clémence gets me into stuff like this all the time.'

'What do you mean?'

'I don't know...Like, what am I doing here, really?'

'I see what you mean,' he admitted.

His sincerity amused her. She kicked off her Converses and sat crosslegged on the bed. Anthony was definitely tormented by her ponytail.

'C'mon, give me that thing,' she said, pointing to the joint.

She relit it and took three quick hits. From then on, the situation became a lot more relaxed. Steph lay back on the bed and gazed at the ceiling. That way, Anthony could look at her legs, the blonde fuzz on her thighs, the sharpness of her shin. Very high up, almost on her hip, a rainbow-coloured bruise was visible. Her right hand dangled in mid-air, holding the joint between her index and middle fingers.

'What about you? You have a girlfriend?'

Taken aback, Anthony said yes. Steph turned to look at his face to see if he was telling the truth, and laughed mockingly.

'What?' he said.

'How old are you?'

'I'm fifteen,' said Anthony, lying again.

'Have you already kissed a girl, at least?'

'Sure.'

'So how do you do it?'

'What do you mean?'

'Which way do you turn your tongue?'

This was a debate that had greatly preoccupied Anthony during the school year. Opinions on the point varied, but he had decided to go with the majority. So he answered that you were supposed to go clockwise.

A mischievous look crossed the girl's face, and Anthony frowned.

'What about you?' he asked after a moment.

'What about me?'

'Do you have a boyfriend?'

Steph sighed. It was complicated and she'd rather not talk about it. So that was what she did and at great length. And Anthony learned that there was this guy, see, who was so hot, who behaved badly but was still so hot in spite of everything. Sometimes he liked her; other times he acted as if she didn't exist. But she understood him, sort of. He was complicated. Besides, he was reading Camus and Go Ask Alice. Anyway, he was driving her crazy. Anthony very soon regretted his curiosity. He eventually took back the joint and consoled himself with it. Steph continued her monologue, happy to revive her pain and display it to someone else. While she talked, Anthony could observe her at leisure. He watched her chest rise and he could see the outline of a bra under her T-shirt. She had stretched out her legs, crossing her ankles at the foot of the bed, a position that accentuated the triangle of her crotch. After a while, she stopped talking. When she did, Anthony noticed that she was rocking gently on her arse. He needed to touch her. He went downstairs to get them something to drink.

He was popping ice cubes from a tray for their Cokes when his aunt burst into the kitchen.

'Who are those girls?'

Three ice cubes shattered on the tiles, shooting chips all over the floor.

'Jesus Christ! You scared me!'

'So who are they? I don't know those girls.'

'They're just friends.'

Anthony mopped up the damage with a paper towel as his phlegmatic aunt watched, remote in hand.

'Where are they from?'

'What do you mean?'

'Did they come here to do drugs?'

'Of course not. They're just friends.'

He put the tray back in the freezer and took the Cokes to go upstairs. But his aunt blocked his path, standing at an angle in the doorway with her shoulder against the frame. She watched as he came closer.

'Is the fat one your girlfriend?' she asked sarcastically.

'She isn't fat,' said Anthony.

As they melted, the ice cubes in the glass made a subtle tinkling. Anthony could feel the cold gradually seeping into his hands. As often happened when he was uncomfortable, he kind of needed a piss.

'Well, she ought to watch what she eats, anyway. So where do they live, these friends of yours?'

'No idea.'

'They're pretty, at least. Tell them to say hello next time.'

Anthony and Steph weren't alone for very long after that. The other two came upstairs looking fresh as daisies; their hair wasn't even mussed. It was enough to make you wonder what they had been doing. Then the girls left the way they came, on their scooter. Clémence gave a little wave before taking off. Steph did nothing at all.

9

On Thursday morning, Hélène got up early. Her son had finally told her the whole story, in detail. She had turned the matter over in her mind every which way and had come to a decision. So she went to Anthony's bedroom, opened the window and shutters wide and sat down on the edge of the bed. Outside, you could hear birds singing, and the hum of the motorway in the distance. It was going to be a beautiful day. Hélène had given a lot of thought to what she would say to Anthony. She felt that her family's whole future depended on the impact of her words.

'We're going to go to this boy's house,' she said. 'I'm going to talk to his father, talk to the boy. I'm sure we can work things out.'

'You're completely crazy,' said Anthony.

He tried to talk her out of it, but it was a waste of effort. Once his mother made up her mind about something, there was nothing you could do about it. She left for work on time, all dressed up, in high heels and blue eyeshadow. Now that she had come to a decision, her worry had almost completely dissipated.

Anthony mulled the thing over all morning while squeezing blackheads in the bathroom mirror. Hélène came to fetch him in the early afternoon, as agreed. He didn't say a word during the entire journey. He'd told her a dozen times that there wasn't any point in discussing things with those people. She didn't agree. They would talk things over like grown-ups, she said; everything would be fine. She felt confident, but not so confident as to park right next to the towers. They covered the last stretch on foot.

The ZUP housing estate where the Boualis lived wasn't especially impressive. It wasn't like those huge developments, the maze-like dormitory towns in Sarcelles or Mantes-la-Jolie. This one consisted of fewer than a dozen low buildings, which seen from the sky were arranged like five pips on a dice, and three higher, fifteen-storey towers, including the famous Manet tower.

Built during the prosperous Trente Glorieuses years between 1945 and 1975, the ZUP had been steadily losing tenants recently, and the ones who stayed thought it perfectly natural to extend their personal domains into the vacated apartments. By swinging a sledgehammer, they created nice five-room apartments for themselves, with two kitchens, two bathrooms, and a bedroom for each kid. The rents, meanwhile, remained unchanged, since the housing authority office chose to ignore this private property expansion. Anyway, there was nothing you could do about those towers. Between the satellite discs and the clothes lines, you could see peeling stucco as rust spread to the balconies, lined the gutters and stained the facades. Anyone who could get out was long gone, to Luxembourg or the Île-de-France, or back to their home countries if they had pensions. The luckiest ones were able to buy themselves a house, the fruit of twenty years of sacrifices. The shabby ZUP buildings reflected the world and its architects' failure. They would be coming down soon, and not in some grand collapse, like on television. They would be bulldozed one wall at a time, as if attacked by insects. Like in London during the Blitz, the gutted buildings would display flowered wallpaper, rebar, Formica and open cabinets. In two weeks it would be all over; fifty years of life turned to rubble. And the sooner the better, thought the planners. Meanwhile, though, the place was still very much alive in its modest way, with long-settled families that had been living there for at least thirty years.

Before going upstairs, Anthony and his mother paused under the Picasso tower arcades across from the Cézanne tower. He wanted to piss and wash his hands. The life and luck lines on his palms were filthy. He felt sweaty and bloated.

'Stop fidgeting like that,' said his mother.

'I need to pee.'

'So do I. Just hold it.'

To buck herself up, she popped a Tic Tac in her mouth.

'Okay, let's go.'

Anthony groaned, but she was already crossing the street. It was just after three o'clock. Ahead of them on the right, kids were playing in a playground, riding spring-mounted pandas and watched by weary mothers sitting on benches. Some of them rocked pushchairs with sleeping babies. When Anthony and Hélène crossed the street, the mothers looking in their direction saw a tall brunette in platform shoes and a boy with a backpack walking by. They looked like thieves.

In the lobby, mother and son were surprised by the coolness of the concrete. They took the stairs. The silence was total. On the steps, their soles made an unpleasant squeaking that echoed in the stairwell. They stopped on the third floor and checked the names under the doorbells. The Boualis lived in the first apartment on the right.

'So?'

'Go ahead.'

Hélène rang the doorbell, and a shrill sound rose to the upper floors. In the tomb-like silence, it felt as if the entire building suddenly had goose bumps.

'That's enough, stop it!' said Anthony, grabbing her arm.

The echo of his voice paralysed them. Within these walls, every sound betrayed them. They waited for a response, but nothing came. Anthony and his mother were alone with their fear in enemy territory, their boldness quickly draining away.

Then the lock began to make metal clicking sounds. Complicated mechanisms were activated behind the door, which opened to reveal a small man with a moustache, dressed all in denim. Hélène tried to smile; Anthony hung his head. In the hallway's yellow light, Malek Bouali looked misshapen, with a big head and over-large hands. His face was marked by deep, concentric wrinkles, in which his eyes glinted weakly. He observed them peaceably, looking mildly intrigued.

'Good afternoon, sir,' said Hélène apologetically.

Curious and alert, the man said nothing. When Hélène asked if Hacine was there, the furrows on his brow deepened.

'No, he is not here.'

'Do you know if he will be home soon?'

'You want what?'

Hélène and Anthony were aware of the emptiness of the stairwell behind them, the building's silent verticality, a numerous, mobile presence, a dull agitation. A whole group of underemployed people on the lookout, held by TV sets, drugs and distractions, heat and boredom. The smallest thing could rouse them. Hélène answered that she wanted to talk to Hacine, that it was important.

'What is happening?' asked the man.

'I would prefer to discuss it when your son is here, sir.'

There was something suspicious about Hélène's politeness. It suggested the calculated distance of a *notaire*, or the tone of a doctor with bad news to deliver.

'He is not here,' he repeated, and started to close the door.

Hélène blocked it with her open palm, then her shoulder.

'It's important. I really have to talk to him, Monsieur Bouali.'

Hélène had sensed vacillation beneath the man's exterior. She asked if they could come in for a moment. Bouali wasn't sure. He was worried. Mostly, he just didn't want to be bothered. Hélène insisted.

'No,' he said. 'Leave me alone.'

One floor up, a door opened and young foreign voices could be heard, joined by the rattle of a chain, panting and the growling of a dog. At that, Anthony firmly pushed the door open and pulled his mother inside.

'Come on.'

'What are you doing? You have no right.'

Bouali staggered as the intruders pushed their way in. He gaped at them in disbelief.

'You are crazy! Get out!'

Anthony closed the door behind them and locked it. The three of them were now squeezed into the narrow hallway. The man caught the scent of Hélène's hair. It was a fresh, spicy lime perfume, the smell of a woman. It stirred him. She was looking at him wide-eyed, a finger to her lips, begging him to keep quiet. The neighbours came downstairs with their dog, chatting cheerfully in Arabic. Anthony's need to piss was getting stronger by the minute. When the other people were far enough downstairs, he asked:

'Do you have a bathroom I can use?'

The question disarmed the old man. He told Anthony to go to the end of the hallway and turn right. Hélène took advantage of her son's absence to tell Bouali everything. She had rehearsed her story for a long time and now told it smoothly, stressing the points that mattered. She said the word 'thief' twice, but in a gentle, consoling voice. Bouali's face gradually changed. All at once he felt responsible and terribly old. He and Rania had emigrated from a poor country and found something of a refuge in Heillange. At the steel mill, he had taken orders for forty years, while being punctual, falsely docile and an Arab, always. He very quickly understood that the hierarchy at work was determined by more than skills, seniority or diplomas. Among the workers, there were three classes. The lowest was reserved for blacks and North Africans like himself. Above them were the Poles, Yugoslavs, Italians and the least competent French. To get any job higher than that, you had to be born in France; that was all there was to it. And if by some unusual circumstance a foreigner did become an apprentice or a journeyman, an aura of suspicion always hung about him, some vague quality that forever put him in the wrong.

There was nothing innocent about the way the mill operated. At the outset, you might think that efficiency would dictate workers' assignments and the use of their strengths, that the logic and brutality of production and mandatory shifts would be enough. In reality, behind the ideals that were held higher and higher as the valley became less and less competitive lay a tangle of tacit rules, coercive methods inherited from the colonies, seemingly natural classifications and institutional violence, all of which guaranteed that the oppressed were disciplined and knew their place. Malek Bouali and his people were at the bottom of the pack, regularly called the afros, niggers, ragheads and wogs. With the passage of time, this contempt for him and his fellows became more covert, but it never disappeared. Bouali even got a promotion. But a stew of anger had been simmering in his gut for forty years. Today, it didn't matter any more. He was collecting unemployment and was using his Metalor lay-off bonus to build a little house back in Morocco. Rania had returned there before him. They had worked so hard. And what about their sons, who, even when they were very little, knew more and understood better? What had happened?

Malek Bouali cleared his throat and said:

'I will make the tea.'

He headed for the kitchen, leaving Hélène in the little hallway. In a moment she heard a cabinet opening, water running, a gas stove being lit.

They drank their tea in silence from hot little golden glasses that left circles on the oilcloth. Their host said little. Staring at his glass, he was ruminating darkly. Hélène, meanwhile, was fascinated by his meditative face, as furrowed as a field, and his workman's hands. He reminded her of her father, oddly enough.

'You are mistaken. Hacine is not like that.'

He was looking at her without pity. He wasn't lying, but neither was he interested in the truth. He was just doing his job as a father. Later, he would do that job with Hacine; that was to come. In the face of Bouali's stubbornness, Hélène again laid out the facts and he listened. Then he smoothed the oilcloth with both hands and turned his cloudy eyes to her. Hélène's shoulders were bare; she was beautiful. Nothing here was simple.

'You come to my house and you insult me.'

'I think we're well past that by now,' said Hélène. Outside, a blackbird kept singing. Anthony told himself that if the old man tried anything, he would tear his head off. He'd been stamping his feet, jiggling his thighs, and tapping his heels under his chair since they arrived. He wondered when Hacine would come home and imagined what would happen then. Anthony was always telling himself stories like that, about settling scores and throwing punches. But Bouali just closed his eyes.

'So where is this motorbike? I do not have a motorbike here.'

'I don't know,' Hélène admitted.

'So?'

'I want to talk to your son. I've been saying that right from the start.'

'He is not here.'

'I'm very sorry, but I'm not leaving without the motorbike.'

'You are going to leave now,' said Bouali in his husky, gravelly voice. 'Right away.'

Across the table, he and Hélène were sizing each other up. They were now down to the nitty-gritty. 'Parenting' is a big word. You can put it in books and flyers, but in reality, each of us does the best we can. Whether you slave away or don't give it a thought, the outcome always involves some degree of mystery. The child is born, you have plans for them, you have sleepless nights. For fifteen years you get up at dawn to take them to school. At the dinner table, you constantly remind them to close their mouth when they're eating and to sit up straight. You find them entertainment, buy them trainers and swimming costumes. They get ill, fall off their bikes. They sharpen their willpower on your back. As you're bringing them up, you lose strength and sleep; you become slow and old. And then one morning you discover you have an enemy in your own home. That's a good sign. They will be ready soon. And that's when the real troubles begin, the ones that can cost lives or end up in court. This was the stage that Hélène and Bouali had now reached: salvaging anything they could.

'When Hacine comes home, I will talk to him,' Bouali promised. 'If it is him, he will give the motorbike back.'

Hélène decided to believe him. She even felt a brief moment of tenderness for this decent, humiliated old man.

He stood up and added, 'You can trust me.'

Bouali picked up the three glasses and put them in the sink. Then he gestured towards the way out. Each of them covered the exact distance required by protocol. At the front door, they all shook hands.

Once he was alone, Malek Bouali leaned against the wall. His lips had begun to tremble and he felt his legs failing him. He stuck his hand in his mouth and bit down hard. He drooled. Later, he put on his shoes and went downstairs to the basement. There wasn't much in his storage area besides suitcases and his tools. Certainly no motorbike, anyway. He took his time now, first picking up a shovel, then a pickaxe. He tried a hammer. He hefted each tool, judged his grip, manipulated the object in the light from the bulb hanging from the ceiling. At last he made his choice. After wedging the pickaxe against the wall, he sawed the handle off just below the head. Then he went upstairs with his axe handle, sat down in front of the television, and watched the Olympics. The Americans were winning everything, the men's and women's 200 metres. Carl Lewis finally beat Mike Powell in the long jump. Time passed and night fell. Bouali dozed off a little before ten o'clock and was awakened by his son's return. He looked at his watch and muttered something in Arabic. He had to push on his knees to haul himself upright.

'Is that you?'

'Yeah, yeah.'

The young man was taking his shoes off in the darkness. He was a bit stoned and hoped the old man wasn't going to bore him with his complaints: Where were you, what were you doing, did you see your brother?

'I have been waiting for you.'

'I was with friends. I'm really tired. I'm going to go to bed.'

Hacine felt someone moving behind his back. When he turned around, he saw his father holding the axe handle above his head. Before he could say a word, it crashed down on his skull, producing a surprisingly hollow sound. As a follow-through, a second blow hit his elbow. Hacine fell to the linoleum floor, protecting himself with his hands as best he could. The blows continued to fall, and pain stabbed at his fingers, his ribs, his lower back. He could hear himself pleading. His father said nothing. He was breathing, taking his time, putting something into each blow, giving it the weight of work.

When it was over, Bouali locked his son in his room. There, Hacine examined the damage in the wardrobe mirror. His brow was smashed, and he had bruises pretty much everywhere. He could barely move his fingers. He carefully stretched out on his bed. He hurt so much all over that he started nervously chuckling. Soon an unusual murmur rose from the room next door. He put his ear to the wall. In his bedroom, his father was praying. That's how serious the situation was. Hacine pulled the sheet up over his head. He racked his brains, trying to think what his father could be angry at him about. He was in pain and he felt ashamed. Eventually, he fell asleep. At one point during the night he needed a piss but found the door locked. He had to relieve himself in the wastebasket. Next morning at six, his father came to him. They had a discussion, man to man. His father said that if he ever did something like that again he would kill him with his own hands. Hacine had nothing to say to that. However, he was going to make sure he found that little queer and his cousin. That much was absolutely clear.

10

By the time Steph woke up, the house was already empty. She padded into the kitchen barefoot, still very sleepy and in a bad mood. Her mother had left a Post-it note on the table asking her to turn the oven on at 11.45 and to remember to make an appointment with the orthodontist. Caroline had drawn a little heart at the bottom of the note and stuck it to Steph's bowl.

She poured herself some fruit juice and walked out onto the patio with an old copy of *Voici* under her arm. She was just wearing a pair of oversized boxers and her Snoopy T-shirt. She began leafing through the magazine while sipping her juice. Johnny Hallyday, Julia Roberts, Patrick Bruel – same old, same old. She and Clémence were fond of the two Monaco princesses, whom they called the mussels, a pair of idiots clinging to their rock. Those girls had nothing else to do and couldn't even snag themselves a decent guy.

Just then, the telephone rang. At that hour it had to be Clémence. Steph had forgotten to bring out the cordless phone. She could have got up and run to answer it, but she was comfortable where she was. You could see the last drops of dew glistening on the green grass. The warm air was gradually getting heavier. Soon she would be feeling the heat weighing on her stomach, yellow and oppressive. The whine of a motor rose from their neighbours' place. That was odd, because the Vincents were away. They'd gone to Ramatuelle for three weeks, as they did every year. The noise grew louder and Steph soon spotted a slim man pushing a lawnmower. She watched the play of his shoulder muscles under his skin, and his broad, ripped back. She lifted a foot onto her chair and absent-mindedly began to play with it. She'd put on nail varnish the night before. She ran her index finger between two toes and sniffed it. A discreet, sweetish smell, her body's familiar odour. While she was at it, she smelled her armpits. At night she would wake up in a sweat, hair plastered to her forehead and temples, because she couldn't stand sleeping without a sheet. She had tried to, but when she did, all her childhood monsters came out from under the bed.

The guy mowing the neighbours' lawn was taking a break now. He lit a cigarette and pulled off his T-shirt, draping it over the mower's handle-bars. His chest was taut and muscular, with blue tattoos. Steph thought of Serge, who also had a tattoo, a very faded seahorse. But Serge didn't have a body shaped by work like this, to say the least. He spent his days sitting on his backside in his executive armchair, and when he moved, it was to go and eat lunch with his colleagues or with service providers who picked up huge restaurant tabs in the hope of selling him software solutions. Serge did a little mountain biking on Sundays – with Steph's father, Pierre, in fact – but after a few miles, the men were just as happy to go and have a drink in the shade.

Across the way, the man stubbed his cigarette out on the sole of his shoe, pocketed the butt and resumed working. His back was tanned from the sun and his hair was thinning on top. Despite being under an open umbrella, Steph could feel a drop of sweat sliding down her right side. She vaguely felt like eating something but didn't know what – sugar, maybe. She pinched her thigh, hard. The phone began to ring again. Sighing, she decided to go and answer it. The patio chair left rectangular marks on her back and thighs.

———

Clémence didn't even bother saying hello.

'So?'

What she wanted was news about the previous evening. Serge and his wife, Myreille, had come to dinner at the house, and whenever that happened, it sent the two girls into a delirium of high-flying invention.

'So, what?'

'Don't be coy! How did it go with Porco Rosso?'

'It didn't go anywhere,' said Steph.

'Yeah, right! Spit it out, you hussy!'

Steph chuckled.

'Did he show you his dick?'

'Stop it! You're completely nuts!'

'I'm sure he showed it to you.'

'He just told me to be careful.'

'What a filthy pervert!'

The girls started to giggle. Serge Simon had become their whipping boy ever since the evening, after drinking two whiskies and the equivalent of a bottle of rosé, he dared ask Stéphanie if she shaved her pubes. Everybody around the table pretended to be shocked, but it was just for show, because, after all, the question was worth asking. Serge had read in VSD magazine that girls were all shaving their pussies nowadays. 'Heeeeeyyy!' Steph's father, Pierre, had cried, but he was even drunker than his buddy.

Stéphanie had known Serge Simon ever since she was a little girl. He was an old friend of the family. He would come over for drinks and go hunting with her father. The two men owned a boat together that was anchored in the Mandelieu-la-Napoule harbour. Serge had two daughters. The elder was finishing pharmacy school in Lyon. The other one was in the United States, where she claimed to be studying, but was mainly having a good time on one of those campuses like you see in the movies with manicured lawns and tall buildings, both historic and brand new, not to mention all those athletes, each dumber and more attractive than the next. Or at least that's how Stéphanie imagined it.

Two years earlier, Serge Simon was still teasing her, pinching her nose and telling dumb jokes. For her fourteenth birthday, all he could think of to give her was a Swiss Army knife. But for some time now, a curious reversal had been taking place in their relationship. Steph would sometimes catch him staring at her legs, or gazing into her eyes. It wasn't exactly lecherous but it felt like a fixation. When fat old Serge realised he'd been caught in the act, he would pull himself together and let out his weird, strangled laughter. Stéphanie and Clémence had turned it into a gimmick. *Heh-heh-heh* . . . A forced, chesty laugh. Their verdict: an IQ of five and all in his dick.

That's what the girls told each other, anyway.

Serge and his wife had come to dinner the night before. When Myreille was there, he generally behaved himself. Which was why Steph had painted her toenails and worn a super low-cut top. Aside from that, she hadn't done anything special to turn him on. She actually didn't say anything all evening, just acted grumpy, strolling around the house barefoot in her top, like a guy at a loose end.

It was funny, how men talked to her now. They used that bass voice, deep and well modulated. Especially Serge. They would go through the same routine each time. Steph would leave the table after dessert and at some point during the evening Serge would come and find her. He would stick his head into the living room, or crack the door to her bedroom and say, 'Goodnight, sweetie-pie.' Yeah, right. It scared Stéphanie a little, but at the same time she didn't mind feeling this successful man's eyes on her.

It was too weird, having men circling you with their heavy bodies and hulking shoulders, their cigarette breath, their strength, their hairiness, and their heavy, sexy, sickening hands. Stéphanie found it confusing; she was wary of them, but drawn to them. She also thought of what the men could do, with their big German cars and their credit cards. These were guys who supported a family, paid exorbitant business school tuition for their clueless offspring, had a boat nearby, gave their opinions, and thought that being the mayor of their village wouldn't be a bad idea, with their mistresses, their debts, their enlarged hearts ready to burst, their little whiskies with friends and their XXL Ralph Lauren shirts. Yet all that power would shrink to nothing because of some girl.

What did they imagine was going to happen?

Sniffing and vain, they could sense that the girls' first time was coming soon, and it moved them, made them angry. They, who were headed for the end of the line with their pointless business deals and carcinogenic responsibilities. One of these days, those slender young girls, with their perky breasts and legs that looked like they'd popped out of a mould three seconds ago, would get into bed with boys. They would spread their thighs and take pink cocks in their mouths. The imminence of this event left the older men dazed and inconsolable. Innocence was about to be lost in sweat, and the men would have liked to have had the privilege of erasing some of that virginal whiteness one last time. They were tormented by the girls' sleek lines, their flat stomachs, their skin so tight you'd think it was spray-painted on. These men, who had won it all, now realised that the only thing that mattered was the beginning.

Steph was now in the shade on the balcony. She leaned on the railing and continued chatting with Clémence. When the girls weren't together, they spent all their time on the telephone. Indeed, arguments regularly erupted between Steph and her mother, Caroline, who claimed the phone bills would bankrupt them. Steph's father instinctively defended her, at which point Caroline turned on him. The rivalry between mother and daughter needed to be resolved, but Pierre ducked the issue out of magnanimity or cowardice. So they all stopped talking to each other, and each retreated to a different part of the house, which fortunately was large. The father, especially, started arranging distant jaunts to avoid being hassled. His workshop had gradually become an office and was beginning to look like a small studio apartment. He even got an estimate to install a shower next to the garage. This highly political plan was the object of a maternal veto, however. Recognising the outsized scale of his intentions, he settled for a chemical toilet, which was fine.

'What do you want to do this afternoon?' asked Clémence.

'I don't know.'

'Yeah, right.'

'I just don't know. I don't think I'm even on his radar right now.'

'You're kidding, right? He's crazy about you, he wants you. It's perfectly obvious.'

'You think so? I don't,' said Steph, savouring her false modesty.

'For real...'

Steph didn't know what to do about the guy. She and Simon had been in year four together. He'd been a good student, noisy and pretentious, who wore 501s and Kickers. But he had changed a lot since then. Now he wore a leather jacket, smoked all the time, and looked sad. Through him, Steph had discovered Leonard Cohen and the Doors. She listened to them constantly. It was too beautiful.

'Well?' asked Clémence, getting impatient.

'Let's just go to the park.'

'You're kidding, right?'

'Well, what else is there?' asked Steph placidly.

'We went there yesterday.'

'Okay, but I'm warning you right now, I'm not going to go back to that guy's house.'

'Yeah, definitely,' admitted Clémence.

Her visit to the cousin's place hadn't been exactly memorable. That was the trouble with bad boys; as often as not, they lived like gypsies. That said, the cousin was really hot. Besides, he was the only guy to have any hash in this whole shitty town. Clémence wanted to see him again.

'And what about that mother of his?' snickered Steph. 'Seriously, did you see her? Totally gaga.'

Clémence didn't pursue it. She and the cousin had a date to meet that very evening near the decommissioned power plant. They'd already met a couple of times. He hadn't dared do anything yet, but she was confident. She shivered just to think about it.

The two girls remained without speaking like that for a few moments. Steph was pacing back and forth. The tiles felt cool under her bare feet. It was pleasant in this heat. She went back out to the patio. The man with the mower was gone, leaving behind a pile of fresh-cut grass. She caught the smell; it was delicious, spring-like.

'Man, I really hate this town.'

'I adore it.'

'The sooner we get out the better.'

'Just two more years.'

'We'll never make it.'

'Well, if you keep dicking around in school I'll obviously have to leave by myself,' said Clémence.

'What would you do without me? You'll never be able to fuck them all.'

'You might start by managing to fuck Simon.'

'Yeah, that,' said Steph, feeling depressed. 'All right then, we'll go to the park.'

By park, they meant the skate park the city had recently built near the fire department barracks, on the road out of town. It consisted of a ramp, three flat rails and two low walls. It attracted a disparate fauna, from rich kids to notorious punks. They did a lot of skating and even more drinking and when the time was right you could find good hash and really gorgeous girls. Despite a wooden style on his board, Simon did the best ollies in town, to the point that he pretty much neglected all the other tricks. He wore Vans with holes in them, jeans that showed his underwear, and a different T-shirt every day.

'We've already gone four times this week,' said Clémence with a sigh.

'So what?'

'I dunno ... It's always the same thing.'

'I just hope that fat whore Christelle won't be there.'

'Relax, that girl's nobody. He couldn't give a shit.'

'You think?'

'Seriously.'

Stéphanie started on Simon again, excited, desperate, talkative to the point of exhaustion. She had to go over it all again, analysing each encounter with him, his slightest gesture, his smallest inflection, like last night, the night before, like tomorrow. Clémence was a really good friend. She let Steph go on for nearly forty-five minutes. At the end of it, Clem announced that she would come pick her up around three, as usual.

Steph made herself some lasagne and ate it alone while watching a re-broadcast of *Cap Danger*. Then she went up to her room, feeling weary and a little sad. At times, she was sick of everything, even of her bedroom, though it had been the fruit of an epic struggle. When she was little, her room was opposite her parents'. Then, when she was twelve or thirteen, she started pestering them for a change. Various solutions had been considered, the most expensive of which involved converting the attic. That was the one they settled on. Unfortunately, the temperature up there fell below zero in winter and was over thirty during the summer. Insulation, ventilation and air conditioning quickly ran to fifteen thousand francs. But Steph now had a place of her own, with an unbeatable view and a little corner with cushions near a mullion window, like in America. Not to mention her own bathroom.

To relieve her boredom, she told herself she ought to do some reading. Everyone was after her about that: you had to read. Her bookcase mainly had the required stuff for school: Zola, Maupassant, *The Imaginary Invalid*, Racine. But she also had other books that she liked better. For the past month she'd been trying to get into the strange plot of *Le Grand Meaulnes*. The little love story was pretty nebulous and hesitant, but she liked it. It had an atmosphere that sometimes suited her when she was tired or had eaten too much. She opened her bedside-table drawer and found a package of Balistos. She took one, slipped it into her mouth, and felt the chocolate melt on her tongue as she returned to her reading. It was warm in the room, whose open windows let in a little breeze, stirring the pastel-coloured curtain. She ate two more Balistos before falling asleep. Twenty minutes later she woke up feeling hot, with an unpleasant taste in her mouth. Though it wasn't even two thirty, Clémence was outside, honking the horn on her scooter.

'I got the hell out of the house,' explained Clémence. 'My father was nagging me again about taking a *préparatoire* course.'

'Don't you want to do *prépa*?'

'Sure I do, but this is the sixth of August, so right now I couldn't give a flying fuck.'

Steph laughed. Clémence was a funny one, with her upper-class airs and her gutter ways, her daring and her insolence. Still, she would be starting senior year with an A average, and Steph was nowhere near that.

'On the other hand, I left in a rush. I forgot about bringing you a helmet.'

'Oh well, no problem.'

'Yeah, sorry. C'mon, get on.'

Steph straddled the scooter and put her arms around her friend's waist. From a dozen feet away, it would be hard to tell them apart. They wore the same kind of clothes, the same flip-flops and they both had ponytails. With a nasal whine, the scooter carried them off.

At that time of day, there weren't many people on the road. People with jobs were in their offices, at their machines or at campgrounds. Old people stayed home to keep cool. Only teenagers would be out looking for adventure in this heat. That said, speed softened the air and made the wind silky. The girls could feel its caress on their bare feet. Steph looked at the motorway over her friend's shoulder. Speeding along on the motorway, microscopic and in movement, the girls felt free, silently counting the promises that life owed them.

When they arrived, Simon, his brother Romain and their weird long-haired friend Rodrigue were sitting in the shade of the skate ramp. With them was a girl nobody had ever seen before.

'Who's that?'

'I don't know.'

Steph absent-mindedly redid her ponytail while Clémence put the scooter on its stand.

Everybody said hello, even the girl, who was smiling. The mood wasn't exactly welcoming. Steph looked at the new girl with deep distrust.

She and Clémence didn't dare sit down.

'What are you guys up to?' asked Clem.

'Nothing special.'

Simon's brother was holding a freshly lit joint.

'So you have hash now?'

'It's Anne,' Romain said, pointing to the girl who had shown up out of nowhere.

'She's Belgian,' added Rodrigue, as if that explained everything.

'Is that so?'

Steph did her best to smile at her. The girls still hadn't managed to sit down. They were standing there like a couple of twits.

'She's staying at the campground with her cousins. They're crazy, they smoke non-stop.'

'Cool.'

'Where are you from?'

'Brussels,' Anne answered.

'Great,' said Steph.

She was studying the girl's legs and face. For somebody from Brussels, the bitch looked awfully Latin. Her pale eyes almost clashed with her skin colour. And her hairstyle was all over the place. Steph and her friends wore their hair long, with hairclips and scrunchies. It was their pride and joy, and they were forever pampering it. By contrast, this girl sported a style that said well-mannered punk: half fringe, half Patti Smith. And naturally, no bra under her blue T-shirt. Steph could've wept.

So when Rodrigue offered her the joint, Steph didn't need to be asked twice, even though she'd sworn to herself to cut back on dope after the Drimblois party. That evening, or as much of it as she remembered, had left her with a bitter aftertaste. She had drunk beer, smoked weed and done poppers. At one point, Simon joined her when she was almost comatose on the sofa. He'd whispered intimate things into her ear, paid her compliments, told her secrets. Flattered and weak, she had let him take the lead. Suddenly, he was kissing her. Later, they wound up in a bedroom upstairs. Simon was holding her by the waist and neck. His hands were all over her. His kisses came as a surprise. They were lively and sweet, really delicious, like an overripe peach. While she was running her fingers through his hair, he very deftly attacked her bra. When he pinched her nipples, she found herself suddenly softening, becoming liquid, a lake. Maybe she told him no, but that wasn't very clear in her mind. She remembered Simon's warmth on her cheek, her neck, her swollen chest, the sound of a belt being loosened. He put his hands in her jeans and she spread her thighs. She sighed while he searched through her knickers for the damp bulge of her pussy. Then he pushed the cotton aside and found the soft lips. Steph seized his wrist to guide him. She was breathing through her nose, in a hurry, warm all over. She wanted to feel him inside her. Put them in, finger-fuck me. When he was done, he showed her his index and middle fingers, as wrinkled as if they'd just come from a bath. After that, she didn't remember much. She eventually went for a swim, feeling a little sad, happy, with that yucky feeling like after you've eaten too much and you regret it. Since then, nothing, he'd ignored her. It was shit.

Simon and Rodrigue were skating bare-chested while Romain and the girls hung out at the top of the ramp, legs dangling in mid-air. The repeated slamming of the boards' trucks ran through the whole structure and thumped in their chests. Romain started shamelessly coming on to Stéphanie. His putting the moves on her was especially annoying because it confirmed Simon's indifference; otherwise his brother would never dare. It made her feel ugly, sweaty and cornered. Worse, she had to keep looking good, what with the horrible new Belgian girl there, skinny as anything. At one point Romain tried to put his hand on her back, and she told him to fuck off.

'Just who do you think you are?' he snarled, stung to the quick.

Everybody heard the brush-off, and from the expression on his face, he clearly wasn't going to let it go. At that point, Clémence stepped in.

'Stop that!' she said. 'Like right away.'

She had gone out with Romain in year eight, and that sad experience had given her a kind of hold over him. If she didn't overdo it, and struck fast and accurately, she could put him in his place without too much trouble. But this time, she had gone too far by snapping at him so sharply. He stood up and walked to the far end of the ramp. Standing there with legs spread, he started to piss.

'You are seriously disgusting!'

'Ew, gross! Stop it.'

Romain took his time and ostentatiously shook the last drops off before zipping his flies.

'You got nothing to say to me.'

'You're disgusting,' said Clémence. 'Really, that's just not okay.'

'Oh yeah? And hooking up with weirdos is okay?'

Touché. Clémence paled. How did he know about that? What about the others? Did they know too? Since nobody reacted, she assumed that her affair with the cousin was common knowledge. Bummer. She promised herself she would end it very quickly – as soon as she'd got what she wanted, anyway.

Anne suggested that they smoke a joint, to lighten the mood. It was well intentioned, but Steph refused and so did Clémence, mainly out of solidarity. Besides, it was starting to get late. Steph was always careful not to be too stoned when she went home. Her mother had the soul of a customs agent and a stopwatch instead of a heart. If Steph had bloodshot eyes or wasn't home by seven, she'd be treated to litanies about respect and the future. Being five minutes late took on a premonitory aspect. It would spell her future ruin, unwanted pregnancies, drunks, dead-end careers or, worse, a sociology degree leading to a civil service exam. Not that her mother herself had exactly set the world on fire at law school. She made up for it by marrying Pierre, a man with the Mercedes concession and exclusive rights over the whole valley and dealerships as far as Luxembourg. At Stéphanie's house, people compensated for the shortness of their academic careers by telling themselves tales of strong arms, self-reliance and the value of work. The story wasn't completely inaccurate, but it greatly embellished the historical reality. To build his little automobile empire, Steph's father was lucky enough to count on a family inheritance, which was very welcome after three failures in his first year at medical school.

'Good!'

Simon had just landed very close nearby. He was standing there, one hand holding his skateboard upright, jeans low, his muscular stomach shiny with sweat. Steph looked up at him. His cheeks were glowing, his hair damp.

'Want to go?'

He was talking to the Belgian girl. She said yes in her heavy accent and stood up, sluggish and very tall, taking time to brush the dust from her arse. Her breasts flopped freely under her T-shirt. You could tell they were big and round. Stéphanie was steaming.

'So where are you off to like that?' asked Rodrigue teasingly.

Anne turned her back on him. Simon, who was wiping his armpits with his T-shirt, didn't answer either. He stepped off the ramp first, then helped the girl down.

'Have fun,' said Rodrigue.

Steph looked down, her nose prickling. The tears were coming; it was uncomfortable; it was the same thing every time. Besides, Clémence was watching her. But she held on, focusing on the bracelet she was twisting around her wrist. As soon as she was able, she stood up in turn.

'Are you heading off, too?'

'Wait, I'll drive you home,' Clémence offered.

'No thanks, I'm good,' said Steph.

'C'mon, I'll give you a lift.'

'I told you, I'm good.'

'You aren't gonna walk all the way home like an idiot.'

'Just leave me alone, okay!'

Clémence realised that they were close to boiling point. She didn't insist.

Steph set off across the undeveloped open space between the skate park and the old workers' housing. It was a hilly, grass-covered stretch that wasn't good for much except ditching broken fridges or riding ATVs. It would take Steph a good half-hour to get to town. The lake was at the end of the earth and her house wasn't much closer. Steph didn't care.

Rocked by her steady pace, she followed a dusty little path that wandered through this useless territory. Her heart felt as heavy as an anvil. She was keeping it together, but the waves of pain and heartache were getting bigger and bigger. She tried to run but tripped and wound up falling full-length in the dust like a klutz. Standing up, she realised her hands were bleeding a little. At that, the dam broke all at once and she started crying for real, a true ugly heartbreak, with snot, hiccups and make-up gone to hell. It left her breathless. Afterwards, she felt relieved, though very tired. While in that state, she was surprised to hear the sound of an engine and turned round to see. It was the other scumbag.

11

After their visit to Malek Bouali, Anthony and his mother hurried to leave the ZUP and get back to their car. They had to cross a landscape of car parks, flower beds and grassy mounds, mothers with pushchairs, graffiti-covered park benches and endlessly circling mopeds. Tenants watched them in silence from their windows. In the distance, you could see the viaduct that spanned part of the valley. The cars on it were driving to or from Paris at 130 kilometres an hour.

'See, we did well to come,' said Hélène. She was pleased with the way things had worked out. Something had clicked between her and the old man. 'Don't you agree?'

Anthony slouched along without saying a word, his head sunk into his shoulders. He looked grumpy, as if ashamed. His mother thought he was swaggering like some sort of thug. It made her want to slap him.

'Stop that thing you're doing. What kind of way to walk is that?'

Anthony glared at her.

'We'll never see that motorbike again!' he said. 'It's gone. It's somewhere overseas by now.'

'You don't know that. Those stories are stupid.'

'Come down to earth, for fuck's sake!'

'We did what we had to.'

He rolled his eyes. Once again, his mother found herself in the presence of a stranger. To think that ten years earlier he was making her macaroni necklaces for Mother's Day. He'd always been a good boy. He didn't exactly shine at school, of course, and he got into fights, but overall she knew what to expect. When he was very little she used to sing 'La Rivière au bord de l'eau' to him. He loved blueberry jam and those cartoons with the little Indian, Zachari or something. She could still remember how his head smelled when he fell asleep in her lap on Saturday evening in front of the TV; it was like warm bread. And then one day he told her to knock before coming into his room and from then on things went downhill in unexpected ways. Now she found herself with this semi-brute who wanted to get a tattoo, whose feet stank, and who swaggered around like a thug. Her little boy.

Finally, Hélène blew up.

'You stupid idiot! Do I have to remind you who took the motorbike in the first place?'

Anthony looked at her defiantly, almost with hate.

'You can't trust those people. That's what you don't get.'

'Will you stop that? You sound like your father.'

Curiously, he felt flattered by the remark.

'At least I know what I need to do,' he said.

'What do you mean?'

They were walking down the hill towards town. Below them, three roads met at a roundabout. One led to the Grappe housing development where the Casatis lived; the others led into town and to the motorway. Anthony picked up the pace to get away from his mother. Hélène grabbed him by the collar. She was ready to kill him.

'Why are you being like this?' she snapped. 'I can't stand it! I can't stand it, you understand?'

'Let go of me and leave me alone!'

He yanked free and Hélène was suddenly struck by how ugly her son was. In the months since puberty started to work its changes, she had privately accumulated a fair amount of disgust for him. It was like an ugly secret. He looked stupid; he was always in a bad mood. His drooping eye, which used to make his face appealing, now looked like an infirmity. And every so often, in his gestures and the way he spoke, she could recognise that other one, his father.

'I can't stand you any more! You hear?'

A car driving up towards the ZUP slowed as it reached them. There were kids inside. They honked cheerfully.

'Do you need any help, madame?'

Anthony took advantage of the distraction to ditch his mother and started running. The young guy in the car asked:

'Want us to bring him back?'

'Oh, leave me alone!' snapped Hélène, with a gesture as if swatting away a mosquito.

Anthony sprinted down to the roundabout and took the road to the left. It wasn't the one that led towards home.

He continued running like that for a while, but he didn't know where to go and had no intention of going home. He was angry at the whole world. Not that long ago, eating popcorn while watching a good film was enough to make him happy. Life was its own justification, even when it was repetitious. He got up in the morning, went to school, fell into the rhythm of classes and friends; everything linked up with disconcerting ease. His biggest stress might be a surprise test. But now he had the feeling of being stuck in mud, trapped in a prison of days.

As near as Anthony could recall, the fever first hit him in biology class. The teacher was using extraterrestrial words like 'monozygote' and 'scissiparity', when suddenly he didn't think he could stand it any more. Capucine Meckert in the front row. The colour of the linoleum. His deskmate. The smell of caustic soda and soap in the labs upstairs. His chewed-up fingernails. The energy constantly burning under his skin. He just couldn't stand it, that's all. Anthony looked at the clock on the wall. There was a good half-hour left in the class, and that half-hour suddenly assumed oceanic dimensions. That's when he sent everything flying: pencil case, books, notebooks, even his stool.

The visit to the principal's office wasn't as bad as all that. Monsieur Villeminot fully understood what made these kids tick, locked inside all year long, the victims of their hormones, pressured into earning useless certificates that would destine them for more or less prestigious career paths, but which all put the kids through the mill, and from which they emerged either accomplished or broken, but ready. Monsieur Villeminot no longer got upset over the fits of rage, the kissing in the corners, or the clandestine consumption of drugs and alcohol. He merely applied the rules mechanically, without anger or leniency. Anthony got a three-day suspension, since his outburst had followed quite a few others.

From then on, life had taken on a strange aspect. Anthony found himself waking up in the morning even more tired than the night before. Yet he was sleeping later and later, especially at the weekends, which infuriated his mother. When his friends got on his nerves, he got angry, started punching. He constantly wanted to hit things, hurt himself, smash into walls. He would take off on his bike with his Walkman and listen to the same sad song twenty times in a row. While watching *Beverly Hills, 90210* on television, a deep melancholy would suddenly overwhelm him. California existed, somewhere far away, and he was sure that people there were living worthwhile lives, whereas he had spots, trainers with holes in them and his lazy eye. Plus his parents, who ruled his life. He got around their orders and constantly defied their authority, of course, but even then, an acceptable future remained out of reach. Anthony sure didn't want to end up like his old man, drunk half the time and yelling at the TV news, or arguing with an indifferent wife. Where was life, for fuck's sake?

By dint of walking, Anthony had reached the edge of town. He'd gone far enough to see a depressing landscape of dense hillocks and yellow grass. For people with imagination, the abandoned shopping trolley over there might seem romantic, but that wasn't how he saw it. He was about to turn back when he spotted Stéphanie.

Immediately, his heart leapt.

She was alone on the little path to the new skate park. At this distance he was just guessing it was her, but from the ponytail and the arse, it had to be. A little scooter with its characteristic *pet-pet-pet* was slowly bumping along behind her. It was Romain Rotier, the other arsehole, riding his tiny Chappy. Steph stopped and waited for him. The distance between them quickly shrank. Anthony felt disgusted; he could already guess what would happen next.

Instead, it was the exact opposite. Steph clearly had no desire to talk to that idiot, and their conversation degenerated almost immediately. She wanted to go on her way, but Romain wasn't about to let her. He followed her, zigzagging on his scooter and tweaking the accelerator to stay level with her. He would veer off and then come back to block her path. What he was doing looked creepy and when he honked at her, Anthony could no longer stand it. He put his head down and charged.

He hadn't realised they were so far away. He had to run for almost a full minute to reach them and they had all the time in the world to see him coming. It was a curious spectacle, this short, stocky boy, heavy through the shoulders, pounding across the landscape at a dead run. Romain put the Chappy up on its stand and grabbed his helmet by the chinstrap, ready for anything. Steph could tell he was nervous. She wondered if Anthony was going to grab him by the throat; it seemed possible. When he finally reached them, dusty and out of breath, he was smiling.

'What do you think you're doing here?' snapped Romain, his lip curled.

Anthony stood with his hands on his thighs, trying to catch his breath. He had the sun in his eyes and couldn't see very well. Still, he immediately realised that Steph had been crying. Her face was dishevelled and her eyes were puffy and red.

'Are you all right?' he asked.

'Yeah.'

'Is there a problem?'

'Of course not. I'm fine.'

She had snapped at him. Romain was amused.

'What are you thinking, droop-eye? That she needed you?'

'What did you just say?'

A few more exchanges of that sort followed, along the lines of 'What do you think?' and 'Who do you think you are?' Romain had taken two steps towards Anthony and seemed to be planning to smash him in the face with his helmet. Which was exactly what Anthony expected. But Stéphanie cut them off:

'I'm sick and tired of both of you. I'm going home.'

Seeing that she really was heading home left them with their pride but without an audience. It seemed kind of a shame. Romain put his helmet back on.

'You were lucky this time.'

He walked back to his motorbike and gave Anthony the finger before heading back the way he'd come. The bike's *peeeeeet pet-pet-pet* sound faded, and Romain disappeared in a small cloud of dust.

In the other direction, the open space, suffocated by the reigning calm, was making motionless waves, and the sun, as it slipped away, lit the valley with a ripple of bronzes and golds. In the distance, Steph's figure had already become much smaller. Anthony decided to follow her. He didn't plan to catch up with her, just wanted to follow her a little. So he started walking, escorting her in silence, careful to leave a good hundred metres between them. Steph soon noticed that she wasn't alone. She stopped and Anthony couldn't avoid catching up with her.

'What are you doing?'

'Nothing.'

'Why are you following me?'

'No reason.'

'Do you have something to tell me?'

'No.'

'Are you a pervert or something?'

'Of course not.'

'Well then?'

'Nothing.'

He continued following her all the same. Steph was feeling more and more weary and depressed. She didn't want to be seen in town with this retard and she also didn't want to be all alone at home. Evening was falling, and she started to feel vaguely anxious. The two of them were now on the motorway to Étange. Steph was walking in the dry grass on the shoulder. Anthony was doing the same, thirty metres behind her. Once again, she let him catch up.

'Just how long do you plan to follow me like this? Aren't you tired of it? Don't you have anything else to do?'

Anthony shrugged. She was now talking without animosity, more to tease him than anything else.

'What exactly are you hoping for?'

'Nothing. I wanted to talk, that's all.'

'Do you often follow girls this way?'

'No, never.'

'You realise you're weird, right?'

He tried to give her a reassuring smile.

'I didn't want to scare you.'

'Yeah...okay.'

She seemed to be looking for something in the landscape. From all the times she'd criss-crossed the area on foot, by bicycle, scooter, bus and car, she knew the valley by heart. All the kids were like that. Life here was a matter of trips. You went to school, to see your friends, to town, to the beach, to smoke a joint behind the pool, to meet somebody in the little park. It was all comings and goings. Same for the adults: to work, to run errands, to the babysitter's, to Midas for a tune-up, to the cinema. Each desire implied a distance; each pleasure required fuel. People wound up thinking of the place as a road map. Memories were necessarily geographical.

Suddenly, Steph had an idea.

'Feel like having a drink?'

They retraced their steps and took the steep, winding road up to the overlook. It was lined with trees and pretty houses recently built by people who worked in Luxembourg. As they climbed towards the summit, the vegetation became denser, as did the shade. They walked along side by side, occasionally bumping elbows. Gradually their legs began to feel the fatigue of climbing. They walked in silence. Anthony was happy. He had so longed for something like this to happen.

Soon they spotted the statue of the Virgin Mary that stood at the top. The Wendel family had paid for the ten-metre monster of piety that watched over the sleep of the workers below. Now, decades later, with her bent head and outstretched arms open, she continued to bless Heillange. When you stood at the foot of the statue, it really was pretty impressive.

'A shell hit it during the war,' said Anthony.

'I knew that,' answered Steph.

This was their shared history. Steph told him to wait for a moment and disappeared behind the statue's base. Looking up, Anthony studied her benign expression, the heavy folds of her robe, the smoothness of metal that was beginning to rust. When Steph returned, she was holding a bottle of vodka.

'What's that?'

'We came up here drinking the other day. We left a bottle behind.'

'Cool.'

It was a new one, and the cap made a crack when she unscrewed it. She raised the bottle to her lips.

'It's warm,' she said with a grimace.

'Let's see.'

Anthony drank in turn. It was really disgusting.

'Pretty awful, isn't it?'

'No kidding.'

'Let me have the bottle again.'

Steph took another big slug before walking over to the circular view-point map at the edge of the cliff. She climbed onto it and sat looking out at the landscape, legs dangling. Anthony jumped up to join her. She held the bottle out to him.

'Hits the spot, doesn't it?'

'Yeah.'

They could see the Henne flowing in the distance, twisty and glittering. In the valley, it was clearly getting late now. The slanting light underscored the imperfections on Anthony's face: the down on his upper lip, a spot on the side of his nose. A vein pulsed at his neck. He turned to Steph. The two of them represented nothing in this space, which itself wasn't very much of anything. A tributary flowed through a valley where people had built six towns and some villages, factories and houses, families and routines. In this valley, the geometric fields of wheat and yellow rapeseed imposed a precise patchwork onto the hilly relief. The remains of forests ran between the plots, connecting hamlets, bordering the grey roads that ten thousand trucks drove on every year. In some places, a lone oak growing in the vivid green of a small valley stood out like a blotted ink stain.

People had become rich in this valley, building tall houses that mocked each village's daily reality. Children had been devoured by wolves, wars, factories. Now Anthony and Steph were there, assessing the damage. Life was coursing right under their skin. Just as a subterranean history was unfolding in this dead valley that would eventually demand allegiances, choices, movements and battles.

'Would you like to go out with me?'

Steph almost burst out laughing, but Anthony's seriousness stopped her. He was looking at the landscape without blinking, stubborn and handsome. The vodka had kicked in and Stéphanie no longer thought him so small after all. And getting used to his face changed it. She was seeing it in profile, without its head-on irregularity. He had long brown eyelashes and tangled black hair. She forgot to keep her distance. Feeling himself being observed, Anthony turned towards her. The half-closed eye reappeared. Steph smiled in embarrassment.

'What makes you ask me that?' she said.

'I don't know. You're beautiful.'

The light was gradually fading. They couldn't go home now. Anthony thought he ought to take her hand. Sensing that, she moved away a little.

'Where do you live?'

He showed her.

'What about you?'

'Over there.'

She gazed at the jumble of roofs, the intertwining of lives down in the flats, under the bridge. She had come here hundreds of times and knew this panorama by heart. She could find landmarks immediately, and could see how inadequate it all was.

'I'm getting out of this dump. As soon as I pass my *bac*, I'm gone.'

'Where do you want to go?'

'Paris.'

'Really?'

For Anthony, Paris was something abstract and empty. What was Paris? The *7 sur 7* broadcast. The Eiffel Tower. Belmondo films. He didn't quite understand what the hell she would do there.

'I don't care, I'm just going.'

For Steph, on the other hand, Paris was black-and-white. She liked Doisneau photos. She'd gone there at Christmas with her parents. She remembered window-shopping and the Opéra. She would be a Parisienne some day.

They drank some more, and then Steph announced that she had to go home.

'So soon?'

'It's almost eight o'clock. My mum's going to kill me.'

'Want me to keep you company?'

She took a step back and threw the bottle towards the city in a high, long, beautifully ballistic curve. The two of them followed it with their eyes until it disappeared a few dozen metres down below in a rustling of leaves.

'No,' said Steph, 'that's okay.'

After she left, Anthony watched the sunset. He wasn't crying, but not because he didn't want to.

12

Hélène Casati was treating herself to a personal day, as she did from time to time. She did what she always did in those cases: be the first one up at six and eat breakfast while listening to Europe 1. She enjoyed Philippe Aubert's show. He was funny and he knew how to talk about women, especially about Mathilda May.

A very precise routine regulated morning activities at home, dictating the use of the kitchen, bathroom and toilet. The goal was to avoid face-to-face meetings, because nobody in the Casati household woke up in a good mood. But meals are a special moment in family life, according to Madame Dumas, the social worker they were assigned after the accident. Hélène remembered her, a fat, energetic woman who talked through clenched teeth. When Mme Dumas sat down in the kitchen, her thighs took on alarming proportions. She dispensed advice while going through their household accounts. Hélène couldn't stand seeing her stick her nose into their affairs.

'I am a bookkeeper, you know.'

'I'm well aware of that,' answered Mme Dumas. 'But we can always do better.'

The perennially even-tempered Mme Dumas smiled then, as she picked her way through chequebook stubs, periodically wetting her index finger. She was really in her element. The judge had assigned her to the Casatis 'for the good of the child'. To some extent, Hélène could understand taking that step. Even Patrick was making an effort. Everything had all happened so fast.

'Do you realise that you need help?'

The couple answered yes. Anthony got used to playing with the toys in the corner of the judge's office. He once complained that he couldn't find the Smurf with glasses. Some other kid must have taken it.

Of course they needed help. In the meantime, Mme Dumas could drive you crazy with her fixed smile and relentless benevolence. Hélène had thought she didn't have a shred of affection for her husband left, but the social worker's behaviour nearly made them reconcile. The fat woman was forever listing his habits, the number of beers he drank, the number of cigarettes he smoked, his friends, his rifles, the motorbike, the language he used in front of the child, even his way of moving. She corrected each of his little ways so as to make the family function properly. 'We're making progress, we're making progress,' said Mme Dumas, a leitmotif she repeated immediately before blaming and prescribing. Patrick and Hélène had no choice but to go along with it. 'What do you talk about during meals? Do you ask your wife how her day went?' Patrick puffed out his cheeks. How could he answer that? 'You can go to the museum, too. It's free for the unemployed.'

Though barely civil in the morning, the Casatis were forced to try having breakfast together. They were eaten American style, with cereal and fresh fruit. Hélène still remembered the sound Patrick made as he slurped his coffee. She could still see Anthony stirring his muesli; he couldn't have been more disgusted if you'd served him mud. Hélène finally told him to go drink his Nesquik in front of the television. She and Patrick ended up alone, unable to say a word to each other, feeling humiliated.

Another time, Hélène had organised a trip to Europa-Park. To endure the long lines at the rides, the heat and all the arseholes, Patrick drank beer continuously, maybe five litres in all. That was the advantage of German theme parks: you could find Spaten on draught everywhere. Hélène took the wheel for the drive home, and they'd had to stop five times so he could relieve his bladder by the side of the road. Anthony had been happy with his day. He was still little; he didn't understand.

When the period of administrative supervision was up, Mme Dumas submitted a report that wasn't very favourable. But the juvenile court judge was handling nearly 150 cases a year, some of them a lot more serious. So they were left in peace. What really saddened Hélène was to see that their completely made-up story about a serious fall had become the truth in everyone's eyes. Even Anthony supported this version of events when he was asked. But Hélène had a good memory.

She had very nearly cancelled her personal day off. First, because there'd been a storm the night before and there was no point stealing a day for yourself if it meant just staying indoors at the cinema. And then the business about the motorbike was driving her half crazy. Hélène thought about it day and night in the weeks since it disappeared, and jumped every time Patrick opened the door. The bike wasn't worth anything; it served no purpose. They couldn't even afford to insure it. But she knew that the moment her husband found out what had happened, he would go berserk. To think that he was once prepared to go over to their neighbours' with a tyre iron because they were slow in returning a raclette grill.

But she needed this day, needed a break.

So she left the house first, while Patrick was in the shower and Anthony was still asleep. At the wheel of her old Opel Kadett, she'd headed for Guérémange. She felt excited; it was like bunking off. She was now driving on the departmental motorway. Through the windscreen, thin clouds emphasised the blue of the sky. Over there, a plane taking off left a contrail that promptly faded away. She rolled her window down to enjoy the earthy smell of rain on dry soil. The wet, dark scent reminded her of the first day of class, the smell of the next day, of nostalgia. It was going to be a beautiful day; they'd said so on the radio.

She first stopped at Carrefour to buy something to eat: bread, a tomato, a bottle of mineral water and a copy of *Femme actuelle*. Then she drove on. When she reached the swimming pool car park, she looked at her watch. It wasn't even ten o'clock. She had the whole day in front of her. She felt far away and free; it was perfect. She punched her ticket at the front desk, where the woman was an old school friend. They recognised each other and exchanged a knowing smile; that was enough. Then Hélène went into the cabin and put on her yellow bikini. She had bought it a few years earlier, but it was still in style, cut high on the thighs and going up pretty high on the stomach. To wear something like that, it was best to be a bit tanned, which Hélène was all summer. To finish, she tied her hair in a bun and wrapped a sarong around her hips. She picked up her bag and walked out to the open-air pool, sunglasses perched on her head instead of a headband. Her feet barely touched the ground. She was even humming to herself.

The Guérémange swimming pool was a model of the kind, both shabby and modern: dug in the 1970s, fifty metres long, with cement starting blocks and gravel tiles, two metres deep at the deep end. There weren't a lot of people early in the morning except for the hard-core ones who swam laps before it got crowded. Hélène chose a chaise longue with a view of the swimmers as they emerged from the changing rooms. Along the way she gave a little wave to a pair of sexagenarians who were permanent fixtures at the pool. The woman was knitting while the man read a newspaper unfolded at his feet. They spent most of their summers there, oiled from head to foot, caramel brown and greying. After lunch they treated themselves to a little nap in the blazing sun. Then you could see the soles of their feet, which gave you some idea of their original colour. Those two came from a nearly vanished era, when sunbathing was considered healthy. They didn't drink or smoke and they went to bed early, yet they baked in the sun every day.

Hélène unwrapped her sarong, spread out her towel and lay down. A sigh of pleasure made its way between her lips. She tried not to think of anything. She watched her long, seemingly smooth body relax. She studied it critically, inspecting her buttocks and thighs, raising some skin with the palm of her hand. It dimpled but, when released, reverted to perfect smoothness. Very gradually, Hélène's skin had become a complex surface, a memory. The changes were undetectable day by day, but then one morning she would notice a variation, a wrinkled patch, an unexpected garnet-coloured capillary. Her body seemed to be living a secret life of its own, mounting a gradual insurrection. Like many women her age, Hélène made herself follow seasonal diets. A strange pact struck between her and her body, with privations becoming legal tender in a barter economy. You traded suffering for vitality, emptiness for smoothness, restraint for fullness. The results were mixed, to be honest. Hélène patted her stomach and fingered the inside of her navel, producing a little round pop. She stood up, smiling. Time was passing, so what? Her bum still fitted into those tattered 501s she'd found in the back of her wardrobe. Men still turned to look as she walked by.

In the pool, the swimmers' movements raised a distant swish of foam, a glittering blue backwash. When the more experienced ones reached the wall, they did a quick flip turn and shot back underwater, extended and wavy. Hélène could feel the sun slowly baking her cheeks and nose, stinging her thighs. She was hot; she felt good. She stood and walked over to the pool. Balanced on the edge, she raised her arms over her head. The rules said she should be wearing a swimming cap. She dived in.

Hélène did the front crawl through the cool water, with gestures she'd learned at school thirty years before. In rediscovering their idiotic repetition, she reconnected with an undeniable sense of wellness. Very quickly, she felt warmth in her joints and shoulders. The effort produced a protected cocoon and she happily curled up in it. She could feel her stomach becoming leaner, her shoulders stretching. Every breath she took at the surface was a kiss.

After one lap she held on to the edge to catch her breath. Millions of reflections dancing on the surface stung her face. She blinked to get rid of the drops pearling on her eyelashes. Her skin grew goose bumps in the breeze. It was a miraculous pleasure. Everything that confirmed the existence of her body filled her with joy.

Because every day, everything conspired against that body. Her husband, who no longer fucked her. Her son, about whom she worried herself sick. Her job, which was making her dull by dint of immobility, meaningless tasks and endlessly repeated trivialities. And of course time, since that's all it knew how to do.

So she resisted. It had already been the same story when she was seventeen. She and her sister loved to dance. They picked up boys, skipped classes, bought pointy bras, listened to *Âge tendre* on the radio. In the neighbourhood, people already called them the sluts because they refused to follow the proper stages in dispensing favours, the careful progression from first to second base and beyond. Hélène had the most beautiful arse in Heillange. It was a power you were given by luck and couldn't refuse. The boys gaped at them, became stupid and prodigal; you could choose among them, line them up, go from one to another. You ruled over their foolish desires. In France in those days, a time of DS cars and Sylvie Vartan songs, when girls were stuck in the kitchen or working in shops, this was practically a revolution.

The most beautiful arse in Heillange.

That's what Gérard told her as he was bringing her home one evening. He was a gorgeous guy with a fur-lined leather jacket. He wore it as if weightless and she loved how light she felt in his arms. He was twenty and worked in a metalwork shop. On Saturday he would pick her up on his motorbike. He took her out and they would make love in dark corners, standing up behind refreshments stands, in the countryside on Sunday afternoons, wherever they could. Gérard was ambitious. After he finished his military service, he planned to work abroad. Each time, as he buttoned up his jeans when they were out in some rapeseed field, he would lay out his career plan. He would go and work on building sites overseas; they would have kids, seaside holidays, build a three-bedroom house. When he was on a roll he would even list the tools hanging in his imagined workshop, which would be next to their two-car garage. In the winter they would have a fire in their fireplace. With luck they might even go skiing; it would depend. Lying on her back, her eyes lost in the blue of the sky, Hélène listened. She could feel something warm dribbling between her thighs. She hoped it wasn't what she thought. She asked him. He'd taken precautions, no problem. And anyway, would it be that bad? No. A family, two cars, living here, it would be great.

Hélène started on another fifty metres. Her legs hurt already. She was short of breath and felt old. But after the depressing stiffness of the first ten lengths, she knew that a second wind would kick in and chase her gloomy thoughts away. The trick was to overcome the cold and the breathlessness, and the weariness that dragged you down. You had to hang on, to persevere in the absurd repetition of the laps. Thoughts passed through her mind, memories, melancholy. Swimming is a sport of endurance and therefore boredom. She stared at the bottom of the old pool and its missing tiles. The sun hit the water at an acute angle that produced glints, shadows, flashes of light. Each lap contained its own stages. Hélène swam.

The first time she met Patrick, his leg was in a cast. She was eighteen and wearing a gingham dress. A cousin of hers was getting married, and Hélène had put on high heels. She wasn't used to them, and it made her look a little silly, as clumsy as a baby giraffe. The other girls chattered behind her back. They were all in a group with her sister.

Hélène was used to having the other girls envy and slander her. With her arse, face and shock of hair, she knew that she threatened minor equilibriums, positions and comforts. If she felt like it, she could get Bernard Claudel into her bed, for example, even though he'd been going out with Chantal Gomez for nearly eighteen months and they would be married next year. Calling her a slut meant she was a threat and could use her body to solve certain problems. The term 'slut' determined an unfair power she was envied for and which people wanted to curb, out of caution, for fear of seeing certain things they relied on suddenly becoming fragile, turning to sand. In this instance, morality was pursuing a political project that didn't speak its name, that of limiting the possibilities for disorder that Hélène contained. To restrain the effects of her beauty. To curb the excess power at her disposal thanks to her arse.

Gérard hadn't been able to come to the wedding where Hélène met Patrick. So he didn't see the looks they exchanged. Patrick was hobbled with his immobilised leg. He wasn't able to dance and stayed in his corner.

He looked sad, or thoughtful, which made him look appealing in a Mike Brant kind of way. When the wedding party broke up, Hélène managed to get herself into the Simca that took Patrick home. After that, they had to see each other secretly, reconcile their families, behave themselves. It was easy. At that time in their lives, love could do anything. Later, they rented a little apartment and made plans. A family, two cars, living there; it would be perfect.

As it turned out, Hélène would never see Gérard again. Twenty years later she learned that he indeed did go abroad to work, to Tunisia, Egypt, and as far as India. He became a master welder, working for aeronautical, nuclear and agricultural corporations. These would gradually become more powerful than countries and afforded Gérard the kind of lifestyle and protections once dispensed by nations that printed money and declared wars. Hélène learned that Gérard had settled in Paca, somewhere between Toulon and Dragnignan, where he built himself a two-storey villa and drove an Audi. That he married an Antilles woman with short hair, which didn't stop him from voting for the National Front once or twice. Two children, friends, kidney stones, a neighbour whose tall hedge annoyed him – Gérard wasn't bored. Hélène learned that he'd caught the travel bug, meaning that once a year he would go on-site to verify the existence of landscapes he'd seen on television: Vegas, Madagascar, Vietnam. Hélène would learn all that at a funeral. That's always where you run into old acquaintances.

Hélène could feel herself catching the second wind she was waiting for. The difficulty diminished, giving way to a sense of expansion, acceptance and rebirth. She could easily cover another thousand metres, she told herself. Afterwards she would feel slim and energised. All she had to do was get past that hurdle to where the body surrenders and the spirit soars. Right now, everything was fine. Hélène would soon turn forty. People sometimes still called her 'the slut', but less often. She still had her looks and saw no reason why she should hide her legs or belly, much less her arse. Above all, she still wanted her share of love. At that thought, she smiled into the water, which kept the secret of her undiminished appetite for men. When driving, she would sometimes need to suddenly stop by the roadside to caress herself and come very quickly while some thirty-two-tonne lorry roared by, shaking the Opel Kadett. It was all still there in her belly, intact, her need for hands and eyes and the possibility of pleasure between her legs that defied the rules of the office, the rules of the road, her marriage contract and most other laws. They weren't taking that away from her.

Hélène had been sleeping with a co-worker for some time now. He was an uncomplicated man who wore Eden Park shirts and pleated trousers. She used to watch him walk by when he went out for coffee. He had a nice arse and also hair, which past a certain stage really matters. She'd drunk too much at the Christmas party and, as they were saying goodbye, more or less kissed him on the mouth. They began to circle each other. One evening as they were closing the year-end accounts she stayed late and he waited, in his office. They found each other and started kissing. Hélène had almost forgotten those deep, quick feverish kisses, with intertwined fingers and a panicky heart, like kids. She took his cock out of his pleated trousers. He entered her pussy almost immediately. Standing up, fully clothed, agitated and clumsy, it only took a minute. The very next day they went to a hotel. In the heat of the action, he fucked her while she was kneeling on the rug. Hélène had no problem with the concept, but changed her mind later, when she saw the carpet burns on her knees. Patrick didn't even notice. But after that, fucking on all fours on the floor was out of the question.

Thirty lengths was already fine, Hélène told herself. She swam over to the edge, her heart full of that pleasant feeling of a job well done. Kids had arrived while she was swimming, alone or in pairs, boys and girls between fifteen and seventeen. They sat on the concrete benches along the pool. She recognised some of them by sight. Around here, you always ended up recognising a face. Looking at them, Hélène felt a twinge. They were chatting; they were in a good mood, carefree and perfect. The water and the hours of training had created bodies built for speed. The girls with their tapered thighs and wide shoulders. The boys with childish heads perched on bodybuilder chests.

Conceding gracefully, Hélène smiled and went back to her chaise longue to dry off in the sun. The coach arrived and gave assignments to the swimmers, who lined up behind the starting blocks. The first ones dived in. The rest followed, synchronised and disciplined, barely raising a few drops when they entered the water. She watched their long underwater trails. Soon the two lanes were filled with their regular strokes. Under the sun, they went fast, they were young, and death didn't exist.

Hélène lost herself in her magazine and let her mind wander. It was past eleven and the edges of the pool began to buzz with people. After lunch she dozed awhile under the parasol. Around three o'clock, a kind of torpor settled on the pool. The heat was sweltering. You had to walk on tiptoe to get to the toilets. People sought refuge in the shade. In the water, a jumble of children splashed and yelled.

A little before four, the tall guy with the pale eyes arrived. He had an odd gait, awkward and rolling, like John Wayne or Robert Mitchum. Hélène wasn't waiting for him, exactly, but she'd still hoped he would come. He set his things down on the steps before his swim. Hélène was one of the regulars at the pool and so was he. Once, she and Line had enjoyed checking him out and imagining things about him, his job, his name, his voice, the sounds he would make during sex, whether he had children, his little habits – that sort of thing. They even came up with a name for him, Tarzan. That big, strong, clumsy body. Hélène watched him swim for a while, then forgot about him. When he came out of the pool, she studied his long arms, broad shoulders, and the water running down his stomach. He glanced in her direction and she felt a great void in her gut. She brusquely returned to her magazine, wanting to hide. He was going to come over. He was coming. Obviously not. He went back to his spot and dried himself off before leaving the pool. Next time. She felt ridiculous, as gleeful as a kid.

The parenthesis had ended.

Going home, Hélène still felt light as a feather. She drove slowly, in no hurry to get back, one elbow out the window. A sad Dalida song was playing on the radio. She should arrange this more often; these little escapades did her a world of good. Passing her parents-in-law's house, she remembered a Christmas Day party with the whole family, the afternoon they spent around the table. They'd been dead for quite a while now.

Everything was there; every street spelled her history; every building held a memory. She cruised by the fire station, drove around the primary school. Then a tall column of black smoke in the distance caught her eye. As she got closer to home, she saw it grow and began to catch whiffs of melted plastic and burning petrol. A worried frown furrowed her brow. It was very close to their place. She began to pray that nothing bad had happened. Once in their development, she drove past two blocks of houses before seeing a crowd of neighbours. They were all looking at the fire. It was the motorbike: broken, burning, melted and unmistakable.

Hélène yanked on the handbrake and shot out of the car without bothering to close the door behind her. She could barely stand. People watched her coming. She looked gorgeous, her hair flaming, electrified in the heat, tangled after her swim. As she passed, someone said, 'This is another job by those little wogs.' A voice called to her:

'Hélène!'

Évelyne Grandemange had extricated herself from the little group of bystanders, holding her eternal Gauloises. She was wearing a white blouse smudged by the smoke. She looked to be in shock and was trembling.

'Your husband is looking for you everywhere,' she stammered. 'He took the truck. He's looking for you everywhere.'

Hélène thought of her son and ran towards her car.

'Wait!' said Évelyne. 'What are we going to tell him?'

'I'll be right back,' Hélène promised.

'Wait, the firefighters are on their way.'

But Hélène had already driven off. She had to find Anthony. She was in such a panic, it was nearly a minute before she shifted into second gear.

13

To start a scooter without a key, all you need is a screwdriver, and Anthony had one. He'd swiped it from the Romand garage on rue Général-Leclerc, where he dropped in from time to time to watch the mechanics working. Didier would sometimes let him take a bike out for a spin, which was how he got to drive a Honda CBR 1000. Those things could shoot you straight to the moon.

Right now, Anthony was walking downtown, carrying a backpack and with the screwdriver in his pocket. He was walking fast, staring straight ahead. He had stopped by to see Manu, who'd seemed delighted to help him out. 'I told you, there's only one way to deal with people like that.' The weight of the MAC 50 in his backpack was unmistakable.

After walking along boulevard Sainte-Catherine, he turned into rue Michelet. He saw what he was looking for at the end of the street: a row of scooters on the pavement. There were always a few parked in front of the Metro. As he approached, he counted three scooters and a motorbike. Only the 103 had a lock. Anthony still had a fifty-franc note in his pocket and figured he may as well play one last game of pinball before he went. He pushed the Metro door open.

Inside were two rows of arcade games and players, mostly young guys furiously duelling in a stifling atmosphere. On the back wall, a huge mirror extended the perspective, repeating the smoked-glass shimmer of the electronic screens. The owner sat in a kind of glass cage in the middle of the room. His main job consisted of giving change while smoking Marlboros. Teenagers actually came to the arcade as much to smoke without being seen as to play *Space Invaders*. The place was pretty empty at that hour, but it was jammed after school and on Saturday afternoons. Anthony asked for five-franc coins and headed for the pinball machines at the very back. He could see himself coming in the mirror, a short figure in the blue glow of the screens. He put twenty francs into *The Addams Family* and played briefly and badly, his mind elsewhere, balls dropping one after another. He bought another five credits, which produced the same result. After wiping his hands on his jeans, he hesitated for a moment. Two heavily made-up girls were sipping Cokes near the entrance. A guy was logging his initials among the *Arkanoid* high scores. And two sweaty, silent boys were excitedly playing a Japanese fighting game. The younger one was pressing his controller buttons at phenomenal speed. From time to time a drop of sweat ran down his nose before falling to the floor. When the music stopped long enough to change CDs, you could hear the powerful roar of the exhaust system. Anthony played a last, equally disastrous game while listening to the Beach Boys, then kicked the pinball machine, which tilted ostentatiously. He didn't have a cent left. He felt nervous, irresolute. His stomach had been aching for hours.

Things had taken a pretty definite turn since the night before. Anthony had been eating chips at Antalya when his mother suddenly appeared out of nowhere. In her car, she promptly did a U-turn across the central reservation to drive up to him, in the process nearly wiping out part of the Turk's terrace and two of his customers.

'Get in!'

'What's going on?'

'Get in, I said!'

Anthony quickly obeyed. His mother had already been looking for him for a while. She looked shaken, and her hair was a mess. Her bag lay spilled open on the floor. One of the car's side mirrors was dangling in mid-air. Anthony was dying to ask her what was going on, but she was busy wrestling the Opel's stiff steering wheel to get them back on the road, everybody was looking at her, and she was on the verge of tears.

Later she announced:

'We're going to my sister's. There's no more motorbike. They burned it.'

She told him everything and for Anthony, it almost came as a relief. The world of fait accompli had its advantages, after all. At least the dread of a catastrophe was lifted. They now had to get organised, manage supplies, think about money, clothes, food and where they were going to sleep. After a week of holding his breath, it almost struck him as an improvement.

When Irène opened the door, she could hardly believe her eyes. It had been so long since the two sisters had stopped speaking. She served them tea and cake. Actually, playing magnanimous hostess was her big chance. She was never better than in melodrama. At one point the telephone began to ring and everybody around the table looked at each other for a long time without saying anything. The cousin took it upon himself to close the ground-floor shutters. It felt as if they were waiting for a tropical storm. But Patrick didn't come over. The phone rang and rang and Irène finally unplugged the line. Towards midnight, a heavy peace had settled on the house and they were able to eat something: some chicken breast, a little cheese, apricots so juicy they left your chin and hands sticky. It was still hot, and as the night gradually enveloped them, they started yawning despite their anxiety. They had to get some sleep. Irène unfolded the sofa and put a mattress on the living-room floor. Unable to sleep a wink, Hélène kept turning everything over in her mind without finding a desirable outcome.

In the morning, the whole family gathered in the kitchen for breakfast. Hélène and Anthony didn't say anything. They couldn't leave and they couldn't stay. Like refugees, they now depended on the revocable

143

goodwill of a foreign power. And Irène had her own ideas about what should happen next: they had to call the police, shelters, a lawyer. Delighted and venomous, she called her brother-in-law 'that bastard', 'that brute', and 'the louse'. Hélène didn't reply. She just stirred her coffee, looking sombre. She was gradually recognising the scope of the damage and thinking of logistical and practical solutions to her misfortune. At one point, Anthony left the room, grabbed his backpack, and climbed out the bathroom window.

He was now looking at his reflection in the Metro's big pale green mirror. A strange peace filled his chest. The time had come. He absent-mindedly touched his right eye and headed for the exit.

Outside, he chose the fastest scooter, a BMW with a Pollini exhaust. The area was deserted, but he had to act fast. He began by unscrewing the fairing. When one of the screws resisted, he used the screwdriver as a lever, and the plastic yielded with an unpleasant crack. He checked again to make sure no one was coming. Five hundred metres of blank wall stretched along the narrow street. His hands were now a little sweaty. He attacked the steering lock with his screwdriver, then grabbed the handle-bar and gave it a sharp yank. Now he just had to kick-start the bike. He gave it a firm kick, and the motor immediately snarled to life. Passing through the custom pipes, the exhaust produced a high, cutting whine. The familiar sound alerted the BMW's owner, who came running out of the Metro.

'Hey!'

He was a guy in sweatpants and a cap, one of those country no-necks who cruised the departmental ring roads, tough, scrawny teenagers, ugly as sin, whose love of noise was the bane of retirees and high schools. Other players spilled out of the arcade hall as backup. Anthony twisted the accelerator all the way and left everyone in the dust. Rue Michelet was perfectly straight, and he revved the motor until the speedometer started flirting with eighty kilometres per hour. At the end, he slowed to take the turn before heading for the upper part of town. His heart was thudding. At least he wasn't questioning himself any more. In the distance, a light turned red. He was tempted to ignore it but decided it was wiser to wait for the green. He was counting the seconds there when a voice surprised him.

'What in the world are you up to? What's that scooter?'

It was Vanessa, his cousin Carine's best friend. She walked towards him with a pair of ice skates slung over her shoulder and inspected his scooter. The light turned green. She wore her usual slightly mocking expression and stood very close, one leg bent, like a dancer.

'Did you steal it? Is that it?'

'No.'

The motor was idling slowly, with a neutral purr. When she noticed the state of the fairing, Vanessa burst out laughing.

'Bullshit! You did steal it! I can't believe it!'

Unlike what usually happened, Anthony remained unmoved. Vanessa searched his off-kilter face for an explanation for this surprising calm. Simply put, he didn't give a damn. Which unnerved her. Anthony was discovering how indifference could be very helpful in attracting girls.

'What are you up to?' she asked.

'Nothing.'

Anthony had never noticed how dark, golden and provocative her eyes were. He asked what she was doing with ice skates in the middle of August.

'I just had them fixed.'

The skates were heavy and she set them on the ground. As she bent down, he glimpsed part of her bra through the opening of her top. His stomach tightened.

'So where you headed on your stolen scooter?'

'Nowhere.'

'Want to give me a lift home?'

'I can't.'

'Come on, take me home. These are really heavy. My shoulder's all bruised and I'll be stuck with thirty minutes of walking.'

True, the laces had bit into her skin. Just the same, Anthony shook his head no. He had a lot on his mind right now. For once Vanessa was being nice. And her skin was really brown.

'Just tell me what's going on.'

'It's nothing at all,' Anthony repeated. 'I gotta go.'

The light had turned red again. She frowned. He remembered her hand and the coolness of her fingers when she'd touched his cheek that other time.

'Anthony, just wait for a second.'

So she knew his first name. He cranked the accelerator and the scooter shot off with a long, rising whine, a heartbreak.

After that, everything happened in a headlong, one-way rush. Anthony steered by his heart, faster than fast, feeling the road's slightest imperfection in his arms. On either side of his field of vision, the buildings were just a grey streak, and he enjoyed that panicky feeling of being nothing more than a moving point. When he drove, he stopped thinking, was content with being mobile, seeking the most extreme point of his thrust. He was discovering his machine's limits. His willpower itself was turning into trajectory. At that point, falling became an illusion; an accident, virtually impossible. Anthony was riding.

Unfortunately, the ZUP estate was at the top of a very steep slope, and the scooter began to labour on the way up, getting louder as it slowed. To slough off the feeling of being bogged down, Anthony drove around at the foot of the towers for a bit, but something in his momentum was broken. He soon spotted the courtyard with the painted carousel and its heat-struck trees. A bunch of relaxed young guys were lounging under the shelter. Anthony put a foot down, watching them from a distance. Everything was calm, the scooter's motor idling smoothly. He started up again slowly, his heels grazing the dusty ground.

For their part, the boys were half dozing, their heads in the clouds. That very morning Eliott had finally scored two 250-gram bars of Moroccan hash, cut to hell but smokable. After weeks of shortage, it was like Christmas in midsummer. So everyone had been smoking non-stop since ten in the morning, everyone was there, about a dozen guys, all seriously loaded and mellow. Eliott was in the process of assembling a six-sheet blunt, a joy.

'What's that?'

Seb was the first to notice the odd little guy on the scooter, but he didn't venture to leave the shade of the shelter. The guy was coming up slowly. Seb wanted to lick his lips. His mouth felt full of cardboard. His eyes narrowed to slits, he repeated his question:

'Hey…who's that son of a bitch?'

'Your mother.'

'No, seriously.'

The little group gradually had to face the fact that the guy wasn't there by accident.

'Hacine!'

'What?'

'The guy there…Come see.'

'What guy?'

The scooter was still approaching. Hacine stood up. With the sun, he couldn't tell who was riding it. The guy didn't have a helmet and was short, kind of stocky. Hacine was in a relaxed, friendly mood. He felt like going home to drink a Coke and quietly space out in front of his TV. It was so great to have dope again. Just thinking about it, his heart lightened a little. Meanwhile, his eyes gradually adjusted to the bright glare on the courtyard. The guy began to take shape. His face came into focus.

Shit.

'So who the hell is it?' asked Eliott.

'A nut job, seriously. Look at him. He's a nut.'

Hacine left the shelter and walked straight towards Anthony. Soon there were just a few metres between them. Unable to stand it any more, the gang started cursing in three languages. A couple of guys had already taken the initiative of leaving the shelter as well.

'You've got some nerve, coming here,' Hacine said flatly.

Anthony slid the strap on his backpack, opened it, and reached inside.

'Uh-oh!' someone said.

Anthony's hand emerged holding the MAC 50. The boys all scattered back under the shelter.

'Who the fuck is that?' yelped Eliott, who suddenly felt in deep shit, being stuck in his wheelchair.

Anthony aimed the pistol straight ahead, his left eye closed.

'Don't get excited,' said Hacine as calmly as he could.

He had the sun full in his face but could make out Anthony's square head, his closed fist and the gun's muzzle perfectly. Around them, the buildings observed the scene with a plastic detachment. Hacine felt fear coming. It gave him bad advice, urging him to beg or to run. But ever since he was a kid, experience had taught him that in his world, the price of cowardice is higher than that of pain. Running away or ducking a punch condemned you to the pathetic fate of victim. It was still preferable to face the danger, even if you regretted it later. That lesson, learned a hundred times over, kept him standing there, facing the MAC 50.

Anthony cocked the hammer and felt the trigger acquire an almost sexual sensitivity. He remained calm, the scooter's motor vibrating gently under him. Someone shouted from a window. Shooting at this distance, he couldn't miss. A tiny pressure would be enough. This would produce a dull bang and the expulsion of an eight-gram metal slug that wouldn't take even a thirtieth of a second before hitting Hacine's skull. From that entry point, about ten millimetres across, the projectile would burn a not insignificant part of the gelatinous tissue that allowed Hacine to breathe, eat Big Macs and fall in love. At the end of its trajectory, the nearly intact projectile would exit his head, leaving behind an irregular red gap, a mass of flesh and bone. This mechanical and anatomical sequence now shaped the relationship between the two boys. They couldn't formulate it quite that precisely, but they both understood it. Anthony sighed. He was going to do it; he owed his father at least that much. A drop of sweat ran down his neck. Now was the time.

Then the scooter stalled.

Oddly enough, that insignificant change made Anthony's gesture unthinkable. He felt his arm relaxing. He was drenched from head to foot. But he couldn't leave it at that. Hacine was still standing in front of him, aflame, ashamed, very close to pissing himself. Anthony did the only thing he could think of: he spat in Hacine's face.

He had to use his screwdriver to get out of there, which made for some awkward fiddling. Hacine didn't dare wipe himself off. He could feel the saliva on his nose and mouth. Anthony finally fled. It was all so unforgivable.

TWO

1994
you could
be mine

1

Anthony found Sonia in the storeroom. He should have guessed she would be there; it was the worst place to hide. She was in a bubble: she had her headphones on, listening to rock 'n' roll while staring at her chewed-up fingernails. She didn't even hear him come in.

'What the hell have you been up to? I've been looking for you for half an hour.'

Since she didn't respond, he snapped his fingers under her nose.

'Hey, I'm talking to you!'

Sonia deigned to glance up. Ordinarily she didn't look all that great, but this time she was a real mess: puffy, red eyes, make-up smudged.

'What's going on with you?'

'Nothing.'

'Has Cyril been giving you a hard time?'

'No.'

Sonia didn't have a childcare or lifeguard certificate; she didn't have her baccalaureate or a driving licence. At fourteen, she wasn't even legally old enough to work. In other words, she wasn't much use and had no business being there. It was her father who insisted that she be given a job. He was the sailing club association's treasurer, so Cyril, the manager, didn't have any choice. Sonia helped out, washed a few dishes at the bar, delivered messages and generally dragged her funereal mood from one end of the beach to the other, while listening non-stop to stuff like Barbara or Depeche Mode to cheer herself up.

She'd apparently had a difficult year, involving a lot of problems with maths and repeated heartbreaks. Her parents were worried, especially about the maths. Anthony liked Sonia. She was smart, quite funny, super-pretty despite her best efforts, with steel-grey eyes and full lips. She was also fun to talk to. But for the last couple of days she'd seemed completely out of it, hiding in corners while waiting for her shift to be over, unable to smile, even paler than usual and scary thin.

'Is it a guy? Is that it?'

She shook her head no. But what else could it be? Anthony was especially worried that she might be in love with Cyril. The manager was a fool, but he had style and might impress some girls with his salt-and-pepper look and his Breitling. He was just the kind of sleazy guy who screwed teenagers to make up for going bald. Just thinking about it drove Anthony crazy. She was only fourteen, for fuck's sake.

'Come on, don't stay there. There's gonna be a lot of people coming through today.'

She took the hand he'd extended and followed him to the bar, dragging her feet. She did take the trouble to lower the volume on her Walkman and Anthony appreciated the effort.

'What do you want to drink?'

'Nothing.'

'Just drop the bullshit, okay? You're not about to slit your wrists, so stop it.'

The girl shrugged. She would slit her wrists if she felt like it.

He took a Schweppes from the fridge, poured her a glass and drank from the bottle. It had been open for a while and didn't have many bubbles left, but at least it was cold.

Anthony had been on the go ever since that morning. It was one of those sweltering days. Everything was heavy and stagnant and the skies low and overcast. The few stirrings of air brought only a stench of mud, succulents and petrol.

'You can't pull a major meltdown on us now,' he said. 'Cyril is hyper stressed. With tonight's party, you'd think he was catering the Parc des Princes.'

Sonia was staring at the little 'Licence IV' sign above the percolator. Something flitted across her face that might have been a smile. No, her eyes were starting to well up.

Anthony suddenly felt very sorry. He tried to think of some way to help.

'Listen, just go and hang out in one of the bungalows. No one'll look for you there.'

After a moment, he tried again:

'Are you in love?'

The young girl's face abruptly changed. The question so shocked her, she forgot she was unhappy.

'You really are a loser sometimes,' she snapped contemptuously. 'How old are you, anyway?'

'Oh, forget it,' said Anthony as he put the Schweppes bottle and her untouched glass away. 'I really don't give a damn.'

'But do you have friends? Do you talk to people? You did go to school, at least, right?'

Anthony gave her the finger and a smile. Sonia was about to go on, but Cyril suddenly burst in.

'Hey, you there!'

He was hurrying in from outside, wearing light jeans and Sebago shoes, with Romain Rotier on his heels. Sonia's face immediately fell.

'What are you doing there, playing tourist?'

'Nothing. We're just taking a break.'

Cyril then launched into one of those management speeches he was so good at. He gave them often and almost therapeutically, thereby relieving his basic impotence. Cyril didn't really know how to do anything, so he was forever dependent on work done by other people, who were less well paid than he was. But he was their leader, and that was the cross he bore, his enviable burden. He was sure it would give him an ulcer one of these days. This time his topic was challenge and personal investment. Sonia and the two boys endured the talk in silence. They were used to it.

Anthony couldn't help wondering what could possibly be going on between Cyril and the girl. The way he ignored her, given how gloomy she looked when she was around him, it made you wonder. Anthony hoped there was nothing to it. He liked this job and had no desire to make waves. For one thing, he didn't start until ten in the morning, which was a major plus. And he spent most of his time hauling boats out of the sheds. It was physical and badly paid, but he met lots of well-mannered people who gave surprisingly good tips. The rest of the time, he loafed on the beach, flirted with rich girls with Romain and drank beer in the storeroom while waiting for the day to end. Besides, he and Romain got along like theives.

That had turned out to be a pleasant surprise. Anthony remembered Romain as a real jerk, arrogant and menacing. But he was pretty cool when you got to know him. He had grown in the last two years and now stood six feet tall. He was a lazy fucker, but when he put his mind to it, he couldn't be beaten. Anthony had seen him drag 300-kilo boats up the slope to the boathouse by himself; it was pretty amazing. Besides that, he was generous, always in a good mood, spent money freely, and knew everybody. Anthony loved driving around town in his dad's Audi Quattro, showing off big time, totally Guns N' Roses. With the car windows open, they were kings.

His lecture finished, Cyril said he hoped he'd made himself clear. Anthony said, 'Yeah'; Romain, 'No worries.' Sonia spoke up:

'I'd like to talk to you.'

'What about?'

'Just five minutes.'

'I don't have the time now.'

'It's important.'

Remembering who Sonia's father was, Cyril turned to the boys and said:

'I want you two to set up the chairs, the trestles and the tables. And make sure the florists do exactly what I said. I asked for bougainvilleas to decorate the refreshment area and they brought clematises.'

'Anyway, it's gonna rain,' said Romain.

'What?'

'Nothing.'

Cyril gestured to Sonia to follow him into his office, and closed the door. Anthony stood there for a moment, staring at it. A sign at eye level read 'Private'.

The boys got to work in spite of the heat and soon had everything ready. They set up tables for the buffet and ten rows of plastic chairs on the lawn between the beach and the clubhouse. The refreshment area would double as a bar. Since there were no bougainvilleas and the clematises wouldn't do, palm fronds were used. They looked fine.

Later, two vans arrived to deliver the food. Cyril had naturally turned to Bellinger, the best caterer in the valley, who had an outlet in Heillange and another in Étange and hoped to expand into Luxembourg. His impeccably white-clad assistants, who looked as if they'd been dusted with talcum powder, came and went unloading trays of shellfish, crudités, charcuterie, fresh fruit, party loaves, and all sorts of delicacies to be spooned out of little glass cups. There was enough to feed a regiment, and Monsieur Bellinger himself had come along. The association's new president was being inaugurated that evening, and a classy crowd was expected, since the sailing club membership included the town's lawyers and judges, doctors, businessmen and influential civil servants. So the caterer was keeping a watchful eye on proceedings. This would be the wrong day for the food to spoil.

For their part, Anthony and Romain unloaded the beverages onto dollies. Ten cases of Mumm champagne had even been ordered. There was also a white Moselle to be drunk very cold, Bordeaux, Sancerre, mineral water, Cokes and fruit juice. Everything was ready by four, so the boys treated themselves to a smoke break in the shade of the pine trees. Sonia hadn't reappeared, and heavy clouds were now scudding across the surface of the lake. The air prickled. People felt damp, itchy, restless. Even the catering assistants were starting to look wilted.

'It's gonna come down,' said Anthony.

'Oh, by the way, I talked about you last night.'

'Who with?'

But Anthony knew perfectly well and his pulse briefly quickened.

'Steph. I saw her at Algarde yesterday. She was eating with her parents.'

Anthony gazed at the sky while chewing on a blade of grass. He was propped up on his elbows with his legs crossed. He smelled of sweat and enjoyed the pleasant feeling of relaxing after hard work. It was so overcast it almost looked like night.

'So, what?'

'So, nothing. I'm sure she'll come by this evening.'

'Cool.'

Romain chuckled.

'Yeah, cool. She remembers you very well.'

'Oh yeah?'

'Yeah. She asked me how you were doing.'

'Seriously?'

'Of course not, moron.'

'You're a dick.'

After a moment, Anthony asked:

'You sure she's coming?'

'I think so. Her father seemed to be counting on it, anyway.'

'Oh, yeah, her father. That's right.'

Anthony had almost forgotten. Steph's father was none other than Pierre Chaussoy, the new president of the association that ran the club. He'd been a candidate in the municipal elections the year before and had taken a serious licking in the first round. After that, he managed to get a seat on the municipal council, in the opposition. He'd since been trying to work his way into the fabric of the local community organisations.

Anthony felt he needed a hot shower.

'I'm going to have a wash. I stink of sweat.'

'Wait, we still have to bring in the 420s.'

Romain pointed to two almost motionless boats in the middle of the lake.

'We'll take the Zodiac. They'll never be able to get back by themselves. There's no wind at all.'

'Yeah,' said Romain. 'I'll drive.'

'That would surprise me,' said Anthony.

They raced each other down to the beach, bumping shoulders and elbows. Anthony wound up in the water. Romain took the tiller.

The first guests arrived a little after six o'clock. They came in couples or alone, more rarely with children. Most were wearing light-coloured clothes. Cyril had put on an elegant Parma jacket to greet them. Given the forecast, tents had to be rented at the last minute to protect the buffet in case it rained. They'd had to put all this up in a hurry and Anthony didn't have time to wash. He just gave himself a quick splash in the kitchen and put on a clean T-shirt. It wasn't nearly enough.

Outside, torches standing here and there gave off a powerful smell of citronella. The tablecloths, chairs and drapery were white. Champagne buckets stood awaiting their bottles. The overall impression was one of order and cleanliness. A little music was playing from the speakers. Cyril had brought in a DJ from Luxembourg. Once it was dark, there would be dancing. All in all, everything seemed to be going fine. Except maybe for the big mound of crushed ice for the shellfish, which was already rapidly melting. Anthony watched for Stéphanie's arrival with growing impatience. When he spotted Sonia, he ran over to her.

'Hey, where d'you get to? Is everything okay?'

'I quit.'

'You're joking!'

'No. I'm stopping. I'm out of here. *Finito.*'

She didn't seem to be in a better mood for all that.

'So when are you leaving?'

'Right away.'

'That's heavy. You could've talked to me about it.'

'There's nothing to say.'

Still, she had bothered to change for the evening and was wearing a little flowered top and a diamond in each ear.

On the other hand, she was still wearing her Walkman headset around her neck and her Doc Martens.

'You look good like that,' said Anthony.

'Thanks.'

'It's a change from black.'

'I got it.'

'You gonna hang around for a bit?'

'Yeah. I still have to see Cyril about something.'

'What is this thing you have with him?'

She shrugged. There was no thing.

'Okay, see you,' she said.

'Don't leave without saying goodbye to me,' Anthony insisted.

'Sure, don't worry.'

She put her headphones back on and left.

Pierre Chaussoy and his wife arrived a little after seven. He was paunchy and affable, with sharp features and grey hair combed flat. When he talked and smiled, his features would jerk upwards, as if a puppet master was pulling strings attached to his face. At his side, Caroline Chaussoy was a moderately dazzling bottle blonde wearing lots of rings. She was heavy in the knee but had the well-preserved face of an outdoorsy Swede. Cyril chatted them up for a while, until they turned away to pursue more meaningful handshakes. Two waiters had started to circulate with coupes of champagne. Cyril went to find Anthony.

'Things aren't moving along. Find your friend and work the buffet. Try to get them to drink water. They're getting out of hand.'

The guests were already talking loudly, holding each other by the arm, laughing inappropriately and draining their glasses the moment they were filled. All this was happening in an electric atmosphere that was almost intolerable, with the low sky hovering ominously. The crushed ice had almost completely melted by now, and water pouring from the buffet had turned the shellfish area into a swamp. Drinkers who approached got their feet wet. A few women even took their shoes off to enjoy the coolness. Anthony and Romain started filling people's glasses. They also offered them Badoit but got no takers. Soon Caroline Chaussoy came over to get a glass. Recognising Romain, she exclaimed:

'I didn't know you were working here.'

'Sure am.'

'Still, not a bad way to spend the summer.'

Romain nodded politely and offered the blonde woman a coupe.

'Ah, that's perfect,' she said, pleased.

Anthony would have liked Romain to introduce him, but it didn't occur to him. On the other hand, he had the presence of mind to ask if Steph would be there soon.

'Oh, with her, you know…'

They chatted for a few more minutes, mainly about mutual acquaintances. Then a crackle came from the speakers. The new president had climbed onto the small stage set up for the purpose.

'Your attention, please!' he said.

The hum of conversations stopped. Pierre Chaussoy raised his hands and again asked for silence and the crowd quickly settled down to listen to him.

'I'll be brief. To start with, I want to thank you all for coming in spite of the rainstorm we're expecting.'

These thanks preceded others. The speech went on. It was skilful, familiar, with well-chosen moments, winks and outstretched hands. An occasional witticism raised a smile, and the damp, motionless spectators snuck glances at their neighbours. Cyril had taken a position at the very back, from where he watched people's faces with deep anxiety. From time to time he nodded approvingly at something the president said. Standing off to one side, Caroline Chaussoy listened while twisting a white gold bracelet around her wrist. Suddenly Anthony thought he glimpsed a squirrel scampering along. It was Sonia. He looked for her, but she had already disappeared.

The president had promised to be brief; that was a lie. Instead, he recounted the history of the club, which had once been threatened, then saved, revived, and today was flourishing. Naturally, that destiny was part of a broader panorama, one that was national, economic and global. Pierre Chaussoy said the words 'deindustrialisation', 'stakeholders' and 'modern'. People applauded.

'Hey there!'

Cyril had stationed himself behind Anthony and grabbed his arm. He seemed in a complete panic.

'Did you see the ice?' he said. 'It's dripping everywhere, the shrimp are falling onto the ground, it's disgusting. You've got to clean that up for me. Go and get buckets from the kitchen. You can toss the shellfish in the bin. It's all over for tonight. Get going!'

Anthony hurried away. Onstage, Pierre Chaussoy was searching in his pocket for the piece of paper where he had jotted down a few thoughts.

'Yes… What I especially wanted to tell you was that the time for tears is over. We've been mourning Metalor's closing for ten years now. Whenever people mention Heillange, it's to talk about crisis, poverty and society breaking down. Enough of that! Today we have the right to think about other things. About the future, for example.'

Again, people applauded. Anthony, who wasn't completely indifferent to these arguments, stopped on his way to the kitchen to hear the rest. After all, he, too, was tired of this whole remembered industrial past. It made people who hadn't lived through it feel like they'd missed the big event. It made any enterprise seem laughable by comparison, any success minuscule. The iron men and their good old days had been a pain in the arse for too long.

The president continued. The sailing club was a perfect example of the valley's possibilities, he said. Recent improvements had restored the campground to its former glory, and the place had been nearly full ever since. Next year, an aquatic complex would be built there with a wave pool, a waterslide and a twenty-five-metre lap pool. Productivist notions were out of date; the future lay in leisure activities. When it came to recreation, the Henne Valley enjoyed some major assets. In summer, it had a remarkable number of sunny days. Its lake, forests and countryside were as fine as any other. It was blessed with a first-class motorway infrastructure. Its proximity to richer countries like Luxembourg and Germany was a real boon. Not to mention Heillange's time-honoured tradition of hospitality, since it had once welcomed the down-and-out from the Continent and the Mediterranean to run its famous mills. Chaussoy also mentioned Holland, Belgium and Switzerland, which weren't all that far away and could provide an admirably solvent customer base. One could also count on subsidies from the region, from Paris and from Brussels. Depressed areas had the right to appeal to the country's generosity. Studies would soon prove what he was saying, and subsidies would follow. The programme was an attractive one. People applauded again, at length. The audience of notables gathered that evening was tired of the prevailing melancholy. They had no reason to despair, after all. They recognised that thirty years of devastation had reshaped the world of work, the nature of jobs and the bases of French prosperity, and they sympathised, but they were full of dynamism. It was time to forge ahead. The support structures would appear.

'Hi there.'

Anthony was standing in front of the bar with a bucket of crushed ice in each hand when Stéphanie came in the door.

'Hi,' he said.

Romain had vanished, so he'd had to do all the cleaning up by himself. He threw out four thousand francs' worth of shellfish, the equivalent

163

of a month's salary. The smell stuck to his hands. It had taken him five round trips to pack out the remaining ice, and he was soaking wet.

'Am I too late?' asked Steph, hearing the racket outside.

'No. It's more that they started early.'

In fact, the president's speech had unleashed unexpected powers of optimism. People had relaxed and were having fun, almost excessively so. A customer with allergies had thrown up, and a service manager tossed her glass over her shoulder. There wasn't a drop of champagne left. For his part, Cyril was going along with the disorder. At least people were having a good time.

'So you're working here now?' Stéphanie began.

'Yeah.'

'It's funny.'

'What is?'

She took her time before answering.

'You've grown.'

It was nice to hear, even if she was sort of treating him like a child. They didn't have much to say, just looked at each other.

'Are you in college now?' Anthony asked.

'No,' she said. 'I just took the *bac*.'

'Did you pass?'

'With honours.'

She gave a dismissive little wave to express how silly the thing was. Just the same, she was proud of herself. Anthony found her even more beautiful than before. Her face had lost its chubby, childish look. But she still had her incredible hair and that famous ponytail. Her eyes seemed larger; she must have been making them up differently, better. Also, she was wearing a low-cut sleeveless white blouse that displayed her cleavage. Anthony was making a great effort to look her in the face.

'I think I'm going to go,' she said.

'Yeah. See you later.'

'Yeah, later.'

As she walked by him, Anthony thought of the smell of shrimp and stupidly held his breath. He was hoping for a last glance back before she went out the door. But they weren't in a movie.

From then on, Anthony's evening mainly consisted of searching for Steph among the guests while pretending to pick up empty glasses. At every instant, he spotted her ponytail, thought he saw her shoulder, glimpsed her eyes or face, found her in places where she wasn't. He was reconstructing her from scratch, starting with nothing, making it all up, and would then unexpectedly bump into her in the frenzy of the party. Stéphanie got tipsy fast and soon joined in the game. Anthony kept getting a hard-on. She was returning his glances. Smiling. Her cleavage glowed like the sun.

For his part, the famous DJ from Luxembourg had tried in vain to get the guests interested in various kinds of music. Nobody felt like dancing. It was too hot; they were tired and drunk, besides. A little breeze was now raising moire ripples on the dark waters of the lake. People still expected rain. Lubricated by alcohol, men who were normally restrained by their ambitions allowed themselves sarcastic pronouncements. Their wives often tried to hush them, without success. The debriefing would come later, in the car. Going home, they might argue, have a shower, or make love, being careful not to wake the children. It would still be a pleasant evening.

Past midnight, things with Steph began to move faster. She had taken to seeking Anthony out as well. She was playing up to him; they had brushed by each other. It should be said that there were no other young people their age at the party. Anthony was enjoying a miraculous but very temporary exclusivity. He had to take advantage of it. At one moment Steph even came to find him in the kitchen, where he was washing some dishes. In the harsh neon light, he saw her as he never had before. The fuzz on her thighs, her shiny skin, the armature of her bra, a minute crop of acne on her forehead and cheeks under her make-up. Faced with the raw reality of this imperfect body, he found himself desiring her more than ever.

'What are you doing afterwards' she asked.

'Nothing special.'

'Could you give me a lift home? I've been drinkin' all evening. Apparently there are police everywhere now.'

'Yes, of course.'

She said all this with a disarming neutrality, leaning on her right leg, hip cocked a little. She had painted her fingernails and toenails. It was crazy, how girls focused on those details in their desire to be beautiful, their hunger to please. It was all part of a nuptial dance as old as time. In the end, the entire species depended on those meticulous touches.

'How soon will you be done?'

'In half an hour, if that works for you.'

'Yeah, half an hour's good.'

'Cool.'

'See you later.'

Watching Steph as she walked out of the kitchen, Anthony gazed at her arse and hips and started flipping out for real. Everything suddenly seemed possible, and at the same time so uncertain. This window of opportunity was becoming the chance of a lifetime. And here he was, reeking of shrimps and Paic dish soap. He absolutely had to have that shower.

After making sure Cyril wasn't monitoring him, Anthony took off for the bungalows. They called them bungalows, but they were actually just spruced-up changing rooms. There were three wooden cabins set back a little near the road, with toilets, showers and a patio with chaise longues for show. It gave the place a kind of safari atmosphere that the clients loved. Anthony had brought a bar of soap and a clean dish towel to dry himself off. He didn't have any more fresh T-shirts, unfortunately, which really bothered him. He first hurried, then started running, caught up in his excitement.

But a light in the distance stopped him dead.

It was shining through the cracks in the first bungalow, outlining a shutter and a door. He approached cautiously. Nobody had any business being there. He thought about the inbreds, about prowlers. He should have turned round and gone back, but cowardice didn't seem a reasonable option at that point. He crept closer and listened through the closed door. He tried to open it, but the door was latched.

'Who's in there?'

He tried the handle, and shook the door, but the latch held fast. From inside he heard footsteps, murmurs, rustling, a load of noises spelling confusion and concern.

'Open up!' Anthony shouted, more to give himself courage than for any other reason. He wrapped the bar of soap in the dishcloth to make a kind of sling, but it didn't have much heft.

'Okay, just a minute,' said a voice.

The door opened and there stood Romain, with Sonia behind him, her eyes downcast.

'What the fuck is this shit?' asked Anthony.

'What?'

Suddenly Romain wasn't so friendly any more.

'She's fourteen years old! Are you out of your mind?'

'Take it easy, okay?'

'What the fuck's your problem?'

Romain walked up to Anthony and shoved him backwards.

'I told you, take it easy.'

Stunned, Anthony took two steps back. He could feel the shove vibrating through his whole body. Its power surprised and humiliated him. His anger increased.

'I'm out of here,' said Sonia, seeing that things were taking a nasty turn.

'I'll take you home,' said Anthony.

'I wouldn't bet on it,' she said.

Anthony tried to follow Sonia as she was leaving, but Romain's large hand clapped him on the shoulder.

'You're staying here.'

With his other hand, Romain grabbed him by the nape of the neck like a puppy. Anthony struggled to get free, first annoyed, then suddenly enraged. He wanted to punch Romain in the face, but that face was too far and too high. He was trapped, and he couldn't see clearly. Romain slapped him hard, hitting his eye. Anthony immediately felt tears welling up, stinging his nose.

'Stop it!' Sonia shouted.

It was too late; Anthony's pride had taken over. He fought harder, grabbing for Romain's eyes and mouth, trying to bite him. The two boys tumbled backwards and started trading blows randomly. But the punches didn't carry. They lacked power and accuracy and the boys were hampered by being on the ground in darkness. They were rolling around and Sonia was screaming. In the end, the two bodies tangling awkwardly looked pretty ridiculous. Anthony was biting at random. Then Romain yanked him up, slammed him down on his back, and punched him twice.

'You're both crazy! Stop it!'

The taste of blood filled Anthony's mouth. It was metallic, a sharp, disgusting taste like iodine or ether and it calmed him.

The bungalow light went out. He thought of Stéphanie. He still had to take her home.

Hacine was driving a Volvo estate, but if you'd asked him what colour it was, he couldn't say.

He was heading home.

Two years earlier, Hacine and his father had gone to Morocco with their car crammed full of stuff. They were taking perfume, coffee, bars of soap, clothes bought at Kiabi for their little cousins and a few pairs of Levi's to be resold over there. On the ferry, his father cut Hacine's hair, then took new clothes and leather shoes out of his suitcase for him. He had to look good.

His mother had been waiting for them on the other side of the Mediterranean. She took Hacine in her arms. It was embarrassing at his age, especially since the entire family – the whole scary rogues' gallery – was waiting a little off to the side. At first glance, Hacine found them ugly and dusty, looking as if they'd stepped out of the grave, right down to their wrinkles, their clothes, their misleading robustness and the critical way they looked at him.

After all these years, the house his father was having built still wasn't finished. They visited the construction site. It looked ridiculous. Partly framed walls, pipe ends, steel rods sticking in the air. Every one of the construction people had an excuse: not enough time, not to mention the weather and the authorities. You always had to get an extra permit, pay an unexpected baksheesh. Bouali said nothing. It was his fault. He should have been there to supervise things. Even in France, you had to stay on top of workers, otherwise the delays went on and on. You could wait forever for the carpenter to keep his promises or for the plumber to show signs of life. The roofless house stood like an accusation: Hacine's father was living far away from his wife. He was living like a bachelor.

As a result, ten of them ended up all living in the apartment belonging to Hacine's uncle. The place was hardly more finished: wires stuck out of the walls, and there were holes in the stairs. The water ran only intermittently, so the bathtubs were always kept full, just in case. One night, someone shouted, 'It's happening!' Pipes moaned and taps began to sputter. The water started to run, at first in a thin, brown stream; then it cleared and became flowing and warm. The kids watched with delight, as if witnessing a miracle.

Now, two years later, Hacine was going home to Heillange.

Near Niort, he left the motorway to get some coffee at a little Total service station. It was past six o'clock in the evening and he'd been driving nonstop since the morning, without saying a word, scrupulously obeying the rules of the road. When the urge to piss got too strong, he relieved himself in a water bottle that was now rolling around on the carpeted passenger-side floor.

He was going home alone, still young, with plenty of money in his pockets and his heart empty. His face had lost some of its early hesitancy. His upper lip no longer bore that shadow of moustache, and he now combed his hair straight back. He was wearing an expensive Armani shirt and white trousers. His belt alone cost half a week's pay at minimum wage.

Hacine filled up with unleaded, threw his piss bottle away and went to park in front of the cafe. Through the windows he could see a post-card display rack, shelves of magazines, coolers full of drinks and tasteless sandwiches. Two guys in uniform were busy behind the counter. The cafe door opened and a girl of about twenty came out. Blonde, small breasts, denim shorts, espadrilles down at the heel. Her tangled hair looked like straw. She walked past the Volvo without a glance and went over to a Mercedes SUV.

In his rear-view mirror, Hacine saw the petrol pumps, the yellow glare of artificial lights, trucks with their hydraulic wheezes, the ballet of cars with empty tanks, their weary drivers watching the litres and francs click by. The sky above the horizon was fading, cut by power lines. The red, orange and blue Total sign reigned over everything.

The SUV manoeuvred to get back on the road. Its number plate began with the number 75. So she's a Parisienne, he thought.

He went into the cafe, sat down at the counter and ordered a coffee. One of the waiters in uniform asked if he wanted sugar.

'Just coffee,' Hacine said.

Each word cost him. The uniformed guy served him in silence.

Over there, people sat on cafe terraces in the evening chatting end-lessly while sipping tiny cups of coffee. Hacine had spent wonderful hours like that with his uncles and cousins. The service station coffee bore only a distant relationship to that bitter brew. He sniffed and looked outside. He felt locked in and blue. Standing up, he asked if they had a payphone.

'Over there,' said the counterman, pointing to a shadowy spot between the toilets and the vending machines.

Hacine paid for his coffee – he'd only taken a sip – and went to the place indicated. He put five coins in the slot and dialled a complicated number. A hoarse voice answered him. He asked for news of his mother. Yes, he said, he was making good time. Everything was fine. He asked about his cats. The voice reassured him again. Hacine breathed calmly. The hoarse voice fell silent. He hung up and stood for a moment without moving. The feeling of emptiness no longer surprised him. He got back behind the wheel. He still had quite a way to go.

When his father left Tétouan to return to France, he told Hacine to look after his mother and to supervise the construction. He was counting on him. Hacine promised he would, though he would've preferred for his father to stay and take care of it himself.

'And if you fuck up again, I will kill you with my own hands,' his father had said.

The words were leaden, heavy, sincere – and empty. He had spoken them too often. When the police showed up at their apartment after the business with the motorbike, for example, they behaved very properly. Sitting in his chair, Hacine's father took on the stubborn, dignified look he always wore when dealing with the authorities, like the family welfare people. At one point, an officer asked to see his papers, and Bouali pulled out his big red folder held closed with rubber bands. It was all there, residency permits, naturalisation papers, work contract, three decades of patiently accumulated documents. Fine, fine said the officer.

Before taking Hacine away, the police wanted to check the basement. They didn't have anything on him except for a few bars of hashish and a knife hidden in his bed springs. They kept him at the police station for five hours. It was both long and efficient. Hacine didn't say anything, not a word, and he walked out a free man. Next day, his father announced they were leaving for Tétouan.

It was funny, when you thought of it. Men of Bouali's generation had left Morocco because they couldn't find work, and none of their problems could be solved there. Yet it had now become the promised land, the hallowed ground where evil was washed away after the corruption and bad luck in France. What bullshit...

From then on, Hacine didn't have a moment of free time. He and his old man did the shops, filled the car with big tricolour bags, and hit the road for the next two days. Halfway there, a few miles from Perpignan, they slept at a rest stop. Three or four hours of bad sleep, in their underwear, doors open, bath towels spread on the car seats. Hacine still remembered the passing lorries shuttling between France and Spain, their dull roar, their headlights sweeping across the night. Exhausted tourists ordering coffee, briefly shivering in the air conditioning, with their children, eyelids stuck shut, the teenagers reading basketball magazines; the Dream Team had won it all at the Barcelona Olympics and Michael Jordan was a demigod.

At dawn, he had found his father in shorts and sandals, standing on a small rise and contemplating the flow of traffic.

'We are going to get going,' he said in his gravelly, monotonous voice.

His face looked drawn, and his stomach ballooned out under his sunken chest. The hair on his shoulders and back had turned white. He looked like a lunatic who had escaped from the hospital, or a retiree who'd lost his way. Hacine considered his father's weakness and said no.

'I do not ask your opinion.'

'I won't go. There's nothing for me over there.'

The man turned to his son. The look on his face ended the debate. There was no weakness there.

'The shame that I had, it is the last time. You will do as I say.'

They barely exchanged two words during the fourteen hundred kilometres to Gibraltar. After the ferry crossing, they reached Ceuta and began the lengthy negotiations with Moroccan customs. Hacine stayed in the car, chewing over his resentment. It must have been fifty degrees. Thousands of cars, waves of people, everyone crowding close, standing up, yelling, holding out their passports. An atmosphere of exodus, of misery, of endless talking, all that shit.

The rest had just been a matter of getting used to it. In particular he'd had to get used to the permanent presence of his uncles and cousins, even at night. And the heat. For weeks Hacine slept on the tiled floor in his pants, trying to keep cool while surrounded by snoring, men breathing, and an absorbing, sexual smell, a mix of dirty feet, cock, sweat and food. The apartment was tiny. You had to share everything, every square metre, even the air.

Hacine also had to endure his mother's reproaches. She constantly yelled at him for being lazy, shifty, cunning and a liar. She worried about what people in the neighbourhood would say about him, and feared for her reputation. Fuck them, he thought. You will drive me crazy, she said. His mother wanted to hit him, but he was too big. Several times, he secretly went out to the stairwell to cry.

Fortunately, there was the sea, its brutal blue neutrality, the beach, the languid waving of leaves, the burning air on his face. Fortunately, there was Ghizlane, his cousin.

She was actually the daughter of a neighbour, but by introducing her as a cousin, they were telling him right away not to get his hopes up. From their very first meeting, they had eyes for each other. She was rounded and soft with amber eyes, full of malice and tricks, calculating and illiterate. Her hair had never seen scissors, and she was forever fiddling with those endless tresses. Depending on the day, she put her hair up in plaits, cornrows or a chignon, or let it tumble down like a waterfall. Its wildness invaded everything. The moment she entered a room, it even got into your mouth. Afterwards, you found hair on the carpets and the armchairs, along with a honeyed, animal, argan oil smell that would intoxicate you for hours. Hacine and Ghizlane didn't speak together more than three times in all, but he wound up waiting for her. For a whole year, he dreamed of her rounded belly, the unbound breasts that her clothes never quite managed to hide. She secretly gave him a pair of striped kittens. And then, without any warning, from one day to the next, she married a teacher named Yazid. They left to go live in Fez.

That was the latest in a number of disappointments and it sent Hacine in pursuit of another passion. Since everything in life was bound to dissipate, slip through your fingers and end in dust, he decided he would get rich. Profit alone seemed to have the power to keep death at a distance. Against life's perpetual haemorrhaging, he was seized by a fury of acquisition. In Tétouan, there was only one way to make money, and he threw himself into it body and soul.

———

Poitiers-Tours-Orléans...Before Hacine, Bouali had made the trip from Heillange to Gibraltar thirty times over his lifetime. Now it was his son's turn to add to their complicated history with Morocco. Hacine had been sent there to expunge a sin, learn how to live, and become a man. He was coming back with forty-five kilos of cannabis resin.

Hacine got lost near Troyes while looking for his rendezvous. He had to take the A6 heading south, then get back on the A5. This took him a good hour but caused no anxiety or impatience. He had all the time in the world. The Swedish estate car cruised ponderously along, its enormous grille spangled with dead insects, the kind of car that could easily make you think life was eternal.

It was almost night when he found the Plaines-Devant enterprise zone. He checked it out, driving slowly with the window open. The place gave off a feeling of elemental newness. Big, hastily erected warehouses stood next to faceless hotels. Franchise restaurants awaited the customers from a monster shopping centre. There were also garden supply centres, two toy shops, a specialised frozen food shop, a pair of hi-fi outlets. A road ran across the zone, linking roundabouts that gave access to the many car parks. Strips of grass filled awkward transitions. Hacine drove slowly, mentally ticking off the reassuring names on the signs: Saint-Maclou, Darty, Carglass, Kiabi, Intersport. In the evening's unusual silence, the deserted shops took on a dramatic quality, looking like a lovely sepulchre. The sky in its infinity lay over it all. Hacine smoked a Winston filter while listening to 'The Girl from Ipanema' on the radio. You don't often get to savour moments like that.

He eventually reached the Carrefour shopping centre's car park, which was as vast as a plain. The last customers emerged from the automatic doors with their full trolleys. Hacine stopped the estate car a good distance away. The air was warm and the noise from the nearby motorway made a pleasant hum. All in all, he felt a bit weary, soothed, not too bad. A couple in a Fiat Panda cut diagonally across the car park. On the other side, a cafe was still open. People, banquettes and the orange globes of old plastic lampshades could be seen through windows streaked with white reflections. The sun was setting behind the shopping centre. A mercantile sadness rose from the earth.

As Hacine entered the shop, a security guard urged him to hurry; it was almost closing time. He went to the garden supply section, where he selected a pickaxe and a handsaw. In the empty aisles, his soles made a little repeated squeaking. Background classical music lulled shoppers who were running late. There were only two registers still open. When he paid, he spoke to the cashier politely.

Once outside, he found there was nothing left to see. Night had fallen, and the endless plain was studded with luminous dots, each streetlight a warm spark in the indigo evening. The red and yellow lights of cars marked slow migrations. The bright green and shiny blue of the neon signs glistened like frost. Advertisements glowed with flat, dull light. This swarm of lights gave vague ideas about mankind's fate and the emptiness of life. Hacine wedged his pickaxe against the Volvo's rear bumper and sawed the handle off below the head. He stowed the saw in the boot and laid the axe handle on the passenger seat. His appointment was here at eight the next morning, a Sunday. He had time. He was hungry.

Hacine pulled into the drive-in and ordered McNuggets, large fries and a Coke, which he ate in his car while listening to the ten o'clock news. The talk was about Hamas, Balladur and Yann Piat. And football, of course. In the day's quarter-finals, Italy was playing Spain and Brazil playing Holland. Like everyone, Hacine liked Brazil.

He found himself a room in a hotel with automated check-in. Before going to bed, he considered bringing the dope in but decided it was just as safe in the boot, and he couldn't see himself traipsing back and forth. His room had its own toilet, but the showers were down the hall. He took his axe handle with him when he went; he needed to get comfortable with it. A truck driver who was brushing his teeth watched him pass in the mirror without saying anything. The water was very hot and Hacine enjoyed it for a long time. After that, he smoked a joint and fell asleep in front of the TV.

When he woke up, he didn't remember having dreamed. Dope did that to you. For years, Hacine thought he had stopped dreaming.

———

He'd been waiting in front of the Carrefour shopping centre for ten minutes when a white utility van appeared at the far end of the car park. It was still early, and the Volvo was parked alone in the middle of the space. The enterprise zones were deserted on Sunday and the same emptiness reigned for miles around. The van drove in a big curve before pulling up right next to him. The driver was a short, standard-issue North African with a pale jacket and aviator glasses. He looked Hacine over and asked:

'So, you're the one?'

'What's inside there?' asked Hacine, pointing at the back of the van.

'Nothing.'

They briefly sized each other up. The little Arab had spotted the axe handle on the passenger seat. His car radio was playing trashy, very up-tempo techno and he was chewing gum at an alarming rate, his mouth open. Right away, you could tell he fancied himself one of those cool hipsters you saw in Ibiza. Hacine gestured for him to turn the volume down so they could hear each other.

'You're awfully young,' said the guy.

'So what?'

'I dunno. I didn't picture you like this.'

He didn't ask what sorts of things the guy had been told. He could easily imagine. Hacine had surprised quite a few people in Tétouan and Algésiras and on the A9. He'd even held a record for a while: Gérone to Lyon in under three hours with five hundred kilos of merchandise in the boot. To do that, you needed an Audi S2 and couldn't value your life too highly.

The guy continued to study him incredulously. Hacine said:

'Well?'

'We'll go and park a little further on. No point in doing it right out in the open.'

The van took off slowly and Hacine followed. They drove for a while through the deserted enterprise zone. There wasn't a soul in sight. Everything was closed. At each roundabout, they had to slow down. The minutes dragged on and Hacine began to get tense. He briefly took hold of the axe handle. It fitted his hand well. He had plans for it. Soon the van's indicators signalled a right turn, and they stopped behind a Halle aux Vêtements department store. The place was out of eyesight, with just enough room for their two vehicles between shipping containers and a stack of empty cartons. The guy jumped out of his van, leaving the engine running. Hacine backed in so the vehicles were back to back, and opened the rear door. Using screwdrivers, the two men started removing the Volvo's trim and the floor of the boot.

'What's your name?'

'Hacine.'

'I'm Bibi.'

They both knew the drill and they worked fast. Still, Hacine said he didn't much like being there.

'There's never anyone around,' Bibi reassured him. 'Honestly, what's the point of going through the hassle of renting a garage?'

It was true, there wasn't a sound, not a car, not a customer for miles around. Tens of millions of francs' worth of merchandise – leather sofas, TV sets, ice-cream cones, jacuzzis – sat in their metal containers, silently waiting for life to resume. Hacine was bothered by the feeling of death and abundance.

It took them a few minutes to transfer the dope. It was packed in little one-kilo bricks and there were a good forty of them, carefully shaped and wrapped in waterproof plastic. They stored them in rigged petrol containers that opened like tin cans. When the containers were full, Bibi topped them up with petrol. Hacine kept five bricks for himself.

'What are you going to do with them?' asked Bibi.

'What do you think?'

Bibi took out a Marlboro and offered Hacine the pack.

'You're not smoking here,' said the latter.

'The petrol? There's no danger.'

'You're not smoking, I said.'

Bibi frowned but put the cigarettes away. Then he asked:

'Why d'you come here in an estate like that? I thought you were supposed to be a driver.'

'I'm done with the speed thing.'

Bibi pursed his lips dubiously. Every week, 400-horsepower cars carrying tons of Moroccan hash raced across France, defying radars, the police and common sense. Doing 190 kilometres per hour the whole way, the drivers were real crazies, winning the admiration of all the little people in the country who made their money reselling those supersonic cargos. In every city and housing estate, there were a hundred guys who saw themselves as ace drivers and future millionaires, with Bibi in the lead. No way that was going to stop.

'So where are you headed now?'

'I'm going home,' said Hacine.

'All right…'

With nothing more to say, they shook hands. But before getting behind the wheel, there was something Bibi wanted to know.

'What are you going to do with that club of yours?'

'Make some room.'

3

Anthony's mouth was bleeding when he left the sailing club. He'd practically fled, forgetting to take his helmet. Since then, he'd been riding on autopilot as fast as he could, not knowing where to go.

He wasn't the hothead he'd once been, though. For a long time he used to pull dangerous stunts on his bike for the hell of it: skirting pavements, doing wheelies, zigzagging between cars, riding in the left lane and only pulling over at the last moment. He was riding for a fall then, seeking contact, seeking the pavement. That period left him with a burn on his right leg that ran from ankle to hip, and a brown patch on his elbow. The asphalt set a limit, at least.

Nowadays, when he saw kids doing stuff like that, he just didn't get it. His screw-up period seemed to be behind him, the burglaries with Steve Mourette and the frenetic drinking, when he used to get bombed in the little park at the edge of the housing development. He occasionally ran into the kid from year seven whose arm he broke, which got him thrown out of school. The boy made it a point of pride not to look down when they met. Anthony was very sorry.

These days, when he rode his Yamaha 125, he aimed for invisibility. Every day, he repeated routes he had carefully chosen for their geometry, the rush of feelings they generated, the possibilities for momentum they offered, and the complicated manoeuvres he loved. From his mother's to the sailing club, from the school to his old man's place. And there was another route, which ran from the Leclerc store through town up to the old power plant. That one combined the pleasures of right angles with a vanishing point. In riding those routes, Anthony aimed for perfection of gesture, early-morning fluidity, tapering to a pure, clean line. Aerodynamics reduced to disappearance, to joy.

But that wasn't happening right now. Anthony's head was full and his mind was racing. He was unable to leave the lakeshore. He kept on riding through the forest and along the road, like a hamster in its wheel. Without realising it, he was drawing an idiotic orbit around Steph's presence. She was there, somewhere and he couldn't bring himself to leave her. Besides, it was starting to get chilly and he was sorry he'd left without taking his sweatshirt. Everything had happened so fast. He had goose bumps and could feel a nervous fatigue overtaking him.

It was when he passed the Léo-Lagrange recreation centre for the second time that an idea occurred to him. He slowed hesitantly, then stopped for a moment. He checked his face in the rear-view mirror. He had some dried blood on his chin and tried to rub it off with spit. He wasn't looking that great, but it would do.

He left the motorbike half hidden in the forest and made his way to the little campground. For the past two years, the recreation centre had offered a nature discovery programme with hikes, classes on fauna and flora, fire rings and tent camping. A kind of secular scouting, led by more or less hippie counsellors. This innovation attracted an amazing variety of kids, from little tattooed dropouts to pony-loving girls in ankle socks. During the two-week sessions, they got to cook their meals, do the washing up, shit in the woods and carry a knife. At the end, the kids emerged exhausted but more mature, with a bag full of dirty laundry and memories to last a lifetime.

When Anthony entered the clearing created for the camp, he could make out a dozen tents and a firepit where a few embers were still glowing. Down the slope, a huge black mass sucked in all of the night's darkness: the lake. Anthony felt nervous. He stealthily walked forward and crouched near the smouldering fire to warm his hands. Sitting on his heels, he searched for landmarks in the dark. It was a moonless night, and this wasn't easy. The camp stood between the wall of the forest and the depths of the lake. Everything was calm and still, not a leaf stirring. The rainstorm everyone had hoped for all evening had failed to materialise in the end. They would have to go on waiting. A diffuse tension remained in the air, a vague feeling of being caught in a trap.

Fortunately, the tents were there, containing living, unwashed teenagers wrapped in their sleeping bags and divided by sex. Anthony came closer. He'd better not make a mistake, or it would be a scandal. He finally recognised the tent he was looking for; it was a bit smaller and off to one side. He knelt in front of it and scratched the fabric with his finger.

'Pssst!'

He repeated:

'Hey…pssst! Are you in there?'

He scratched harder, and a faint female cry came from within.

'Shhh! It's me,' he said.

'Who is that?' asked a not very reassuring voice.

Though he was out of doors, Anthony felt trapped. Behind him loomed the forest's pale green presence. He turned round: nothing. Yet he wouldn't have dared stretch out his arm. It was getting darker and darker. The trees were an oblique, dense presence, the forest a blackness of humus, a swarming that was ancient and indifferent. He shivered.

'It's me,' he said again in a low voice. 'Open up!'

The zip tab ran up, and the tent flaps parted.

'Don't talk so loud.'

Anthony crawled forward and disappeared inside the tent.

'What are you doing here?' said the voice. 'What time is it, anyway?'

Anthony felt his way, unable to see a thing. His fingers encountered something soft.

'Hey!'

'I can't see anything,' he said.

'What are you doing here?'

Anthony's hand continued its exploration. He touched the girl's cheek. She felt all warm, pulled from sleep like bread from an oven.

'You feel soft.'

'You're a dick,' Vanessa answered. 'I already told you not to come here.'

She had grabbed him by the collar and pulled him in so she could zip the tent closed behind him. Anthony found himself sheltered in a tiny space that smelled pleasantly of something like candyfloss, with a warm, less distinct smell behind it, of clothes and sleepy skin. His hand was resting on Vanessa's naked thigh. She didn't object.

'Let me see,' he said.

'What?'

'You. I dunno, show yourself a little.'

When she turned her back to him to rummage in a corner, he took advantage of it to stroke her arse. He could feel the outline of her knickers through the baggy shorts she slept in. He wanted to slip a hand between her thighs.

'Stop it,' she muttered.

A thin beam of light shot from a small torch, and Anthony could see that Vanessa was in a bad mood.

'Is there a problem?'

Instead of answering, she showed him the time on her watch.

'What?'

'You're such a pain. It's past one o'clock. I'm gonna be completely exhausted tomorrow.'

'I wanted to see you.'

She liked that, in spite of herself.

'I'm working, you know. Besides, if they catch you here, I'll be in deep shit.'

She was kneeling now facing him, looking worried and sulky. Her hair, which had been pinned up in a neat bun, now fell across her shoulder.

You could see the almost square nipples of her bare breasts through her Snoopy T-shirt. Suddenly her expression changed.

'What happened to you?' she asked.

Aiming the torch at his battered face, she touched his brow, his nose and his split lip. The examination was also a caress. Anthony closed his eyes.

'Shit. Who did that to you?'

'It's nothing. I got into a fight at work.'

'Who with?'

'The other arsehole. The Rotier kid.'

'He really did a number on you.'

'It's nothing, I said,' snapped Anthony irritably.

She flexed the cartilage of his nose to see if it was broken, examined his teeth, felt his scalp, inspecting him like a mother checking for lice. He submitted with bad grace.

'It's nothing, for fuck's sake. Stop it.'

'So why'd he do this to you?'

Anthony was evasive in his explanations. He was especially careful not to tell Vanessa about taking the time to write a little note at the bar before leaving the sailing club. His face had been bloody and his hands shaking, so he'd had to do it twice. When he was finished, the paper was a mess and his writing almost illegible. Then he had to walk alone and stiff-necked through what was left of the party. When he handed Steph the note, she turned bright red. Everyone was watching them. The club president and his wife couldn't believe their eyes. It was a scandal and an apotheosis. 'What the hell are you still doing here?' Cyril snapped. But Anthony had delivered his little piece of paper, and the rest didn't matter. Two days later he would be waiting for Steph behind the old power plant. That's what the two lines written in blue ink said. Maybe she would come. Finally, he had climbed onto his motorbike and, without looking back, roared off in third gear, making as much noise as he could. As an exit, it wasn't too shabby.

'What about your job?' asked Vanessa.

'It's history.'

'He fired you?'

'Well, duh.'

'Heavy.'

Anthony had stretched out and wanted her to lie next to him.

'Wait a minute,' she said.

She switched off the torch, then lay down beside him.

'I can't see a damned thing.'

'I don't want some kid catching us.'

'What are you afraid of?'

'Nothing. Take your hand away.'

He obeyed, but she caught the hand in mid-air and laced her fingers between his. They were whispering now.

'Your hands are freezing,' said Anthony.

'Shh! What are you going to do about your job? Think you're gonna get in trouble?'

'No. I don't know. I don't give a damn.'

'Stop it,' she said.

Vanessa didn't like it when Anthony started acting like a stubborn child. She planted a kiss on his cheekbone, his nose, his lips. He stuck his tongue out and she took it tenderly in her mouth, a gesture that turned into a kiss. Saliva flowed, soft, voluptuous and heady. She laid her palm on his cock. It was getting hard.

'You taste like liquorice,' Anthony said.

She chuckled; it was the flavour of her toothpaste. She bit him on the neck, searched for his mouth and chin as she felt his hands slip under her T-shirt and squeeze her breasts hard. Without warning, she sat up and turned her back to him, wedging her arse in his lap. He grabbed her by the throat. She couldn't keep from moaning.

'Shh!'

This time, he was the one demanding silence. She played along for a moment. Within the tent's narrow space, they were cruising in the void, isolated, self-sufficient. The nearness of the other tents, the risk of the darkness and the forest all heightened their pleasure. They moved their joined hips in tandem, each feeling desire rising in the other. Anthony held Vanessa by the throat and belly. She softened in his arms, moaning and sweating. 'Harder,' she said, and he tightened his grip. A mewling sound rose from her chest. Then she couldn't stand it any more. She turned round and their mouths immediately met. They gave each other languorous kisses that opened like beignets full of jam. Their tongues were soft, their saliva warm and abundant. Anthony felt a tingling in his balls and his cock swelled further as he listened to Vanessa's quickened, excited panting. She was now breathing with pleasure, through her nose. She turned her face to him, rubbing cheeks, nose and forehead, then the kisses started again. Very quickly they began to give each other deep, more technical, intrusive kisses. They were filling each other. It felt so good.

At a sudden noise, they stopped.

'Did you hear that?'

'No.'

'Are you sure?'

'Of course I am,' said Anthony.

He wanted to get going again very quickly, he was ready. Actually, he was afraid of losing his hard-on.

'I'm scared all the time here,' explained Vanessa. 'I was so freaked out the other night, I went to sleep with the girls.'

'Was that fun?'

'They're twelve years old, you idiot!'

'What are you afraid of?'

'The forest. It makes noises. And the inbreds, too.'

'They don't come over this far.'

'Are you kidding? We found dead hedgehogs hanging in the branches the other morning.'

'So what?'

'Hedgehogs are their thing. They eat them, I think.'

'That's bullshit.'

While they were whispering, Anthony ran his hand down her back. He counted her vertebrae, stroked her ribs and hips. His fingers encountered some pooled sweat in the small of her back. Vanessa was moist and undulating, her words a muffled rustling in the tent's overheated air as fear further sharpened their pleasure. Anthony brought his sweat-damp fingers to his mouth. He wasn't worried about his erection any more. He wanted to press his belly against Vanessa's, to mix their perspiration. He mopped his sweaty brow.

'Aren't you too hot?' he asked. 'We're dying in here.'

Instead of answering, she slipped her hand down between them, unzipped Anthony's jeans, and started to rub his cock through his pants. She was good at it. Anthony groaned.

'Be quiet!'

He looked for the torch and switched it back on.

'What are you doing?'

'Just for a second. I'd like to see you. Please.'

She let him, and Vanessa's serious face appeared very close, velvety and brown. Anthony drew back, the better to see her. She was busy jerking him off. He tried to slip his hand into her knickers, but she pulled away.

'Let me do it,' she said.

She started tugging his jeans down and he helped her. His pants immediately followed. Then she really grabbed hold of his cock, spitting in her hand to make it slippery. For Anthony, a sharp, indescribably fluid sensation rose from his arse up to the back of his neck.

'Shit, that feels good...'

She wasn't listening. Eyes riveted on his cock, she continued stroking it, occasionally slipping her hand under his balls – it really was mind-blowing. She watched him with the detachment of a statue, a maniacal opacity.

'You are going to fuck me,' she announced.

Anthony closed his eyes. He could have come. He could have come, just like that.

'Do you have any condoms?'

'Yeah.'

She straightened up and crawled to the other end of the tent. She had her back turned to him as she rummaged in a bag spilled open on the tent floor.

'Where the hell did I put them?'

As he played with himself, Anthony watched her, then said:

'Don't move.'

'What?'

She gave him a curious glance over her shoulder.

'Don't move, I said.'

'You're a sick puppy, you know that?'

But she was wearing a mocking smile, and the game went on. He brought the torch closer.

'Arch your back a little, so I can see.'

'Come on, stop your bullshit.'

'Shut up, or I'll call for help.'

She stifled a giggle and arched her back. He came closer. She was still on all fours. He pressed down on her lower back to make her arse jut out. Then he roughly grabbed her by the back of her neck. This was their thing. She spread her legs a little to make herself comfortable, and laid her cheek on her arms, which were crossed on the tent floor. Holding her tight, he ran a hand inside her thigh. Vanessa's eyelids closed. He slid his hand up to her pussy, pressed on it, ran his open palm over the fabric of her shorts. She tried to arch her back more, breathing hard, her sighs now coming from her chest, Anthony slipped the shorts down, revealing her white knickers. He pressed against her thigh, rubbing himself.

'Go ahead,' hissed Vanessa.

He uncovered her arse, leaving her knickers halfway down her thighs.

'Take them off,' she said.

'Shut up.'

They were talking in low voices, their chests tight. The tent was now drifting far from the mainland. Hidden and nervous, they no longer felt constrained by anything. For more than a year now, they'd got into the habit of occasionally fucking like this, when they felt like it or the opportunity arose. They didn't ask any questions, made no demands, reproaches or promises. More than anything, the secret of their hidden lovemaking had led to a boundless complicity. It had allowed them to acquire a lot of experience. They already knew a great deal about their predilections, their little quirks, their turn-offs. In bed, you would think they were thirty-year-olds. That progress made them happy and proud and eventually resulted in an unusual affection. Anthony appreciated Vanessa's giving him the training he would need for future conquests (as in making girls like Steph come). Vanessa liked Anthony because he was rugged, naive and malleable. It was a win–win situation, even though they were mismatched. In bed, one good turn deserves another.

Meanwhile, Anthony had grabbed Vanessa's knickers and yanked them up between her bum cheeks. Between being tightly held and the rubbing of the cotton against her pussy, Vanessa thought she was going to go crazy. Displaying herself, she arched her back a little more and spread her legs. The shorts stretched across her thighs suddenly ripped.

'Don't worry about it,' said Anthony.

He tore the shorts off. God, how good it was to feel that strength. In the beginning she'd had to push him a little; he was just a boy, awkward and timid. Even if he'd denied it, she immediately realised she was his first real lover. So she had to show him how to proceed, what to do, and in what stages. Then, once he'd grasped the female basics, Vanessa showed him what she herself needed.

And what she wanted was to be held.

Because, generally, getting what she wanted was what Vanessa had always done in life. She always took the bit between her teeth, made the effort, displayed strength of character. She was known for knowing what she wanted. Talk about a consolation.

Vanessa grew up in an affectionate, stable family, and her parents didn't succumb to the widespread fashion of getting divorced and remarried. They had lived in the same three-bedroom house for the past twenty years with their two children, a boy and a girl. Her father worked in the registry of deeds; her mother was a secretary at City Hall. Every year, they spent two weeks in Sanary-sur-Mer. They were satisfied with decent salaries and reasonable pay rises and didn't try to change their life. They knew their place, favoured the status quo, were a bit shocked at the forces that rejected it, worried about the perils they saw on TV, were content with the good moments that life gave them. Cancer might some day put this static harmony to the test, but in the meantime, things were good. They sat by the fire in the winter and went on walks in the spring.

Thomas, their elder, was studying sports physiology, which his parents thought was fine. On the other hand, they worried about their daughter's unusual aspirations, which threatened to involve expenses that would be hard to meet. Vanessa had been putting on airs ever since she was thirteen. Studying law only confirmed the family's feeling that she thought she was superior.

Still, she had been pretty frivolous until she turned fifteen. And then, when she was in sixth form, something hit. She started studying hard, suddenly horrified at the thought of being stuck in Heillange, where she in turn would lead a comfortable and moderately happy life. Maybe the flash of insight came in sociology class, or when shopping at Leclerc with her mother. Whatever the case, that's when she started distancing herself from her longtime best friend, Carine Mougel, the cousin's sister. As a result, she'd done very well in the baccalaureate and was now studying law. In a state of constant anxiety, she spent all her time holed up at the library with her soporific textbooks, her Bristol index cards and her three-colour felt-tip pen.

When she came home at weekends she found her parents busily leading the life she no longer wanted, with their general goodwill and hackneyed phrases about pretty much everything. To each his own. Where there's a will, there's a way. We can't all be rocket scientists. Vanessa loved her parents deeply and felt pained and a little ashamed to see them just chugging along, with neither triumphs nor failures. She couldn't grasp how much determination and humble sacrifice was required to keep an average existence afloat, to bring home a salary, plan holidays, maintain the house, cook dinner every evening, and be present and attentive, while still giving a novice teenager the chance to gradually earn her autonomy.

Vanessa saw them as small, subservient, constantly weary, bitter, constrained and vulgar. They had their *Télé Star* magazine and scratch-off games. Her father wore his daily suit and tie; her mother dyed her hair every three months, went to fortune-tellers and thought that all psychologists were crooks.

Vanessa wanted to flee that world at any cost. And the anxiety she felt was as strong as her desire to get out, by the skin of her teeth if need be.

Before her first mid-term exams, she studied so hard, she worked herself half to death. Her zeal was partly due to her family's warnings. Her parents said that if she failed her year, she'd be hauled right back to Heillange, because they didn't have the means to support a dilettante. She actually didn't quite believe those threats. On the other hand, she had heard scary stories about university life since she was very little. Kids who up to then had done fine at school suddenly found themselves getting poor grades. The professors' viciousness was limitless, their conceit proverbial, and humiliating students was the rule. Moreover, those students were now on their own, far from Mummy and Daddy, sleepwalking from one class to the next, and feeling depressed amid general indifference. Many of them yielded to the easy temptation to party, spending their time sleeping or fucking, getting stoned in their studio apartments or playing *Legend of Zelda* instead of studying. The stories were enough to alarm even the most hardened souls.

What had especially intimidated Vanessa were the cool city girls who wore trench coats and loafers, with their beautiful hair and their Longchamp handbags. Those girls walked to the campus, while Vanessa endured forty minutes on the bus from university housing. Instead of studying, they spent hours in nearby cafes drinking Perrier with lemon, talking about politics and their winter holidays, while guys from the year above tried to catch their eye. With their innate self-confidence, knowledge of the London and Amsterdam museums, houses in town and refined vocabulary, they scared Vanessa half to death. But at the end of the first term, she saw what was what. Those little show-offs played at being relaxed, but they weren't all that gifted, and the ones who hadn't done a stroke of work found themselves weeping in front of the list of grades. Vanessa hit the medium everywhere, and got an A in consitutional law.

To celebrate, she took herself out for coffee, alone in a beautiful downtown brasserie, sitting nice and straight with an old edition of a Françoise Sagan novel in front of her, which of course dealt with love. For the first time in weeks she felt she was where she belonged.

So when she ran into Anthony, Vanessa wanted to be looked after. She wanted to be taken, held and fucked. She wanted to be hurt a little, to clear her head. She had a boyfriend at law school, a nice boy named Christopher who wanted to take the Sciences Po entrance exam, but that was something completely different. She had trained Anthony to meet her needs. He acted accordingly and never mentioned it to anyone. Basically, she adored him.

He now pulled Vanessa's knickers aside, and she knew he was going to enter her pussy and fill her up. She was dripping, it was really hot. She wasn't thinking of anything any more.

'Put your cock in me.'

'Wait...'

'Come on, fuck me.'

'I'm telling you, wait.'

Kneeling behind her, he bit her on the arse and on the flesh of her thighs. Shivers ran all up her back, she started to tremble and then, feeling his breath on her cunt, she arched her back.

'No, not that,' she said.

'Why not?'

'Stop. It's hot. There's no bathroom here.'

'So what?'

'Stop it, that's all.'

Too late. Anthony's tongue had found the velvet of her pussy. He followed a fold, slid up her groin, tasting her sweat and her slightly tart, deep inner juices. Vanessa could feel herself weakening and forgot to dissuade him. He was holding her firmly by the hips, spreading her cheeks, clutching her thighs. She felt like putty in his hands. It was everything she loved. She started moaning for real. Anthony grabbed her hair. She arched, seeking him with her lap. His swollen cock was there, pressed against the entrance to her cunt. He stopped moving.

'Can you feel me?'

She answered with a sigh. He was being talkative, which annoyed her. Also, she couldn't think only about herself; since he liked to talk, she listened to him. He began to very gently sink his cock into her.

'The condom…'

'Too bad,' said Anthony. 'Can you really feel me?'

'Of course! Go ahead.'

When he was all the way in, he embraced her. She ran a hand behind his neck and he fucked her in silence, in the sweltering heat of the tent, sticky with sweat, forgetting about the dangers and their problems. It felt good, but Vanessa knew that she could never come like that, all dirty, with the kids and the forest just a stone's throw away. So she faked it, rocking faster and faster, enveloped, overflowing, determined.

'Are you going to come?' he asked.

'Yes…'

'Now?'

'Mmm.'

Sweat plastered her back to his belly. She moved faster and faster, burning up, he grabbed her by the throat, she said, 'Now,' and a second later Anthony came deep inside her. Panting, she stopped moving. She could even count the spasms of his cock. They relaxed right away, with him satisfied, almost immediately indifferent. She had to hold him to keep him pressed against her.

'Wait, stay there,' she said.

'Did you come hard?'

'Yes.'

Anthony rolled over on his back and she held his hand. The two of them now gazed at the ceiling of the tent, without saying anything. He was breathing through his mouth. Funny, she'd never noticed that before.

'I'm hungry,' he said.

'You're kidding.'

He yawned, zipped up his trousers and straightened.

'I haven't eaten since noon. Do you have a cigarette?'

'Don't make any noise.'

He stepped out of the tent while she rummaged in her bag. Outside, nothing had changed, but the magic had dissipated. All that was left was the dense materiality of things, the sky's uncaring beauty. Anthony stretched. The fresh air dried his chest. He felt good, his spirit cleansed. He took the cigarette she handed him, and she lit it.

'Aren't you smoking?'

'No.'

Vanessa stayed in the tent. She seemed distant.

'What is it?' he asked, almost aggressively.

'Nothing.'

He was silent for a moment, then casually said:

'I'm going to see my father tomorrow.'

'Cool.'

'Yeah. I always wonder how it's going to be.'

'It always goes pretty well.'

'Yeah, but it makes me feel weird.'

Vanessa stuck her head out, looking sincerely concerned.

'I hardly recognise him,' said Anthony.

'What do you mean?'

'I don't know. He's not like he used to be.'

'What about your mother? What does she say about him?'

'Nothing. They don't see each other any more.'

'It's better that way.'

'Yeah.'

After a moment Vanessa asked him:

'Would you like me to come along? I'm free tomorrow evening.'

Anthony looked at her without understanding.

'What do you mean?'

His tone was needlessly sharp, but she was used to it.

'I don't know. I was just saying.'

'You're not coming to my father's place.'

'Okay, fine. I couldn't care less.'

That's what always happened: Vanessa would go too far and Anthony would immediately shut down. More so this time than usual. Now, all he was thinking about was his meeting with Steph in two days. Anthony finished his cigarette and crushed it into the grass, and gave Vanessa a peck on the cheek.

'See you.'

'See you,' she answered.

She wasn't angry with him.

Later, under a tree away from the clearing, she cleaned herself off with a bottle of mineral water and a T-shirt. She didn't hear any noise or see anyone. But she couldn't shake the strange feeling that someone was watching as she washed her pussy.

4

After going through his pockets, Patrick Casati spilled all his small change onto the Formica bar top. It was mainly two-franc coins and centimes and didn't amount to much.

'Is that all?' asked Georges, the owner.

'Wait, lemme see.'

Patrick searched some more, turning his jacket pockets out. Today was Monday, collection day. He eventually found two fifty-franc bills and dropped one of them onto the pile of change.

'I'm keeping fifty francs for myself. I have to eat, after all.'

'Definitely,' said the owner, who knew about life.

'So, are we good, or what?'

'Let me see.'

The owner turned to the imposing coffee machine towering behind him. In the corner next to it stood a big glass jar that was full to the brim, mainly with change but also a few greyish banknotes. He took the jar in both hands and jingled the coins.

'A very nice sound,' said the barber, raising his glass.

'We can't be too far off, I think,' said Patrick.

The owner set it down on the bar. It was a three-litre jam jar with a waterproof rubber top and a 'Quetsch 1987' label. The damson jam it once held had long since been eaten.

'Want to count it?' asked the owner.

'Let's do it,' said Patrick with a smile.

He came to L'Escale for his coffee every morning. It was a bistro not far from his job, run by Georges and his wife, a dark, unreadable Portuguese couple who worked fifteen hours a day. The wife wasn't around that day. Georges's hair was so thick and bushy that the guys never tired of teasing him about his supposedly North African origins. Portugal was right next door, after all; centuries of invasions had surely made for some hybridisations. Georges just nodded silently, as if to say, 'He who laughs last laughs longest.'

'All right, let's count,' said the barber, 'but first . . . *pfiiit!*'

With his thumb, he mimed filling his glass, which was already empty. The owner went to serve him a little muscadet for the road, the barber's third. He came here every morning as well. Starting at eight, he had his first glass of white wine with a slug of lemonade. It helped steady his hand. In fact, the greatest surgeons did exactly the same thing; he'd read that in a magazine. And nobody had ever complained about his work. Still, a certain Mélodie had set up a salon practically across the street, and his business wasn't as brisk as before. She offered a loyalty card, children's haircuts for fifty francs and a plunging neckline. It was almost unfair competition. The barber considered repainting his shop and replacing the old transistor radio, but those modernisation fancies had vanished at the bistro, like the rest. Aside from that, he was completely bald, and a card-carrying member of the conservative RPR party. He loved meetings, cold meats, his country and Charles Pasqua.

The owner filled the barber's glass, then tipped the contents of the jar onto the counter.

'Whoops!'

A few coins went bouncing onto the tiled floor, but no one bothered to pick them up; they would get them later. The three men began sorting the coins by category, in piles of ten. They had plenty of time.

Patrick didn't start work before 9.30, and the place was almost empty during school holidays. The only people there were the regulars: the barber, Patrick and Namur, a fat man on a disability pension who sat at the back reading the newspaper with his little dog on his lap. Villages don't have idiots any more, but every bar has its designated wreck, a semi-drunk invalid who spends his time drinking from morning till night, right to the very end.

Georges took out a notepad and began the final tally. The men smoothed the notes and started counting the ten-franc coins. They checked the totals twice, wary of celebrating too soon.

'That's really it: 5,268.'

Impressed, the barber whistled.

'New francs?'

'Of course.'

'You never know.'

'Well, then…'

Patrick had to admit it wasn't bad. He had been feeding this piggy bank with the money he saved by not drinking. Over time, it had made a pretty penny. With the feeling of having done their duty, the two other men gave him a brotherly look. His pals.

'This is worth celebrating,' said the barber, lifting his glass.

Patrick gave him a little sarcastic nod, as if to say, 'You don't miss a trick, do you?'

In the beginning, quitting drinking had really put Patrick through the wringer. It was worse than anyone could imagine. Over time, alcohol becomes another organ alongside the others in your body, and no less essential. It's there, deep down inside you, it's intimate, and helps keep things going, as much as your heart, kidney or intestines. Stopping drinking means amputating a part of yourself. Patrick had wept. He had screamed at night. Spent hours in scalding hot baths, his teeth chattering. And then, after two months of migraines, aches and night sweats, he woke up one morning, weaned. Everything had changed, even his smell.

Along the way, his belly had grown a lot from eating sweets, but he slept more soundly and woke up feeling better. He was discovering a whole new body economy, with its profits and losses. He didn't feel so out of sorts when he got up in the morning, for example, but neither did he experience that delicious rush of the first drink, when you put fuel in the boiler, where burning alcohol stands in for having a second youth.

Yet that wasn't the fundamental problem of a life without booze. It was time. Boredom. Slowness and people.

Patrick was awaking from a twenty-year sleep, during which he had been dreaming friendships, interests, political opinions, a whole social life, a sense of himself and his authority, certainties about many things, and, finally, hatred. But in fact he'd just been drunk three-quarters of the time. Sober, he was bereft. He had to rediscover everything, all of life. It was hard to endure seeing the sharpness of lines and that heaviness of human substance, the mud of people that drags you down, fills your mouth, torpedoes relationships. That was the principal difficulty, surviving the truth of other people.

At first, Patrick hunkered down in his little apartment, a place outside town that he'd rented in a hurry after his separation. He told himself he would find something better once the divorce was final. A year and a half later, he was still living there. For days on end he'd wandered around like a beast of burden, heavy and vague, full of strength without an object. From time to time he would stand in front of the bathroom mirror and grab his gut with both hands. He disgusted himself and complained about everything – about the cost of living, about Anthony, who was screwing up left and right, about his bitch of a wife and a thousand other things. And especially, he ruminated over that huge waste, his youth spent in the gutter.

Eventually he bought himself a bicycle. His first step towards something better. It was a nuisance, because he didn't have a garage and had to store the bike in a one-bedroom apartment already full to bursting. But at least he went riding. He rode along the canal and met other cyclists. He sat on the bank and watched the water flow by. That boredom was his delight. And he'd managed to find another job, thank God. It was then that the piggy bank idea occurred to him. Each day he would put in the twenty or thirty francs that he used to spend on drinking. Now, ten months later, he had accumulated more than five thousand francs. Quite a sum.

'So, have you decided what you're gonna do with all that dosh?'

'Ah,' said Patrick, his arm raised dramatically.

As if the other men didn't know.

With the back of his hand, Georges swept the five thousand francs off the counter and into the jam jar. He set it on the counter under the three men's noses, a tower heavy with coins.

'Aren't we gonna drink to this?' said the barber again, whose glass was empty.

'Sure, go ahead,' said Patrick expansively. 'Pour him another shot.'

'Ah, that's more like it.'

Patrick looked over at Namur and asked him if he was thirsty. Namur remained silent. He hadn't finished reading. On his lap, the little Cavalier King Charles spaniel was following along line by line, waiting for his master to turn the page.

'Pour him a kir.'

Georges filled the barber's glass, and Patrick brought Namur his kir. He himself settled for a cup of very strong coffee.

L'Escale didn't have a lot of customers in the summer. It was a school hangout, with table football, two pinball machines, and infinite tolerance for minors who lingered for three hours over a cup of coffee and a glass of water. The cafe was right next to Fourier, the best school in town. At noon, it made croque-monsieurs and sandwiches. A peanut dispenser and a pay-phone stood on the bar. The place was old and brown, with the patina of age. It had stools, a colourful tiled floor, a big mirror, a few plants, fake marble and Formica, and brass railings. Absolutely no music; Georges's wife had tinnitus. And the whole place was clean as a whistle.

Every August, the owners closed for a month to go home to Coinbra, to a sun-struck little village where they spent their time digesting staggering lunches and equally ample dinners cooked by their aunt Bruna. They came back rejuvenated, ten pounds heavier and almost black.

At the moment, L'Escale was practically empty. Through the windows, you saw occasional traffic, the social security office over the road, and what remained of the Palace, a cinema closed for security reasons.

The poster of the last film shown there was slowly peeling off: a Sylvester Stallone flick about a trucker who was an arm-wrestling champion.

Namur's voice broke the silence. Everyone listened up; they were used to this.

'Leo: You are full of energy today, and will take things in hand. Love: You are open to being amazed. Work: Your ambition may hide the essential from you.'

Every morning, when Namur reached the last page of the local rag, he read the horoscopes, starting with Leo, his dog's sign. The barber waited for Aries before raising the question he'd been dying to ask.

'So where do you want to send your wife with this money?'

'She's not my wife any more,' said Patrick.

'True enough.'

Actually, he'd been wondering the same thing.

'I'll see with the girl at the travel agency,' he said.

'With five thousand francs, you should be able to go to Sicily.'

'We'll see.'

Patrick had just looked at the clock hanging on the wall between Benfica pennants. He stood up. It was time.

'Well, gentlemen…'

'So long,' said the owner and the barber.

'See you next time.'

'Work well.'

Wishing everybody a good day, Patrick picked up his jar of coins and left the cafe. His piggy bank was pretty heavy, maybe four or five kilos, though still not as heavy as his guilt. As he walked out, he was happy to notice that Namur had drained his kir without any fuss.

Once outside, he hurried towards the Districan offices. He strode along at a good clip, glancing at his watch from time to time, the loot clinking under his arm. When he got to the office, Caro was already there, standing by the gurgling coffee maker, whose smell filled the whole room. She poured him a cup, then took down an assignment sheet from the corkboard.

'Here, this one's for you.'

Patrick read the document as he blew on his hot coffee. He had set his jar on the table where the office workers ate their lunch at noon. Caro eyed the jar without daring to touch it.

'Are you serious?' he asked.

'Well, yeah. That's the way it is,' she said pragmatically.

'You *are* serious.'

They were the same words, but his tone had taken on more gravity. Caro apologised, all sweetness now.

'We're understaffed, sweetheart. It's July. What can I tell you?'

'Yeah, it's summer all year round with you guys.'

'Go on, complaining won't do you any good.'

Patrick counted thirteen checkpoints and almost thirty machines. Plus, they'd stuck him in the hospital. The place was lousy with vending machines; they had them on every floor and in every corner. It would take him all morning. He glanced at his watch, sighed, looked over the assignment sheet again, then headed for the exit.

As he was leaving, Caro called to him:

'Hey! Your piggy bank!'

What with all that, he'd almost forgotten it. Caro was holding it in both hands. She jingled the coins before handing it over, as if the sound could give her an idea of the total.

'How much do you have in there? Did you win the lottery?'

'Don't touch that,' said Patrick, who was trying to pick up the assignment sheet, the money and his coffee all at once.

'Hey, come on,' said Caro. 'There's no point being grumpy. I'm not the one who assigns the jobs.'

'You are, actually.'

'I work with what I've got. What can I say?'

Patrick felt like saying a lot of things. He tried to find the words. It was a waste of time.

'You'd do better to collect your pennies and take me out to dinner,' she said playfully.

Patrick considered her for a second. After all, why not? It was an idea. Caro wasn't especially pretty, but at forty-plus, she was still in the running. He liked her plain, what-you-see-is-what-you-get look, her tight jeans, her way of being both provocative and proper. She belonged to that category of women with good legs who are shapeless in wintertime, but come fair weather are transformed by a skirt and high heels. Patrick liked the type, episodically sexy, springtime pride, returning swallows. Caro was also a relentlessly hard worker who thought the boss and the clients were always right, didn't count her hours and invariably made excuses for the powers that be. Probably from lack of imagination, she never thought to complain about the way things were. She was bringing up two daughters alone, Nina, seven and Sofia, fifteen. She hadn't had a pay rise in five years.

'So?' she said.

'What?'

'Are you gonna take me out?'

'No.'

'So what's the money for?'

'A surprise.'

'For me?'

'Dream on.'

'Well, ciao then. You're already late.'

As he went out the door, she added:

'And don't forget your cap.'

Every time Patrick opened a vending machine, he had to collect the money from it, wipe it down and restock it with canned drinks, water bottles, packets of crisps and little Papi Broussard cakes, not forgetting the chocolate bars. The machines all had magnetic badges. He registered his passage at each with a scanner hanging from his belt. When he got home, he just had to plug the device into his phone line, and the precious information shot straight to the database that Districan used to organise its services and prepare invoices. As a bonus, that same information let the company measure the pace of work, identify downtime, optimise routes, rationalise charges and fire the lazy.

Patrick had found this job thanks to Adecco and the boss had promptly signed him to an open-ended contract. He cleared a little under seven thousand francs a month and got a meal allowance, five weeks of paid holiday and health insurance. Plus free Mars bars and Cokes.

Aside from the work tempo, the job might have suited Patrick pretty well. He was becoming less and less demanding, in any case. Since his separation, he ate the same thing every day, chicken and rice, and always wore the same clothes. His days had themselves all become identical, including at the weekend. Basically, once he became a bachelor, he had simplified himself. But there was that business with the cap. It was one thing to wear a Districan T-shirt and jacket, but he drew the line at that soft, red, corporate and supposedly adjustable hat. He categorically refused to wear the thing. A quality-control supervisor had caught him bareheaded on the job several times. That's how the problems began. 'Didn't you read the memo, Monsieur Casati?' Patrick answered that it wouldn't help him meet his quota and anyway, no one could see him. The supervisor had been forced to press the point. 'There are rules. It's impossible to follow all of them, of course, we aren't Nazis. Still, some of them involve the company's image. And that's critical.'

From then on, Patrick's relationship with the cap became a soap opera. He wore it, felt himself observed, stomped on it, forgot it in his van and regularly lost it. Behind the wheel, on the job, in the bistro, the office, the garage, he would ask himself the question: Should I be wearing my cap? In the old days, people didn't have to put on costumes, except maybe lift operators, porters and maids. But today, we're all flunkeys, more or less. Silicosis and mine explosions are no longer risks of the job. Instead, you now die by degrees, killed by humiliation, tiny demands, petty surveillance at every stage of your day. By asbestos, too. Since the factories shut down, workers were nothing more than confetti. Fodder for the masses and the corporations. It's the hour of the individual, the temp, the isolated. And all those scraps of employment endlessly orbiting in the great vacuum of work are divided into a swarm of separate plastic and transparent places: bubbles, cubicles, partitions, glass panels.

Inside them, air conditioning tempers mood swings. Pagers and telephones split up friends and erode connections. Centuries-old solidarities dissolve in the great bath of competitive forces. New, poorly-paid, thankless little jobs are replacing work that was gruelling, but shared. Production no longer means anything. People talk about relationships, service quality, communication strategy, client satisfaction. It's all so small, isolated, nebulous and wimpy, Patrick thought. He couldn't understand a world where you didn't have a mate, where discipline extended from gestures to words, from bodies to souls. You were expected not only to provide punctual availability and monetisable labor, but to believe in the mission, echo its spirit everywhere, use an approved vocabulary handed down from on high, spin your wheels. This had the stupefying effect of making resistance illegal and your interests indefensible. You had to wear a cap.

Blue-collar workers no longer counted for anything in this new world. Their glory days were out of fashion. People laughed at their unions, which talked big but were always ready to strike a deal. Whenever some poor slob demanded a less pathetic existence, he was carefully shown how unreasonable his desire to live was. In wanting to eat and enjoy himself like anybody else, he risked slowing the march of progress. But his selfishness was understandable. He was just ignorant of worldwide trends. If they increased his pay, his job would fly off to the outskirts of Bucharest. The famously hard-working, patriotic Chinese would do the work in his stead. He simply needed to grasp these new constraints, which were explained to him by affable, well-paid pedagogues.

That said, there was no danger of a supervisor showing up in the middle of July, and Patrick worked bareheaded. As he'd expected, it took him all morning to cover the whole hospital. He worked through his lunch hour, because Anthony was coming to dinner and he wanted to go home early. After three o'clock, he even elected to swipe a few electronic badges without restocking. With vending machines, it was obviously tempting to pretend to work while just recording your passage. He worked quickly and accurately, making the same moves at each machine, treating himself to a free Coke from time to time. Since he'd given up booze, that had become his vice.

He drank a couple of litres a day, which led to bloating and frighteningly guttural belches. In an empty hospital hallway, they took on almost pyrotechnical dimensions. The best was when they hit when he was stopped at a red light. People would turn to him with quizzical looks on their faces. At the wheel of his Districan vehicle, Patrick would give them a little military salute. That was surely good for the company's image.

Punctual as usual, Anthony arrived at his father's around seven. They hugged on the threshold. They now had to get along far from Hélène's eyes, and didn't know quite how to do it. The kind of dull hostility that had served to connect them had evaporated. What remained in its place was a kind of affectionate embarrassment. They were especially careful to avoid any hot topics.

'So, how's it going?'

'All right.'

'What's that?'

Frowning, Anthony's father was pointing at the cuts and bruises on his son's face. His lip was split, and one eye sported a rainbow-coloured bruise.

'It's nothing.'

'Were you in a fight?'

'No.

'Let me see.'

Anthony pulled away before his father touched him. It was an instinctive movement. Patrick's hand dropped. No point in insisting.

'All right.'

Anthony went to sit in the little living room, facing the car park. He had locked his motorbike right outside on purpose. He liked keeping an eye on it. His father cooked dinner in the kitchen. Anthony recognised the smell of tomato sauce, heard meat sizzling in the frying pan.

'What are you making?'

'Spaghetti bolognese.'

'Great.'

His father smiled. Spaghetti was practical and it was the only thing he cooked when Anthony came over. Make a 500-gram package of pasta, and the boy wolfed it down. Patrick was proud of that appetite and what the kid had become. During his entire childhood, Anthony had been small, below average; you could tell by the charts in his health file. Not to mention his screwed-up eye and the way he always clung to his mother's skirts. Some things did improve with the passage of time after all. Patrick lowered the flame under the pan, added onions and garlic to the meat, then heated everything while stirring it with a wooden spatula. One thing was still bothering him, though. Anthony had been beaten up and he wanted to know why. Put words to the injury.

He heard an official-sounding voice coming from the TV in the living room. It was a wrap-up of the Tour de France.

'Who has the maillot jaune?'

'Indurain.'

'It's getting boring. Same old, same old.'

'The man's a machine.'

'No kidding.'

'He's going to win.'

'I know.'

They ate while watching the news. Anthony was bent over his plate. Patrick cut his pasta, which reminded him of old arguments. Hélène used to say that you shouldn't cut spaghetti; she was a stickler about things like that. Remembering it gave Patrick an odd feeling.

On the screen, bundled corpses were being piled into common graves dug with a backhoe. Goma was short of quicklime and an epidemic was threatening. Father and son listened to the news with dull indifference. Everything that came out of the box seemed far away and a lie. The government's spokesman appeared just then, using high-flown, trans-border phrases. Father and son ate their spaghetti before it got cold. From time to time Patrick tried to say something. 'It was hot today.' 'When does school start?' and 'How's your mother doing?'

'Fine.'

'What about her guy?'

'I don't know. We don't see him much these days.'

'Ah,' said his father, his lips pursed. 'He headed for the hills.'

Anthony shot him a pained look. The old man just couldn't help himself. It all came down to resentments and sniping.

In an effort to make it up to him, Patrick said:

'Well, it just so happens I'm giving your mother a present.'

'How come?'

Patrick left the table and fetched the jar full of money from the sideboard. On the news, people were remembering the first moon landing. An unidentified astronaut took historic little hops in the dust. A phrase that had been heard a million times crackled in the warm living room.

Anthony was startled to see all the money.

'I've been saving up for quite a while, to treat her to a holiday.'

'What are you talking about?'

'Do you know how many times she criticised me for not taking you all on holiday?'

'You can't do this.'

'I don't want any more reproaches.'

'What reproaches? She doesn't talk to you any more.'

'I know what I'm doing.'

'She'll never take it. You're crazy!'

'Whose side are you on, for God's sake? I'm going to treat her to a trip, that's all.'

Anthony could see the old leathery face reappearing, with the prominent cheekbones and the fiery eyes under the bushy eyebrows. It had been a long time. He immediately went back to his plate. The food was almost cold now and each bite cost him.

'Listen, she can do whatever she likes,' said his father, softening. 'Me, I pay my debts, that's the way it is.'

Just then, the phone rang. Patrick checked the time on his watch, and a worried look crossed his face. He stepped into the hallway to pick up. Anthony lowered the volume on the TV. His father was answering in monosyllables, with an occasional questioning 'Yes?'

'Really? When?'

His voice suddenly cracked. Anthony turned in his chair to see. There was his old man standing in his slippers, the phone in his hand, looking stunned. 'Yes...yes...all right.' With a familiar gesture, Patrick patted his thinning hair. In the shadowy hallway, Anthony thought he looked aged and grey, skinny in spite of his gut. At every moment, his voice betrayed his thoughts, this old man's whole inner life, his bitterness and his surprises, which were once unknowable. The first fissures.

The phone call went on for a few more seconds in the same tone of embarrassed disbelief. Then Patrick hung up and, eyes wide, said to his son:

'I have some bad news...'

5

Hacine was early, so he drove around below the ZUP towers for a while. He recognised the courtyard, the dust, the shady places where he'd so often been bored out of his mind. The bumper-car carousel wasn't there. He didn't see any familiar faces. Like it or not, this was home. The heat was stifling.

Because he dreaded that dead time before dinner, he couldn't bring himself to go home to his father's right away. He could've looked for Eliott and the others, but he didn't feel like that, either. He was returning after a long absence in a halo of rumours and questions. He didn't want to dissipate the shaky credit created by distance too quickly.

So he decided to spend some time in town. He parked the Volvo and walked, to stretch his legs. In the three days since he'd left Morocco, he'd hardly said a word to anyone. He found himself in a fairly pleasant state of weightlessness. He had slept a lot, these few weeks. As for Heillange, it looked exactly the way it did before he left. Yet a thousand details contradicted that first impression. There, a kebab stand had recently opened; here, a video-game store. A bus shelter looked abandoned. Brand-new Decaux billboards advertised Parisian perfumes and cheap shoes.

All in all, it was pleasant to stroll along streets he knew so well. Like a good expatriate, Hacine felt envied and important, as if the people who'd stayed here led lesser lives and hadn't done much of anything except wait for him. He had a cup of coffee on a terrace on Place des Flamands, near the fountain. A lady was walking her dog. A nanny watched two nearly naked children splashing in the pool. The people who dared to venture outside looked like tourists on the loose. The sweltering heat was an invitation to wander aimlessly.

When Hacine got back in his Volvo, it was almost five. He felt relaxed, floaty. The mood in town was almost that of a seaside resort, an off-season softness. He savoured the calm a little longer, driving as slowly as possible, one elbow out the window, breathing in the enjoyable smell of a familiar landscape.

Over there, he had also experienced moments like that, of being in suspension, on the evening air. He remembered smoking joints with Rashid, Medhi and the others, while looking at the sea. When he first landed at Tétouan, he was sure he would meet only retards and plebs. But then his cousin Driss introduced him to his mates, and Hacine soon realised that their hobbies were no different from his. Hanging out, smoking blunts and playing video games, laughing, thinking about girls. Except that here, you were at the mother lode. The hash you could get in Morocco was of incredible quality, fat and soft, a beautiful, matchless brown colour. It gave you the munchies and fits of laughter that wouldn't stop, and it was dirt cheap. You smoked it in big three-sheet blunts, or straight, in a pipe, before gorging on pastries that left your fingers sticky with sugar and honey. And then you did it again, drinking mint tea, as the heat outside plunged you even deeper into that state of paranoid lightness and exhausted pleasure. Sitting barefoot in jeans and short-sleeved shirts, leaning against the wall in an empty room, Hacine had spent incomparable hours gazing at sunlight filtering through the blinds. Dust and smoke made marine eddies in the air, the sprinklings of dreams. Muted music carried you far away. Even poverty took on a singular beauty. You watched all that without ever tiring of it. Abdel once brought *The Guinness Book of Records* over. Stoned out of their minds, the boys dwelled on the pages dedicated to record giants and diminutive dwarfs and went off on endless peals of laughter seeing one odd little guy who was barely taller than a telephone handset.

Hacine had often come to Morocco during the summer holidays but never wanted to get involved with the locals. He found them repulsive. There was something medieval about their mentality that scared him. This time, since he was stuck here for good, he learned what was going on beneath the apparent inertia. Each year, the Rif produced thousands of tonnes of cannabis resin. Fluorescent green fields covered entire valleys as far as the eye could see. If the land recorder looked the other way, everybody knew what they could get away with. Beneath their respectable exterior, those cunning men with moustaches and big bellies that you saw on cafe terraces were as voracious as anyone on Wall Street. The money from the traffic sustained the place from top to bottom. The millions were used to construct buildings, cities, the whole country. Everyone got a taste, at every level: wholesalers, bureaucrats, moguls, mules, police, politicians, even children. People wondered about the king, but without daring to say it out loud.

Like everyone else, Hacine wanted a piece of the action. His cousin Driss slipped him a few dozen grams, and he got his start that way, with low-level dealing to tourists, practically in the street, the pits. From then on, things began to click. With that money he bought his first kilo, then invested in shipments headed for France and Germany. He came home in the evening and had dinner with his family, normal as anything. He was adding up dollars and francs in his head while his mother asked if he wanted more vegetables.

And to think he'd been sent here to get reformed. The opposite happened. He got stoned, went with whores, and earned in a day what his old man used to make in six months. As he thought of it, what struck him as funny was the way the business worked. In many respects the traffic mimicked the same old patterns as heavy industry, from its modes of supply, the personnel it used, and the families it supported all over Europe.

A large workforce, concentrated in dormitory towns, poorly educated, often foreign-born, lived off this welcome business, with street dealers instead of factory workers. But that was where the comparison stopped, since this new proletariat's philosophy hewed closer to business school than to class struggle.

Hacine gauged the advantages of his situation against that of his parents. Even leaving aside all the money he was making, he didn't have to endure the long hours, the routine, the crushing repetition from Monday to Friday while waiting for holidays, in an endless cycle that took you from youth to the cemetery in the snap of your fingers. His activity gave him a relative feeling of freedom and flexibility. He could get up late and take it easy. True, the work itself was always the same – each time, you had to score a supply, cut, package and resell it – but the tempo was somewhat sporadic and transporting the dope had a whiff of high adventure. You felt you were both a businessman and a pirate. Not too bad.

The biggest drawback was jail. Everybody did time, even the biggest and smartest guys. Once they were caught, the government confiscated their goods and bank accounts, even went after their wives' jewels. In Marseille and Tangiers, sumptuous properties stood padlocked for months, steadily falling into ruin until some little arseholes broke a shutter, squatted in the bedrooms and shat on 5,000-franc sofas, leaving behind a field of ruins and some anarchist slogans on the walls.

After a year, Hacine came to be seen as a reliable guy within his little network. He had a cool head, plus the enormous advantage of a French passport. When problems cropped up somewhere, in Spain or in France, he would be sent to take a look. He took flights there and back; problem solved. Soon he got the chance to drive some round trips. At first, his job was to lead the way, but he was quickly promoted and put behind the wheel of the main vehicle. The convoy from Costa del Sol to Villeurbanne was well organised. A lead car, five miles ahead, to warn of checkpoints. A sweep behind, to retrieve the dope if necessary. In between them was the cargo car, with five hundred kilos of hash hidden in the doors and boot, driving at top speed with no stopping, averaging 190 kilometres per hour the whole way. Hacine demonstrated some obvious talent at that little game. He also had a lot of luck.

So Hacine was already making tens of thousands of francs each month by the time he was twenty. Dressed in Armani from head to toe, barefoot in his trainers, he was tall and scornful, with no particular aspiration except to get rich. He took to smoking contraband cigarettes and treated himself to a Breitling. He looked sharp. His mother still hassled him a little, but he had improved the lot of everyone in the house so dramatically that she didn't dare ask him to lead an honest life. To give them a little more room, he rented the upstairs floor. He bought new mattresses, two TVs and a washing machine, and had the plumbing fixed. The pantry was overflowing. Moreover, he continued living at home, respecting his elders, and stepping outside to smoke. What more could they ask of him?

Hacine's success in business wound up shaping his thinking about how the world worked. As he saw it, you had a choice in life. You could be like his father, complaining and resenting the bosses, spending your time begging and tallying injustices. Or do as he did, show boldness and entrepreneurial spirit, and create your own destiny. Talent was rewarded, as he himself demonstrated rather brilliantly. Pushed to the margins of society, he adopted its most widespread ideas. Money deserves to be recognised for its extraordinary power of assimilation, which turns thieves into shareholders, traffickers into conformists and pimps into merchants. And vice versa.

The problem was that all that money took up a great deal of space. The boys spent a lot of it and laundered some through friendly businesses. But that still left accounts and bundles of cash languishing in banks. The inactivity bothered Hacine, and he talked about it to Driss. It infuriated the two boys to have their desire to expand stymied. They went looking for legal investments, preferably in property. One of their contacts suggested a deal. The guy in question marketed pre-sold villas to Europeans planning to spend their old age in Saida, Essaouira Nador, Tétouan or Tangier. For every dirham invested, you made three back. The idea seemed excellent. The cousins did their research. The guy had an impeccable background, with dozens of completed projects to his name. They went to check things out on the ground. The villas were neat and white, and the bankers and architects all wore beautiful suits. Moreover, their contact accepted foreign currency, cash, everything. They decided to do it.

Once the man pocketed the money, he vanished without a trace.

It left the boys stunned. The humiliation was so stinging that for several days they couldn't even talk about it. But they soon started getting letters from Saida, Eassouira and Nador, where they had chosen to invest their capital. A bunch of people there were demanding to be paid. Ground had been broken; workers wanted their pay; bureaucrats expected their baksheesh. And Driss and Hacine's signatures appeared at the bottom of every legal document authorising the start of the work. They were being asked for enormous sums of money, on top of what they had already lost.

In the beginning, the boys just ignored them. More letters were sent. These were handwritten and abusive. Threats followed. One evening, a fire broke out in the stairwell of the building where Hacine and his family lived. The boys felt spied on and became mistrustful. Another time, Driss was grabbed near the Beaux-Arts. Two men held him while a third gouged his eye out with a screwdriver. That's when they paid up, and Hacine decided it was all over. Anyway, his father was having heart problems. He decided to go home.

So that was how Hacine was returning to Heillange: with his fear, his shame and the last of his savings.

Climbing the stairs to his father's apartment, Hacine was still brooding over that disaster. He climbed in silence, holding his axe handle. A neighbour kid skipping down the stairs passed him. It took the boy four more steps before it hit him. Looking at the skinny figure slowly climbing the stairs, he realised it was him, Hacine Bouali. It had been two years since he was last seen in the neighbourhood. From what people said, he'd been acting like a bandit. His gang had got postcards from the Balearic Islands and the Costa del Sol and started hating him, while secretly feeling jealous. In any case, everyone thought he was gone for good. The kid hurried to spread the news of his return.

Hacine reached the third floor. He had no chance to ring the bell, because the door opened of its own accord. His father was waiting for him, a big smile on his lips.

'Come in, come in,' he said.

Hacine was happy to see how well his father looked. A little more stooped, maybe, his skin a little darker. For some time now he'd started playing boules with his old work buddies. It gave him something to do and got them outside for some fresh air.

'You are all right?'

'Yes, yes.'

They hugged briefly, and his father glanced at the axe handle.

'What is that for?'

All during the trip, Hacine had been imagining the scathing things he would say to him. But now, facing this old man in the building where he'd grown up, it no longer made any sense. His intentions looked like what they were, strictly for show. His father was an old man, gentle, forgetful and weary. And glad to see him again.

'For nothing,' said Hacine. 'Stupid stuff.'

Once in the apartment, Bouali announced the plan. He had made a big pot of *harira* soup but had forgotten the parsley. And he was almost out of chickpeas. They would do without. He had bought tea, too, from Bourrane, along with fresh mint. Hacine was surprised to find the old man so talkative. He noticed that a slight, unpleasant smell of dust and aged skin had appeared under the house's usual odour. He tried to find where the smell was coming from, but it had no origin. It was being exhaled by the walls, the passage of time, his father's habits. The old man grabbed him by the elbow to get his attention. Hacine felt the strength of that grip and it reassured him.

'Are you sleeping here?'

'No. I'm not staying.'

216

'Where are you going?'

'I have to see some friends.'

'Do you have a place to sleep?'

'Sure, don't worry about it.'

'I got your room ready.'

'Thanks, but like I said, I can't stay.'

After a pause, his father asked if he had a job.

'Not yet,' the boy answered. 'But I'll look for something.'

'That is good.'

They went into the kitchen, which was full of the roux smell of Moroccan soup. Bouali asked for news of his wife, Hacine's mother, even though he called her every day.

'She's fine,' said Hacine. 'She's taking it easy.'

'That is good,' said the old man approvingly.

He served the tea. A new oilcloth covered the kitchen table, decorated with a lovely design of tropical birds on a deep blue background. Hacine listened as his father nattered on and on. He had got into the habit of commenting on everything that he was doing, of saying whatever came to mind. 'Now I am heating the water, I am cutting the carrots, I am going to open the window, I am starting the washing machine.' He was reading his life out loud, afraid of leaving things only half done. Hacine wondered if his father did the same thing when he was alone. Then he went into his bedroom. There, nothing had changed.

'You see, everything is ready,' said his father.

The boy smiled to see his salmon-coloured sheets, the flowered quilt, the tattered old rug. There were still *Body Count* and *Terminator* posters on the wall, his weights in the corner, and his bottle of Jean-Claude Gaultier cologne on the little white sideboard. He had only worn it on special occasions, and the bottle was still three-quarters full.

They watched a little television before dinner. The soup was delicious. For the rest, it was the usual, instant potatoes and defrosted mince. His father's constant chatter proved very useful. It avoided questions and serious topics. Hacine's brother, for example, was never mentioned again. Dinner lasted a long time and it was already nine when his father offered to make coffee. Hacine accepted. It was Nescafé and vile. His father got up to piss three times during the meal. Hacine hadn't taken his eyes off the clock and stood up as soon as he finished his coffee.

'I have to get going.'

'All right. Do you have a car?'

'Yes, why?'

'I need you to give me a lift tomorrow. I no longer like to drive any more.'

His father showed him his eyes. The pupils had turned a milky colour. He could no longer see very well.

'What time would you like me to come and get you?'

'In the late afternoon, around five o'clock.'

'Isn't that a bit late? Are you going shopping?'

'No, I have to go to a funeral. You will drop me off over by Beauregard, near the cemetery. Can you come and pick me up afterwards?'

'Yes, of course, no problem.'

'Good.'

His father walked him to the door. In the hallway, he set his hand on his son's back. He wasn't hurrying him. It was an affectionate gesture, gently consented to, just before leaving.

'You will come back soon?'

'Yes. I'm going to stick around now.'

'Ah, that is good.'

'I already told you.'

'Yes, yes, of course.'

Suddenly his father seemed in a hurry and worried. In any case, he had stopped listening to him.

'What's the matter?'

'Nothing, nothing.'

They hugged again and Bouali hustled his son out without further explanation, then closed the door behind him. Feeling intrigued, Hacine stood motionless on the doormat for a moment. There was no noise in the stairwell, not a murmur. He turned the handle and the door opened. Everything was quiet in the apartment. Some light from the kitchen

218

spilled into the hallway. The boy felt like a burglar, a tomb robber. He stood on the threshold, not daring to go further, feeling almost ashamed. Suddenly he heard a sharp, watery sound, interspersed with groans. His father was pissing again and lamenting his fate. Hacine silently closed the door, leaving the man to the monotonous secrets of his old age.

Out in the courtyard, Seb was the first to spot him. He was sitting on the low wall, busy throwing small stones at a bigger one. He had got pretty good at his little game. It was already almost dark and there were five of them in all, hanging out, same as always. A nearby street lamp cast its pale light on the ground. For the first time, the carnival women hadn't come this year. But the boys were there anyway, contemplating the empty space framed by the towers. They were smoking, talking crap and passing around a bottle of white rum that Steve had brought back from la Réunion. Seb had traded his 49ers cap for a navy blue-and-white Detroit model, the same one that Magnum wore in the old TV series. He had just hit the big stone with a smaller one again when he saw a shadow appear at the foot of the Picasso tower.

'Hey...'

They all looked. The shadow came closer. It was Hacine, holding his axe handle. They'd already known for a few hours that he was back and had been making fun of him all afternoon. Mostly, they wondered what had brought him back to the neighbourhood, since he was leading the life of a mogul in Morocco and Spain. Curiosity stimulated their minds. Steve was the first to notice something odd.

'What the hell's he doing with a cane?'

'That's not a cane,' said Eliott.

With a low hum, his wheelchair drove away from the little group. Eliott's back was soaked, his hands damp. For the last few days, a persistent heaviness had hung in the air, an abscess of wind and lightning, and the crippled boy had been stewing in his shorts. In the morning, his mother had to dust him with talcum powder. Every so often the wind would start to blow, raising hopes for a break, rain showers, the relief the whole valley was waiting for. But each time, it was a false alarm. Everything started up again in the same swollen, sexual immobility, that almost painful suspension. Eliott forced himself to smile.

'Hi.'

'Hi.'

The others came closer. They were now within the white circle cast by the street lamp. The faces looked the way he remembered them, but were no longer the same. Months had passed.

'How're ya doin', big guy?'

'You good, or what?'

Hacine said hello to all of them, casually slapping their hands, ending with Eliott.

'You been back long?'

'You're sure suntanned, man.'

'It's nice to see you.'

'You staying long?'

They were all nodding, attentive, patting him on the back, but weren't really convincing. You could sense their awkwardness.

'What's that stick of yours?' asked Djamel.

Hacine held the handle in front of him, gripping it hard, his wrist firm.

'It's nothing. It was for my father.'

'How's your dad doing?'

'What was it like over there? Tell us all about it.'

'Yeah, c'mon, tell us.'

'Did you bring any dope back?'

'When are you leaving?'

'You got something to smoke, man?'

Hacine answered each of them with a terse word, two at most and his coldness gradually spread to the little group. Eliott was looking at his friend, struggling to recognise him. And yet it was him. When Hacine pulled out a big ten-gram bar of hash from his pocket, something like cheerfulness revived the troops. Everybody started rolling blunts. Ten minutes later, the gang was back on the low wall, smoking and chatting.

Only Hacine remained standing, leaning on his club. He asked how the business was going.

'What business?' It had all turned to shit, his mates said.

They explained to him that the traffic was now in the hands of younger kids, fourteen or fifteen years old. That generation's boldness was frightening. They didn't respect anything, thought only of raking it in. They were seen criss-crossing the ZUP on scooters, picking fights, ambitious, constantly stoned. They used even younger kids as lookouts. Families who didn't want to be involved ended up hiding 250-gram 'soap bars' under the kids' bed or in Grandma's wardrobe. Some of these little hotshots even carried guns. Fights were constantly breaking out and the police had increased their surveillance and the number of patrols, but were careful not to get out of their cars except in cases of serious mayhem. In short, things had really changed.

'What about the wholesaler?' asked Hacine.

After all, those teenagers weren't riding to Holland on their motorbikes. They needed a source, an adult somewhere with contacts and a driving licence to organise the thing and satisfy their appetites.

Nobody dared answer. Hacine waited, puffing on a big three-sheeter. He turned to Eliott.

'So, who is it?'

The fat boy shifted in his wheelchair before answering. It was so fucking hot.

'It's Kader, I think.'

'Where is he?'

Nobody knew, but in general he always came by during the evening.

'We're gonna wait for him,' said Hacine.

Nobody felt like smoking any more. At least now everyone knew why Hacine had come back.

Little Kader finally showed up. It was almost midnight, and the boys couldn't stand it any more. They were stoned and starving and each time one of them opened his mouth, Hacine seemed to condemn them all

221

to death. It wound up being painful. All the more so because intermittent thunderclaps were now echoing across the sky. On the horizon over by the border, you could even see heat lightning. The atmosphere was unbearable. You just wanted to have a shower and go to bed. So little Kader's appearance came as a relief. It was time to end this one way or the other, and as quickly as possible.

'Hi, kids!' cried the new arrival cheerfully.

Kader was wearing a leather jacket covered with zips and big 800-franc Nikes. He came strutting up, looking very pleased with himself, apparently relaxed. Hacine's presence didn't seem to bother him particularly.

'What do you know,' he said. 'Long time no see!'

Hacine's eyes were bloodshot, his mouth clamped shut.

'So you've come back...'

The person in question had to admit that this was so.

The others followed this exchange with suitable expressions on their faces, while inwardly generating predictions and equations. Hacine wasn't all that respected. He'd never been very strong and tonight seemed almost sickly weak, a wobbly invertebrate no one would pick as the future local Pablo Escobar. His contempt didn't change anything; he came across as fragile.

Kader, on the other hand, was short, tough and quick. He'd been doing a fair amount of coke lately and felt very sure of himself, on a roll, aggressively sarcastic. He had contacts in Amsterdam, Saint-Denis and Villeurbanne. He would score a kilo for seven thousand francs and resell it for fifteen thousand, easy. On his BMW 750, the rims alone cost four times the minimum wage. He spat between his teeth. A fresh thunderclap rumbled in the sky overhead. When Kader smiled, you could see that he'd lost teeth on his right side and had them replaced with gold. It was chic.

'All right,' he said patronisingly. 'I'm glad you're here, but—'

He didn't have time to get any further. The axe handle hissed through the air in a perfect curve and smashed the lower part of Kader's face with a mineral crack. With its suddenness and absence of motive, Hacine's move pained each of the witnesses. Silence fell immediately. Someone started to vomit. On the ground, his jaw dislocated, his hands flat in the dust, little Kader sat up. He had the bewildered look of a child lost in a department store. He was panting like a dog, and the harsh, whistling breath through his throat and nostrils blew threads of saliva mixed with blood from his lips. He tried to stand, not yet feeling the pain, not yet realising what had happened, thinking it trivial, that he'd just slipped. But then he tried to speak and felt his lower jaw caught in a disgusting mushiness. Hacine watched him without saying anything. He was so scared he could have killed him right then and there.

6

Anthony's mother asked him to accompany her to Luc Grande-mange's funeral, and he didn't have much choice. It was his first funeral and he'd dressed up: white shirt, jacket and tie. It felt odd to be fitted out like that, looking halfway between a policeman and an executive, but it wasn't actually unpleasant. He was even wearing smart shoes, which they'd had to buy for the occasion. Like weddings, funerals involve expenses. His mother had wanted to buy him shoes that would last; Anthony wanted stylish Kenzos. And luckily, they were on sale.

During the whole drive to the church, Hélène kept fiddling with her hair, a sign that she was extremely nervous. Also, she smoked continuously. Anthony twice had to warn her that a light had turned red.

'It'll be fine,' he said protectively.

She said, 'Yes, sure, nothing to be done about it, anyway.' Behind her big sunglasses, Hélène was hanging in there. She would be seeing Patrick for the first time since their divorce became final. That was a drawback of funerals: you always ran into old acquaintances.

They arrived quite early, so parking in the church's car park was easy. The church itself stood in the very centre of town, not far from

City Hall. It was an impressive Roman-looking building with a symmetrical, pilastered facade and a square belfry tower. The Wendel family had had it built during the German annexation and asked the architect for something with a Renaissance, Italianate feeling, as a slap at the kaiser and his Visigothic leanings. They had spent lavishly on a significant building, probably out of guilt, since they were living in the 8th arrondissement of Paris while Heillange was under German rule. A hundred and ten years later, Saint-Michel d'Heillange now stood as a luxurious relic surrounded by poverty. Each time a family buried a drunkard or a silicosis victim, it felt as if they had somehow earned the right to a national funeral.

The church's little forecourt soon filled with people. Anthony and his mother, who had stayed off to one side, joined the crowd. Hélène led the way. She was wearing a dark dress cinched at the waist by a shiny belt. A small handbag shaped like a seashell hung from her shoulder. In the sea of faces, Anthony recognised a few, mainly people he was used to seeing in town. Everybody was smiling and chatting quietly. You might have mistaken it for a charity bazaar, except for a certain restraint and all the black. A thunderstorm loomed overhead like a promise. This was no weather in which to be wearing a suit.

'Look,' said Hélène.

Vanessa had just spotted the two of them, and crossed the forecourt to join them. She, too, was wearing a dark dress and high heels. She looked pretty.

'So you came?' said Hélène, pleasantly surprised.

'Yes, sure.'

'Do you know the Grandemange family?'

'Not really.'

Vanessa smiled, looking natural and sweet. Hélène was very fond of the girl. She used to come to the house from time to time, and she said hello and stayed downstairs to chat for a few minutes before running upstairs and shutting herself in Anthony's bedroom. She ate dinner with them a few times and always offered to help lay the table or do the washing up. She was intelligent and not a show-off, the kind of girl who could have raised Anthony up. Then she stopped coming and Anthony didn't mention her any more. But it was none of Hélène's business.

Anthony saw the situation differently. As soon as he could, he took Vanessa aside.

'What the hell are you doing here?' he asked.

'Am I bothering you?'

'No, but you have no business being here. I didn't ask you to come.'

'All right, don't get uptight. I'll head off.'

But Anthony kept her from leaving. He was dying of the heat. He loosened his tie and unbuttoned his shirt collar. Searching for some fresh air, he looked up at the close, low sky. It was marbled and grey, as languid as soup.

'It's got to break soon. I can't stand this any more.'

'There's nothing forecast before tonight.'

That was something Anthony was well aware of, having checked the weather earlier. He had a date behind the old power plant that evening at nine and intended to be there come rain, wind or snow.

Meanwhile, Hélène had started making the rounds. Neighbours were there, as well as Luc's family and old workmates. She greeted each person with an appropriate expression, but conversation soon drove away the show of sadness. People caught up with each other's news. So-and-so was dead; that other one's son left for China; the Hartz's bakery found a buyer. Expressions flitted across Hélène's face like clouds. She was friendly, solicitous, always interested in other people's lives, their joys and sorrows. When she raised her sunglasses, you saw the bags under her eyes and her ashy skin, wrinkled by worry and scored by tears, that made her look quite old. She'd gone through a tonne of shit in the last two years.

For their part, Vanessa and Anthony watched as the little crowd complacently milled about in the shadow of the church. Vanessa hadn't said anything for some time. He turned to her.

'Are you in a bad mood?'

'No.'

'Seems that way.'

Vanessa was angry at herself for having come. True, Anthony hadn't asked her for anything. She was trying to make a place for herself in his life, but why bother? He was a dick and a jerk. Ugly, too, with that screwed-up eye. She looked at him to make sure. He really wasn't that ugly, worse luck.

'Come on,' he said, nudging her with his shoulder. 'It's all right. I apologise.'

'You're not so aggressive when you come to fuck me.'

He turned on her in surprise.

'What's that supposed to mean?'

'Nothing.'

'That's a bitchy thing to say! You enjoy it as much as I do.'

This time she turned to face him. In her heels, she was almost as tall as he was.

'Yeah, I just love it when you wake me up in the middle of the night to drain your balls.'

'So what do you want?' he snapped irritably. 'For us to get married?'

'Arsehole.'

It was less of a reproach than a regret. Vanessa didn't expect anything from him, of course. He was a kid, a loser, hopeless at school, always going on about his motorbike, not her type at all. Besides, they had their agreement to get together and fuck, *basta*. Except that after sex, when you're lying there looking at the ceiling, you can't help but confide in each other. When Anthony's mother wasn't home, they sometimes stayed like that for a long time in his darkened room, talking. He had those long lashes, that brown skin. He kept saying that he didn't give a damn, but clearly, the opposite was true. She sometimes thought about him even when she was in her studio apartment in Metz or watching a movie with Christopher. She constantly felt an urge to grab him, pull his hair, bite him. She hated herself for being that way. She had put on her prettiest dress.

———

The little crowd suddenly seemed to part in the middle and began to move in a circle, like a school of fish. Évelyne Grandemange, the widow, had just appeared. Holding her arm was a very tall, slim, hunched man with a pockmarked face. This was her nephew Brice. Everybody knew him; he had that truck and van rental place on the road to Étange.

'She seems to be doing okay,' said Vanessa.

It was true. Évelyne seemed in good shape. She was even doing a bit of a star turn, all smiles, saying hello to everyone, an eternal Gauloise in her hand. Anthony, who hadn't seen her for a few months, was startled to see how deeply she had settled into old age. She looked sunken, withered, her face sombre and furrowed, as if kneaded by the years. Her shining eyes and tireless smile almost clashed with the rest of her looks. Her legs, especially, didn't bode well. They looked like two wooden sticks. Anthony hoped he wouldn't have to kiss her; it would feel cold.

'Do you think we ought to go over?'

'Whatever you like,' answered Vanessa.

'I don't know what to say to her.'

'Well, just tell her you're so sorry. That's all.'

'I don't really feel it.'

'Haven't you ever been to a funeral before?'

'No. What about you?'

'My grandmother, when I was a little girl.'

'Oh, I'm so sorry.'

'Pfff! You idiot!'

They stopped talking and stood there. All in all, Anthony was quite pleased that she'd come. The hearse appeared, bearing the coffin. It was a long, old-fashioned pachydermic Citroën CX, bright with chrome, with lots of windows to show the interior. There was something majestic about its movement and people parted as it passed. It was so quiet, you could hear the sigh of its hydraulic suspension when it stopped. The crowd fell silent as well. A body inside was on the verge of disappearing. A cold future that awaited us all. People stopped messing around.

'Damn, I wonder where my father is,' said Anthony.

'Are you sure he's going to come?'

'I hope so.'

Even after all this time, Anthony still worried that Patrick would show up dead drunk. He had too many memories from before, from his childhood and then the rest, the crises during the divorce, finding his father in a pathetic state, weeping and saying he was going to shoot himself. Best not to think of it.

Two men wearing identical aubergine-coloured polyester suits got out of the CX. The taller one's tennis socks were visible. His shorter partner wore glasses that darkened in sunlight. They lowered the tailgate, and Brice the nephew and another man came over to lend a hand. When they hoisted the coffin, it seemed surprisingly light and too small.

'How did they ever fit him in there?' someone wondered.

'At the end, he was just skin and bones.'

'Still, it's not like they folded him in half.'

The crowd gradually arranged itself into a cortège behind the deceased. The coffin led the way, followed by the widow, all alone. Behind her, people came in twos and threes, walking in silence, with children held by the hand and the old by the arm. In the nave, which was cool and empty, the organ was already playing drawn-out notes that echoed in people's chests and under the stone arches. The pews gradually filled as the coffin was set on stands. Two white candles stood guard on either side.

Anthony, Hélène and Vanessa slipped into a row halfway between the choir and the porch. Unused to being in church, Anthony looked at the stained-glass windows, the sculptures, and the images of agony and glory without understanding any of it. For him and for many others, the meaning of that language had been lost. All that remained was pretentious decorum and empty gestures. At least it was cool.

The priest tapped the microphone to make sure that the speakers worked. He began:

'Dear brothers, we are gathered today to remember...'

Anthony turned round in the hope of spotting his father in the crowd, but he still wasn't there. On the other hand, his cousin was a few rows away, with his girlfriend, Séverine. He and Anthony shared a smile, and his cousin even winked at him. He'd completely dropped out of circulation after he started going out with her. She was a knockout mixed race girl who competed in beauty contests. Even here, dressed in sober black, she still caught people's eye. The cousin was totally at her beck and call. You could understand why. Still, it was stupid.

Aside from that, the rogues' gallery of faces summed up old Grandemange's life pretty well. The family, the neighbours, old workmates, two deputy mayors, business owners, drinking buddies and guys from the Société des fêtes. Gathered at the back were his CGT union brothers, guys who shared a look of cocky aloofness that went with their refusal to get dressed up. And then there was Dr Reswiller, in a houndstooth jacket and black polo shirt, with glasses on his forehead and Paraboots on his feet, as usual. He had suspected that there was something wrong with Luc's pancreas from the very beginning. He ordered some extra tests, which confirmed his diagnosis. Reswiller had been Grandemange's doctor for nearly forty years, and together they agreed to put off hospitalisation as long as possible, since he was as good as dead anyway. When the pain became unbearable, he was put in a double room with a car-park view, television and a morphine drip. Very soon, he sank into a coma. In two weeks, it was all over.

During the ceremony, the priest summed up the deceased's life, which had been neither very long nor very exemplary. It filled a single sheet of paper. To begin with, he had a father and a mother who died during the war, leaving two orphans. Luc was the younger and had a rough time, growing up in boarding schools as a war orphan. For people who had only known him as a big, easy-going mammoth of a guy, always joking and complaining, those memories seemed almost impossible. Grandemange had loved nature, rock 'n' roll and Charles Trénet, hunting and drinking. He met Évelyne in 1966 and married her. The priest then ran through the list of his jobs, which mirrored the valley's economic history: Metalor, Rexel, Pomona, City2000, Socogem. But he said nothing about the lean years, unemployment, lay-offs, union activism, politics, or the most recent campaign, during which Grandemange had put up posters for the National Front.

The priest concluded soberly, noting that for Luc Grandemange 'friendship' wasn't an empty word, and that he had always been deeply involved in the town's life. Seated in the front row, Évelyne listened in silence, her hands gripping a dry handkerchief. Along with that, you had to stand up, sit down, pray. In general, everything that had been said was forgotten. The nephew read a poem by Éluard. People sang, tentatively. Those who wished to bless the coffin did so. The organ played. It was over.

As they went out, Anthony was relieved to see his father standing at the back near the door, hands in his pockets. He'd had a haircut and put on his blue suit. That's when he realised that he'd lost quite a bit of weight, in spite of the belly that stretched his shirt.

'Stay close to me,' whispered Hélène, who was as white as a sheet.

Anthony reassured her. In the distance, his father watched them, a slight smile playing on his lips. Aside from that, he seemed in great shape.

7

Steph parked the 205 with the top down near the train station. This was a functional, century-old building with a clock high on the wall that read 4.10 p.m. Clémence remarked that they were super early. Steph didn't even hear.

She had been waiting and getting herself ready for ages. These last few days she had been careful to drink her two daily bottles of Contrex mineral water. She had lain out in the sun, but not too much, an hour at most, patiently building up her tan so as to get the perfect smooth suntan, a golden skin with a few pale marks on her naked body, a memory of her bikini.

The moment Steph got out of bed, she stepped onto the scales feeling vaguely worried. She liked to eat and party. She enjoyed staying up late and tended to drink a lot. So she had started watching her weight to the gram, tracking how much sleep she got, and taking great care of her body, which was prone to extraordinary changes, depending on the moment, the light, her fatigue and what she'd had to eat. She painted her nails, made up her eyes, treated her hair to two shampoos, first one with seaweed, then one with eggs. She gave herself a facial. In the shower, she scrubbed her skin with coffee grounds. She entrusted her legs and pussy to her beautician. She was clean, appetising, calibrated to the millimetre.

Today, she was wearing a brand-new T-shirt, a striped Petit Bateau number that was so tight, Clémence asked if it was designed for a six-year-old.

'We're going to have to wait for hours,' said Clem, who was already feeling bored.

'Of course we're not.'

'Well, I'm sorry, but we are.'

They went to Platform 2, which was completely deserted. The girls both had long hair and were wearing Converse and skirts. The train would arrive at 4.42, with a two-minute stop, maximum. The Heillange station hardly served any purpose any more but survived as a matter of principle because the deputy mayor had made it a political issue, because a town without a train station was nothing at all. On the shabby walls, illegible posters gave the schedule of the regional TER trains, which no longer stopped here. The advertisements were six months old. The weather was horribly oppressive. Clémence decided to go wait in the shade. A feverish Stéphanie took to staring at the point on the horizon where the tracks converged.

She felt happy. She was about to get her reward.

Steph had been sweating blood these last few months. She had always skated through life, doing as little as possible. Merely acting doleful and looking cute were enough to get her through most situations. Except that as exam time approached, her father had suddenly started harbouring unexpected ambitions. Or maybe he'd begun to panic about Steph's future. Whatever the case, he'd read her the riot act. Unless she passed her baccalaureate with honours, he said, she could kiss her car and her holiday goodbye.

'You're joking, right?'

She still remembered the moment when he delivered the blow. She was standing in the kitchen, eating a strawberry Yoplait. That's probably why she would hate that flavour for the rest of her life.

'I'm just warning you, that's all,' he said. 'Either you pass with honours or you won't get a car.'

'But I already took the written driving test.'

'So what? I saw your friend's father at the stadium yesterday. She's going to take a *préparatoire* course in Lyon.'

That bitch Clémence! Always slaving away on the sly. Whereas with all her screw-ups, Steph was now up against it.

'But she's been working like mad ever since primary school!'

'So what were you doing all that time?'

'That has nothing to do with it! Where in the world is this coming from? I can't make up ten years in three months, that's crazy.'

'I've talked it over with your mother. That's the way it is. Also, you're going to finish your university applications. That's been dragging on for weeks.'

'Okay, fine.'

'When?'

'I'll get to it.'

'Today!'

'Jesus...' Steph groaned.

In disgust, she tossed her Yoplait in the bin, spoon and all.

The ultimatum hit especially hard because she'd just found a little Peugeot 205. It had 225,000 kilometres on the odometer, but it was red and a convertible – and her parents had said yes. She and Clémence had been dreaming non-stop about what they would do with it. And now the dream was imploding just like that, right in their remodelled kitchen.

Ever since he'd started aiming for the mayoralty, Pierre Chaussoy had developed a rabid appetite for conformity. It had got so bad that Steph's mother could hardly go out in a miniskirt any more. And now he wanted an offspring with diplomas. He was less of a pain when all he cared about was cars and getting a new coupé every year.

All things considered, the threat to Steph's holiday was the most serious. If she bugged her parents long enough, she would eventually end up getting a car. It was essential for getting around here and cheap, so they wouldn't give her a hard time. The holiday, on the other hand, was something else. They'd grumbled about it from the start. The plan was a pretty big deal. The Rotiers owned a fabulous house in the Basque region near Biarritz, a sheepfold facing the ocean, to which they invited a chosen few every August. Stéphanie and Clémence had scored invitations for the first time this year, a signal honour.

It should be said that Steph and Simon were now pretty much seen as a couple, despite the break-ups, psychodramas, reconciliations and separations that were their standard operating procedure. She was his girlfriend and that was that.

Starting in April, Steph's life became a sedentary nightmare. She had been counting on passing the baccalaureate with a B– average, thanks to helpful grades in English and P.E. in her oral exams. But her dad's demands had thrown her into homework hell. Worse, she was practising for her driving licence at the same time.

So for weeks on end, Steph endured a series of exhausting days. She got up at six and studied before breakfast, especially history and geography, subjects that demanded an unreal amount of memorising. Yalta, the United States, Japan, the Missile Crisis, the Trente Glorieuses... was there no end to this crap? She bought Bristol index cards, writing notes in blue ink and emphasising dates in red. She had some muesli and orange juice and continued studying in the car on the way to school. Then she had classes, followed by tutoring in maths.

Every subject counted, even philosophy. Plato's *Republic*, seriously? Who dreamed up these insane programmes? In a country ravaged by unemployment, socialism and Asian competition, were younger generations really expected to be interested in that ancient bullshit? In the library, Clémence got a good laugh when she saw Steph aim two fingers at her temple, but that didn't help her understand the allegory of the cave.

After a while, she decided to focus on 'annales', well-edited little study guides that summarised everything you needed to know to avoid being humiliated on exam day. She underlined the main points but was so anxious that she ended up highlighting practically every single line. Sometimes, when she got depressed, she would fold her arms on her desk and bury her head in them. The weather was beautiful and Roland Garros would be on TV soon.

In the evening, Clémence would drop Steph off at the driving school. Her instructor, who wore Bermuda shorts and Pataugas boots, would drape his arm around her headrest. For the whole driving lesson, she had to endure the smell of his armpits and the sweaty presence of this car-mad clown. It was enough to make you weep. The guy had an especially disgusting way of teaching parallel parking. As she was pulling in, he would slide close, watch the rear-view mirror, and mutter, 'Yes…Yes… No…That's good. A little to the right. Gooood. Yes.' What a creep! Once, she yanked the handbrake and ditched him, stalking off without a backward glance.

When she got home, Steph went at it again, studying until nine, if not later. Clémence came over and they would cram together. The girls also spent a fair amount of time working out university courses. Steph had never taken much interest in her career path. She was now discovering a whole nebula of programmes in the liberal professions, secondary degree tracks, dead-end paths and useless bachelor's degrees, and technical diplomas that led to well-paid jobs with no hope of promotion. Clémence, on the other hand, had those career paths down pat, had been preparing for them since forever. Steph was only now discovering that there was no such thing as destiny. In reality, you had to build your future like a construction game, one brick at a time. You had to make the right choices, because you couldn't afford to take a path that required a great deal of effort and didn't lead anywhere. Clémence had all this stuff at her fingertips. Her father was a doctor, and her mother, an education inspector. Those people had practically invented the game.

At times, Steph would space out. Her mind wandered. She started thinking about Simon Rotier, wondering what he was up to. She hardly had a second to devote to him and, knowing Simon, he probably wasn't sitting around twiddling his thumbs. Whenever they ran into each other in the corridor at school, she couldn't help demanding to know what he'd been up to. Their conversations quickly turned nasty. Also, that slut Virginie Vanier was buzzing around him, with her big teeth and her big tits.

Too bad. Steph had to stay focused. Honours. The car. The holiday. The Basque country. Once there, she would go swimming every day. They would go surfing, have barbecues, party non-stop. She and Simon would fuck in the shade of the pine trees, with the taste of salt on their skin, the rustling of the wind, the ocean so close.

'And itchy sand up your bum,' added Clémence.

Steph grinned. She no longer saw her friend in the same way. Now that she was thinking about her future, her options and the way careers were made, she was suddenly becoming conscious of a new fact: the world belonged to the students who were the first in their class. All those kids, the ones people mocked for being followers, timid, studious and conscientious, had the right idea from the very beginning. If you want a crack at the good jobs and later an exciting, respected life with couture suits and pricey heels, it wasn't enough to be cool and born into the right family. You have to do your homework. This came as a real shock for Steph, who had largely relied on her basic don't-give-a damn attitude and a fondness for Winter sports.

With all this studying, strange things started happening in her head. Shortcuts, surprises, insights. Up to now, she had always thought the disciplines she was taught to be diversions, pastimes for channelling the young. But once the force feeding started, it changed the way she saw things. Steph would've had trouble defining this turnabout. She felt both more confident and less certain. Under pressure, a brief *Eureka!* would sometimes light up her mind. Or, on the contrary, some obvious truism would fade away before her very eyes. The world was becoming fragmented, ramified, infinite.

Gradually, she began to enjoy it.

And a terrible worry hit her. She was belatedly realising that her view of success was totally fallacious. Her parents' ideal, with their idea of exponential comfort – the chalet in the mountains and the flat in Juan-les-Pins, their need to be well connected and have status – she now clearly saw as pathetic. To be successful, it wasn't enough to sell luxury cars and know all the rich people in town. That was a horizon for small-timers and the perpetually confused. A cocooned place that hung by a thread.

Steph's folks thought themselves lords, but they were actually mediocre stewards for a rule operating elsewhere.

With Clémence, Steph was starting to see the big picture. France's real decision-makers went through the *préparatoire* courses and private academies. As early as primary school, society started sorting its children, picking the most promising ones, the ones best suited to reinforcing the status quo. The result of this systematic selection was a prodigious underpinning of existing power. Each generation produced its batch of gifted people who were quickly converted and duly rewarded, and who went on to strengthen inheritances, revive dynasties, and consolidate the huge architecture of the country's social pyramid. In the end, merit wasn't opposed to the laws of birth and blood, as had been imagined by judges, thinkers, the rebels of 1789 or the black hussars of the Republic. It actually disguised a huge winnowing operation, an extraordinary power of agglomeration, a continuous shoring up of existing hierarchies. It was a very clever system.

After hours of studying, beating herself up, eating Pepito sandwiches and sitting inside while the sun was shining, Steph came to despise the entire edifice. She and Clémence got enormously worked up, wanting to overthrow the whole system and go and live cheaply, listening to music on some faraway beach. This revolutionary ardour barely disguised their fatigue, their laziness, and the fear that they would fail and find themselves at the bottom of the ladder. In May, they were still burning with this feeling of injustice. Then came the exams. Steph passed with an A average. Her *baccalauréat* with honours in hand, she quickly reconciled with the ways of the world. Nothing remained of her political fervour, including the quickly jettisoned notion of joining the young socialists. Delighted, her father bought her the little red car.

While they were waiting, other travellers had joined the girls on Platform 2. Clémence did her best to ignore them. Steph could hardly keep still. Then the train appeared.

Steph immediately ran to the last carriage. A moment later, Simon stepped down carrying his suitcase, looking fresh. He took her in his arms and they shared a deep kiss.

'I've missed you so much,' she said.

'Me too.'

She looked at him. He smiled. She immediately sensed that something was off.

'I have my car,' she said.

'Cool.'

'I can't tell you how happy I am.'

'Yeah, me too.'

'Did you get a haircut?'

'Yeah.'

They joined Clémence and headed out. Simon insisted on sitting in the back with his suitcase, and they got under way.

Steph had dreamed of this moment dozens of times. They would get into the convertible. They were young, beautiful and free. She had even made a cassette tape mix for the car's Hi Fi, with songs by the Beach Boys and Mano Negra. But instead of that, Simon was acting distant, Clémence was feigning indifference and she herself felt burdened and unwell, as if she were on her period and had just eaten a couple of Snickers bars.

'So, how was it?'

'Cool.'

'What did you do? Did you go to concerts?'

'Yeah.'

'Did you see the Eiffel Tower?' Clémence asked with a straight face.

'Yeah.'

'Super.'

Steph kept asking questions. She already assumed there was some girl behind Simon's laconic answers. But all in all, that was a lesser evil. The Basque country was calling. Distance would quickly make him forget his accidental Parisienne. Besides, Simon went to Paris pretty regularly. He had cousins there. If he had in fact found himself a girlfriend, Steph would just have to keep an eye on him. He said 'Paris', but the cousins in question actually lived out in Rueil-Malmaison. She was a top executive with Danone; her husband worked for Matra, in La Défense. They had three children. Judging by the photos, they looked a lot like the Triplés, the insufferable blond kids in the cartoon strip that ran in *Figaro Madame*.

'So what did you do there?'

'Nothing special.'

'Did you see friends? Did you go out?'

'Yeah.'

'What do you mean, "Yeah"?'

Steph checked the rear-view mirror. Simon was wearing his Quiksilver glasses and looked very superior to everything, as usual, and that indifference drove her completely crazy. She couldn't help it. She wanted to matter to him and right now. She fell silent, in a hurry to be alone with him. She would do whatever he wanted.

Then Simon spoke up.

'By the way, Biarritz isn't happening,' he said offhandedly.

'What?'

Clémence spun round in her seat, and Steph almost stalled the car.

'We aren't going. It's off. I'm sorry.'

'What are you talking about?' asked Clémence.

'Are you serious?' asked Steph.

'C'mon, talk. What the hell is this shit?'

'Yeah, I'm sorry. That's the way it is. The trip is off.'

Steph brought the car to a screeching stop on the shoulder. Another car passed them, honking furiously. The girls gaped at Simon, incredulous. He actually didn't seem all that sorry.

'Explain yourself at least.'

'It's nothing. Drive on, I'll tell you about it.'

Steph set the handbrake instead. Simon looked around the area where they had stopped. It was one of those ambiguous zones where scattered houses with little gardens, fences and coloured shutters formed an intermittent archipelago. There were motorway signs, electric wires, spaces between people. It wasn't the countryside, but neither was it a town or a housing development. A bus stop shelter maintained the fiction of a link with civilisation. Two old people were waiting there – since when?

'So?'

'I'm sorry,' Simon repeated, about as convincingly as before.

'What part of "We want an explanation" don't you understand?' asked Clémence.

'It's complicated.'

'Get out of my car,' said Steph.

'You're joking.'

'Yeah. We're dying of laughter. Get out, right now.'

'Wait.'

'What?'

'I'll explain it to you. It isn't my fault.'

Simon told them what had happened. Julien, the oldest of his cousins, was due to go to the West Coast of the United States for a whole month that summer. It was a big deal and had been arranged a long time ago. But he'd had the bad luck to break his leg roller skating. So Simon stepped in to take his place. He was leaving in three days; his bags were already packed. A month with a family of psychologists in Carmel, California. It was a golden opportunity; no way was he going to pass it up. He was very sorry.

'So you're just ditching us?' asked Steph.

'Well, what would you want me to do?'

'You could start by drowning in your own vomit,' suggested Clémence.

'How long have you known?'

'A week.'

'And you didn't warn us?'

'You realise we made all our plans around you, don't you?'

'Well, yeah. I'm really sorry. That was just it. I actually didn't know how to tell you. I'm really sorry, girls.'

There he was, sitting on his arse, with his white polo shirt and his little head hiding behind his glasses. Steph hated him so much, especially because she couldn't stop finding him hot. That was her drama. For nearly two years now, Simon had made her life a living hell. They had broken up a dozen times. And not just because she caught him kissing other girls at parties. He lied all the time, stole money from his parents, got trashed on TCE and never kept his word. And the worst was that he always managed to land on his feet. Steph had always been the one to initiate their reconciliations. She told herself stories about crazy love and attraction/repulsion, like Dylan and Kelly in *Beverly Hills, 90210*. Simon was tortured, selfish and sexy. In short, a real arsehole.

'You know, I always said he was a born loser,' observed Clémence.

Steph was thinking hard. Things couldn't just spiral out of control this way.

'What about your brother? Couldn't he open the house for us?'

'You can always ask him,' answered Simon sarcastically.

'You're a truly sick individual,' said Clémence.

'You gave me no choice,' he said, frowning. 'I knew you were going to give me a hard time. I've been wondering for days how I was going to break the news to you.'

You had to admit that Simon had a kind of genius for getting himself out of tight spots. You criticised him for something, and two seconds later you found yourself apologising. Steph had had her head turned round so many times, she'd lost count. But this time, she wasn't falling for it.

'You're going to take your little suitcase and fuck off.'

She opened the door and tipped her seat to let him through.

'I'm not getting out here. This is the middle of nowhere.'

Steph looked around. It would take Simon at least an hour to walk to town. With his suitcase and in this heat. The idea pleased her enormously.

'Come on, *raus!* You're getting out, now.'

Clémence was silently jubilant. With ill grace, Simon finally got out of the car. He started walking towards the bus stop, occasionally looking over his shoulder in the hope that they would say, 'No, it's okay, we'll drive you home.' But Steph was too disgusted. She thought about Simon's hands on her arse, her crotch, everywhere. Shit.

'What a loser,' said Clémence.

'No shit.'

Stéphanie got back in the car, released the handbrake, and headed for Heillange under a cement-like sky, in the thickness of July. She drove quite fast, without caution, without pleasure, without a word. Their holiday was fucked. Their last one as schoolkids. A brand-new sadness rose in their tight throats.

8

To close the mass, the organist played a customary Bach toccata. The staccato, tubular, vaguely metaphysical chords rose very high. Despite Anthony's refusal to believe in this biblical fantasia, the soaring stone, the blues of the stained-glass windows and the church's verticality ended up moving him. In the nave a little further away, four men were carrying a corpse sealed in a box. People shuffled towards the light. Thousands of Sundays had been spent this way, in hymns, canticles, anxiety and hope. He shivered. It certainly was cold in here.

Anthony gave his father a hug when he reached him and recognised his cologne. Hélène gave him a peck on the cheek. Then they found themselves outside on the forecourt, dazed, having lost some of their composure. They needed to get orientated. Hélène folded the little yellow pamphlet to help people follow the service and rummaged in her bag for her sunglasses. She avoided meeting her ex-husband's eye. She put on the glasses and crossed her arms under her bosom.

'Are you doing okay?' asked Patrick.

'Yes. How about you?'

'I'm fine. Feels funny, though.'

'Yes, it does.'

He was talking about the dead man; she, about their being together. The kids nudged each other with their shoulders and Anthony nearly took Vanessa's hand.

On the forecourt, the faithful emerging from the church mixed with the people who hadn't wanted to attend the mass. There was a hell of a crowd. It was easy to spot Luc Grandemange's old Muslim co-workers and the union diehards who'd rather be run over by a train than set foot in a church. But for all their acting like know-alls and renegades, they felt uncomfortable. A big chunk of their history was being buried along with Luc. Since he paid his first union dues back in 1963, he'd been a little of everything: union rep, workers' delegate, officer at large, secretary. He even became a movement figure during the big Metalor strikes. He wasn't one of the ideologues, and he didn't have a gift for negotiating. Other guys were brighter, stupider, more committed, had more to lose, or would hang in over the long haul. But Luc had a seemingly superfluous quality: he set the mood. In a struggle, you needed guys like him, to mess about, slap the waverers on the back, call the hotheads 'sweetheart'. Sometimes it was a drag. It wasted time. Luc's jokes were rarely funny, and with him, it was always party time. But in his own way, he created bonds between people and held them together, right to the end.

Since then, his involvement and good cheer had taken a distinctly chauvinistic turn. He gradually began to think that the poor suckers whose cause he served weren't just workers, wage earners, provincials and dropouts. They were also native-born Frenchmen. The real problem was the influx of immigrants. You could just do the maths. The number of immigrants, about three million, exactly matched the number of the unemployed. Hell of a coincidence, right? When you thought about it, a lot of complicated problems got simpler once you realised that those lazy people from abroad were the main cause of our current woes.

Plenty of people around Luc agreed with that diagnosis and pleaded for quotas and deportation flights, a sharp reminder that France was our home, after all. But despite their popularity, those ideas stayed out of sight and under cover. They weren't mentioned in places where you had to behave yourself. A kind of vague shame, like politeness, kept them in check. The priest didn't say anything about those questionable beliefs when he summed up Luc's biography. Nor did they appear in his obituary in *L'Est républicain*. And when they were mentioned within Évelyne's earshot, she minimised them with a sigh and a wave of the hand. Her husband had just been carried away. He was like that about football, too.

Once the coffin was in the hearse, Évelyne's nephew stood at the top of the steps between the forecourt and the church porch and clapped his hands to get people's attention. Évelyne, who hadn't stopped thanking people and nodding gravely, took the opportunity to light herself a cigarette. The flame shot up and her cheeks hollowed as she inhaled the brown smoke.

'We're going to Saint-Michel cemetery,' said her nephew. 'Those who care to are free to follow us. But there may be no point in everyone coming.'

Almost apologetically, he went on to say that there wouldn't be enough room in the car park and that the family would like a little privacy. The forecourt was jammed with people; you'd think the whole town was there. Everyone listened to him impassively. They silently exchanged glances and little signs. At one moment Anthony caught his parents looking at each other without a word. Then his mother looked away. His father stared at his feet.

'On the other hand, we're not going to part like this,' the nephew continued. 'Évelyne is inviting you to L'Usine for brioche. I don't suppose I need to give you the address.'

The comment was greeted by laughter and another murmur went through the crowd when he announced that Évelyne was also paying for coffee and the first round of drinks.

'Champagne!' someone yelled.

Évelyne smiled and the lout was put in his place. The mood had changed, anyway. Death was all very well, but we're going to go have a drink.

'Hey there!'

Anthony's cousin was walking towards them, tightly holding his girl-friend's hand.

'So what's new?'

'I'm okay. What about you?'

'I'm doing great.'

Patrick seemed delighted at this little family get-together. He grabbed the cousin by the shoulder and gave him a friendly shake.

'Been a long time, hasn't it?'

'Yeah, it has,' he said, embarrassed but also pleased.

'Your mother told me that you're moving in together,' said Hélène.

'Not yet; we're looking,' he said.

'We'll find something,' said Séverine.

'Where are you looking?'

'Over by Blonds-Champs. There are some brand-new apartments there. We went to see at City Hall. They don't have anything right now. Anyway, we don't have priority. It's always the same thing.'

They knew what she meant.

Anthony asked a couple of questions out of politeness, but his mother and his aunt had become much closer since his parents' split, so he already knew all about the couple's problems. His cousin had decided to leave school and was working part-time on stupid little stuff, main-tenance, cleaning, odd jobs. The beautiful Séverine wanted to earn a technical diploma, but that was complicated because she hadn't passed the baccalaureate. She'd taken a few vague steps to get an equivalent, but her zeal was greatly undermined by her love for the Spice Girls and her secret conviction that she was destined for a career in show business. She was making the rounds of karaoke bars and local beauty contests, taking acting classes, and sending her CV off to Paris. Anyway, the two of them loved each other. That clearly justified anything.

Once the hearse and the immediate family had left, a kind of wavering ran through the ranks. People couldn't decide whether to drive or walk to L'Usine. Considering the distance, the second option soon carried the day, and nearly three hundred people set out through Heillange on foot. From the church to the bar was about half a mile, down two streets in a row. The crowd poured into the street and very quickly started talking loudly and carrying on. People came out onto their front steps to watch the parade go by. They recognised faces, asked for news.

Some joined the procession, because the dead man's name was vaguely familiar and because they weren't about to pass up a free drink. People wondered how the bar was going to hold everybody. Jokers were already yelling comments in crude, heavily accented voices. The humour gradually turned raunchy. People started laughing, even shouting, as their nerves settled. Life, always lusty and tireless, revived to create red noses and sweaty necks. It was a hot Saturday, a real scorcher. An urge to sing started to fill people's chests. Soon the blast furnace appeared. They were almost there. Anthony had walked the whole way with his cousin, with Vanessa next to him. His parents were walking side by side in front. They weren't talking very much, but at least they weren't arguing.

'Things seem to be going okay,' said Vanessa.

'Yeah.'

'It'll be fine.'

Anthony was living with his mother and wasn't about to blame her, but he couldn't help putting himself in his old man's place. There he was, twenty pounds lighter, dried out, balding and knotty. His fangs blunted. What was left of him? Ashes and fading strength. And, in the end, regrets. Their house had been liquidated in seconds flat. Patrick and Hélène's efforts, twenty years of sacrifices and acrobatic struggles to make ends meet, all gone. The furniture, the knick-knacks, the clothes that had to be thrown away. Plus they were forced to sell quickly, for peanuts. The bank ended up getting the money to settle their debts.

When they were dividing things up, Anthony's father almost got into a fight. He really didn't have a lot of friends, had no real work and only then discovered that he didn't even own the house and that all those ideas he'd had were more or less crap. He thought he was the one bringing in the money, that he was in his own place, that it was his wife, his house, his kid. The notaire bulldozed those preconceptions away. And two years later, Patrick was still coughing up money to pay his lawyer, who had done fuck all except to tell him that he was in the wrong and that the law would decide. In that world of paperwork, lawyers and judges, what was left wasn't a man. Only arrangements.

During this whole wrenching period Anthony had been pressured to take sides. He didn't want to. Each of his parents had their reasons, and he had his. Hélène concluded that he didn't love her enough. Patrick, that his mother had spoiled him. She had passed on her weakness and indecisiveness, that soft virus that all the Mougels carried. Those people never finished anything. The men did whatever their wives told them. They were a race of slaves, and Anthony had embraced the chains. In fact, when they lived next to the Jules-Ferry school, Hélène was always on the alert. From her kitchen, she watched him playing with the other kids in the courtyard. She didn't hesitate to shout to him from upstairs to behave. Once, when she caught him fighting, she came down to stop it. The kids called him pussycat for weeks after that. His mother arranged with the doctor to get him excused from sports. He didn't learn to swim until year four.

'I don't know why she was like that,' his father had said. 'Maybe it was that little Grégory business in 1984. You remember, the four-year-old who was drowned in the Vologne River? The cops thought the kid's relatives had done it, but they could never prove it.'

'So what?'

'You looked exactly like him. You know, in that famous photo? Exactly the same. To be honest, it made me feel weird when they fished him out.'

When they got there, the pavement outside L'Usine was already jammed. The doors had been thrown wide open for once and people were going in and out, waiting for things to get under way. Trestle tables had been set up with white paper tablecloths and all the necessities: a big pump-action Thermos, trays of brioche, non-alcoholic drinks and plastic tumblers. The sky cast a veiled, opalescent light that hurt the eyes. The smell of coffee filled the air. Cathy, the owner, had come out and was greeting people in a friendly, businesslike way. This would be a good day for her, she knew. As she added up the totals in her head, her smile widened.

Stupidly, Patrick decided this was a good time to trot out his idea.

'So, how about that trip?'

'What are you talking about?' asked Hélène.

She had clutched her handbag strap and answered a bit sharply. Patrick's eyes almost completely disappeared underneath his eyebrows.

'I told you. I'm paying for that famous trip of yours. Your holiday.'

Hélène said nothing. She had told him a hundred times that it was out of the question.

'You can let me know when you make up your mind.'

She didn't reply to that, either. Anthony caught Vanessa's eye. She grimaced. This looked like it might be pretty complicated after all.

Two girls hired as extra helpers were standing outside. Chubby goth types, probably sisters. When they started serving people coffee right on the pavement, Cathy jumped on them.

'Stop that! Are you out of your minds, or what?'

It was bad enough that nobody wanted to go into her bar because of the heat; now the street was turning into a terrace. Up the road, cars were at a standstill because of the confusion. The first honking began. People raised their arms to the sky. Relax, we'll all be dead soon enough.

'The police are going to come if this goes on,' said Cathy anxiously. 'Thierry!'

The tall guy with the crew cut standing behind the bar looked up. He was a drywaller in civilian life and lived with Cathy. Just seeing him red and sweating in his shirtsleeves, you could feel the heaviness inside, the stifling air, thirty degrees at least.

'Open the back doors,' she said. 'We need to make a draught.'

Then, turning to the two girls:

'Get people inside, for heaven's sake. We have to clear the street. And go upstairs, we have some fans there.'

Baffled by this barrage of orders, the girls just stood there. Apologetically, Cathy made herself clear:

'Carine, you deal with the customers. Sonia, you get the fans. Can you do that? Do you need a Post-it note?'

Without getting flustered, Sonia asked:

'Where should I plug in the fans?'

She was the chubbier of the two, and the prettier. She had pierced ears, and little rings that ran all the way around the edges. Along with that, she had jet-black hair, nice legs and creamy skin.

'There are adapters in the kitchen. Just figure it out.'

Sonia sighed. Her sister was leading people inside. It was comical. But gradually, under the combined pressure from Carine, Cathy and the cars trying to get through, people crowded into the cafe. Anthony ended up with his parents and Vanessa at a table in the back, not far from the toilets. Everything settled down in a hubbub of chairs and voices. At that point a man emerged from the crowd and came towards them. He was a handsome, knotty old North African, all earth and ochre. He was wearing a pair of big white trainers from which his legs rose like sticks. He looked like a pot plant.

'Good afternoon,' he said, bowing his head.

He had a beautiful, gravelly, hoarse voice. It took Anthony a few seconds to recognise him, then his stomach tensed. His mother was already on her feet, extending her hand. Memories came back in waves. The motorbike, the little apartment where they drank tea. Old man Bouali. When Anthony saw his father getting up as well, he said to himself, 'Now it's all over, we're done for.'

But instead of that, Patrick seized the hand of the man with the big white trainers and shook it warmly. They knew each other.

'Well, I'll be damned!'

'How are you doing?' asked the old man.

'I'm good. It's been ages, hasn't it?'

'It sure has,' said Bouali with a broad wave of his hand. His raised eyebrows had come together and he looked moved. Patrick grabbed him by the shoulder and shook him, laughing to cover his embarrassment. He explained to Hélène and Anthony that he and Malek Bouali had worked at the mill together, on neighbouring stations, until Patrick was assigned to the pour. Those were the good old days. Well, not that good, but at least they were younger. Still, having Luc Grandemange in the cemetery kind of hit you.

The two men then brought each other vaguely up to date, health, children, family, everything was fine, yes, yes, *labes alhamdulilah* – all is well, praise Allah. And they agreed that it was really stupid that they never saw each other, given that they lived, what? Not three miles apart? One of these days, they would have to get together with the others, Michelon, Rosicky, Pellet and the Heizenberger brothers. Sure, sure. Old Bouali's eyes were two dark, liquid expanses. Patrick had stopped shaking him. Before leaving, the old man nodded to Hélène. He hadn't looked at Anthony. Then he went to join some friends across the room. Each of his movements was measured. He was already on the other side, that of slowness and diminution, of long patience and sleepless nights.

'Poor guy,' said Patrick, sitting down again. 'Just think of it. He worked like an animal and this is the result. He's God knows just how disabled, with a miserable pension. And kids who shit on his doorstep.'

At the mention of that problematic offspring, Anthony felt his stomach knotting again. He didn't dare look at his mother. To finish, his father magnanimously added:

'You know, those people aren't the problem. I've never seen guys work as hard as them.'

Across the room, the little troop of Magreb immigrants was gathered around the same table. There were about a dozen of them, aged and low-key, drinking Picon like everyone else, but still not speaking French. Their wives had stayed at home. Nobody paid any attention to them. They'd made the effort to come, though.

'All right, I think I'm going to the bar,' said Patrick, gesturing at the table in front of him. 'We're dying of thirst here. What are you having?'

Everybody chose beer. He went to order three beers, plus a Perrier for himself. Hélène looked at him. She couldn't help thinking, 'What a pity, all those years wasted, ruined by pride and binges.' To end up like this, with him drinking water and wanting to send her on a trip.

Patrick came back with the drinks, passed the glasses around. The beer was cold and delicious. Anthony took a big slug. It did him the world of good.

9

'**I don't care**, you know. I was sure of it, anyway.'

Stéphanie was lying. Clémence let her talk.

After driving around without being able to either separate or settle on a place to go, the two girls wound up at the foot of the cast-iron statue of the Virgin Mary. They were sitting cross-legged on the base, drinking the 7 Up they'd bought along the way from the Prisu behind Place des Flamands. The storm had further tightened its grip on the valley, with its imbroglio of houses, streets and buildings. The light had turned reddish, lending everything the colours of evening and fire. Steph urgently wanted the world to end. She sighed.

'Are you pissed off?' asked Clémence.

"Course not. I told you, I don't care.'

Steph tried to kill a tiny insect that had landed on her shoulder, but without success. She felt sticky and heavy and besides, her back hurt. Stretching out her legs, she thought them tanned and not too bad. She had pretty ankles. That was something, anyway.

'How many times did you fuck?'

'I don't know,' said Clémence, staring off into space.

'Oh, stop the bullshit. I don't mind.'

Clémence pursed her mouth in a funny way, and Steph made a grimace that said, 'You just decided to go for it, didn't you?' Clem was tempted to laugh.

'Frankly, I've forgotten. Quite a few times.'

'You're too much.'

'What can I tell you? I didn't keep track.'

'Where was it?'

'How do you mean?'

'You didn't fuck in the street, did you? So tell me where you did it.'

A secret that been growing between the two girls for weeks had burst into the open just ten minutes earlier. They were both feeling confused and undecided. But mainly relieved.

Steph had definitely sensed that something fishy had been going on. Clémence had acted strange, blushing the moment you asked where she had been. It involved a guy, for sure. Yet now that Clem had finally owned up, it didn't seem that important.

Clémence and Simon had been fucking.

After her confession, Steph had sworn at her, of course, the whore. But curiosity very quickly gained the upper hand. Now the two girls were savouring their restored equality and the wonderful possibility of telling each other everything and better yet: comparing.

'Come on,' Steph insisted. 'Where did you do him?'

'I don't know, wherever.'

'What do you mean, wherever? Did you go to his place?'

'Once or twice.'

'What about your place?'

'Once or twice.'

Steph was wide-eyed, appalled, dying to know more.

'But not in his car, right?'

'I don't remember.'

'Of course you did, it's obvious!' cried Steph, shoving Clémence with her shoulder. 'What a slut!'

'Oh, give me a break! Once or twice. Quickies.'

'So he basically screwed you every which way.'

'Damn, you're right,' said Clémence, the realisation dawning.

Steph burst out laughing.

'You bastards...'

'I'm...I'm really so sorry,' said Clémence sincerely – and feeling forgiven.

Steph leapt to her feet. This whole business infuriated and upset her, but it felt great to luxuriate in their renewed complicity. She couldn't stand it any more. She wanted to know everything.

'How long did it go on?'

'I dunno.'

'Come on, it's okay. Spit it out.'

'A few weeks.'

'Or a few months, right?'

'Yeah,' admitted Clémence, pretending to be dismayed.

'That shit! He was fucking us one after the other.'

'The same day, sometimes.'

'You're not serious?'

'I swear.'

'The bastard.'

'A piece of crap.'

'What a dog.'

'A psycho.'

'A real pervert.'

'No kidding.'

And now, having laughed their fill, the girls got down to brass tacks.

'So?'

'So what?' asked Clémence.

'Well, was it good?'

'It was okay.'

'Oh, give me a break! Why would you fuck him for weeks like that if it wasn't any good?'

'Well, it was good but...I dunno, he's sort of into his own thing.'

'Yeah, he doesn't actually take you into account.'

'Honestly, he thinks he's in a movie.'

To illustrate the problem, Clémence put on a dazed expression, grasped an imaginary ponytail, and gave a few empty hip thrusts. Steph couldn't help herself.

'Yes, that's exactly right!'

'Besides, he's got a weird one.'

Clémence raised her eyebrows very high and looked innocent while holding out her curled little finger.

'That's it!' said Steph. 'You'd think it was a Yorkie's dick.'

'Stop it!' Clémence exploded. 'You're the one who's crazy!'

The two girls were baiting each other like sisters now, pushing and pulling, their breath coming hard, panting. Steph couldn't help herself.

'Yeah, yeah!' she said.

Looking disgusted, she showed an unflattering distance between her thumb and index finger.

'And it's so ugly, all pinkish and damp,' she continued.

'Oh, come on! You're too much!'

Just the same, Clémence wanted more, too.

'And didn't you notice?' asked Steph. 'When he comes?'

'Notice what?'

'I dunno. He does this thing, breathes through his nose.'

Steph imitated him: *mffff, mffff, mffff!* Nostrils flaring, she sounded like a calf and a choo-choo train.

'Ha ha! Yes, that's it!' exclaimed Clémence in delight.

Sharing these kinds of secrets was a deep part of their friendship, along with their childhood memories, endless phone calls and eating tubs of coconut ice cream while watching *Dirty Dancing*. And the absolute certainty that the other one would be there if she needed her.

Ever since they were teenagers, the girls would compare notes on how their bodies worked, debrief on their dates with boys and give each other tips to avoid UTIs and thrush. A girl's body was such a complex machine that it was far easier to understand when there were two of you. The intimacy of this female safe space had gradually extended to every domain, and they took a feverish pleasure in describing their nights, dissecting guys from head to toe. The boys had heard that girls were worse than they were, more blunt and pitiless, and much more precise. They didn't want to believe it. They were wrong. To be fair, it should be said that the girls applied this anatomical ferocity to themselves with a vengeance. They went to great lengths inspecting themselves, comparing themselves with each other and with magazine photos. They swelled with pride at a tightened pore and felt that gaining an extra kilo was an excellent reason to kill themselves.

Clémence had this obsession with her vagina, for example. Her labia spread out like butterfly wings and this alarmed her, as if it were a sickness or deformity.

Steph had already had to reassure her on several occasions. Each time Clémence was about to sleep with a new guy, her obsession returned. Unable to stand it any longer, at some point Steph asked to see for herself.

'What do you mean? Your pussy's very nice.'

'But there, it looks like steak.'

'You're sick. It's fine.'

'Yeah, but yours is perfect.'

'True,' said Steph.

Finally, they raked Simon Rotier over the coals together. He was stupid, micropenile, pretentious, arrogant, disgusting, impotent and unfuckable.

'Yeah, but he's hot.'

'Incredibly hot.'

'In the meantime, though, he's really taken us for a ride.'

'Yeah,' Clémence admitted.

Steph handed her the 7 Up bottle. The drink was warm, but Clémence drank some anyway, to make her happy.

'Are you angry at me?' she asked.

Steph wasn't quite sure any more.

'He's an arsehole, that's all.'

'You going to dump him?'

'That's the worst part of it. I can't even do that.'

'Why not?'

'I don't even know if he's really my boyfriend. We never did anything to make it official.'

'Like what? What do you mean?'

'I mean his parents, they think we're just friends.'

'Are you serious?'

'Yeah. He never really introduced me that way. I'd come to his place, it was the same thing. I could have been a guy.'

'What about you? Did you introduce him to your folks?'

'Not really, now that I think of it. In fact, he treated me like dirt right from the start. We never went anywhere, just the two of us. He fucked me when he felt like it. And he saw too many other girls while we were going out. When we got together, it was almost always just the two of us, never his friends or mine. He never skipped a party to come and see me, never once took me out to a restaurant. Basically, he never gave a shit.'

'What about you?'

'Hey, you already know the whole story.'

That was true; Clémence did know it. And had known it from the time when every other conversation revolved around Steph's great love, her hopes, her suspicions, all that stuff. Once, last year, Steph had hit rock bottom. She stopped eating for a couple of weeks and had to be sent to a shrink. The guy gave her minimal treatment: got her to talk about her father, then prescribed Prozac.

Clémence really couldn't stand Simon, that pretentious little shit. It was all about him, all the time, and his relationship with the world was that of a taker, pure and simple. His little head, all that money, his phoney rock 'n' roll, totally rotten side. But he was hot, which was a drag.

The first time he came on to Clémence was at a party at the Rochand place. The guy's dad was a notary, and his mum a certified master teacher. They lived in a big, really gorgeous downtown apartment, full of mirrors and parquet floors, trendy modern paintings and furniture that was a mix of classic reproductions and designer pieces. Every year in February they went skiing in Chamonix. But this year they'd left their eldest son at home for once, because of some business involving his need for maths and physics tutoring. The poor guy was hopeless at science, yet his parents absolutely insisted that he do a science module, even though he would eventually study law like his father. Whatever the case, this denial of winter sports led to a series of parties at the Rochands' place. They were actually pretty low-key, because in those days everybody preferred smoking hash to drinking vodka. That was when Simon tried his luck with Clémence. He trapped her against a worktop in the kitchen, even though Steph was in the next room. She had caught his smell, felt his hips against hers.

'Just where do you think you are?'

'What?'

'Stop it! Steph is six feet away from us. Seriously, what's your problem?'

Simon couldn't care less. He was so sure of himself, so disdainful. Clémence thought of slapping him. But instead, she didn't resist when he kissed her. A kiss so incredible, she immediately wet her knickers. Crazy, all those things that you initially think are unacceptable and disgusting but then something happens inside you, under your skin and in your guts, and you find yourself feeling like the ocean, all depths and wavelets. She and Simon ran to lock themselves in the bathroom at the end of the hall and started kissing hot and heavy, their jeans open, their hands roaming, and their mouths locked together, endlessly sucking. Clémence had heard so much about this guy Simon from her friend that she'd started feeling a kind of envy, a mirrored desire. She had to have him. That was how things started. Over the next weeks she swung between sweet madness and total remorse. She couldn't stop hating and wanting him, usually at the same time.

'So what do we do now?'

Steph didn't know. She felt as if they had just found each other again. She smiled at her friend. It wouldn't have taken much for them to embrace.

'Are you going to see him again?'

'Nah,' said Clémence. 'He's dead to me.'

Steph wanted to believe her, at least. She walked over to the viewpoint map that identified the valley's landmarks. It bore several inscriptions in waterproof marker: 'Kurt Cobain forever', 'No future', 'Motherfucker'.

'Do you remember the guy from that summer?' asked Steph. 'The one with the cousin.'

Clémence didn't know quite who she meant.

'Sure you do. The two of them showed up at the beach in a canoe. You went out with the older one, for fuck's sake. You know, the house with that crazy mother of his.'

'Oh, yeah. So what?'

'I saw the younger one.'

'The one with the screwed-up eye?'

Steph nodded. The landscape before her offered only ruins, stale ideas, boring, predictable weekends and too-familiar faces.

'I'm never coming back to this shitty town,' she said.

'What does that have to do with the guy?'

'Nothing. I just saw him at the sailing club the other evening.'

'What was he doing there? The family doesn't have a pot to piss in.'

'He was working. He sort of got into a fight with Romain.'

'Yeah, those guys are real lowlifes.'

'Well, he sure had changed, anyway.'

'Hey, come on! You aren't doing one of those losers, are you?'

'Course not. I'm just saying he's changed a lot.'

Clémence stood up in turn. She swung her arms around in the air to get the stiffness out of her shoulders and to wake up a little. Though evening was gathering, the temperature still seemed to be rising.

'His cousin was hot, though.'

'Mainly he was a dick.'

'Come on! He was really handsome.'

'Yeah, but that house and his mother...That was a red flag.'

'Yeah, so? What about the other one?' asked Clémence.

'I dunno. He has potential.'

'In any case, we'll be gone in two months and they'll never hear of us again.'

'That's for sure,' said Steph.

She looked at her watch. It would soon be six o'clock. Anthony had said to meet him behind the old power plant at nine. Maybe she would go. After all, what was stopping her?

10

By the time Hacine reached L'Usine to pick up his father, people had already been drinking for a couple of hours. He parked a good distance away and walked the rest of the way. He very quickly understood what was happening. From fifty metres away he could see dishevelled men staggering in the street, talking. The tables set up for the occasion were now littered with empty cans and plates, with brown circles that looked like constellations on the white paper tablecloths and plastic tumblers rolling in the gutters. Women's laughter rang out. Inside, voices joined in the opening bars of 'Les lacs de Connamara' *pam papam, papppam!* and then trailed off, replaced by a busy, cheerful hubbub.

Before making his way inside, Hacine thought he'd better take a look first. The place was rammed and lively, reeking of beer, tobacco and bodies heated by alcohol and promiscuity. He entered as if into a sauna, looking for a face and was promptly caught in the whirl and deafened by the noise. It was odd to see these red-faced women in their Sunday best, and men in shirtsleeves with loosened ties sprawled on chairs, telling each other funny stories or talking about politics, about Bernard Tapie and Balladur. Over-excited children were racing between the tables, and from time to time a mother would nab one and give the kid a good shake. This was no place to be running around like that. But the game very quickly resumed. People had long since stopped drinking coffee and jugs of cold beer glowed on the tables. The waitresses, as shiny as seals, endlessly cruised the room, topping up glasses and emptying William Lawson ashtrays the size of dessert plates. Behind the bar, Cathy stood anchored to her beer taps. They had already had to change the barrel. She was earning six months' receipts in a day. Speakers were playing Polnareff's 'Holidays' on the Nostalgie station in the background. Elsewhere, a man was resting six feet under. Here, his nephew had stood up several times to propose a toast in his memory but was now asleep in a corner, his head resting on his bare arms. Underfoot, Hacine could feel the resistance of the floor sticky with beer.

'Hacine!'

His father spotted him first and waved from a table on the left at the back, near the door to the pool room behind the bar. Hacine joined him. The Arabs had all gathered together, of course. They hadn't drunk as much as other people but were in a very good mood just the same. Hacine recognised several of them, neighbours. He said hello.

'Is this your son?' asked one, a bald man with a lined face and a gleaming, caramel-coloured pate.

'Yes. Sit down for a moment.'

'I'd rather we took off now,' Hacine answered.

'Sit down, I am telling you. Come on.'

Hacine gave in and ordered a Coke. He felt ill at ease amongst these men, who'd all been born over there and were full of naive ideas. They had worked like animals, yet wound up stuck in their little corner: welcome, but not all that welcome.

Hacine never discussed this with his friends, but it was a thorn in their side just the same. The boys had all grown up fearing their fathers, men who didn't fool around. Yet they couldn't really take seriously what their fathers said. The men mostly misunderstood the real rules of French society. They spoke the language badly. They laid down rules that were out of date. So their sons were caught between the respect they owed their fathers and a certain understandable contempt.

Besides, what had these fathers, who had tried to escape poverty, really done? They all owned colour TVs and cars, they had roofs over their heads and their children went to school. But in spite of those things, satisfactions and accomplishments, no one could say they had succeeded. No material comfort seemed able to erase their initial poverty. Was it due to professional vexations, being given menial work, being marginalised, or just the word 'immigrant', which summed them up wherever they went? Or was it the fate of being stateless, which they couldn't admit to themselves? These fathers, hung suspended between two languages and two shores, were badly paid, disrespected, uprooted and had no heritage to pass on. From this their children, and especially their sons, developed an abiding feeling of disappointment. So to do well in school, succeed, have a career and play the game became almost impossible for them. In a country that treated their families like a minor footnote to society, the least honest effort looked like an act of collaboration.

That said, Hacine also had plenty of former schoolmates who were getting technical diplomas, taking sociology and mechanical engineering classes, earning business certificates, even studying medicine. In the final analysis, it was hard to sort out the impact of circumstances, personal laziness and general oppression. He himself tended to favour explanations that let him off the hook and justified the liberties he took with the law.

Hacine finished his Coke. It was nearly seven o'clock. All this was dragging on. He didn't like this place, didn't like these people, didn't like the atmosphere. Besides, he had to see Eliott a little later to explain how things would go down from now on. He was at the start of a delicate period. He had to prime the pump. He thought he could probably get at least four thousand francs for the kilo he'd brought back. With that, he would launch the business. When you bought directly from the grower, right at the farm, you could buy a kilo for twelve hundred francs. He knew good middlemen, but he wasn't fooling himself: he would have to pay five to six thousand francs. With a 20,000-franc investment, he was sure to get three or four kilos, which he could sell for 20,000 francs each. Then the business would be up and running. Hacine would drive the first trips himself, but planned to turn that lousy job over to other people as soon as possible. He wasn't one of those idiots who kept racing across Europe for the excitement, flooring it, even after they'd become millionaires. He would concentrate on tasks with significant value added: negotiating prices, stocking raw material, organising logistics, and managing teams in the field. He had gone over his calculations a hundred times. The graphs followed a lovely exponential curve. The more money came in, the more he would move to the background. The mediocre prestige of being a big shot didn't interest him. On the other hand, he still had that gnawing hunger to be rich. It was no longer a matter of success or comfort. He needed the money to avenge himself, to wipe away the spittle.

Hacine thought he could eventually get a big slice of the pie between Reims and Brussels, Verdun and Luxembourg. There was competition, but he wasn't worried. As he had with little Kader, he would do whatever it took. All that was left was to whip the local labour force into line. For starters, he had a little money and no scruples. But the first months would be critical. Like old-time merchants in Bordeaux, Bristol and Amsterdam who bet everything on a first ship, he knew that a single storm could doom all his hopes. That risk stressed him out so much that he ground his teeth while he slept. He would wake up with a sore jaw, wondering what had happened. He and Eliott drew up lists: babysitters, lookouts, sellers, managers. The people he had to convince, the people he had to mess up. Make a couple of examples. It would work. His stomach hurt and he'd had diarrhoea for days. He felt emotionally dead, or nearly so.

He leaned over and spoke into his father's ear:

'We ought to go.'

'Yes, yes. Just a minute.'

The old man was enjoying himself. Hacine had time to take a piss. When he stood up, he saw Hélène.

At first, it didn't quite register. She was a middle-aged woman with thick hair falling to her shoulders. She reminded him of someone, but who? They looked at each other for a second. Hacine racked his brains. In Heillange, you were always running into the same people. Then the boy sitting next to her stood up. He was very young but quite strong, with a drooping left eyelid. Hacine jumped out of his chair.

'Where are you going like that?' asked his father.

'I'll be right back.'

For her part, Hélène immediately recognised the tall, brown young man, as spindly as an insect, who had just stood up. He held her gaze for a moment and gave a polite nod. His dark eyes were disturbingly unreadable. His face was absolutely blank. Hélène had drunk quite a few beers and her head was spinning a little. Patrick was talking to his neighbour. Around her, she saw only red faces and open mouths, all that racket and smoke, the women fanning themselves with the yellow pamphlet handed out in church. Anthony got to his feet and she had to move her chair to let him by.

'I'll be right back,' he said in turn.

Anthony headed for the men's room nearby. The young brown man crossed the room and followed him in. The door to the toilet closed behind them. My God, thought Hélène, suddenly frozen.

'Patrick.'

She grabbed him by the arm, but he couldn't hear her. Especially since he was talking about football. For the last several minutes she'd been hearing a chorus of foreign names: Baggio, Bebetto. Dunga, Aldaïr.

'Patrick!' she repeated.

Now she was pleading with him.

The men's room at L'Usine looked like a corridor. Anthony went to stand at the only urinal and relieved himself, tracing loops and curlicues on the porcelain. He had drunk five beers and pissed on and on. Behind him was a stall with a door that didn't close well, and next to him a tiny washbasin with a bar of soap on a metal rod. To dry your hands, you did the best you could, which usually meant wiping them on your trousers. Daylight entered through a barred window. That was it. Anthony began to whistle light-heartedly. He was a little loaded and feeling especially glad that things between his parents were going so well. After months of hatred and insults, their politeness was already a wonderful improvement. And his father was sticking to his pledge, even in a bar. Anthony felt an unusual burst of optimism. Then the door opened.

'Hello,' said Hacine.

Anthony quickly buttoned his flies, feeling some wetness dribble along his thigh. The walls suddenly seemed very close and the smell of ammonia, unbearable. He looked around. Aside from the barred window, there was no way out. He felt fourteen years old again.

'How are you?' asked Hacine.

He took the time to close the door and push the little bolt home, though it was already almost torn off. He was standing a few metres from Anthony and looked very calm, impassive and tanned.

'What d'you want?' asked Anthony.

'What do you think?'

Anthony honestly didn't have the slightest idea. That was all so long ago. Behind the door was the world and his father. He could hear the low hum of conversations, the clink of glasses. He tugged at his shirt, which was sticking to his back, and decided to leave.

'Where are you going?'

'Let me out.'

Hacine pushed him back with the flat of his hand. It was a languid gesture and it made an unsettling impression, the way a spiderweb feels on your face. Anthony could feel anger rising in his cheeks. He was still stewing over the humiliation of the other day with Romain. He thought about his father again, just outside the door.

'Leave me the fuck alone.'

At that point Hacine's appearance underwent a curious change. He perched on one leg like a heron, brought his other knee to his chest, raised his fists to eye level, then suddenly kicked. His foot hit Anthony in the solar plexus with a dull, flat thud. Surprised, he flew through the air and found himself sitting on his arse with the breath completely knocked out of him. The sole of Hacine's shoe left a distinct print on his beautiful white shirt. Anthony could feel the piss-stained tiles and the rough grain of the ceramic under his hands. He couldn't believe what had just happened. It took him a good ten seconds to get his breath back and to stand up.

'You bastard,' he said.

An exchange of feints followed, until Hacine stepped back a bit and started firing a series of middle kicks at Anthony's ribs. His shin struck with amazing speed, but the blows were mainly for show and had no impact. Hacine wasn't heavy enough to do any real damage and Anthony took the kicks without any trouble. Soon the boys found themselves face-to-face, breathless, snarling and ridiculous. Hacine kept his guard up, swaying from side to side with his fists raised. Anthony would've been happy to call it quits, and Hacine was nearly of the same opinion.

Just then, the door rattled on its hinges. Hacine took a step aside. The door handle jiggled, the bolt yielded and Patrick came in.

'What's this all about?'

He saw his son with his white shirt soiled, looking confused and dishevelled. He turned to Hacine. Hélène had explained everything in a few words. So it was him. In Patrick's head, the links of evidence had implacably come together: the motorbike, the theft, the divorce.

'It's nothing,' Anthony tried to say.

Patrick glanced at him with a look of regret. Then he turned back to the tall arsehole with the duck-bill mouth and kinky hair. A wog, wouldn't you know. With that dull, empty gaze, no way to know what was going on behind it. Right now, Patrick wanted to hurt him.

'So you're the one?' he said flatly.

'I'm the what?'

Anthony was the first to understand. His father had taken on that stone-like density, that look of stupidity and mineral solidity. Anthony wanted to say something, but Hacine spoke first:

'We're good here. Don't bust my balls.'

Patrick gave a kind of chuckle and threw the first punch.

It came from a long way off, from his shoulder and back, rising from his kidneys and deep in his belly. It carried ancient pains and frustrations.

It was a fist heavy with misery and missed chances, a ton of misspent living. It smashed Hacine full in the face. Even Patrick was surprised by the effect it produced. A pétanque ball couldn't have done better. Under the impact, the boy's head snapped far back and hit the wall. He bounced off and fell to the floor on all fours. Thick blood mixed with saliva immediately started dripping from his lips between his fingers, which he had raised to his mouth. With his tongue, Hacine explored the extent of the damage. He turned his head towards Patrick and opened his shattered mouth. What Patrick saw displeased him. Hacine's left incisor was cracked, and the other one was missing. The boy spat between this gap in his teeth. Was this little shit defying him?

'Go and stand in front of the door,' he ordered his son.

'What?'

'Do it.'

Hacine was still on his knees, bent double, able to breathe through only one nostril, which made a spitting, hurried whistle, like pipes. Tiny bone fragments pricked his tongue and he spat again. That's when he noticed the pattern of the floor tiles. The little white and brown squares hadn't been laid at random. They formed an ingenious weave of curves and loops, something ample and floral. As he felt the pain rising, Hacine thought of the guy who had once knelt there long before him, composing these delicate patterns piece by piece, just to receive footprints and piss.

'Don't make me say it again,' said Patrick.

Anthony came out of the men's room first. He looked ashen and his shirt was ripped. His mother stood up.

'Anthony!'

He didn't hear her. There was too much noise, people standing, music. He muscled his way through the crowd, using his shoulders and hands. Along the way he bumped into a guy who spilled some of his drink onto his torn shirt. The guy in question made as if to protest – 'Hey there, take it easy, no need to shove' – but it was more for show than anything else. In any case, Anthony couldn't see anything or anybody. He went out of the door in a rush and didn't turn back.

When Patrick emerged in turn a few seconds later, he seemed surprisingly calm. He carefully closed the men's room door behind him, then headed for the bar. There he grabbed the first drink he saw, a half-empty glass of beer and looked around. Cathy the owner was chatting with a woman with spiky, mousy blonde hair, her elbows on the bar. Thierry was hard at work pulling on the beer taps and handing glasses to customers. Around them, you caught smiles, wrinkles, details. And always, that exhausting racket. Patrick ran a hand through his hair. His temples and neck were wet. A boy, his chin resting on a table, was studying a wasp trapped in his glass of grenadine. Life flowed on, without malice, determined to destroy, day after day, always unchanging. Patrick raised the glass to his lips and downed the beer in a single gulp. A terrible peace spread through his belly, the silence of an ossuary. He gestured to the bartender and ordered another glass. The same again, but with Picon this time.

11

The old power plant was the worst possible place for a date. A ruin perched on a hill, it was covered with ferns and weeds, choked with brambles, and littered with fire pits, condoms and broken glass. Steph was already regretting she'd come, especially since the little idiot was late. She stood waiting, caught in the greasy immobility of that summer evening. She glanced at her watch again. She felt thirsty and horny.

He finally arrived.

Anthony rode up on a tinny, *putt-putt*ing motorbike, legs spread wide. His shirt was in tatters, he had pointy dress shoes on, and he looked completely dazed. When he was within a few metres, he cut the engine and coasted. The bike rolled to a stop near Steph, swaying gracefully on its shock absorbers. Anthony looked like a child on a rocking horse.

'Hi.'

'Did you forget?'

'No. I'm late, I'm sorry.'

He pulled the bike onto its stand and climbed off. He stuck his hands in the back pocket of his trousers, which emphasised his shoulders in a not unattractive way. Steph looked him over.

'Did you get into another fight?'

'No.'

'What about your shirt?'

'It's nothing.'

She let him stew for a moment. Anthony looked a little stupid, but he felt like a nice change after slimy Simon's low-down tricks. Besides, he was attractive. His shy roughneck side had its charm. She made him wait a little longer, then said:

'All right, come on. You're getting on my nerves.'

She pointed the way and they walked to some steps behind the power plant. From there, at least you got a view of town, with its scattering of street lights, an occasional car on the maze of roads and the ZUP estate with its flickering, bluish windows. The narrow steps led to some old changing rooms. They sat side by side, elbows touching. Anthony looked at his hands and thought about his father. He had come in spite of everything. Steph lit a cigarette.

'So what happened to you?'

'Just a thing. It's nothing.'

The silence fell again, thickened by the heat. In this weather, everything took on the consistency of oil. As Anthony stared at his chewed-up fingernails, Steph studied him. The red marks on his neck. The outline of his cheekbone, his smooth cheeks, the black eye, that youthful, velvety skin, his smell.

'You're no fun,' she sighed.

'It's too hot. Anyway, I don't know what to say.'

He said this with an impatient gesture, as if he were tossing coins on the ground. He felt self-conscious and hesitant. Steph decided she would have some fun with him.

'So, what did we come here for?'

He looked at her. She was very brown, had her hair up and was wearing shorts, a sleeveless blue blouse and Converse trainers. He recognised her perfume, the one that smelled like candyfloss, and saw the golden fuzz on her thighs. She had put her question to him as a challenge. She knew perfectly well what he wanted. She went on:

273

'Try something, at least.'

'What do you mean?'

'You're not just going to sit there, are you?'

'What d'you want me to do?'

'Hey, it's not my job to tell you what you should do.'

'Do you want me to kiss you?'

'Try it and you'll see.'

He considered this. She really had a lot of nerve. Steph's eyes were full of mischief, but not so much as to totally discourage him.

'Haven't you ever slept with a girl?'

'Of course I have!' he said indignantly.

'Well, then, what did you do with other girls?'

'I don't know, it just happened.'

'And with me you're hung up?'

'Well, I'm not about to jump on you right here on the steps.'

Steph burst out laughing. No way was she going to have sex with him, either on the steps or anywhere else. But she could still have fun turning him on, and then give him a quick consolation peck at the end of the evening.

'All right, then. What shall we do?'

'You want to go somewhere?'

'Wait a minute. Try something, at least.'

'Like what?'

'Whatever you like.'

'Whatever I like?'

'You have carte blanche, I promise.'

'Anything at all?'

'It's an open bar, I'm telling you.'

She was smiling and so was he. For Anthony, this was as much an opportunity as a chance to mess everything up. He had to play it just right. He took her right wrist and pulled her hand close. Steph felt tempted to laugh. What was this idiot up to? He brought her fingers to his lips and kissed them.

'Shit, a romantic.'

'Yeah.'

'You're really too much of a gentleman.'

'Too true.'

Meanwhile, he was still holding her wrist and she didn't pull away. It was a soft bit of shared skin-to-skin contact. Steph's eyes were sparkling. They were now entering that blessed realm of play. The timing was good. Night was coming on. All in all, things weren't turning out too badly.

'Oooh, I think I'm in love,' she said.

'That's normal.'

'You're dumb, you know. You could've touched my breasts.'

'Or your arse.'

'Or even worse yet.'

'Seriously?'

'No, you're crazy.'

She pulled her wrist back and playfully pushed him away. Through the gap in her blouse he glimpsed the taut strap of her bra, the roundness of a breast, and a mole near the edge of the fabric. She was desirable, the way a beach is desirable, or a pastry, or chocolate.

'Do you want me to help you?' she asked.

'It's okay, I didn't do anything.'

'Come on, let's go somewhere.'

Steph jumped to her feet and turned towards the silent town. She brushed off her bottom and put her hands on her hips. There she was, firmly planted in front of him. A statue, an Eiffel Tower.

'Where do you want to go?' he asked.

'I don't know. It was stupid not to bring something to drink.'

'We still can. We could just drop by the club.'

'To do what?'

Anthony checked his watch.

'It's closed at this time of night. I know where the key is hidden. We'll slip in, grab a bottle and take off.'

'Think so?' she asked, coming closer to him. 'Kind of risky, isn't it?'

Anthony had also stood up and was stretching, happy to be taking some initiative.

'No, it's okay. But I only have one helmet.'

'I've got my car.'

'I'd rather we went on the bike. It's simpler.'

'Can two of us ride on that thing?'

Anthony sighed. Of course they could.

'You'll bring me back here afterwards?'

'No problem.'

'Wait a sec.'

Steph ran to her car and fetched a little canvas shoulder bag that she slung across her chest. They were ready to go.

'Hang on, okay?'

'Yeah, but where?'

'Anywhere you like.'

She put her arms around his waist and he abruptly took off. As he rode down to the road, she cried:

'You won't drive like a maniac, okay?'

They flew through the warm evening air, enjoying the perfect smoothness of motorways. Steph soon began to shiver. Speed rose from everywhere, in her thighs and her belly. She clung to Anthony, trying to lean into the turns, her cheek against his back, eyes closed. Daylight gradually faded from the surrounding countryside, leaving only a timid pallor at the horizon. They crossed open areas, forests and fields. All along the way she breathed in the boy's sour smell. He had been drinking, running and sweating, and he smelled. It was physical and vaguely off-putting, but in the darkness that smell became her landmark. The night rushed into her. She let herself go.

When they got to the sailing club, Anthony left her alone while he went to get a bottle from the storeroom. It wouldn't take long, but Steph started to freak out the moment he disappeared. The night was pitch-black and she was stuck by the side of the road in shorts. At the first car that came along, she panicked and ran to hide in a little grove of trees nearby. She waited there, crouched down without moving, her hands on her shoulders, heart pounding. Branches rustled gently overhead, even though there wasn't a breath of wind. When Anthony reappeared, the relief she felt was so sharp she could have kissed him.

'Shit, where did you go?'

'Nowhere. Hey, take it easy.'

She took Anthony's arm, instinctively seeking contact with him.

'It's a jungle in there,' she said. 'I was scared.'

By way of an answer, he showed her the bottle of vodka and some old newspapers he'd found to start a fire with.

'Can you put all this in your bag?'

'Sure. Give me the bottle. I need a drink now.'

He handed it to her. It was Eristoff, and not even cold. It brought back memories. The screw cap cracked when Steph twisted it off. She took two good swallows before returning the bottle.

'Does a body good.'

'C'mon, let's get going,' he said. 'I don't feel like hanging around here.'

He stuffed the newspaper into Steph's bag. She climbed on behind him and they left as quickly as possible. She now hugged him tightly.

All around the shore, the lake was dotted with the bright pin-points of campfires. Youngsters were partying or camping on the various beaches. Theoretically, you weren't allowed to camp or drink there, but custom won out over the rule. So in summer, kids would come almost every evening to light fires, get wasted and sleep under the stars. This led to all sorts of nuisances: fights, wear and tear and a lot of rubbish. So City Hall launched public information campaigns, plastering the area with signs reminding people of the relevant prohibitions. Sometimes, a patrol would even fine offenders. But everybody in Heillange could remember once sleeping overnight on a beach or sharing a kiss in the moonlight. And, by and large, you couldn't do anything against that tradition.

Anthony and Steph actually had to walk quite some distance on the American beach to find a quiet spot. Along the way they passed several small groups of laughing teens playing guitars and flirting around the campfires. They finally settled near a circle of big blackened rocks. Anthony gathered branches and crumpled the newspaper, then lit a match. The flames shot up, yellow and bright, redefining their faces and lengthening their shadows. Steph sat on the sand, her knees pulled up. Anthony came close to her and they started drinking. They didn't have much to say to each other, but that was okay, they felt good and Stéphanie no longer wanted to be elsewhere. But in the silence, Anthony started thinking about his old man anyway. He wondered how the business at L'Usine had turned out. This time it was Steph who wanted to talk about the weather. Which was handy, as a subject of conversation. You just made statements.

'I can't stand this heat any more.'

'Yeah,' said Anthony.

'I can't sleep, even though I have air con in my bedroom.'

'It's driving everybody crazy. Did you see in the newspaper, about the guys over by Blonds-Champs?'

'No,' she said.

The idea already amused her. Appalling things were always going on over there. At that, she downed a big slug of vodka.

'There was a family living there with a lot of kids, grandparents, dogs everywhere. Nobody had a job. Anyway, you know what I mean. And they were all naked.'

'What's that supposed to mean?'

'It was too hot. They'd stopped getting dressed.'

'No way!'

'I swear. The neighbours called the police. They couldn't stand seeing the whole tribe like that, walking around without any clothes.'

'Ha! You can't be serious.'

'It's true, I swear. My mother showed me the article. The whole family, naked. Apparently the police had a lot of trouble taking them in.'

By then, the alcohol had taken them under its wing. Seeing Steph laughing, Anthony started to get his hopes up. They began telling more anecdotes like that one; the valley was full of them. Incestuous families where brothers, fathers and cousins all got mixed up in tangled family trees. Post office hold-ups with crowbars, high-speed Massey Ferguson chases, dances that ended in blasts of buckshot, the inbreds, benefit scams, incest over three generations – local colour, in other words.

Over on the far shore, a light went out.

'Look,' said Anthony.

Steph rested her head on his shoulder. It was only the two of them, just drunk enough, protected by the night, the fire, the lake. After that, everything followed wonderfully. She kissed him, a nervous kiss with the medicinal taste of the vodka. Very quickly they tipped backwards and stretched out on the coarse sand, their legs tangled. When she squeezed his cock through his jeans, he pulled back.

'What is it?' whispered Steph.

Without even realising it, she was moving against him. She wanted it. She kissed him.

'Don't worry, it'll come.'

'I know,' he said.

Steph chuckled, then sat up to take off her blouse. Underneath, she was wearing a little bra without any underwire. You could make out her nipples through the fabric. She stood up to get rid of her shoes and shorts. Her nearly transparent white knickers were tiny relative to the volume of her thighs. Her full, overflowing body looked like one big cleavage.

'Come on,' she said. 'Let's go for a swim.'

'In there?'

'Come on, I'm telling you.'

She helped him stand, then pulled him towards the water. As she walked, her arse swayed unctuously. He wanted to take his shirt off.

'Fuck!' she suddenly shouted, and started hopping around.

'What's wrong?'

'I don't know. I stepped on something.'

She dropped to the ground to examine her wound.

'Get out of the light. I can't see anything.'

Sitting on the ground with her right foot drawn up on her left thigh, she studied the thing with a look of dismay. Anthony crouched down to see. She had a neat little almond-shaped cut in the very pale skin of her plantar arch. It looked like a mouth.

'It's not very deep,' he said. 'But I think you'd better not go swimming.'

'Carry me.'

He looked up at her.

'Bring me to the water. I don't want to get sand in it.'

Anthony took the time to pull off his jeans, then helped her climb onto his back. As she wrapped her arms around his neck, Steph caught his smell again, the one she'd breathed on the road. She laid her forehead on his neck. She was becoming simple, patient. The water rose around them. When they were in up to their waists, she slid off and came round to face him. They kissed again. She held him in her arms and wrapped her legs around him. He was supporting her, his hands under her legs, brushing the fabric of her knickers. The water was quite warm, almost cloying.

'Feels good, doesn't it?'

'Yeah.'

Steph was now talking quietly. She let herself lean against him. The water blended with the sky. Anthony thought of all the filthy things crawling under the water, like fishes, and catfish, and that boy Colin's rotting corpse. He could feel the mud squeezing between his toes as they went further. He shivered.

'Are you cold?'

'No.'

She put her head against his collarbone. Anthony kept walking. The water was deep now. Very soon, it would be over his head.

'Hold me,' she said.

'I'm holding you,' he answered.

They floated, insular and white in the darkness of the water and sky, and life really felt worthwhile.

'Stop,' she said.

'Are you scared?'

'A little.'

He planted a kiss below her ear. Imperceptibly, she had started to wriggle against him. They felt good, the water was delicious after all, and the rain wasn't coming. He rocked her gently, taking advantage of her heavy, malleable arse.

'Wow, you're really hard...'

She had said that under her breath. Anthony wanted to show her just how true it was.

'Don't move,' she said.

She was very gently swaying against him. Through the fabric of her knickers, he could feel the furrow of her pussy, that call within. She rubbed against him and her breath gradually quickened. Under the water, he tried to push the fabric aside, so he could enter her.

'No...' said Steph.

She hugged him hard, urgently, languid. The movement between them had given rise to a kind of regular lapping. He dug his fingers into her flesh, feeling a tremendous urge to knead and enter it. He must have hurt her a little; she moaned.

'Again...'

'What?'

'Do it again,' she said. 'Hard.'

He did so and she moaned again, louder. Despite his excitement, Anthony was experiencing a strange impression of solitude and seriousness. Steph's face remained hidden. He was alone in confronting the darkness, the lake's animal presence, the weight of the sky. Huddled against his chest, she was using him, her hips producing that maddening female swaying. Anthony could hardly stand it. His cock almost hurt, he so badly wanted to plunge into that meaty softness, that pulsing, blood-warmed heart, Steph's vagina. He freed one hand and grasped her by the waist. She arched her back. He tried to push into her in spite of the fabric. Again, he tried to free his cock.

'Tch!' she said.

'I want to.'

'Be quiet. Stay like that. Hold me, dammit.'

He tightened his grip. She was now breathing really fast, and her hips were moving in rhythm with her breath. It was now, he told himself. She was going to come.

'Wait,' he muttered.

He wanted to come too. But at the same time it wasn't so easy in this water, and this darkness. She held him with all her strength and an odd, almost grotesque sigh rose from her chest.

'Wait,' he said again.

But he could already feel Steph's body slackening in his hands, becoming like a piece of cast-off clothing. She let go, stood facing him, looking. He very quickly lost his erection. The silence around them had an almost unbearable relief.

'Take me back now. I'm exhausted. I'm cold.'

He watched her step out of the water. Her clearly outlined silhouette was solid, she was limping a little bit, and this jerky movement gave her flesh a pointless, sexual quivering.

'Are you angry?' she asked.

She was rubbing her arms and hopping in place, waiting to dry off.

'No.'

A few minutes later, they were able to pull on their clothes. They headed for the motorbike, leaving the fire behind them to die. This time, Steph held on to the saddle. As a farewell gesture at the power plant, Anthony was treated to a peck on the cheek. For a few days he tried to convince himself that he had fucked her. But it was really the other way round.

THREE

14 July 1996
La Fièvre

1

All in all, things had fallen into place pretty automatically.

Anthony turned eighteen in May. Then in June he passed the technological baccalaureate without having to take the orals, and also without any illusions about what would happen next. In any case, it no longer mattered. In March he and his class all went to a career fair in Metz. Colleges had come to the freezing exposition hall there to push their offerings. Technical and engineering diplomas were touted; the universities made their pitches. There were lots of daunting possibilities Anthony knew nothing about. The army had a booth as well. He took a prospectus and talked to the woman there, a cheerful blonde in uniform. She gave him a CD and showed him images of a marine, a submarine, a helicopter pilot and jungle warfare training in Guyana.

Anthony signed the enlistment papers in April. He was leaving on 15 July. Tomorrow.

Meanwhile, he did his daily ten-mile run in the cool morning of 14 July. He crossed the Petit-Fougeray woods, then ran round the lake before following the motorway to the Relais des Chasseurs, where he retrieved his Opel Kadett. His head was empty; he felt light and hard. He felt good.

His mother had given him her old car as a reward for passing the baccalaureate. Some present! It broke down every chance it could. Fortunately, Anthony could take it to the Munsterberger brothers, who ran a little garage on the Lameck road. They rebuilt his clutch for free, then fixed the spark plugs, carburettor and brake pads, all still for free. But during an oil change, Cyril Munsterberger finally decided that enough was enough.

'We'll show you how to do it, so you won't go on being such a pest.'

The brothers were mates of his father, big guys with bum cracks on permanent display. They were rough-hewn and nice, with hands that never got clean. Hélène called them the scrap dealers. Their mother took care of the paperwork. She was still young and dressed well. From her glassed-in office, she watched to make sure the shop ran smoothly. Anthony now knew how to fix his car himself. These days when he went to see the brothers, it was to have a cup of coffee and talk.

Once at his mother's place, Anthony went directly to the small garden at the back. Hélène had found herself an attractive little terraced bungalow and the rent wasn't too high. The neighbourhood had been built on the site of an old orchard. A few sickly trees remained from that rustic past, including a plum tree that Anthony had hung his pull-up bar on. He took off his T-shirt, strapped a weighted belt around his waist, and began his series: five sets of twenty. It was ten in the morning, and despite the plum tree's shade, sweat immediately began to run down his sides and back. He continued with sit-ups, press-ups and stretching. His back, arms, thighs and belly all felt sore. He was satisfied. He checked out his reflection in the glass door to the kitchen: slim body, well-defined muscles. He flexed his deltoids. His mother opened the door.

'What are you doing right now?'

'Nothing.'

'Help me fold the sheets, then.'

Anthony picked up his gear and followed her into the living room. The shutters were closed, and she was doing the ironing while watching Laurent Cabrol's TV shopping programme.

'Here,' she said, handing him the corners of a fitted sheet. They backed up, tightened the sheet, then folded it.

'Is your bag ready?'

'Yeah.'

'Did you think to go to the station, to check the timetable?'

'Yeah.'

He was lying. For the last week she hadn't stopped pestering him about this. For Hélène, preparations for his departure had taken on a nearly existential dimension. She made lists, couldn't sleep, feared unlikely calamities. The train timetables in particular were the topic of constant concern. Anthony let her talk. She spent all her time worrying anyway.

Once the laundry was folded, he went into the neat little kitchen. He opened the fridge, took a bottle of Contrex mineral water, and downed it almost in a gulp, his head thrown back, naked to the waist, his hair wet.

'Hey, the fridge . . .'

Anthony closed it with his foot, then stretched his arms overhead, fingers laced and palms out. Hélène didn't like what she saw. From dorsals to trapezius, he was all of a piece, a dense, veined pattern that gathered at the shoulder to burst out in his triceps. To Hélène's eyes, it was just violence in reserve. Beneath the muscle, she sensed the possibility of punches. She'd seen too many of them and now hoped only for peace, a calm paradise without shocks or remorse. A dreamy grey flatness.

'You're going to hurt yourself, with all that exercising.'

'I'm going for a shower.'

'Think about your bag.'

'Okaaaaay!' he said, spreading his arms wide. 'Enough! Stop it!'

'Haaa!' she growled irritably, shooing him away like a fly.

She hated his weightlifter look, those beefy arms angling out away from his body like the Michelin Man. She hoped the army would know what to do with that big, idiotic body. Anthony saw things differently. Like thousands of poor kids who had never been happy in school, he was going off to make his way, learn to fight and see the world. To fit the idea that his father had of what made a man. Watching all those Clint Eastwood films hadn't been in vain. He had explained this to his mother. Hélène just laughed. She had seen plenty of boys sign up, hoping for combat and exoticism. They came back disgusted with the discipline, bureaucratic and nitpicky, having never left their barracks except to go and drink bad beer in small-town bars.

After his shower, Anthony shaved. In the mirror, he no longer saw his lazy eye, only the taut cabling of his shoulders, the flat vertical of his pecs, the obliques, the biceps that bulged even at rest.

The skittering *pschtt* of the pressure cooker valve could be heard, and a smell of cooking spread through the house. Hélène was listening to Radio Europe 1, as usual. Hit parade titles alternated with falsely cheerful chatter. Anthony recognised 'Gangsta's Paradise'. Then the phone rang while he was brushing his teeth. He turned off the tap and cracked the door to listen. Between the pressure cooker and the music, he couldn't hear much. Hélène was talking quietly, 'Yes...No...Yes...Yes, of course.' She called up to him:

'Anthony!'

He stood in the doorway without saying anything, toothbrush in hand. The mint flavour tingled on his tongue. He held his breath. After a few moments, his mother repeated:

'Anthony!'

'What?'

'It's your father!'

'I'm in the shower.'

'No you're not, I can hear you.'

'What does he want?'

'How do I know? Come on.'

'Tell him I'll call him back.'

'Come down, for God's sake.'

'No, I'm naked.'

'Then get dressed, dammit!'

He slammed the door, so she would get the message. Then he went back to the washbasin, spat and rinsed his mouth. His forehead knitted in a worried frown. He looked at his reflection in the mirror for a moment. He really didn't see how he could avoid it.

When he joined his mother in the kitchen, she was smoking a cigarette and leafing through an old copy of *Point de vue* that her neighbour had given her. The table was set. The pressure cooker was still hissing. The windows were steamed up, and you couldn't see out. Anthony sat down facing her, waiting for Hélène to decide to look up. She didn't.

'So what did he want?' he asked after a moment.

'What do you think?'

She looked at him over the top of her glasses (on sale, two for the price of one) with that expression, both annoyed and satisfied, that he found so irritating. He forced himself to breathe calmly. This would all be over tomorrow, no point in getting angry.

'He's your father.'

'I know.'

'When do you plan on going over?'

'I don't know.'

'You're leaving tomorrow.'

'I know.'

She took a drag on her cigarette, carefully stubbed it out, then stood and walked over to the stove.

'I made a roast and green beans. Would you like some pasta, too?'

'Yeah, sure.'

He needed slow sugars for energy and protein to build bulk. Anthony's nutritional regime had become a big thing. Hélène had to cook him meat at every meal. His bodybuilding was a bottomless pit.

'What did you tell him?'

'That you were in the shower. What else could I say?'

'What did he say?'

She filled the pot at the tap and took a packet of macaroni from the cupboard. The bluish gas flame hissed as she waited for the water to boil. Hélène still had her back turned to him. He saw her shake her head no.

'He didn't say anything special.'

'I'll stop by later,' said Anthony.

'And this evening?'

'What about it?'

'You aren't going out, are you?'

'I might go out for a while.'

'Let me remind you: you're leaving tomorrow.'

'I know.'

Hélène wheeled round, holding the macaroni. She wore that face of hers, the face of the devoted, self-sacrificing mother. She had been struggling to make things work for so long and nothing did, and in the end, there was so little you could do. Over time, she could no longer stand the way other people acted, the conflicted functioning of the world, the way obstacles to her great dream of peacefulness were constantly popping up.

'You know that if you're late, you're considered a deserter.'

'Oh, give me a break!'

Fortunately, the timer rang just then. Hélène served lunch. Anthony didn't lift a finger to help. He complained that the meat wasn't salty enough. Hélène got up to get the salt.

'Here.'

'Thank you.'

'What time is your train?'

Bent over his food with an arm folded between him and his plate, Anthony ate one big forkful at a time. The food in his mouth was hot and comforting, with a taste of butter he'd grown up with.

'I've told you a hundred times, it's the ten fifteen.'

'If I were you, I wouldn't go out this evening. Stay home and take it easy. Rent a video. We could have pizza.'

'For God's sake, Mum!'

He had straightened up and was talking with his mouth full, eyes wide, as if his gaze could compensate for his trouble speaking.

'Today's Bastille Day,' he said. 'It's stupid to just stay at home.'

'Thanks for calling me stupid.'

'I never said you were stupid!'

'How else do you expect me to take it?'

'Oh, for fuck's sake...'

The meal continued in silence. Hélène barely touched her plate, choosing instead to contemplate this son of hers gulping down the food she had cooked for him, one bite after another. Just the sound of chewing, his breathing, the clicking of his fork on the plate. He served himself seconds of meat and macaroni, then ate two Danette yogurts for dessert. Finally, she told him he could do whatever he liked; it was his life, after all.

As she loaded the dishwasher, he turned on the TV. The Olympic Games were starting soon. You saw the same faces, big David Douillet, Marie-José Pérec, Jean Galfione and Carl Lewis, old now but still looking great. From the air, Atlanta looked like a glittering Monopoly board, bristling with tall glass-and-steel towers. Everything was the colour of mercury, clean, sharp, exorbitantly modern, under a blazing sun reverberating a thousand times, forty in the shade. Fortunately, this was the Coca-Cola city, so there was no shortage of refreshments. The hum of the dishwasher forced Anthony to turn the volume up a little. When she was finished, Hélène wiped her hands on her apron and lit another cigarette. She looked at her son, then came over to sit down.

'It does feel strange, all the same.'

Anthony's eyes were glued to the screen. With his tongue, he was trying to free a little piece of meat stuck between his teeth.

'What does?' he asked absently.

'No, nothing.' After a few moments she added: 'You might want to take your things up to the attic.'

'What things?'

'All that iron junk.'

'Yeah, sure.'

Hélène meant Anthony's weightlifting gear, the dumbbells, barbells and weight bench, all put on a Sofinco credit card. At least he wasn't smoking dope when he was working out.

'Not "Yeah, sure",' she said. 'Right now.'

'Okay, okay. I'm watching the news. You can wait two seconds.'

'Right now. It can't be done after you leave. It's too heavy. I can't do it all by myself.'

Anthony took his eyes off the screen for a second. His mother wore that imperious, bruised expression that had become her shield and her sword. It was her way of saying, 'I may be a drag, but this is still my house.' Since the two of them had been living together, she'd given in to Anthony on almost everything, and objectively he had taken total advantage of it. That's how he ended up with a motorbike, a PlayStation, and a TV in his bedroom, not to mention three pairs of Nike Airs gathering dust in the front hall cupboard. At the same time, by some mysterious phenomenon of compensation, his mother was punctilious about details, strict about schedules, and frighteningly demanding about keeping the floor clean and his wardrobe neat. This yawning divide led to ever-renewed arguments. Like an old married couple, they bitterly endured each other. Which was also what had made Anthony decide to get the hell out of there.

'Now,' ordered his mother, her arms crossed and holding a cigarette.

Sighing, he stood up. But she had to have the last word:

'And don't do it in boots! You'll track in all sorts of dirt.'

True, his equipment took up a hell of a lot of room. In fact it was because of that they parked their cars outside. He stored the weights in big tricolour shopping bags, sorted the bars and dismantled the bench. Gradually, Anthony's irritation subsided. He had to admit that his mother had gone through a lot. First the divorce, then his father's trial. Patrick hadn't gone to jail, but that had seemed the only logical outcome, and they'd dreaded it until the very end. In any case, the violent fight had cost the family what little money it had left. Patrick would be in debt for the rest of his days. It was barely even worth his working; he would never be able to pay what the lawyers and the courts demanded of him. Between the fees, the fine and what the loss of his job cost him, he was ruined.

Basically, it was an incredible lesson. If you step out of line, society has a whole set of tools to bind you for good. The lawyers and your bank are only too happy to arrange it. When you're carrying a six-figure debt, there's nothing to do but go drinking in a bar with other arseholes just like you, and wait for the end. Patrick Casati didn't have the slightest excuse. He'd proven himself stubborn, drunk and brutal his whole life. Still, the result was stunning: he'd been made an outcast, without appeal.

During the trial, old Bouali was called to testify. He answered all the questions politely and softly in his beautiful, gravelly voice. He came across as both overwhelmed and dignified, which greatly appealed to the judge. At the end, she gave him the chance to talk directly to Patrick, his former workmate. Did he want to tell him or ask him anything? Bouali answered that he had nothing to say. His passivity looked like wisdom. But maybe he was simply tired.

'What about you, Monsieur Casati? Do you have something to say to Monsieur Bouali?'

'No, Your Honour.'

'But you do know each other, right?'

'Yes, madame.'

'All right...' she concluded, twice tapping the file before her with her ballpoint pen.

Each side departed with its story and its grievances. Their failed meeting weighed heavily when the verdict was delivered.

After the period of the trial, Hélène Casati had to face further indignities. The management of the company where she'd been working for twenty-five years decided to reorganise its administrative functions, now newly renamed support functions. Her supervisor made her take a battery of tests to be sure she knew how to do the job she was already doing. Then an outside auditor, a guy from Nancy who wore Ted Lapidus suits and used hair cream, decided she didn't, quite. So she had to drive all the way to

Strasbourg for training, her stomach in knots, to relearn what she already knew. She became a child again, gently rebuked, who needed to be helped along and introduced to new tools in a changing world. When all was said and done, her job still consisted of tracking salaries, that is, adding lines that produced a total down on the lower right-hand side of a page. Only now the whole surrounding apparatus had abruptly changed, becoming opaque, sententious and anglicised.

A new manager soon showed up at the office. She was twenty years younger than Hélène, had ideas and had just earned her MBA in the United States, a fact she pointed out every chance she got. She was forever lamenting the pointless obstacles that in France still stood in the way of the essential forward march of a whole civilisation. In Berlin, a wall had fallen. Since then, history had been made. It was now time to use office software to overcome the final remaining difficulties and organise the peaceful melding of the world's five billion human beings. The promise of endless progress and the certainty of amazing unity were on the horizon.

It didn't take Hélène long to work out that she was one of the brakes slowing this historic movement. Which led to a feeling of resentment and in turn to a two-month work hiatus and a prescription for anti-depressants. When she returned to her job, she found that her office had been given to colleagues two levels higher on the food chain, newly hired marketing staffers. She was assigned a desk in an open-space work area. She'd had to write a registered letter to the work inspection service in order to be allowed to display a green plant and photo of her son on her desk.

From then on, Hélène didn't do much. She was forgotten. She kept boxes of biscuits, sweets and peanuts in a locked drawer, and nibbled. She put on eleven kilos. Fortunately, she had a healthy metabolism, and the recently acquired fat was spread around in a fairly harmonious way. Besides that, she was diagnosed with thyroid problems and put on Levo-thyrox. She often felt tired, depressed, uninterested in anything. She felt hot, but her office mates didn't want to open the window, since they had air conditioning. She found a new boyfriend, however. Jean-Louis wasn't all that bright and his glasses were constantly sliding down his nose, but he was nice. He worked in a restaurant and always carried a whiff of chips. At least he was good in bed.

It took Anthony nearly two hours to lug all his gear up to the attic. After that, he needed another shower, but decided to deal with his bag first. Time was marching on. It was already three o'clock.

When he went into his bedroom, he found all his things laid out for him. On the bed stood a stack of ironed T-shirts, two shirts, underwear and socks, a clean pair of jeans and a brand-new toiletries bag. He opened it and saw that there, too, everything was in perfect order: razor, deodorant, toothpaste, cotton swabs, et cetera. His mother had thought of everything. She annoyed him. He was touched.

He took his big sports bag from the wardrobe and started stowing his things in it. When he lifted the pile of T-shirts, he found two Snickers bars underneath. He picked them up and his throat tightened. This time he was leaving for good. Childhood was over.

Anthony had certainly taken advantage of it. How many times had people told him, 'You're lucky you're a minor.' All those years of looking for trouble, getting involved in drug deals, stealing scooters, hanging out and skipping lessons, and cheerfully degrading the built urban infrastructure. But being a minor has this ambiguous virtue: it protects you, but when it ends, you're suddenly tossed into a world whose ferocity you hadn't suspected. From one day to the next, the reality of your behaviour is shoved in your face, you don't get second chances, and people are fed up with you. Anthony had dreaded that turning point without really believing in it. The army was another bosom where he could go and hide. There, all he had to do was follow orders.

Most of all, it was the way to escape. He wanted to leave Heillange at all costs, and finally put hundreds of miles between himself and his dad.

After the trial, Patrick had been forced to move again. He now lived in a twenty-square-metre ground-floor studio apartment in a converted barracks on the motorway out of town towards Mondevaux. From his window he had a view of the health services office, a roundabout, railway tracks, and a billboard urging him to shop at Leclerc or Darty, depending on the day. Anthony once found himself doing community service in the neighbourhood and saw his father coming out of the off-license carrying a case of beer. Check it out, said Samir, the guy who was pulling weeds with him. Patrick staggered under the case's weight. It was Aldi, cheap beer. He went to open his apartment door, put the beer down, searched his pockets, found his key, opened the door, and forgot the case outside. Two minutes later, he came out to get it. Samir laughed.

Over the last two years, Anthony had several times found his father asleep in his bed, fully dressed and half comatose. It was a sickening sight. The stained pillow, the open mouth, the sleep like death. After checking that he was still breathing, Anthony took the opportunity to do some housekeeping. He filled black bin bags with empty bottles, vacuumed, changed the sheets, put the washing machine on. He left when he was finished, locking the door behind him; he had a key. From time to time he also came by with food that his mother had cooked. Patrick didn't drink when his son was there. Anthony heated the plate of lasagne and watched him eat it. He didn't stay long. At the end of the meal Patrick rolled himself a cigarette. His hand was steady. He was scarred, but that was it. Somewhat thin in the arms and legs, a puffy face, eyes that occasionally vacillated. He was still Patrick, only harder and more secretive. Anthony watched him vanish in the smoke of his hand-rolled cigarette and said, 'Okay, I'm on my way.' 'Go ahead,' said his father. It suited him, he was thirsty.

During this whole period, night and the pleasure of riding his motorbike helped Anthony keep it together. He went *putt-putt*ing along, precisely driving down streets that over time had become written in his guts. He'd been roaming the area since he was a child and knew every house, every street, every development, even the rubble and the potholes. He'd gone on foot, by bicycle, on his motorbike. He had played in that alley, been bored sitting on that wall, French-kissed in this bus shelter, and wandered the pavements along those huge warehouses where in the evening refrigerated lorries waited in dead silence.

In town, he saw the little shops that sold clothes, furniture and household appliances and that would soon be killed off by the new des Montets enterprise zone. There were the well-crafted apartments downtown, rented for a song to professors and prefecture officials. Palatial houses that stood empty now that the NGOs had shipped out with their regiment. And this was not including all those little shops along the street, IT service outlets, clothing stores, bakeries and pizzerias, kebab stands, and a good fifteen pavement cafes, with table football, pinball, TV, scratch-off games, a few newspapers, especially the local ones, and often a dog lying in the corner. Anthony made his way through a landscape that was as familiar as a face. Speed, the grey blur of building facades, the intermittent flash of street lights, oblivion. He would then find himself on the departmental motorway and would continue straight ahead, there, to the end. From school to the bus stop, from the swimming pool to town, from the lake to McDonald's stretched a world, his world. He covered it without let-up, at top speed, pursuing a risk, a straight line.

Tonight he would take his 125 out for the last time; he would go to the party. He would drink and dance. And tomorrow at 10.15, the train. *Ciao, tutti.*

The phone downstairs rang again. His mother answered it. Then he heard her call up to him:

'Anthony!'

'What?'

'It's your father.'

2

When Hacine woke up, his first thought was for Coralie. His second was for his teeth, which weren't in his mouth any more. He had spent the night on the living-room sofa bed and his back felt a bit sore. The curtains were flapping, framed by the open window. In the distance, you could hear the low rumble of cars driving across the aqueduct. Hacine lay there for a moment without moving. He was thinking.

Seb, Saïd and Eliott had come by yesterday and spent the evening. The first two left around three in the morning. Eliott stayed and slept over. He was still sleeping, stretched out on an inflatable mattress on the other side of the coffee table. He had kicked off the sheet in his sleep, revealing his fat chest, white pants and legs as thin as a corpse's. They were skin and bone, with a crop of very black hairs.

Hacine raised himself on his elbows and was immediately hit by the terrible smell filling the room. He looked around. The dog must have shat in the corner again. They'd had him for nearly two months now, and despite their walking him, punishing him and rubbing his nose in it, he couldn't stop. Just the same, Hacine thought it funny, and smiled as he imagined the little wretch quietly doing his business while everyone was asleep.

His pals had arrived around eight, as they had every evening since Hacine and Coralie got back from their holiday. It was the same routine as usual: blunts and pizza, followed by playing *FIFA Soccer* on the PlayStation and drinking Tropico. The living-room carpet was littered with Domino's pizza boxes, overflowing ashtrays, game controllers and scattered clothes. Hacine contemplated this war zone with a touch of melancholy. He was going back to work tomorrow. They had spent their last laid-back evening together; the holiday was over. And Coralie hadn't given them any grief, for once. She let them play the World Cup without saying a word. Anyway, you could always negotiate with her if she had her dog and got the blunt when it went round. At one point they had to change to *Super Mario Bros*. That was kind of a drag, because without a three-way splitter box, the change involved unplugging the PlayStation to switch to the NES, a manoeuvre that could take up to twenty minutes when they were really stoned.

Hacine fetched a bin bag from the kitchen and started collecting everything that was lying around loose. He wanted the place to be clean before Coralie got up. She had fallen asleep on the sofa bed a little after midnight, her usual time and he'd carried her into their bedroom. For Hacine and his friends, that meant the party could really get started. Being just among guys, with Eliott continuously rolling super-loaded blunts, they could talk shit and laugh until their sides ached. Especially since Seb still dreamed of winning the World Cup with Cameroon.

'No way, man, not even if you played for a hundred years!'

'Yeah, but what's the fun in winning with Brazil? Where's the challenge?'

'You're the challenge!'

'Shut up! Who're you choosing, Brazil?'

'Yeah, Brazil.'

'You're such a pussy! Take Holland, at least.'

'Why Holland? What the fuck do I want with Holland?'

Eliott had a soft spot for Argentina. Hacine alternated between Mannschaft and England, solid teams that played a long game, could make forty-metre passes side to side, fire volleys and bing, bang: goal! It saved him from having to feint and dribble in midfield. Hacine played a 4-2-4 formation and took every shot he could, no patience. Saïd had cast his lot with the Squadra Azzura. Nobody had ever picked Les Bleus. Ever since Platini hung up his boots, the French hadn't been able to win a damn thing.

Hacine finally located his teeth at the foot of the halogen lamp. He sniffed them and went into the bathroom. He was barefoot, wearing pants and a T-shirt with *Just Do It* on the back. He brushed his denture with toothpaste and put it on his upper jaw. As they did each time, the teeth felt mechanical and uncomfortable for a moment, then settled into their proper place. Hacine looked in the mirror. The teeth were straight, beautiful. And fake.

On his way back to the living room to wake Eliott, Hacine passed the bedroom. Coralie was asleep in her bra and pants, because he hadn't dared to completely undress her. Nelson lay curled up against her belly, panting. He was part fox terrier, part something else. Coralie had pestered Hacine for nearly six months for them to get a dog. He wasn't too keen on the idea. 'They stink,' he said. 'A dog costs money, plus you have to walk it, and what will we do when we go away?' 'We never go away,' she said. As a result, they now had this cute, demented mutt living with them, and they'd had to find a dog sitter, because they actually did go away after all.

To his great surprise, Hacine enjoyed their stay at the seaside. Coralie had found a camping resort at Six-Fours with parasol pines, three swimming pools, and lots of regulars and their families. The two of them drove across France in their Fiat Pronto to spend two weeks doing nothing and hanging out, being cheated by the local merchants and annoyed by the noise of children, while drunk on cicadas, heat, cold rosé and crowds. Hacine let himself go with the flow. Mornings, they got up early and had breakfast in front of their tent while chatting on relaxingly neutral topics. Their neighbours popped by to say hello. Hacine and Coralie spent whole days in flip-flops, practically naked, breathing in the wonderful dark, sweet smell of sap that rose from the pine needles covering the ground. They then drove to the beach, where Coralie did crossword puzzles and an incredulous Hacine watched people sitting out in the blazing sun. They took turns going swimming, to keep an eye on their things. Then they ate lunches of tomatoes and roast chicken, fried aubergines, rice salad and sardines. A life of disconcerting simplicity. After lunch they sat dozing in their canvas chairs as the heat settled on them like silence. It was called a siesta. Nearby, shaded by their tent flap, a pair of fifty-year-olds in swimming costumes listened to the Tour de France playing quietly on an old transistor radio. More sounds came from the pools, a mixture of muffled splashes and kids shouting.

Hacine was familiar with that feeling of torpor, the smothering heat of noon and the pleasure of doing nothing. But France was completely different from Morocco. The French brought a particular zeal to their holidays. There was something about their organised laziness that didn't ring true. Whether in the air-conditioned supermarkets, on the beaches, going to the showers, or doing the dishes, Hacine found them too focused, almost anxious to succeed. And lurking under the surface was that certainty of having to return home. It was like a threat or a safety catch that limited your authorised *far niente* happiness.

Going back home surprised him even more. Whenever Hacine returned from Morocco with his family, he always felt caught between two kinds of rootlessness. As he and Coralie drove up the A7, he now experienced a completely different kind of melancholy. In the traffic jams, at service stations and tollbooths, he felt accepted, as if he belonged wherever he was, just like other people. These periodic migrations, the famous French *chassé-croisé*, where the returning July holiday makers cross paths with the outbound August ones, acted as a huge unifying force. As they headed home, already missing afternoons under village plane trees or evening strolls along the waterfront, millions of shorts-wearing citizens enjoyed the pleasant fiction of being free people. That was where French identity was really created, more than at school or in the voting booth. Still, there was another side to this integration by paid holidays: you had to go back to work.

Today was Sunday, 14 July, and his job started again tomorrow.

As Hacine drank his coffee in the kitchen, gazing vaguely out at the landscape, he considered this inevitability. It was almost ten and Eliott was still asleep. Hacine had cleaned most of the mess and mopped up the dog shit. The fridge was nearly empty. Also, he hadn't done any of those essential jobs they'd hoped to do during the holidays. Theoretically, he was supposed to deal with the bathroom basin, which was cracked and needed to be replaced, and also the bedroom window, which let draughts in. He and Coralie had gone to the Mr Bricolage and Leroy Merlin shops, but came back empty-handed every time. Hacine didn't know anything about DIY and was afraid of being cheated, which made him mistrustful, so he wouldn't talk to any of the salespeople. Fortunately, there were other shops right next door where you could buy home furnishings, clothes, video games, hi-fi gear and exotic furniture, and then have a bite to eat afterwards. That was the beauty of the area's outlying commercial zones. You could spend the whole day blowing money you didn't have to brighten your life, without asking yourself any questions. Hacine and Coralie even went to King Jouet and roamed the toy shop's aisles, thinking of how much they would've enjoyed that when they were kids, if they'd been able to afford it. As a result, the apartment was full of candles, little plastic lights, fleece blankets and Buddhist-style knick-knacks. Coralie had also treated them to two rattan armchairs with white pillows. With the yucca and the plants in the corners, they gave the place a certain cachet. It would be even better when Hacine got round to putting up a nail to hang the photo of the Brooklyn Bridge that stood waiting at the foot of the wall.

Coralie got up around noon, having waited for Eliott to leave. It was a whole rigmarole when his mother came to get him, and she preferred to stay in bed. Eliott was supposed to be eligible for a handicap subsidy soon, and he and his girlfriend could move into their own apartment. The sooner the better, thought Coralie, who was tired of seeing him squatting here. She walked into the kitchen barefoot. She had been maintaining her suntan every day since they'd got back, at the pool and at the little park at the foot of the building, and her white cotton underwear stood out against her brown skin.

'Hi there.'

She was smiling and in a good mood, even in the morning, even on Mondays. Hacine liked her long body, her muscular legs, her flat stomach. In the winter Coralie wasn't much to look at. She was a bottle blonde with a nose a bit too big, her eyes moderately light. She wore too much make-up, boots and hoop earrings, and bundled herself in improbable cashmere sweaters. But once the nice weather arrived, she displayed a slender model's body: a small chest and perfect shoulders, and not an ounce of fat. Two dimples on her lower back saved her from looking too thin.

Hacine served her coffee and she stretched, as happy as a cat.

'Did they leave late?'

'Yeah. Fatso slept here.'

'Oh yeah? Something stinks, doesn't it?'

With his chin, Hacine pointed to the responsible party, who had walked in after Coralie, paws clicking on the parquet, nose in the air, looking innocent. She chuckled before sitting down. She immediately dived into her bowl of coffee and Hacine buttered a slice of bread for her. Nelson gazed at him with pleading eyes. He tossed him a scrap of bread.

'Here you go, you bastard.'

'Don't call him that,' said Coralie.

'It's a joke.'

He cleared the table. As he was putting his cup and the plates in the dishwasher, he asked:

'What do you want to do today?'

'Nothing. I don't know. Let's fuck.'

He swung round. She often enjoyed embarrassing him that way. They had been going out for nearly eighteen months and sharing the apartment since the spring. She had insisted on that. When they first met, Hacine was still living at his father's place. The old man had gone back to Morocco but continued paying the tiny rent, and everything went on as before. Where work was concerned, Hacine had got a temp job with Solodia, a big industrial clearance company that landed the famous Metalor account.

The old steel mills owned dozens of residential buildings in the valley, little terraced houses for workers and a few big ones for the engineers and bosses. Since the shutdown, all this property had been so neglected, it was literally falling into ruin. It took a long time for Metalor's holding company to recognise its responsibility and decide to deal with the problem. Solodia had won the bid, and they now had at least three years' worth of work. For Hacine, it was simple. In the morning he and two or three other guys showed up at a building armed with buckets, sledgehammers and crowbars, and they started smashing whatever they could. At first, it was an enjoyable kind of destruction game. You knocked down plaster panels, smashed brick walls, ripped out old lead plumbing. It was childish fun to see a wall come down, then tip the whole thing over with a kick of your heel. By noon, there was practically nothing left to see. Thick dust hung in the air; the guys protected themselves with paper masks. When the initial work was done, you had to clear the rubble. The men took turns. One group filled the buckets while the other hauled and emptied them in the dumper truck. You carried beams and pipes on your shoulder.

At first, Hacine worked like a maniac. He hustled in the stairways, confusing aggressiveness with strength, taking the steps at a run, always in a fever, worried, in a hurry to finish. Jacques took him aside. He wasn't the boss, and he didn't earn much more than anyone else, but he was the guy who gave the orders.

'Listen...'

Jacques told him what was what. This job has no end, he said. After this bucket, there will always be another bucket. After this apartment, another apartment will come along. There will be other walls to knock down, other places to demolish.

'Your alarm clock goes off at six every day. No point in knocking yourself out.'

At that moment, Hacine was tempted to punch him on the nose. But he already felt sore all over, and besides, Jacques weighed a good hundred kilos. Hacine's anger settled with the dust. Heading home in a truck, he felt like shit, weary and misunderstood. He watched the grey landscape endlessly rolling by the window. The sky didn't promise anything else. Jacques was right. There was no point in hurrying. Hacine studied Jacques in the rear-view mirror, his Rica Lewis jeans, old-fashioned work boots, and big, rough hands. He worked with a flannel belt around his lower back. He didn't talk much.

The following Monday, Hacine struggled to get up, and he arrived late. The others gave him a hard time. 'Slacker!' Jacques told them to leave him alone. And he took Hacine aside again.

'When it's time, it's time,' he said.

Hacine gradually caught the rhythm by watching the older man. He noticed that Jacques followed certain rituals to pace himself and break up the day. A cigarette at eight, another one at ten, with coffee. At eleven, he turned up the volume on the radio because it was time for his favourite broadcast. He tried to do most of the work during the morning, so as to take it easy in the afternoon. Similarly, he put in the most effort early in the week. There were all sorts of tricks to conquer this desert, this uniform stretch of time that awaited you when you got out of bed and then extended forever, until you retired. Hacine understood that. His time didn't belong to him. But you could always trick the clock. On the other hand, there was nothing he could do about this basic fact: minds other than his own were making the rules for his body. He had become a tool, a thing. He was working.

Hacine probably wouldn't have held on all by himself. When he thought about it, nothing had ever accustomed him to holding on. And besides, was it even a good idea, to hold on, to become a reliable person, a poor slob like his father? But there was Coralie.

Honestly, he'd been lucky. On paper, their relationship made no sense. She had a technical diploma, a good job at the prefecture, and was really pretty. Plus, the first time Hacine met her at Derch, he was completely drunk. Two months later he was having lunch with her parents. Her father did maintenance at a secondary school. He was a very likeable guy, big talker, union man, hair all gone, sweater. Her mother worked at Solin, the last silk mill in the area. She had thoughtfully cooked fish. The old man was less subtle. He simply took out a bottle of Bordeaux, and Hacine drank it without any fuss.

Since then, his life was in balance. Buying household appliances compensated for the travails; the prospect of a holiday made the long days bearable. Coralie broke up the week's monotony, and his mates, weed, the Canal subscription and *Tomb Raider* did the rest. All things considered, it amounted to a perfectly acceptable little life.

Anyway, since losing his teeth, Hacine no longer made waves. They had found him in the L'Usine men's room, lying in a pool of his blood. His father knelt down and took him in his arms. At the hospital, he came to see him every day. Then, after the trial, Bouali went back to Morocco, for good this time. When Hacine got him on the phone these days, he heard the voice of a stranger, a man being erased, barely touching things, dissolving. Hacine had promised himself he would go and see him soon for months now. But he was afraid to find himself face-to-face with a ghost. Coralie helped him with this, too. The impossible heritage, with death hovering nearby. She would take his hand and say, 'Fuck me hard, honey,' simple things that pierced his loneliness.

But Hacine was going back to work tomorrow and felt as heartsick as a schoolboy. From his kitchen window, he could see the valley, all those idiots crowded together in happy families, and on Sunday, besides. The new little apartment building on the heights where he and Coralie lived was nice. It was half owned, the rest subsidised rent, with concrete courtyards, gas central heating, double glazing, and common areas that still smelled new. Coralie had found it, of course. The view was terrific; you could see the whole town and as far as Guérémange to the east. Oddly enough, the panorama made Hacine depressed. Looking down and seeing other people like ants made you ask yourself the big questions.

Having finished her coffee, Coralie stretched and yawned widely, her head thrown back, legs stretched, slippers dangling from her toes. The image reassured Hacine.

'Seriously, though, what are we doing?' he asked.

'I don't know. We could stay home.'

Again, she reached for him, smiling. He leaned over and took her fingers, and they kissed above the table. A noisy little peck. Coralie looked him over.

'What's the matter with you?' she asked.

'What do you mean?'

'You have that look...'

She imitated his scowl, and he shrugged.

'Come on,' she said. 'You're not gonna screw up the whole day just because you're going back to work tomorrow.'

'That's not it.'

'I know you.'

He stiffened. Even now, years later, Hacine still had that funny way of holding his body, a posture that made him look like an offended chicken. Coralie couldn't help giggling.

'What now?'

'What, nothing. Come on, it's our last day!'

She stood up and began to get busy. She walked into the living room and it immediately seemed cleaner and brighter, without his quite being able to say why. Hacine had witnessed those instant metamorphoses a hundred times. It took very little – some item, the fall of a curtain, practically nothing – but once Coralie had gone through a place, it was completely different. She'd left for three days of training in March and the apartment became a shambles, almost turning into a cave. On the last evening Hacine even preferred to eat at McDonald's rather than stay at home.

Her little worker-bee job done, buzzing in the corners and bringing in sunshine, Coralie decided what they would do next. While she got dressed, Hacine made sandwiches, packed a blanket and filled the cool box. An hour later they were on the shores of Le Perdu lake. They picked a spot in the shade, spread the blanket and stretched out with her head in his lap.

'Did you think to bring the Coke?'

'Yeah.'

'And the crisps?'

'Yeah.'

'Do you love me?'

Hacine kissed her hand, which he was holding. It was nice to be lying on the grass under this old tree, watching the water's metallic sheen, the windsurfers, the children crouched in the muddy sand.

They ate with their fingers, then went swimming. Coralie was usually talkative, and Hacine enjoyed listening to her. She would often hatch plans and he would end up saying, 'Yeah, that's a good idea.' But for once they didn't talk. It felt like the day after a drunken party. They touched each other lightly, happily. Hacine wanted her. He stroked her shoulder, his index finger following her collarbone. He could feel her skin, sticky and soft under his fingers. At one point, a big raft cruised by in the distance. It had been cobbled together with boards, with drums for floats and a mast stuck in the middle. The kids on the raft wore life jackets and were paddling with pieces of wood. You could hear them a hundred metres away. A big French flag flew from the mast.

'Today's Bastille Day, you know,' said Coralie.

'So what?'

So there would be fireworks at the American beach that evening and Coralie wanted to see them. The city government had arranged a dance. Hacine had never gone there.

'Why not?' Coralie asked.

'I dunno. What the hell does it have to do with me?'

'It's good fun. Not even when you were little? You've really never seen the fireworks?'

'Never, I'm telling you.'

Neither had any of his friends. It just wasn't their thing. In his family, the question had never even come up.

'Why should I give a fuck about the Fourteenth of July?'

'Stop that! For a kid, it's magical. There's music, you have a few drinks. It's great.'

'Yeah, right. But I have to work tomorrow.'

He was frowning, so she gave him a punch.

'Don't do that thing again.'

'But—'

'We won't stay late. Come on!'

Besides, he had to get up at five because they started early in the summer. Jacques had warned him that they would be on a truly crappy worksite, with a risk of asbestos. Hacine had no desire to go dancing. The

Bastille Day celebration would be sure to be full of red-faced idiots, police everywhere, brass bands and soldiers. In a word: shit.

As he laid out his arguments, Coralie rolled her eyes.

'My poor baby...' she said.

Hacine understood that it was all settled, and there wasn't much he could say about it.

On the way home, he did manage to wring one concession from her. They wouldn't dance.

'All right,' said Coralie. 'But we're going to Sophie's next Saturday.'

Sophie was her friend who lived in a farmhouse out in the country that she and her boyfriend were restoring. They had four kids, including a newborn. It was hell. Each time they came back from there, Coralie's head was full of plans for the future.

3

Stéphanie's father had finally built his swimming pool.

It was rectangular and blue, surrounded by wooden furniture, flowers and umbrellas – the kind associated with television personalities featured in the pages of *Paris Match*. Steph considered the thing from the terrace. Standing nearby, her mother awaited her verdict.

'Well?'

'It's nice.'

'It is, isn't it? Those chaise longues, they're teak. Rot-resistant. They stay outside, even in winter.'

Caroline was seeking her daughter's approval. In vain. Steph remained hidden behind her sunglasses. She had kept her distance from her parents since coming home, barely speaking to them. Her mother was trying to do the right thing.

'Do you want to go swimming? I can get you a towel.'

'Maybe later.'

The two women were about the same size, with Steph maybe a little rounder. Her mother was dressed in white and smoking a Marlboro. Each time she raised the cigarette to her lips the gold bracelets on her wrist jangled prettily. In the distance you could hear the steady hum of the pump. The light cast thin white reflections on the water. Nobody ever went swimming.

'I'm thirsty,' said Caroline. 'Want to have a drink?'

'Sure.'

'Okay, I'll take you into town.'

'Oh.'

'I'll treat you to champagne. As a celebration.'

'What are we celebrating?'

Her mother made a funny little noise with her lips that might have sounded like a fart, and meant that they were sure to think of something. The response amused Steph. The more her father embraced respectability, the more her mother seemed to loosen up. With her daughter away and her husband hustling, Caroline found herself on her own, or with friends. It didn't bother her. She had decided to have fun.

'Where do you want to go?' asked Steph.

'Let's go to Algarde.'

'You sure?'

'Oh, don't be a snob. He'll be happy to see you.'

She looked at her daughter with desperate eagerness. Since Stéphanie had come home, Caroline wanted to take her everywhere, to show her off. People were calling her 'the Parisienne'. It was both flattering and annoying. They had even gone shopping in Luxembourg City. Anyway, Steph didn't really have much choice. She had already cut her visit down to nothing, four days, and then was leaving with some friends for Florence, Rome and Naples. She hadn't been home since Christmas. And her parents were still footing the bills.

She and her mother took the Golf to drive into town. Steph had mixed feelings about being back in Heillange. In spite of herself, she enjoyed seeing these places again, the Metro, the Commerce brasserie, the little shops that would close when their owners died – a milliner, a haberdashery, a tiny fruit and vegetable stand – and also the post office, with its 1970s furnishings, City Hall, which was decked out for the national holiday, pedestrian streets, the bridge across the Henne and finally her old school. In this shrunken, permanent landscape, Steph felt proud of herself. She kind of wished people knew it, that there was something that could set her off, now that she belonged to other places. Her whole attitude said she was just passing through.

When they reached Algarde, the owner immediately left the counter to come and greet them. One of those eternally youthful men, Victor had the latest trainers, rolled-up sleeves and gorgeous teeth, thinning hair but not a single wrinkle. He didn't flash his money around, but he still drove an SUV accompanied by an updated wife, with two kids in the back who looked almost exactly like him, except they had hair with lots of gel in it. Caroline hung out at Algarde, which she'd made her headquarters, coming in for drinks with her friends and eating there at weekends. She took Victor's arm and gave him a kiss.

'So you brought us your Parisienne!' he said.

Steph smiled at Victor but was careful not to kiss him. He was giving her the eye with a little half-smile, seductive but distant. His cheeks had that burnished lustre you see on men who shave twice a day. He was attractive, but in an unsettling way.

He eventually led the two women out to the terrace. The weather was beautiful. Victor asked them for their news. Steph's mother answered playfully, without telling him anything in particular. He found them a table shaded by a big umbrella, quite far back from the street and the occasional passing car. They had some trees behind them to keep them cool and a panoramic view of place Mortier, the handsomest in town, with its old houses, paving stones, and a fountain designed by some contemporary artist.

They chatted for a moment, out of habit. Basically, Stéphanie was at the centre of a somewhat meaningless society game. Her mother showed her off, people pretended to be interested, and Steph played along. A kind of fake currency was being circulated that helped lubricate relationships. In the end, nobody really gave a damn.

Victor was treating them to drinks, so they gave up the idea of champagne. Caroline ordered a kir; Steph had beer. It was almost eleven in the morning. They sipped their drinks slowly, looking around. It was crowded. For some time now, downtown Heillange was being pulled in different directions. Businesses were heading out to the periphery while the historic core, with its streets and buildings, was being renovated at great expense. The mayor was ambitious and he had accommodating bankers. There were practically no factories left in the valley, and young people were leaving for lack of jobs. As a result, the mass of workers who once formed the majority in municipal elections and shaped the area's politics had become the smallest share of the electorate. So City Hall was exploring new development approaches with the help of the regional and state councils. Tourism would spark a renaissance. After upgrading the campground, enlarging the sailing club and swimming pool, and creating a miniature golf course, the city was now multiplying pedestrian streets and bike paths and had announced a brand-new iron and steel museum for the year 2000. The surrounding area had lots of hills and trails, which attracted hikers. Moreover, several companies – local, German, and Luxembourger – had been persuaded to support the idea of an amusement park. The overall plan was simple: invest. The means: take on debt. The inevitable result: prosperity.

Steph's father, Pierre, now a deputy mayor for culture, was totally committed to this laudable adventure, whose repercussions were yet to be felt. At the municipal council, people stuck to the official line. Priming the pump required time and effort, but once the machine was launched, we'd be set for a century of full employment. In the meantime, when a councillor was challenged by an inquisitive voter, a budding economist or a reporter, he blamed the state or the previous administration, Communists who had brought the town to its knees.

'What they've done isn't too bad,' commented Steph's mother.

'Yeah.'

'Everything used to be grey in this town. It was ugly.'

'For sure.'

Buildings throughout the area had blossomed in light red, green, fuchsia and baby blue. The fashion even reached the prefecture, which was now painted a dusty rose. Driving through town, you sometimes felt you'd stumbled into a Jacques Demy movie. Everything that remained of the old city – its steel mills, its memories of wars and their dead, its republican mottos and what remained of its Catholicism – was gradually disappearing under new paint. The urban landscape that resulted from these renovations gave the inhabitants the odd feeling of living in a theme park. But they accepted it in the name of that most tenacious of ideas, progress.

Steph was thinking about all this and much besides, when she felt a hand on her shoulder. She looked up. Clémence was standing right behind her.

'What the hell are you doing here?'

'Well, nothing,' said a delighted Stéphanie.

'Don't you ever tell people when you come home?'

'I arrived on Tuesday. I'm leaving tomorrow night.'

'And I'm spending nearly the whole summer here,' said Clémence, with mock dismay.

'Oh, poor you.'

'Yeah.'

'Aren't you leaving?'

'As soon as I can, in August. But I'm working all of July.'

'Where?'

'At the law firm, with my father. I'm subbing for the receptionist.'

'That's nice.'

Clémence was still standing behind her and Steph was looking up at her, which made her friend's face look strangely reversed. She was amused at having such trouble recognising her old friend.

'Sit down,' suggested Caroline. 'Have a drink with us.'

Clémence gladly accepted and took a chair from the next table. The women began gossiping enthusiastically, like actresses in the limelight, speaking loudly or softly depending on the topic. Steph learned that their classmate Clarisse had twice screwed up her first year at medical school and was at the end of her tether. On top of that, her boyfriend, who'd been at Paris Dauphine University, was leaving for London for a graduate internship. It was crap. As for Simon Rotier, he was loafing his way through a business school in the Paca area, where his main interests were windsurfing and electronic music. He had just got back home, and Clémence had run into him.

'And?'

'The same as ever.'

'A total prick.'

'There you have it.'

The girls laughed. Was Steph planning on seeing him? Clémence wanted to know.

'Not on your life!'

Still, just thinking about it made Steph feel funny, sort of weak. The two girls continued the roll call of people they knew. Rodrigue was studying law in Metz; nobody saw him any more. Romain Rotier was a star in a sports physiology programme. He'd started doing triathlons and was winning metals. Steph's mother had seen his name in the paper a couple of times.

'Problem is, he's going to end up working as a coach.'

'That's right. The guy's going to spend the rest of his days wearing slip-ons in some smelly gym. Awful.'

Caroline giggled. She had already finished her drink and was having a very good time. She wanted another one and ordered a bottle of a very cold white wine that tasted like electricity. The mood was definitely excellent. Steph was happy to find Clémence the same as always, lively and desirable, with an extra something that was hard to define. It looked like arrogance, but maybe it was actually just strength. Whatever the case, it made her irresistible. Being there was delightful and the three women intended to make the pleasure last.

'Let's have lunch here,' said Caroline after a while, glancing at her watch.

It was almost half past. They hadn't seen the time flying. Clémence said she was expected somewhere. Caroline insisted, she would treat her. Well, in that case. Victor brought the menus. Around them, people were lingering over drinks. Thirty-somethings in T-shirts enjoyed the sunshine. Children ran to and from the big fountain in the middle of the square. There were also a few old people with tartan shopping bags, visitors eating sirloin steak and quiche. The two girls wanted salads; Caroline was inclined to salmon tartare. But they kept drinking and eventually ended up ordering pizza. The conversation flowed on, more and more lively, cheerful, unstoppable. Clémence had tons of stories about her father's law practice and the crazy people who passed through it. To hear her tell it, a medieval court of miracles had nothing on the waiting room. Alcoholics, pensioners, indigents, silicosis victims, the obese, varicose veins sufferers, people crippled or otherwise hurt, incomprehensible foreigners and French people who were hardly more articulate.

'One woman showed up, she had three children, all handicapped. One, I can understand, but three, what the hell is that about?'

It was funny, though not really. Making fun of weirdos was pretty routine and increasingly widespread. It was partly for laughs, but partly to ward off evil, the insidious tide ever rising from below. When you ran into those people in the street, they weren't just local colour any more, a few weirdos or inbreds on the prowl. A bare-bones economy was being set up for them dedicated to the management of poverty, the extinction of a species, with housing, Aldi supermarkets and health clinics. You would see the people wandering ghostlike from social security office to ZUP estate and from bistro to canal, carrying plastic bags, laden with children in pushchairs, legs like posts, huge bellies, and extraordinary faces. Once in a while a particularly beautiful girl would be born to them, and you could then imagine things, promiscuity and violence. Still, she was lucky, because her body might serve as a passport to a better world. Those families would also produce incredibly tough guys who refused to accept their fate and lashed out. They would have brief, deviant careers and wind up dead or in prison.

There were no statistics to measure the extent of this collapse, but the number of hungry people fed by Restos du Coeur was growing exponentially as social services crumbled. You had to wonder what kind of life those people could be leading, in their shabby housing, eating fatty food, hooked on video games and soap operas, spending their time making children and trouble, lost, enraged and marginalised. It was best to avoid asking yourself the question, or counting them, or speculating on their life expectancy or fertility. They were scum, hovering below the poverty line, tossed occasional scraps of welfare, destined to frighten and to disappear.

Victor suggested dessert, but the three women were full. They had shared a carafe of Côtes-du-Rhône with the pizzas and were feeling very relaxed, sleepy and heavy. Steph's mother announced that she couldn't move and the two girls were doing no better. Coffee came with the bill, and Caroline laid her Visa Premier card on it. While they'd been chatting and laughing, the terrace had emptied out. Only an English couple who came in late remained, with some teenagers smoking Chesterfields and drinking a Monaco. In the torpor of this early afternoon, it was very pleasant to contemplate the emptiness of July.

'Hey, look!' said Clémence, pointing down rue des Trois-Épis.

Steph's father was coming their way. His sagging belly hid his belt and stretched his blue-and-white-checked Eden Park shirt. He strode along carrying a briefcase and staring at his shoes. He looked at his watch and quickened his pace. Steph's mother stood up to wave at him.

'Hey there!' she called, clinging to the back of her chair.

'Are you all right?' asked Steph.

'Sure, sure. I've been a lot worse.'

Caroline raised her hand, and her bracelets slid down her forearm and made their pleasant jingle. Her husband gave a quick wave and came over. He looked black as thunder and immediately started telling them what was bothering him. The three women pretended to listen.

Pierre Chaussoy had just come from the American beach, where he'd checked on the final preparations for the festivities. The fireworks weren't set up yet. The firefighters were giving him a hard time and so were the municipal workers, who wanted triple-time pay because this Bastille Day fell on a Sunday. The mayor was waiting for him to report back. As he talked, he swiped pieces of pizza crust from his daughter's plate. Steph watched him doing it. He won't last long at this rate, she thought.

'You're coming tonight, aren't you?' he asked. 'There'll be a big turnout.'

Steph and Clémence played up to him. In fact they weren't too keen on the idea. Oompah music and fist fights really weren't their idea of a fun evening. But he was so persistent that they finally promised to come. Then he went on his way, pudgy, panting, briefcase in hand. The mayor was waiting for him and, in one way or another, the whole town needed him.

'Okay then…'

Caroline and the girls didn't have anything more to say to each other. The two avoided looking at her and she got the message. She got to her feet and picked up the bill.

'Do you have a car, Clémence?'

'Yes.'

'I'll leave you, then. I still have lots of stuff to do.'

Caroline asked Clem to say hello to her parents for her and went inside to pay the bill. She couldn't walk very straight, but then again, she couldn't see very well, either. Her car drove her, rather than the other way round. Steph and Clémence smiled as they watched her go, a talkative fake blonde with an overdone suntan and lots of gold bling. Before leaving, she gave them a last little wave goodbye.

'So, what do you feel like doing?' asked Clémence.

'I don't know.'

'Yeah, this place is still such a drag.'

'Too true.'

They were silent for a few more minutes, enjoying the three o'clock drowsiness and the effect of the wine on their heads and the food on their stomachs.

'Still, you could have called.'

'I haven't stopped running around since I got here. My mum is dragging me everywhere.'

'Yeah, okay then.'

They decided to walk a little to stretch their legs. All the shops were closed and the few restaurants were closing up. An occasional open window gave glimpses of modest interiors, a couple watching television downstairs, a teenager's bedroom with *Top Gun* posters on the wall.

Clémence started to talk about her life and studies and about living in Nancy. After a failed start at the *préparatoire* in Lille, she'd switched to medical school and had just finished her first year. Overall, things were going pretty well, though she'd really suffered in her first term. She had arrived in midstream, lost in the mob of 1,600 students before the exam results. The professors' methodical contempt, the phenomenal amount of work – it was awful. Until March, one day had followed the next with neither light nor pleasure, a grey tunnel, not to mention the fatigue, the competition, and the city of Nancy, which was nothing but a string of pretentious buildings and pathetic bars. She ended up on Prozac. Since then, she'd caught the rhythm and had created a little gang of supportive, hard-working friends: Capucine, Marc, Blanche, Édouard and Nassim. They all went to the library together, partied together, did some casual fucking. It built connections. Come August, Clémence planned to go camping with them in the Cévennes for two weeks.

'So, do you have a boyfriend in all that?' asked Steph.

'Not really. Anyway, we have so much work.'

Then it was Steph's turn to talk. She was evasive, though she and Clémence hadn't seen each other since the summer of the baccalaureate. There was a lot to tell.

After passing her bac with honours, Steph had a flash of insight: studying law was suddenly out of the question. She had sensed that for people like her, law school offered too much freedom, too many opportunities to lose your way. Part of this last-minute rejection had a touch of snobbery. She couldn't see herself spending five years in enormous lecture halls, being just one of hundreds of other idiots who'd wandered in from the sticks.

Unlike Clémence and their other classmates, who had been oriented towards attractive academic careers from childhood, Steph had never thought ahead. From primary school to her final year in secondary school, she'd been happy to do as little as possible, and towards the end, her obsession with Simon had practically become a full-time occupation. So when the time came to make serious choices, she found herself at a loss. She regretted this and blamed her parents.

The Chaussoys had managed to build themselves a comfortable, petit-bourgeois life without too much culture, and hadn't laid out any specific plans for their only daughter. Pierre had just made that single, eccentric demand, that she pass the baccalaureate with honours. After that, they supposed she might go into business, they would get her internships, a job, help her buy a couple of good local properties with garages to rent out and she would gradually build her nest egg, as they had.

But Stéphanie wasn't about to settle for those modest aspirations. She now understood how things worked, even if she was a little late coming to the party. School functioned as a kind of classification yard. Some kids left early, destined for manual labour in jobs that were underpaid and unfulfilling. True, one of them might end up being a millionaire plumber or a rich garage owner, but in general, those career paths didn't lead very far.

A second category, about 80 per cent of a given age group, passed the baccalaureate and went on to study philosophy, sociology, psychology or economics and management. After the brutal first-term thinning out they got mediocre diplomas that promised endless job searches, civil service tests taken as a last resort, and a variety of frustrating destinies, like teaching in a low-income school district or doing PR in local government. They would go on to swell that category of bitter citizens who were overeducated and underemployed, who understood everything and could do nothing. Disappointed and angry, they would gradually give up on their ambitions and turn to other outlets, like building a wine cellar or converting to an Eastern religion.

Finally, you had the hotshots, the ones with top honours on the baccalaureate and a solid-gold CV, a real launchpad to desirable careers. Those people would follow narrow tracks and, under pressure, go fast and climb very high. Mathematics was a major asset when taking those accelerated courses, but there were also a few tracks for abstract thinkers, historians, dreamers, artists and clowns of that ilk. Steph wanted to be part of this third category.

Given her CV, though, hoping to get into a public *préparatoire* school was unfortunately out of the question. So her father started looking for a backup plan. On the advice of a Reims Mercedes dealer, they settled on a private school that prepared students for the entrance competitions for the big graduate institutions like Essec, HEC and Sciences Po. Problem was, the establishment in question was in the 6th arrondissement of Paris and cost an arm and a leg. A little more than three thousand francs a month, to which you had to add food, lodging and travel. So Steph was given an ultimatum: her parents would pay the freight costs, but she would be brought straight home at the first screw-up.

In early September Pierre rented a little van to help Steph get settled in her studio apartment. They drove down together, for once just the two of them. Her father talked about his life and his youth. He even told her about some of his old girlfriends. At one point Steph asked if he still loved her mother.

'Not much, any more.'

He said it without bitterness, and Steph was thrilled that they were dropping the pretence for a few seconds. She felt appreciated. And she was careful not to ask him why they stayed together, or stupid questions like that. Being an adult means knowing that there is more than having the love of your life, or the other bullshit that filled magazine pages: doing well, living your passions, being a big success. Because there's also time, death, and the endless war that life wages against you. Being in a couple is clinging to a lifeboat teetering at the edge of the abyss. Father and daughter said nothing more about it. In the car, Pierre said he was proud of her and Steph felt like a grown-up. They stopped at a McDonald's in La Ferté-sous-Jouarre and she insisted on paying.

Steph's first autumn in Paris was awful. She was attending a place called the École Préparatoire de Paris that was full of rich little snots who thought only of sitting back and doing E. Her class included the son of the ambassador of Benin, the child of a Thai minister, girls with hyphenated first names, and all manner of well-coiffed, stuck-up kids of the rich. In the eyes of her new classmates, Steph was a total bumpkin. For example, they particularly made fun of her for wearing Achile socks, which in Heillange were considered classy. At her very first oral exam, the professor advised her to get rid of her accent, saying it would seriously hurt her at the competitive entrance exam.

Besides studying, Steph had to shop, cook, and clean her apartment, though at sixteen square metres, this didn't take long. At weekends, when she wasn't studying for classes, she treated herself to trips around Paris. She had always thought that she and the city would have a great romance together. She was sorely disappointed. Of course, Paris remained a little like a stack of profiteroles, with its curves and its excessive, overstuffed, sickly side – at least, that was the case in the central arrondissements. It was only there that you really had the feeling of being at the centre of things. But Steph was forced to recognise that the city – with its flood of bodies, explosion of buildings, windows and lights, glowing streams of vehicles, comings and goings in the Metro corridors, the beauty of the monuments and the ugliness of the streets – was completely beyond her grasp. A gap yawned between her and Paris. You had to have been born there. Or to succeed there. And succeeding is what Steph planned to do.

She started studying like a lunatic. She hadn't had any illusions when she arrived, but neither did she think she was slower on the uptake than anyone else. Yet from her very first classes, she had the feeling that she'd landed in a foreign country. References, vocabulary, expectations – she didn't understand any of them. The first week, she cried into her pillow every night. Plus, she didn't have a TV or a telephone. To call her mother, she had to go downstairs to a phone booth. She felt weary and found the professors haughty and pretentious, and her fellow students semi-moronic. Steph, who'd never had trouble sleeping eight hours at a stretch, was now waking up twice a night, feeling sweaty, with her jaws aching. She squeezed her spots in the bathroom mirror under the harsh neon light. When she was finished, her face was covered with red blotches. She thought she looked ugly, and her hair lost its sheen. Worse, she was in the bad habit of snacking while she reviewed her notes. Her arse doubled in size in no time at all, and so did her arms. At the end of December, the balance sheet was grim. She had screwed up all her oral exams, was scary pale, and the scales said she'd put on seven extra kilos.

It was on a Saturday morning, during a six-hour written exam, that she came across this subject under general culture:

The progress made by insomnia is remarkable and exactly follows all the other kinds of progress.

PAUL VALÉRY

She felt her throat tighten. That naked sentence, that feeling of the undeniable.

Steph was aware that up to now she'd been very lucky. She'd been born in the right place at a rather benign period in the history of the world. She'd never in her life had to fear cold or hunger, or even a hint of violence. She had belonged to desirable groups (well-off family, cool mates, students without major difficulties, a few hotties), and one day had followed the next with its dose of minor obligations and repeated pleasures. As a result, she had always viewed the future with a kind of relaxed indifference. So now that she was on her own and far from Heillange for once, she found herself completely out of step and ill-prepared, her only baggage being some naive ideas from primary school, and the pride and overly thin skin of a spoiled child.

She reread the Valéry sentence and considered her three-part essay structure. Then, without a word, she got up to go to the toilet. The invigilator was used to this sort of thing. He'd gone this route himself, and merely smiled knowingly as he watched the girl with the loose chignon walk by. Upstairs, Steph locked herself in a cubicle and had a good cry. She was at the end of her tether. She found herself fairly seriously wondering which would be easier, to jump into the Seine or under the wheels of an RER train.

Except that she went back. 'Feeling better?' asked the invigilator. 'Yes, I'm okay.' On her way back there were tight smiles and worries. Everybody knew they were more or less threatened by the same drama, sudden collapses were multiplying – even the clever ones wouldn't last much longer. It was time to buckle down and either hang in there or give up. For that first year, Christmas would be their Cape Horn.

Steph hung in there.

She even started nailing her maths tests. That wasn't a total surprise, since she'd always been good at it, but still, what a breath of oxygen!

After the Christmas holidays, she kept up her steady pace. She stopped doubting herself, just did her work without reluctance, until one o'clock in the morning if need be. She spent less time making herself attractive. She looked at guys less. She took notes. She graduated to the second year.

During the summer holidays she kept up her efforts, knocking off a good chunk of the reading that her professors had recommended. *Race et histoire*, Winock on the 1960s, Aron, *L'Histoire des droites en France*, even Robbe-Grillet and Giono. That said, she stalled on Proust. The whole business of flowers, stained-glass windows, the slightest oscillation of the heart…give me a break. Then she spent three weeks in Bristol, with a family who hosted paying foreign students. The house was vast, with carpets everywhere, even in the bathroom, which gave you something to ponder as you sat on the toilet. Most of the other guests came from Japan or Korea. They behaved like their stereotypes, polite and hard-working, and the girls covered their mouths when they laughed. They were forever nodding, as if they wanted to nail down with their foreheads every word they said.

Steph got along well with the Asians. For them, being there was like being on probation. After spending a year visiting Europe and perfecting their business English, they would have to go home to become managers. Yuki, a boy she slept with three times, told her about his future as a 'salaryman'. Each time, they had fucked at six in the morning, having come back from a club. He had very stiff, dyed hair, which was apparently the fashion in Tokyo and Osaka. He worked so hard to make her come, it was touching. Big drops of sweat dripped from his forehead and Steph had to close her eyes. Once, when she told him to relax, he promptly lost his erection. When it was over, they chatted. Yuki's parents had invested a good part of their savings so that he could get the Japanese equivalent of the international English certificate. Everybody was counting on him. Soon he would have a good salary, responsibilities, fourteen-hour workdays and a tie. At last, everything was settled for him. Steph told herself that in Europe you were still lucky enough to be able to disappoint the people who loved you.

As a result, she hadn't seen any of her old Heillange pals during this studious summer. She kept to herself, afraid of interference. She also didn't want anyone seeing her wrestler's thighs. She laid low.

Second year was characterised by its flatness, a neutral expanse like grey Canson art paper. Steph had the feeling she was digging a tunnel through a Himalaya of work. She experienced the discouragement of this absurd task, but also the pay-off of each foot cut through the rock. She knew that at the end she would find her Eden, a career. She would take her rightful place, and with a vengeance. She pinned some postcards above her desk, Sisley reproductions, Caravaggio's *Judith Beheading Holofernes*, a picture of Virginia Woolf, a bare-chested Belmondo in *Breathless*.

She also found herself some friends, Renata and Benôit. From the very beginning professors had pushed working with others as a remedy for everything. There were all kinds of formulas for success, even say-ings. One suggested that if you're in a relationship, you'll drop out: if you couple, you'll buckle. You had to make sure to get enough sleep, study with a partner, team up with the most driven students, set aside free time to decompress. Steph and her friends chose one approach: they wrote the titles of the chapters to be studied on little pieces of paper, put them in a shoebox, and took turns drawing them out. On Saturday afternoons they played a few games of ping-pong in a little neighbourhood youth club.

Being organised gradually began to pay off. Steph's grades were good, she was making progress in all areas, even in philosophy and it was cost-ing her less and less effort. Discipline had gradually seeped into her and arrayed her faculties in order of battle. She no longer woke up at five in the morning, could knock off twelve hours of work without complaint, and had lost weight, besides. The only shadow in the picture was a residual languor when she had a little free time, a kind of fog of anxiety, a why-bother worry. But she didn't have that much free time, anyway.

More than anything, her gift for maths had come to the fore during this second year. At school she'd never had any problem keeping up, in spite of her dilettantism. But in *préparatoire*, she came into her own as a maths whizz. Not only that, but she didn't have to work at it. Mathematics seemed to flow out of her in a quasi-miraculous way, like in those stories where heathens touched by grace suddenly start speaking in tongues. And in the world Steph was aiming for, maths was practically the lingua franca. Mathematics not only made planes fly and computers work, but also ordered civilisation, certified intelligence and founded innovation.

Monsieur Moineau, her economics professor, was the first person to give Steph a sense of how lucky she was. He took her aside after an oral exam, and they went for an espresso in a little cafe on rue Notre-Dame-des-Champs. He asked about her study habits, the amount of time she spent on her homework. He wanted to be sure she wasn't getting outside help. He also asked her what her parents did and whether she was seeing anyone. He used the English word 'boyfriend', probably to minimise the intrusiveness of his question. The word seemed so out of character, it amused her. How had he come up with such an expression?

Moineau was old-school, with a crew cut and rimless Affelou glasses, and casually dressed. He taught his classes with sarcastic detachment and wrote corrections in green ink. Rumour had it that he'd had a drinking problem. Apparently, he'd done Polytechnique and run the real estate department at BNP Paribas bank before his downfall. The tumble must have been a big one, because he once told them that he had twenty-five more years of contributions before he could retire on a full pension. And he was at least forty-five.

On the day they had their coffee, Moineau wore a very handsome tartan jacket that made him look like a green woodpecker, and a blue knitted tie that accentuated his pot belly. He seemed weary, as if he could use a sabbatical. Steph noticed tiny purple veins on the sides of his nose and thought she could never sleep with a guy who had that skin, that nose, or those yawning pores. If he ever made a pass at her, she would do her best to duck him. At worst, she was prepared to make a few concessions to keep up her average in economics – give him a handjob or let him feel her up. She wouldn't go so far as to blow him, however. Her sex life amounted to so little, anyway. But she was wrong about him. After a moment of intense thought, Moineau merely said:

'Good, good... In that case, aim high, Mademoiselle Chaussoy. Aim high.'

In May, Steph got to visit the HEC business school campus with a little group of her classmates, as a way of getting a feel for the place. She saw brightly lit offices, well-tended flower beds, high-tech equipment, and professors who were lively, prophetic and better paid than marketing directors. Steph's attention was especially drawn to the students. They were as lean as athletes, devoted to power and beautiful, just by knowing they were the best.

For Steph the visit served as confirmation. This was exactly what she wanted to do. This was exactly how she wanted to be.

She'd always had the feeling that outside of Paris, people only led second-class lives. Seeing this caste of hungry young people reinforced that impression. They alone knew; they alone were properly trained to understand how the world worked and how to move its levers. Everything else was crap, and the physicists, social sciences stars, *agrégés*, politicians, philosophers, lawyers, film stars and football players were all blind, impotent idiots. The people who intimately understood the machine and spoke the language of their time, those who embraced a perpetually accelerating era, exponential by nature, all-devouring, infused with light, speed and money, they were here, the economics princes and future business leaders in their blue shirts, with their smooth, sleek bodies, their terrifying drive.

Steph took her entrance competition exams in the spring and got her results in early July. The letters arrived one after the other. She was accepted at Lille, Lyon and Essec. There it was: the launch pad. She could relax.

Acting blasé and without a smile, Steph only told her that she'd succeeded in the entrance competition for Essec.

'Wow!' exclaimed Clémence.

'Yeah, gotta admit.'

'When I think that you didn't do shit at school.'

'True. But it seems so long ago.'

'What happened to you?'

'I don't know. I didn't want to come back here. I'm never coming back.'

'You amaze me.'

'There comes a time when you just gotta go for it.'

'Yeah, too true.'

'I don't care. I know what I want, and I'm not ashamed to be successful.'

They walked a little further to the white Peugeot 106 that Clémence drove when she was in town. It was her parents' runaround car, insured for liability only, dented but sturdy. Her father sometimes took it to the woods, hunting. The rest of the time it sat mouldering in the garage. The seats gave off an unpleasant smell of mildew. The girls rolled down the windows for some fresh air.

'Where are we going?'

'I dunno.'

'There's a pool at my place now,' said Steph.

'Well, that's it.'

'Cool.'

Steph was happy. In the last two years she hadn't experienced this kind of relaxation, the feeling that nothing needed to be done. She had nothing to study, no daily obligations to meet. Her parents had even stopped pestering her to clean her bedroom or wash the dishes. The future looked complete, ideal. She could just coast until classes started. She was enjoying this unaccustomed state of weightlessness when she said:

'You know, the timing of this dance is actually pretty good.'

'Why?'

"Cos it's been months since I've had sex.'

Clémence slapped the steering wheel and laughed.

'Are you serious?'

'Yeah. I was working like crazy. And the guys in my class, forget about it. Rejects.'

'Yeah, but still.'

'I dunno. I didn't even want to any more. My libido completely vanished.'

'So it's back now?'

'Fuck, yeah,' she said with a leer.

Clémence laughed again.

'But still, on a Bastille Day in Heillange, who are you going to get it on with? Some army private? A gypsy?'

'I don't care,' said Steph. 'Even your father, if worse comes to worst.'

4

Patrick Casati wanted to do things right. He got up early to buy fresh bait from Lamboley's and came back with his old Nesquik can half full of weevil grubs. Crawling around in there, the larvae looked really disgusting. He put the pierced cover back on and laughed, remembering how they so revolted Anthony when he was little. He got his fishing poles ready. Those bait tins must be almost fifteen years old by now. They dated from the time the boy still drank hot chocolate, holding his bowl in both hands, a cowlick on his head.

Patrick hadn't ever taken him fishing that often. It was a good idea to do it now, before he left.

He then didn't have much to do with his morning, aside from waiting. It was pretty easy to not start drinking before noon. He plopped down in front of the TV and started rolling his cigarettes for the week. He would roll them in advance and store them in an airtight metal box. He eventually dozed off with the tobacco and the roller in his lap. He'd spread a towel underneath so as not to spill stuff everywhere. He slept like that for quite a while, with his mouth open and his chin on his chest. The parade finally woke him up. On television, tanks were rolling down the

Champs-Élysées. Bands were marching, planes flying overhead, troops striding along as usual, geometry on the move. Seeing Chirac standing up straight in his Jeep and looking silly, he couldn't help laughing.

'Ah! The big guy!'

Patrick was now living in a studio apartment that supposedly was on the ground floor. In reality you had to go down five steps to get in, and the windows looked like basement windows. In all, he had a three-by-four-metre room at his disposal that served as a living room, kitchen and bedroom with a bathroom where the toilet was in the shower. He was handy with tools and had fixed the place up a little, in particular by building shelves, which freed up space. He slept in a twin bed that doubled as a sofa.

Patrick grabbed a tin for lunch, the first tin he came across. The cupboard over the sink was full of them. Cassoulet, boeuf bourguignon, couscous, ravioli – the basics. He poured the ravioli into a pot and heated it on the gas camping stove. It was ready in two minutes. And practical, with almost no dishes to wash. It wasn't like he ate right out of the pot, but it was close. He added a healthy shake of salt and pepper, then poured himself a big glass of red wine. Eaten from a tray in front of the TV, the meal didn't take much longer than its preparation. Since he'd misplaced the remote and was too lazy to get up, he had to watch the entire news programme. He ate an apple for dessert and treated himself to another glass of wine, full to the brim; it was a small glass. According to the little alarm clock at the head of the bed, it was almost two. The boy would be here any moment now. Patrick drained his glass, had a third one for luck, and fell asleep again.

Patrick was living a lethargic life on benefits in his studio apartment. He'd found a nice little job working for a private building manager, twelve hours a week at minimum wage. It consisted of doing the housekeeping at a couple of quiet residences, taking out the rubbish, mowing the lawn, weather permitting – being present, basically. It wasn't much, but old ladies would ask him to lend a hand from time to time. He would do a little carpentry and fix things and they would tip him. In the beginning, he felt crappy about the job because he would sometimes run into people he used to know. Mopping a floor in front of an old classmate was still something of an existential trial. But all in all, the job was as good as any other. Patrick had big debts and a tiny income, received a housing subsidy, and had the town's permission to cultivate a patch of land behind the Renardière football stadium. He tried to grow potatoes and onions, some parsley and had even planted strawberries. Each time he went he would take a case of beer with him. After the third can, he would put down his spade and sit in a camp chair, smoking cheap tobacco and looking at the turned earth. He could stay like that for a long time, without saying anything, doing nothing but drinking. As the sun set behind the stadium benches, he would be there, slumped in his chair and occasionally laughing to himself, surrounded by empty cans. He felt good.

As result, when the time came to harvest his potatoes, the yield wasn't that great. He mainly ate out of tins anyway. He went fishing, too. It was a diminished, anaesthetised life and he didn't ask himself too many questions. That's the way it was.

Patrick soon woke up, his mouth dry. The phone was stuck under his armchair. He pulled it out, grumbling. His mood had changed. Everything got on his nerves. On the TV, a guy was pitching mobile phone service in front of Mont-Saint-Michel. You could get a network connection everywhere now, apparently. Patrick was no more tempted to buy one of those filthy phones than fly to the moon. He turned the volume down and dialled his ex's number. He plugged his other ear, the better to hear.

'Hello.'

'It's me,' said Patrick.

Hélène said yes, she recognised him, she was used to it. Since they'd got over their coldness, he called her often. He would ask her to fill out his tax form or make him an appointment at the ophthalmologist. Among men of Patrick's generation, relations with the outside world went through the women. Those guys could pour a cement slab or drive two thousand kilometres without sleeping, but they found it almost physically impossible to invite someone to dinner.

'So is he coming, or not?'

'I'm sure he is, since he said he would.'

''Cos I've been waiting for him.'

'I know. Stop worrying.'

'I'm not worried.'

'All right.'

A silence followed.

'Did you watch the parade?' he asked.

'Yes.'

'The *légionnaires*.'

'Well, yeah. I saw them.'

'Feels funny, though.'

'What does?'

'That he's going there.'

'Yes, I know. I didn't sleep a wink last night.'

Hélène always had a good reason for not sleeping, worries, unless it was the phase of the moon. To hear her, she hadn't slept since May 1991.

After hanging up, Patrick had another glass of wine. He did the dishes. Because he was expecting Anthony, he had collected the empty bottles, five full bags and driven them down to the recycling bin. The apartment was immaculate. Then he opened the windows and smoked a cigarette lying on his bed, the ashtray perched on his chest. The television was still turned on, the volume low. Outside, the summer was beautiful. Patrick had known enough of them to know. It wasn't raining. In the clear sky, the few passing clouds served only to show the wind direction. Today was like yesterday and like tomorrow. He remembered the summers of his childhood, a veritable continent that his brothers and their friends moved to, emerging only when classes started again. Those were followed by summers broken up by jobs, girls, motorbikes. Then adult summers, almost unnoticeable, three weeks of mandatory paid holiday that always felt failed and inadequate. When he was unemployed he experienced other ones – slow, guilty summers spent stewing and brooding. And now this. He didn't know any more. He felt out of it. It both relieved and angered him.

What he especially couldn't stand was the waste of his strength. His father hadn't gone to school beyond the age of twelve; his mother, not much longer. He himself had dropped out at fourteen, and had consoled himself later by claiming that his certificate was worth more than a baccalaureate. During his whole childhood, his parents had raised him to dread idleness, to be contemptuous of *far niente*. He learned to cut wood, make a fire, lay tiles, fix a tap, patch a roof, maintain a house and garden, even do basic carpentry. He and his brothers spent their whole youth in the open air, gathering mushrooms and picking blueberries and plums. He had learned to ski thanks to Catholic youth programmes, even though he didn't go to church. In his world, people looked down on indoor occupations. They preferred leading collective, hard-working lives outside. Even the steel mill, that gigantic operation, was a kind of outdoors. Anything except sitting in an office holding a pen, debilitated by the act of thinking.

So he had ended up by himself, alone most of the time. He spent gloomy evenings sipping Picon-bière and falling asleep open-mouthed in front of the TV. He would wake with a start at three in the morning, a cold ache cutting across his lower back. The next day, he would struggle to get up and then had to work all day. After that he didn't feel like doing anything except going home. And there, it was the same thing all over again. Just one glass, that's what he promised himself. And then his willpower would weaken and he would polish off the cans one after another. This housebound repetition now made up the greatest part of his life. Sometimes, sunk in his armchair, he would look at his hands. A few brown spots had appeared on their backs, but they were still heavy and nice-looking. He felt empty, exhausted. He didn't feel like going out or seeing anybody. He'd got into fights with almost everybody, anyway. He would have liked to put those empty hands to work. Wrap them around a handle. They were made to use tools, to shape things. At times like that, fevers and anxieties would rise, turning him into a killer.

But Patrick Casati was happy, for once. His son was coming to see him and he felt proud. The boy would soon be in uniform, in Germany. He didn't tell himself that the boy was becoming a soldier. And he thought about war even less. Just one word went through his mind: 'military'. It carried a whiff of moderate heroism, order and discipline, and especially the same steadiness as a civil service job.

The poor kid really hadn't had much luck. They'd had him very early. Then there were the problems at the mill. Fear of what might happen tomorrow had wormed its way into their lives. The lack of money, the worries, the struggle fought on the line that separates the lower-middle class from the long-term poor. And finally the urge to drink, which had always been there.

When Patrick met Hélène, she was seventeen. She and her sister thought they were the sweethearts of the valley. They were kidding themselves. The Kleber girl was prettier. So was Chantal Durupt, who went off to Paris; they saw her in a Petula Clark Scopitone film. People didn't know what became of her, but with legs like hers, a good marriage or a career as a stewardess wasn't out of the question.

Except that Hélène had something else, something alluring and dangerous. Looking at Hélène was a little like having sex with her. At the time all the boys were sniffing around her, and she ordered her crew of idiots around like a conductor. That game had lasted decades. Hélène had never really wanted to give up her power over men. Nowadays, it was Patrick's turn to laugh. The witchcraft had completely dissipated. She had cut her hair; her arms had gone soft; her cheeks were sunken. Not to mention her breasts. He was happy. Hélène was neutralised.

And to think they weren't even fifty yet.

Their turn had come and gone quickly, and they hadn't got much out of it. This feeling of retreat had produced a new kind of understanding between them. It wasn't love any more, but a kind of weary tenderness, a disappointed faithfulness. They wouldn't hurt each other any more now. It was too late.

After a while Patrick fetched his present from the cupboard under the sink. He set it on the tiny desk and sat on a chair. It was almost three o'clock. 'That kid just doesn't give a shit about anyone,' he muttered. Patrick sat staring at the shiny wrapping paper and curly ribbon. His chair wasn't very comfortable, but he didn't dare go back to his armchair, for fear of falling asleep again. After half an hour he got up and snapped a can from the pack that had been intended for their men's outing. He drained three beers, eventually lay down and fell asleep as suddenly as if he'd been clubbed.

When he came to, it was past eight, he felt stiff all over, and the day was shot. The grubs were still busily crawling around in the Nesquik tin. The washed-out sky promised only emptiness. It didn't feel as pleasant as before. He closed the window and walked to the kitchenette. His lips were pursed, and you could hear him breathing from three metres away. It was a congested breath, heavy with thirty years of tobacco and full of gravel. He stared at the gift for a moment. Then he tore off the wrapping paper, opened the rectangular box, and grasped the beautiful hunting knife it contained. A superb weapon, it had a wide, almost black blade whose oblong, swollen shape looked like a Judas-tree leaf. Patrick had tested the edge on his forearm; it was razor-sharp. He slid the knife into its sheath, then slipped the sheath into his belt. Since Anthony hadn't come, he would go find him.

Before leaving his apartment, Patrick took a couple of beers for the road. He got into his 205 hatchback and headed for the lake. He was going to give him his present, like it or not. His fucking son.

5

So there they were, maybe not everyone, but a lot of them: the French.

The old, the unemployed, the big shots, the kids on motorbikes, the Arabs from the housing developments, the disappointed voters and the single-parent families, the prams and the owners of Renault Espace, the executives in Lacoste, the last workers, the sellers of chips, the babes in shorts, the slicks and, from further away, the rustics, the inbreds, and of course a few drudges for good measure.

They were coming to the lakeshore en masse, having parked for a few kilometres along the departmental motorway, in the fields, even in the forest. They moved in clumps, migrating, cheerful, frighteningly diverse and irreconcilable, yet side by side and ultimately pretty friendly.

They were all going in the same direction, towards the American beach, as it was called, though nobody could remember why. The name went all the way back to the sixties, when a guy who ran a military surplus store and sold imported jeans decided to build a drive-in there. He claimed to be from Texas and wore cowboy boots. That was all it took. His cinema didn't survive, but the name stuck.

When they got there, Stéphanie and Clémence found that things were already well under way. The stage had been set up for the speeches, and the city worker doing the sound check would send a blast of indifferent feedback over the crowd from time to time. There wouldn't be a band this year. It was too expensive and corny besides. A DJ would do just as well. There was also a big refreshment area, with long tables flanked by wooden benches with a guy under a plastic canopy selling chips and sausages. Theoretically, he had a monopoly, since he was the only one with a petty cash drawer and the necessary permits. Other people would still show up later though with a little barbecue or a deep-fat fryer and a transformer, and try to earn some scratch on the sly. By and large, the authorities turned a blind eye.

Some spectators had come early to get the best spots. They set up folding chairs along the shore and drank cold beers from colourful coolers while waiting for the show. A barge loaded with rockets floated a little distance offshore. The lake's surface still reflected the pale sky, but the light was already beating a hurried retreat, leaving behind a feeling of disorder and shadow, a rustle of trees surrounding the horde of spectators. A pleasant smell of barbecue, that summertime scent, drifted over all this. People seemed patient and were enjoying themselves. Steph and Clémence wandered around.

'Where should we sit?' asked Steph.

'I don't know. Let's just walk around.'

'I'd just as soon not run into my dad here.'

Before coming, the girls had stopped by Lamboley's to buy something to drink. It was Sunday, all the shops were closed, so the old guy was their only recourse. He had anticipated that. His garage, which offered the most unlikely groceries and never closed, was bursting with food and alcohol this evening. No one was quite sure he had the right to sell all that stuff. In blue overalls and T-shirt, he and his son and daughter served the clientele day and night. Even when the steel curtain was rolled down, you could just ring; there was always a way.

When the girls arrived they found all the local idiots standing in line. Young people mainly, but not only. Lamboley's efficiency was remarkable.

A guy would take his turn, ask for a case of beer and some guacamole. The old man would say, 'Of course.' His son would rummage in the jumbled back storeroom with its freezers and metal shelves, and return with the purchases. The customer would pay through the nose and it was on to the next. When it was Steph and Clémence's turn, they asked for a twelve-pack. Thirty-five francs.

'That's expensive!'

'That's the way it is.'

The old man, his blue overalls, his two kids. They paid.

On the way to the beach, they listened to the same song over and over, 'La Fièvre', with the lyrics *For hours, but she gave me the fever*. The girls were excited, in a mood to have fun, drinking beer as they drove. Steph was in charge of the Rewind button. Each time they heard the lyrics, it made them even crazier.

Before they got to the beach, they drank two more beers by a little country road that wandered through the woods. Then evening fell and the forest turned chilly. The girls felt nervous and drove on, leaving the beer behind. Squeezing into a parking spot, Clémence bumped the cars in front and behind. The girls were still laughing. Their flyaway hair got caught in their mouths. They finally reached the beach, which was already crowded. They were having a little trouble walking straight.

'Shit, if I run into my mother in this state, let's make a move.'

'No danger of that, with all these people.'

'Yeah, crazy how many losers this attracts.'

'Well, it looks like they all came. It's carnival time.'

'Yeah, totally. I'm wondering what we're doing here.'

'Hey, didn't you want to fuck?' asked Clémence sarcastically.

Steph grimaced. Suddenly she wasn't all that sure any more. She felt worried, compromised. She told herself she was going to ease off on the beer. She would walk around a bit, then ask Clémence to drive her home.

Gradually, they merged with the crowd. There was the smell, the music, the hubbub, the ceaseless blinking of faces. The girls were walking together, not talking any more. To them, everything was a spectacle. After a little while they bought a portion of chips and went to sit on some logs to eat them. Some guys passed and checked them out, yokels with shaved heads and Rangers. They wore sleeveless denim jackets over heavy metal T-shirts. Some of them were trying to grow beards, without much success. They got pushy, so Clémence gave them the finger and they moved on.

'Metalheads are funny. Soon as you check them out, there's no one home.'

'Yeah, well, everybody's pretty much the same. C'mon, let's move. I've had enough of this.'

'You're such a drag all of a sudden.'

Steph didn't respond. It was true, she was feeling weird.

'There are too many people.'

'Do you want to leave?'

'I dunno.'

Clémence stood and pulled her friend up by the arm; she weighed a tonne. They walked on, continuing their slow progress through the crowd.

Coralie and Hacine were walking hand in hand, with their dog. In other words, Hacine was in agony. Once they were past the refreshment stand, he told himself, he would drop her hand. They passed it. He didn't dare. They had already run into some friends from the old days, and it was awkward. He didn't quite know why, but he just couldn't get used to the business of being in a couple, walking around, kissy-kissy in the street. Girls were so weird. You wanted to fuck them, and then they got you to sleep over, and one thing leads to another, you start signing papers and making plans, and one bright day you don't recognise anything around you. You never go to any of the places you used to hang out. Childhood friends become complete strangers. And you start being mindful about putting the lid down before leaving the bathroom.

To be honest, Coralie hadn't demanded anything, and in fact was totally cool. As proof, Hacine's mates had played video games at their place for half the night. But a kind of slow slide had taken place, and Hacine had gradually dropped a thousand of his habits. He didn't regret it. His life was better, no doubt about it. When he felt blue, he wasn't alone to wonder if his life was less good than it could be, or if other people were better off than he was. Thanks to Coralie, he no longer experienced that gloomy feeling of total failure, of a wasted life. She distracted him, and sex with her was terrific. Even his in-laws were nice. It was just that when the two of them went into town, he was always afraid of being found out, as if he had something to blame himself for. Once in the light of day, this love story felt like a masquerade and he realised he was a poor actor, and all wrong for the part. He had dreamed of being a made man. He couldn't get used to this job of being a companion.

He sometimes wondered what had happened to all those people he'd lost sight of, Mouss, and Raduane, the gang. They were probably leading their lives as losers and petty criminals without him. Little Kader did some time in jail, two years for assault. Some stupid business about a fight at a red light. Hacine would have enjoyed seeing him again.

Coralie wanted to eat some chips and have a beer. Hacine paid, counting the money. Everything becomes expensive once you have to earn your living honestly. In the beginning there was something reassuring about getting a salary, compared with the unpredictability of business. But Hacine soon realised that for honest people, those tiny sums weren't a beginning, they were the standard. So you start calculating in shopping trolleys, or comparing the cost of your homeowners insurance with a trip to the Balearic Islands. Life becomes a series of anticipations, tiny nibbles and painless deprivations compensated for by pleasures that are never sufficient. For example, Coralie had been pestering him with the idea of going to a seawater therapy spa for a while now. A weekend for two cost almost five thousand francs. Hacine earned 7,240 francs a month. How could you enjoy two days in a bathrobe and flip-flops if you had to bust a gut for two years to afford it? Just thinking about it gave him a pain. And Coralie kept saying, 'You'll see, it'll do us good.'

Around nine o'clock the music paused, and she pulled Hacine closer to the stage. The mayor had climbed up and was flanked by an elegant woman with the face of a rodent and a fat, rotund man who was clearly in a very good mood, Pierre Chaussoy. Behind the stage you could see the smooth surface of the lake, and the ragged silhouettes of trees on the far shore. The speakers crackled.

'If I could have your attention…'

Silence fell, and the mayor started his speech. He was happy that people had come in such great numbers. He was happy with everything that was happening in the area. During the winter, they'd had the Christmas market, the new indoor gymnasium, and the auto show, which this year had beaten attendance records. In the summer, Heillange of course had its natural assets, and people had apparently come from far away to enjoy them. Saint-Tropez had better watch its step. But, beyond that, there was the canoe trail through town, the skate park, tennis courts, renovated swimming pool, miniature golf, campground, et cetera. And the mayor didn't intend to stop, now that they were on a roll. The town had other ambitions; it wanted to forge ahead. Pierre Chaussoy took the microphone and announced the big news. Next summer, Heillange would host a regatta. The announcement left the audience a bit dubious. What exactly is a regatta? asked a few curious people.

'I know that it might seem pretentious,' Pierre Chaussoy said very enthusiastically. 'It isn't really part of our region's culture. But I'm convinced that we have all that it takes to hold a prestigious event. I went to check out Annecy, Lugano and Lake Como. They don't have anything we don't.'

Though we might envy Lugano's low taxes, said the mayor with a straight face. The fat man resumed talking, stressing the benefits that were sure to be generated by such an event, but Hacine was no longer listening. He had started looking around. The other spectators were no more attentive. You could see mild amusement on their faces. A few jokers were laughing. At one point a drunk yelled, 'Get naked!' which amused his neighbours, but not his wife. After all, people didn't really care about Heillange's social and cultural life. They'd come for the noise, the light and the drinking. They were politely waiting for the speeches to be over. Hacine suddenly glimpsed something, but didn't have time to grasp what it was. The familiar face with the drooping eyelid had already disappeared.

Anthony had come by himself. He didn't want to see his father, or any of his friends, especially. He just wanted to savour the certainty that he was done with Heillange once and for all. It was a new feeling to be walking around with his hands in his pockets, almost like a tourist, in a landscape and a crowd that no longer concerned him. He was leaving tomorrow, at last.

As he listened to Steph's father's final words, he caught himself looking around for her. He would have really liked her to be there. It was the ideal moment for a last meeting. They would be playing as equals this time. Pierre Chaussoy wished everybody a good evening. The mayor did the same. The woman with the rodent face hadn't said anything and seemed disappointed.

'While waiting for the fireworks, I leave you in the expert hands of our DJ,' the mayor concluded, introducing a chubby young man in a white T-shirt with headphones around his neck. He started playing standard FM radio music that everybody already knew. Along with five thousand people, Anthony resumed his stroll. He was finishing a warm beer when he spotted his cousin. He was walking with his sister, Carine, and her boyfriend, Micka, flanked by a buggy and two kids; Killian was three and Julie was eighteen months. Anthony shook hands with the men, kissed Carine and the children. They exchanged a few simple words, awkwardly. It was nice to see them, anyway.

'So that's it, you're leaving?'

Carine said this with a look that was both a reproach and a compliment, her daughter on a hip, one hand on the buggy. Anthony found her profoundly changed. Her pregnancies had acted on her like a revelation. Back in the day, you would have thought her the ultimate lazybones. And now she belonged to the category of selflessly devoted mothers. With her first child, she plunged into her new role, leaving nothing of her teenage self behind; the girl had disappeared under a pile of nappies. At only twenty-two, she already displayed that power of resignation and tenderness, that unstoppable haemorrhage, overflowing with milk, tears, love and fatigue. Without any warning, she cut the bridges with her previous life to devote herself without regret to her progeny, becoming a full-time homemaker in the snap of a finger.

Carine's days now all followed the same rhythm of meals and naps. She woke the children up, warmed their milk, washed and dressed them, then did the ironing. The hissing pressure cooker sounded the noon whistle: potatoes, string beans and pork. She drank her coffee while absentmindedly watching the kids play. Around two o'clock, she treated herself to a little break, eating chocolates and watching her soap opera while the kids napped. The afternoon held its own series of chores and repetitions. Wake the kids, feed them, take them for a walk, come home, make dinner. Going out always meant going from the house to the doctor's office, to Leclerc, or to the playground. At home, the television was on twelve hours a day. There were three sets in the apartment. Her boyfriend, Micka, was a long-distance lorry driver and gone at least three nights a week. When he came home, exhausted, he plopped onto the sofa, where the children came to snuggle with him. By tradition, there was ice cream afterwards. Together, the family watched the screen with the nice taste of vanilla in their mouths. How could you hope for anything better?

Just looking at Carine, Anthony felt sick. It made him phenomenally depressed to consider generation after generation of these women getting beaten down, practically turning into nursemaids, doing nothing except ensuring the persistence of a progeny destined to the same joys and the same ills. In this dull obstinacy, he sensed the fate of his class. Worse, the law of the species, perpetuated through the unconscious bodies of these stay-at-home women with their wide hips and fecund bellies. Anthony hated the family. It promised nothing but a hell of continuation, with neither goal nor end. He himself would take trips and work miracles. He would let himself do things, though he didn't know quite what.

Meanwhile, he'd started chatting with his cousin. It was nice to be able to talk a little, even though Anthony was still getting all the news through his mother. After a while they decided to have a drink. Everybody sat down at the end of one of the long tables in front of the refreshment stand. There wasn't much room, so they squeezed together. Micka volunteered to get the drinks. He was a nice guy, with calves like posts that emerged from cut-off Adidas shorts. Anthony's cousin was pretty talkative, for once. He'd had quite a few setbacks in the last year and talked about them in a fairly detached way, like a guy who had seen it all. Which couldn't hide his basic disappointment. He had finally separated from his idiotic girlfriend. Anthony was hardly surprised but kept the comment to himself. Aside from that, he had a new job in Luxembourg, delivering lunches to decision-making executives in glass towers.

'Everybody there drives a Bimmer,' said his cousin. 'They've got it all worked out.'

Anthony agreed. Like everyone else in the valley, he was forever hearing about Luxembourg and its astronomical salaries, ridiculously low taxes, and that terrific perk, the company car. The need for manpower in the duchy was such that the authorities arranged things so that workers on the other side of the border could commute in a Mercedes, a BMW 5 Series or an Audi Quattro without spending a centime. Seen from Heillange, it looked like heaven on earth.

That wasn't the cousin's situation, unfortunately. He lived close to the border in a small two-bedroom place and had to get to work by his own means. Micka came back with the beers. Excited by the imminent fireworks, the children were out of control. Carine alternated threats and promises, starting all of her sentences by saying, 'I'm warning you...' without much result. When they raised their beers, she drank hers nearly in one gulp. Everybody bought a round, and Anthony insisted on buying chips for the kids. The adults nibbled from the chip boxes. The table was soon covered with food and tumblers. Everybody was in a good mood, even though the children were squealing and writhing. Anthony and his cousin gazed at the lake with a touch of nostalgia. Important things had happened there. Anthony needed to take a leak. He was drunk. He was getting more and more thirsty.

'I'll be back,' he said.

'Hurry, it'll be any moment now.'

He stood up and tried to stay straight as he walked to the chemical toilets that had been set up for the occasion a little further on. The guy in charge of the sound was clearly a big fan of the group Indochine.

Anthony had already recognised 'L'Aventurier' and 'Trois nuits par se-maine'. 'Canary Bay' was playing for the second time. 'This is my last night,' he thought.

Patrick had taken a little walk before bumping into Rudi at the bar and they started to drink, sitting side by side. Rudi didn't have much money, so Patrick was buying. Soon, the barber joined them. Leaning against the counter, the three men enjoyed the spectacle, drinking un-hurriedly, watching the other customers, the aquatic movement of the crowd and the young brunette serving the beer. She was dressed in black, moving fast, answering the wisecracks with a smile, not that pretty but sexy and, as a barmaid, the centre of attention. Rudi, especially, was obsessed with her. At one point, as she set three fresh glasses in front of them, he touched her wrist. She jerked her arm back and went to say a few words into the owner's ear.

'You're an arsehole,' said the barber.

'What do you mean?' asked Rudi.

The owner told them to watch their little friend, or things would get ugly. Patrick promised he would.

'I'm warning you, if he does it again, I'll punch his lights out, handicap or no handicap.'

'I'm not handicapped,' said Rudi.

'Yeah, right.'

The owner had a moustache so big you could barely see his lips under it. Patrick knew him from rugby; the guy coached the little kids. Anthony had been enrolled for three years when he was small.

'We'll keep an eye on him. No problem.'

The barber went 'Heh-heh', and they left it at that.

'Stop messing around, Rudi. Are you out of it or something?'

'She was looking at me.'

'The hell she was.'

'You don't usually bother girls. What's going on?'

'I dunno. I thought she was looking at me.'

'We all need love,' said the barber philosophically, raising his glass.

'That's for sure.'

Patrick turned his back to the bar and resumed studying the crowd. He enjoyed the state he was in, drunk, bitter, all-powerful. There wasn't much chance of finding his boy in this flood of faces and light, anyway. He grunted and took another swallow of beer. Rudi had turned round as well. His unblinking eyes shone like lead in his hedgehog face. He was staring, lost, his mouth agape.

'Over there!' he said, pointing.

Patrick tried to follow his gaze, and in fact a figure that could well be Anthony had just left a table full of people. Rudi's finger was still in the air. Patrick didn't even bother asking him how he knew. Drunks, idiots and saints, all those people basically belonged to the same natural order.

'I'll be back.'

He emptied his glass and tried to make his way through the crowd. It wasn't easy. He grumbled as people kept coming in the other direction. He checked to see that the knife was still there, stuck in his belt under his polo shirt. He eventually found the cousin and Carine, along with some kids and a little fat guy who looked vaguely Hispanic.

'What do you know!' he said.

'Hi there.'

The cousin offered him a seat. A baby was perched on Carine's thigh. The other guy had a nice smile and was playing with another kid. Introductions were made. Patrick discovered the extent of this family, which had grown in his absence. He remained standing, feeling chagrined. The kids were sweet, even if their noses were running and they looked scruffy from playing under the table. He pretended to steal little Julie's nose between his fingers.

'Bingo!'

The girl's eyes widened. Patrick caught Carine looking at him askance. He was just a drunk, after all.

'So what's happening with you?'

'Not much. What about you?'

'I'm gettin' by.'

'Lotsa people, eh?'

'Yeah.'

Patrick looked for cigarettes in his pockets. The cousin offered him one.

'Here.'

He gave him a light. 'Thanks.' 'You're welcome.' Patrick no longer quite knew what tack to take. He was thirsty already.

'How's your mother?'

'Same as always,' said the cousin.

Patrick drew thoughtfully on his cigarette and nodded slowly.

These kids, he'd known them since they were this high. They had played at his house. He had treated them to carousel rides and swum with them at the pool. He cleared his throat.

'You haven't seen Anthony, have you?'

This caused an odd exchange of glances over the table. Nobody wanted to speak. Eventually the cousin took the plunge.

'Yeah, he was here five minutes ago. He went to take a piss.'

'He was supposed to come and see me,' Patrick explained.

The young people didn't react, of course. Why the hell should they care? Patrick suddenly felt a little weary. He stubbed out his cigarette and smiled.

'All right, I'll leave you to it.'

'Have a good evening.'

'If you see Anthony...'

'We'll tell him, no problem.'

He made his way back to the bar, carefully putting each foot firmly on the ground. He didn't want them to see him swaying. This whole thing was beginning to seriously piss him off. Reaching the counter, he found Rudi and the barber, along with his tin of cigarettes. He lit one and gestured to the moustachioed owner to serve him another beer. He didn't ask the other two men if they wanted something.

Anthony quickly sized up the situation. If you wanted to take a piss, the beach had a grand total of three toilets, blue plastic cabins, with a queue twenty-five metres long in front of each one. Women, mostly. Once they saw the line, guys headed for the woods. Anthony did the same. He wanted to find himself a quiet spot, but even there, it was crowded. He went deeper among the trees. Soon the darkness of the forest closed around him. At his back, the party was nothing more than a muffled yellow pulsing. He took a few more steps. The foliage barely rustled. He unbuttoned his flies.

Whenever he found himself in this kind of situation, he started thinking of the inbreds. He couldn't help it. When he was ten or twelve, he and his cousin used to spend entire afternoons watching horror movies. They closed the shutters, sat on the floor and gazed up at the screen. The game consisted of seeing how long they could stand it. At times, the fear became so intense that Anthony closed his eyes. That only left the sound, and the fright took on a superlative dimension in his mind. After that he would have nightmares for days. Even at school, or at home, he would feel presences, sensing things lurking in dark corners. He jumped at the slightest sound, refused to go to the toilet by himself. His mother even talked of taking him to a therapist. Luckily his father scotched that idea. Then the boys moved on to pornos, the cousin taped Ashlyn Gere and Christy Canyon on Canal, and Anthony's sleep improved.

Being there in the woods with his cock hanging out brought back all those vague fears. A shiver ran down the back of his neck. It wasn't really cold, but there was a prickly dampness in the air that fell from the branches and slipped under your collar to your skin. He thought he saw a shape passing between the tree trunks in front of him. Eyes wide, he stared into the emptiness. Something pale again caught his eye. His scrotum promptly tightened. The hairs on his forearms stood up. Then he recognised the familiar wet sound of urine hitting the soft soil of the forest.

Only he wasn't pissing.

Breathless, he buttoned his flies. He didn't dare move.

'Hey there!'

Anthony jumped, and whipped round to see where the voice was coming from. A guy was just pissing behind a tree, only a few metres away.

'Oh, man, I really freaked out!'

'Heh-heh,' said the guy.

Just hearing him, it was as if someone had turned on a light. At that, Anthony was able to go back to doing what he'd come for. He pissed for a long time, with pleasure, reassured by the presence of the other man, occupied just as he was in relieving himself against a tree. When the other guy was finished, he took a step towards Anthony, and said:

'I can't stand this place.'

'The beach?'

'No, the forest. I don't know, it gives me the creeps.'

'Me too.'

Anthony couldn't see the man but from his voice he imagined he was young, friendly, and a little loaded, just like him. In the distance the first notes of 'La Bamba' could be heard. He shook off the last drops and buttoned his flies. The other guy was waiting. Out of politeness, in a way. Anthony wiped his hands on his jeans and joined him.

'Shit.'

He and Hacine had bumped into each other for the first time in a long time. Somewhat stunned, they remained speechless for a long moment. They didn't know quite how to handle the encounter.

'So what do we do?' asked Hacine.

Anthony didn't have the slightest idea. Fortunately, just then the music stopped and the lights at the beach were switched off. The two boys found themselves in total darkness. A murmur ran through the motionless crowd of spectators as the first rocket soared above the lake, drawing a long curve of glittering sparks. It exploded very high up, very far away, amazing. The opening lyrics of 'Who Wants to Live Forever' rang out pompously. Anthony found himself alone again. Hacine had left. Behind him, the forest weighed like a memory. He hurried back to his cousin and the others.

6

On the beach, a thousand faces were lifted to the sky, reflecting bursts
of red, blue and white light. Roman candles shot up through the night,
sparkling and rigid, before thumping people's chests and blasting their
eardrums. It was a swarm of light, a cascade of colour and thunder. City
Hall had gone all out this time.

Even Steph and Clémence couldn't find anything to mock, despite
the deeply gregarious atmosphere, despite Céline Dion and Whitney
Houston. The sound and light captivated them, and they forgot to keep
themselves detached. Nearby, a father held his daughter in his arms as
she said, 'Beautiful red one … Beautiful blue one,' her finger pointed at
the sky. Even the police had their noses in the air. The whole valley was
looking in the same direction. It was 14 July, Bastille Day.

The final display was launched to the strains of 'Que je t'aime'. Steph
felt Clémence leaning against her. Their eyes were shining with the same
damp spark while the lyrics *my body on your body* kneaded their bellies
with a brute, animal emotion, an irresistible grip.

And then it was over, people whistled and applauded, and everybody rushed off to get a drink. The audience had worked up quite a thirst. Now the dancing could start.

Very quickly, the mood changed. What had begun as ambling goodwill turned into a kind of frenzy. Bodies heated by alcohol, noise and fatigue mindlessly attracted and repelled each other. On the dance floor, couples began to sway under garlands of light bulbs. The DJ, who knew his classics, started the dancing with the Jackson Five, then Gloria Gaynor. If you looked, you could glimpse beads of sweat in their cleavages. The old people cast an affectionate gaze over all this disorder. Some of them were nodding off. The teenagers, on the other hand, were in no danger of falling asleep. Tightly wound and pretending to be cool, they watched each other along the edge of the dance floor, their eyes like daggers. For each generation, desire had to overcome the same shyness. It's such a drag not knowing how to do that.

Steph and Clémence had also stepped onto the dance floor. Anthony found them there when he came back from the forest. They were dancing, a little shakily, copying each other's moves, arms in the air, doing a whole number, and looking very pretty. After a couple of songs, they whispered something to each other and Clémence left the dance floor.

This seemed like the right time.

'Hi there,' he said.

Steph turned to him. It took her two full seconds to realise who he was.

'Damn, look who it is!'

She was smiling broadly. They tried to talk, but the music was too loud. She took the initiative to leave the dance floor.

'So what have you been up to?'

'I'm in Paris now,' she said.

'Cool.'

'Are you joking? I'm studying like a maniac. I've put on ten kilos.'

Anthony looked her over. Much of the extra weight had clearly gone to her breasts. The strap of her top was cutting into the skin on her shoulder, the way her bikini strings once cut into her hips.

'Hey there!' said Steph, snapping her fingers under his nose.

'You're beautiful.'

'That's so stupid...'

All the same, hearing this pleased her, and she struggled to hide it. Just then Clémence came back carrying two tumblers of beer.

'I couldn't find you. Where were you?'

'I was here.'

Steph didn't know what to say. Anthony kept quiet. They'd got off on the wrong foot.

'Am I in the way, by any chance?' asked Clémence.

'Of course not.'

Nothing was happening. The music blared. Anthony chose to sacrifice himself.

'I'm getting myself something to drink. I'll be back.'

'Right,' said Clémence.

There you had it: dead in the water again. Anthony tried to look cool as he walked away, though he felt completely disgusted. He'd come here to enjoy himself, to take one last breath of this shithole town before leaving forever and Steph had screwed everything up, as usual. He couldn't even turn round, because she and her bitch friend were probably watching him. He went to join the queue for the bar. He was dying to look over his shoulder but didn't dare. It all made him feel like hitting something, hurting himself, though he thought he'd got over all that. Girls...what a plague!

'Hey!'

Anthony turned round. Steph was walking towards him, alone. Her friend had disappeared. A miracle.

'Can you drive me home a little later?' she asked.

'Of course.'

'Clémence had to go, and it felt like a drag having to leave.'

'No problem.'

'Okay, but don't go getting any ideas.'

Too late. Anthony was already hoping for everything. He got his beer and they went off to one side, at the edge of the woods, to talk. Actually, talk mainly meant sitting on the grass, waiting. Steph asked him questions. He answered yes or no, evasively, almost unable to look at her. He in turn tried to find out what she'd been doing these last two years. She wasn't much more talkative. None of this was happening the way it was supposed to.

'You're a pain,' said Steph.

So he turned and kissed her. Their teeth banged together. It was a rough kiss, one last chance. It hurt her and she grabbed him by the hair. They nearly lost their balance. They closed their eyes, their tongues tangled, their hearts beat fast. Gradually, the clumsiness fell away. They tumbled over onto the scratchy grass, him on top of her. He kissed her cheeks and her cheekbones, breathed into her neck. He was heavy and Steph felt herself yielding under this weight of a man, opening up to him. She wasn't thinking about anything any more for once. And neither was he. They were excited, and it was the end of the world. But as he began to fumble in her knickers, she changed her mind.

'Wait.'

'What?'

'My parents are here. I don't want them to catch me getting off with some guy.'

'They can't see us. We're cool here. We're not doing anything wrong.'

'Still…'

To get out of it, Steph said the first thing that came to her mind:

'Anyway, I want to dance.'

'Are you serious?'

'Come on, I love this song.'

'I don't feel like dancing.'

But it was already settled. She pushed him aside and quickly straightened her clothes.

'Come on. It's not late, you can fuck me later.'

In his career as a drinker, Patrick Casati had known various eras. The era of mates and parties, which left you with a patchy memory and was dealt with in the morning with two aspirins and a Coke. Later came the binges that lasted several days, followed by self-pitying repentance, where he went so far as to lecture his friends and consider returning to the Church. He had also known the phase of continuous, medium-intensity drunkenness, bottles hidden in the changing room and chewing gum for breath, the thousand slip-ups at work that his friends covered up for him, the good times laughing at the bistro and the gloomy return home. Those ended in shouting matches, sleeping on the living-room sofa, and the boy seeing it all. After Metalor shut down, there was therapeutic drinking, to relax, cheer yourself up, forget your problems; even the unemployed have a right to have a little fun, for fuck's sake. There had been times when he stopped for good, not even having a drink at the weekend. Which basically consisted of waiting for the backsliding, when a drink would eventually do him in – just a splash of port, and then the deep dive. At times like that, when he wasn't drinking, Patrick didn't want to go out or see anybody; Christmas became a threat. He was afraid of his friends, afraid of happy hour each evening. Around seven, the need would make itself felt, always. Nothing to beat yourself up over, but the temptation of a drink, just one. It couldn't do any harm. The drink had its moments, and also its voice. That of the friend who knows that life is short, that we'll all wind up in a hole, may as well enjoy ourselves. So Patrick would take just one break, and the next day find himself completely screwed up, and having to start all over again.

Those phases had followed each other again and again, in confusion, he had experienced them all. But they were nothing like what was happening now. Now he was drinking like an athlete aiming for a personal best, like a bodybuilder seeking the weight he couldn't lift, the one that would leave him drained. And during this whole effort, until he fell asleep, Patrick lived like a king. All-powerful, brutal, generating fear and trembling because you knew at a glance that he was capable of anything and that his thirst had no other end except the cemetery.

'All right, this isn't the whole story.'

He and Rudi had found themselves a little spot where they could watch the dance floor without people seeing them. They quietly emptied a bottle they'd stolen from one of the tables. It had practically nothing left. They lay stretched out, leaning on their elbows, legs crossed. They weren't waiting for anything; they were just there.

'I'm gonna go.'

'Where?' asked Rudi.

'Nowhere. If I stay here, I'll fall 'sleep.'

'So what?'

'I don't wanna fall asleep, tha's all.'

Patrick stood up as best he could. He was swaying on his heels. He patted himself down.

'What are you looking for?'

'My knife.'

'Where d'ya put it?'

'Rhaaa.'

Patrick knelt down, felt around and found it. He slipped the knife back in his belt and pulled his polo shirt over it. Then he grabbed the bottle.

'I'm finishing this.'

Rudi didn't react. Not that he had any choice. Patrick was looking the way he did on bad days, anyhow. His mouth shrunk to a bitter slit and the skin tight over his cheekbones, he looked like a corpse. He didn't have many more drinks ahead of him, and firmly intended to down them all. He raised the bottle to his lips and drained it.

'That's some more that the Germans won' get.'

He was now in a state of terrible drunkenness, buzzing and metallic. He looked at the idiot with his spiky hair, his already deep wrinkles, his poignant, dazed look. Poor Rudi was useless, just getting nowhere and no woman would ever give in to him. He would be just as well off dead.

'Home safe,' said Rudi.

Patrick snickered and made a move. He was stooped, breathing hard, still holding the bottle. Soon he was weaving between the tables. He had to use his shoulders and hands to make his way through. People didn't want to move their arses. They stepped on his toes. Some kids shoved him. Little niggers, even. Need just one last drink, then go home. He was sure he'd find someone to drive him back. He stopped for a moment at a table, sitting down astride a bench. He looked over the table. There were abandoned tumblers with dregs of beer and red wine. He drank everything he found. He noticed some people looking at him. A whole family, with the grandparents and the kids.

'What?'

Nothing. They didn't have anything to say. Cowards. He wanted to stand up but his legs got tangled in the bench, and before he knew it, he lost his balance and smashed face first onto the ground. The father of the family hurried over.

'Wait, don't move!'

Patrick's face was pressed against the ground, his legs in the air. He was trapped. He let the guy straighten him out.

Once on his feet again, he touched his forehead. It didn't hurt, but blood had started dripping onto his polo-shirt and his shoes. The whole side of his nose was scraped. He felt it with his finger, which sank in. Facing him, the man grimaced in a way that said a lot.

'You're pretty banged up, you know.'

'Is it deep?'

The guy took Patrick's wrist and pulled his hand away, the better to see.

'Yeah, it is.'

Patrick checked his teeth with his tongue. He had a taste of metal in his mouth; he was bleeding. But no damage, apparently.

'It's nothing,' he said.

He looked at his hands, his clothes. The guy's wife pulled a pack of tissues from her handbag, and her husband offered them to him.

'It'll be okay,' he said.

'Still, it's really bleeding a lot.'

Patrick felt a little foolish, his legs wobbly. He held his hand out to see if it shook. Tomorrow, he would have no memory of this, only scrapes and bruises. His hand was shaking hard.

'Let's go and see the medics.'

'Nah, it's okay. I've been though worse.'

He wiped himself with a tissue. When it was wet with blood he stuffed it in his pocket and used another one. It took two more before the bleeding stopped. The guy was insisting that they go and see the paramedics. He was a friendly, corpulent man with a pitted face and grey hair. His whole family was watching him. A regular hero.

'Leave me alone, dammit!' said Patrick.

He wrenched himself free. He wasn't very steady on his feet.

'I'll manage.'

And he left, one step after another.

The shock had woken him up a little. He wandered over to the dance floor. The light had been turned blue to accompany the slow numbers, and he fell to studying the entwined couples shuffling around on the plywood. His hands felt like anvils at the end of his arms. He mopped his brow with a tissue from time to time. That gesture alone cost him the last of his strength. It was past midnight. Long past.

That's when he saw his son, dancing with a girl. He was holding her tight, and the two kids were moving with the slowness of a jellyfish. In his nasal voice, Eros Ramazzotti was singing about the pain of love, and every embracing couple seemed overcome by the serious sense of their destiny. The women were remembering vague sorrows. Even the men had lowered their guard, and their faces showed a baffled awareness, like disappointment. By the light of this poor tune, life suddenly appeared to them as it was, a muddle, a series of false starts. The Italian's sad song was whispering in their ear the secret of ill-lived lives, diminished by divorces and deaths, worn out in work, gnawed everywhere, sleepless nights and loneliness. It gave you something to think about. You loved and you died, too; you were the master of nothing, neither your best efforts nor your end.

That kind of thought had no room in Anthony's head, however. He was dancing with his girlfriend, they were glued together, indistinguishable, mixing their hair and their sweat. Patrick saw the boy's hand slide up his partner's back. His son spoke into the girl's ear. The song ended. And they disappeared, without holding hands or anything.

Patrick stood there for a moment like that, panting, unable to move. He wasn't even thirsty any more. He just knew one thing: he didn't want to go to sleep.

7

Hacine was totally fed up. Coralie had run into some friends from work, and there was no escaping them. He'd been forced to sit down and have drinks with them. There were three couples, and if there was one thing Hacine hated in his new life, it was having to hang out with other couples. Sooner or later, the men would always wind up together, talking among themselves. You had to play the game. A guy wearing boat shoes and a Mise au Green shirt started talking about how he planned to upgrade his apartment so he could buy a bigger one. Seriously, why the fuck would anyone care about that? Besides, Soizic and Romain had just bought a dog, a totally moronic pug that kept bothering Nelson. Hacine would have liked to fire a load of buckshot at it, to see how he liked it. He couldn't even do any real drinking, since he was going back to work the next day. Coralie, who must've realised that something was wrong, put a hand on his knee. She gave him a squeeze from time to time to remind him to behave. He got the message.

Hacine was all the angrier because when he went to take a piss, he ran into that little shithead with the twisted eye. Granted, the valley was narrow, gloomy and inbred, but this was really too much. On top of that, he'd had to slink off like a coward, because he had to rejoin the other morons at their table. Ever since, he'd been feeling weird, like being on probation and especially like he was being spied on. He constantly glanced at his watch and looked around to see if someone was about to jump him. Meanwhile, Rémi and his girlfriend were trying to convince Coralie and him to go skiing with them. Hell.

'Just for a weekend.'

'I've got an agreement with the head of my company. Three days at the chalet, and it doesn't even come to five hundred francs a head.'

'But I don't ski,' said Hacine.

'That doesn't matter. You'll see, it's beautiful in the mountains.'

Coralie insisted and Hacine's misgivings became less and less audible. You'd think he was crazy to pass up such a wonderful opportunity to freeze his balls off.

'No, I mean it. You guys can go without me.'

'But it's just two days.'

'Two days is nice. We'll make fondue. You'll drink mulled wine.'

This went on and on, to the point where Hacine began to wonder if they were doing it on purpose, just to annoy him. He finally dropped out of the conversation and let his gaze wander. There were already fewer people around. On the dance floor, the DJ was playing a series of slow numbers, as much to get people to dance as to calm them down. A man was staggering along the edge of the dance floor.

'No…' Hacine muttered under his breath.

'What is it?' asked Coralie.

Hacine was on his feet. He recognised the man over there, who seemed about to fall down. It was the guy who had destroyed his mouth.

'Oh!' said Coralie, trying to grab his hand.

Hacine's face had totally changed. It almost scared her.

'Is something wrong?' asked Soizic.

He couldn't really make out the man's face, but that didn't matter. He would have recognised that look anywhere, even in the dark with his eyes closed. Five weeks of hospitalisation and two months of convalescence had written it in his guts.

Around the table, everyone had fallen silent. The two other couples exchanged meaningful glances. Speaking in a low voice, Coralie tried to salvage the situation:

'Stop it! What's got into you?'

The man at the edge of the dance floor still seemed unsure whether to stand up or lie down. Then he started walking again. Hacine immediately stepped away from the bench. Coralie tried to stop him. Her hand closed on emptiness.

'It's nothing,' she said with a weak smile.

They all acted as if that were true.

Meanwhile, the man began walking at a good clip in spite of his drunkenness and at first Hacine had trouble keeping up. Then they moved away from the dance, and the festivities gradually faded behind them. Soon they were alone, and all that remained was a dull murmur in the distance. They continued onwards, heading south, with only twenty or thirty metres between them. The man swung close to the shore and his lurches sometimes left him splashing in the water. But he kept stubbornly on, relentlessly moving towards the end of the beach. It was the lake's biggest, almost three kilometres long. There was something in his determination, his drunken heaviness, that suggested a beast of burden, like he was accomplishing a task almost in spite of himself.

In ten minutes they reached the point where the sand turned to mud, a swampy tangle of rushes, brambles and tall grass. Only then did Hacine dare look behind him. Without realising it, they had covered quite some distance. For his part, the man walked on, then found a flat rock and sat down on it. With legs bent and arms draped over his skinny knees, he gazed out at the lake and the night. Hacine bent over and got closer, then knelt down to watch him. What he saw between the rushes and the grass was a motionless shape, like an Indian. The man wasn't doing anything. Every so often a croaking sound broke the silence. Hacine waited for the right moment.

Then the man seemed to pass out. His head became too heavy and slumped onto his chest. Hacine thought this was it, now. But the man almost immediately awoke and shook himself, grumbling. He got to his feet, still muttering what sounded like curses and criticisms. He continued to complain as he removed his shoes, with some difficulty, before taking off his shirt, trousers and socks. And finally his pants. Once naked, he cautiously walked into the water up to his waist. He stretched out on the surface, first on his back, floating like an otter. Then, without warning, he started swimming away from shore.

'What the fuck is he doing?' wondered Hacine.

The man's pale arms were flailing in clumsy strokes, but he was swimming. Hacine stood up, the better to see. But the man's shape was already almost out of sight, disappearing in the distance, in the mix of water and darkness for lack of a horizon. Hacine glimpsed a sort of whitish band, then nothing.

He hurried over to the flat rock where the clothes were piled. The water lapped gently at his feet. He couldn't see a thing. Everything was black as ink. His heart was thudding against his ribs.

'Hey!' he shouted.

Then again, in a laughably childish way:

'Hey, you!'

But his calls didn't ring true. He waited a good long time, scanning the expanse of water and night stretching before him. He would have liked to leave but couldn't bring himself to do it. Something in him, some incongruous hope, resisted. Finally, he searched through the things the man had left on the flat stone. There wasn't much; no watch, no wallet, just his clothes and a knife, a beautiful hunting knife that Hacine slipped in his belt. He had nothing to feel guilty about. He then walked through the woods to the road. During the whole way back, he thought about the man and his son. Hacine felt he had the soul of a killer. It wasn't unpleasant.

8

The Opel Kadett was parked far away and Anthony and Steph were walking along the departmental motorway, tired now, and not as drunk. From time to time they had to step aside when a car passed; it was quite late, and the motorway shoulder was empty. Their hands touched occasionally. Everything became serious and precious. They kept quiet, thinking of what was to come. Neither of them wanted it to end like this, unresolved.

'Here we are,' said Anthony.

He had spotted his car in the distance, alone on the side of the road. They covered the last metres dragging their feet. Steph got in on the passenger side, and Anthony sat down behind the wheel. He was about to turn the ignition when she said:

'Wait.'

He waited. You couldn't see anything through the windscreen. They might as well have been lost on the high seas. Steph lowered her window a bit to get some fresh air, turning the squeaky crank. The moonless, indifferent sky weighed down on the little car's square roof. From the surrounding countryside came tiny, continuous rustlings.

'It's sweltering.'

'Yes,' said Anthony.

'What time are you leaving tomorrow?'

'I'm getting a train a little after ten.'

'Come here.'

She leaned towards him and their mouths met above the gearstick. Anthony, who had closed his eyes, reached for Steph's breasts. Touching her body through the bra, it felt almost solid. He pressed, and Steph giggled.

'What?'

'Nothing.'

'C'mon, what is it?'

'It's nothing. You're touching my breasts like they're made of plastic.'

'They are a little like plastic.'

'Idiot!'

'Really, they're super hard.'

'They're firm.'

She arched her back, showing off.

'Come and see.'

He felt them again.

'So?'

He felt her through the vest top, then touched the bare skin in her cleavage with his fingers.

'Now here, it's soft.'

He ran his hand across the naked space between the straps of her vest top, and slipped his index finger into the dip between her breasts.

'You're sweating...'

Steph reached behind her back and unhooked her bra. She slipped the straps off her shoulders, pulled the thing out the side. Then she took the top off over her head. The faint starlight just barely revealed the oval of her shoulder, the weight of her breasts. Anthony had wanted to see them for so long. He took them in his hands. The feeling was incredible – and almost immediately inadequate. Breathing hard, he hurriedly started exploring, then bit one of her nipples. Steph gave a little cry. He

364

had hurt her. Her knickers were getting wet. She hoped he wouldn't waste too much time feeling her up. Guys tended to get lost doing that, and she preferred to have them slip a hand into her knickers and really caress her. She wanted to spread her legs wide. She grabbed Anthony's face with her hands and the kisses started again. For once she needed speed, to wrap it up. Also to repress a strange urge to weep that was rising in her, though for no good reason. It was late, she was tired. She hung on to him and Anthony took her in his arms. That is, he tried to, because the gearstick was definitely in their way. They got increasingly annoyed, driven by a fierce hunger, kissing like high-school kids, their hands wandering everywhere, the car's interior full of sighs and rustlings. Their cheeks and foreheads met. She bit him. She was dying for it. She sobbed.

'Something wrong?'

'I'm fine, it's nothing. I'm just tired.'

She climbed over the gearstick and straddled him.

'Hey, there…' he murmured consolingly, wiping away her tears with his thumb.

She bumped him with her forehead.

'Stop it. I'm fine, I'm telling you. I want it. Fuck me now.'

She tackled the flies of his jeans, which had buttons, what a nuisance. 'Help me.'

He arched his back to open his flies and Steph's head nearly hit the car roof. But she didn't care, she was rubbing against him, she could hardly wait.

'Hurry.'

She thrust her hand down between them, touching his cock through his pants. She was languidly rocking against him. He felt hard against her knickers. She pulled them aside, freeing her pussy. They were almost there when a noise distracted them.

'What was that?'

'Wait.'

A buzzing could be heard behind them, nasal at first and steadily getting louder.

'What is it?'

'It's kids. Don't move.'

She flattened herself against him. He used the occasion to pull off the elastic holding her hair.

'Hey, not so fast!' she said.

'Shh!'

Headlights appeared in the rear window, their beams lighting up the inside of the car. It was delicious and freaky. Motorbikes passed them, snarling and insulting, then went off down the departmental motorway, leaving only the red wavering of their tail lights in the distance, which disappeared in turn.

'That was weird, wasn't it?'

'They didn't see us.'

'Yeah, but I dunno...Did you get the feeling they were slowing down?'

''Course not.'

'Who were they?'

'It's nothing, don't worry about it.'

Still, it had cooled things a little. Steph was thinking.

'I'm going to take off my shorts. That way, we'll be ahead of the game.'

Anthony laughed. She was right, it was a good idea. But to do it, Steph had to overcome a number of obstacles, namely the tightness of the passenger compartment, the lack of light, and the awkward gearstick. She finally managed to get onto her knees and slip her shorts off. She had plain cotton knickers on underneath. A roll of her belly hung over the elastic waistband.

He touched her thighs. The skin was soft, the flesh underneath smooth and generous. His fingers sank in deep.

'Stop that.'

'It's a turn-on.'

'Well, so much the better. But stop it. I feel like a fat cow.'

She got back into position over him and he grabbed her hips.

'You have any condoms?'

'In my pocket.'

He handed her the condom and while she was unwrapping it, he reached around a buttock and found the swelling of her pussy lower down.

Through her knickers, he could feel her vagina gradually softening. He pushed the fabric aside to check. It was juicy and viscous. Steph's face was hidden by her hair, but he could guess at the effect of pleasure on her crotch and the redness of her cheeks. His fingers dipped deep inside her. She finally got the condom out of its wrapping. Holding it between her lips, she grabbed her knickers with both hands and ripped the seam.

'Pull down your jeans,' she said.

He arched his back to get his bum free of the seat and slid his trousers down.

'Take it easy,' said Steph, whose head was against the ceiling. 'Stop. Don't move.'

He couldn't see her crotch but felt the nearly unpleasant prickling of hairs against his cock. The sensation of warmth was incomparable. Despite the darkness, she slipped the condom on him easily, pinching the reservoir just the way it says in the manual. Then she raised herself up and suddenly he was inside her – a sensation like diving that barely lasted a fraction of a second. Lowering herself, she took him all the way in, pressing down with all her weight, open and heavy, trapping him with her arms, her hair spread across his face. Some got into Anthony's mouth, and he blew to spit out a strand. He could barely move. She was holding him in her body in a vice-like grip.

The sound of the motorbikes rose in the distance again. In the darkness, the noise was terrifically sharp, like a dentist's drill. Steph held Anthony even tighter.

'Don't move,' he said.

She didn't answer. He wrapped his arms around her.

She was frightened. He could feel her breathing against his belly. With all this going on, he was going to lose his erection, he thought. The motorbikes approached. They slowly cruised past and for an instant their lights filled the inside of the car with dusty brightness. The noise came in through the lowered window. It felt as if they had been there all along. Anthony was afraid they were going to stop. Then they rode off again.

'This isn't good. I'm sure they spotted us.'

'I don't care,' said Steph.

'I don't like it.'

'Be quiet.'

But she could tell that he wasn't as much in the mood any more. She gathered her hair and tied it in a knot, baring her neck and face. Above him, she arched her back. He could see the angle of her jaw, the outline of her ear. A girl is full of so many details. Meanwhile, his erection was definitely on the way out. She leaned over to kiss him and he set his hands on the small of her back. He could follow the damp track her sweat was making along her spine. Catching the smell of her pussy, he roamed over her breasts, his hands constantly surprised by a swelling or an unexpected fold. And under her skin and the soft rolls of flesh, something intense, boiling, and whirling. Drops of sweat ran down her sides. His own arse was stuck to the seat. He ran his hands up to her deep, damp armpits. Steph was overflowing. He had an urge to bite her, to break her skin, to drink her juice. He wanted to smell the salt of her sweat. He took her buttocks in both hands and spread them. She couldn't help sighing. She started swaying back and forth against him very fast, drenching him. She was so full, slumped and open, he couldn't even tell if his cock was still stiff. He raised himself up to match her movement. They were fucking. It was official now. Hard to believe. Steph had started to moan rhythmically and he pounded hard against her, his back arched and his arms rigid. Her pussy was like a bath. She told him to come, told him to spurt, said other words that stung like slaps. But he wasn't ready yet and began to work harder.

A dull thud echoed on the roof of the car.

They froze.

Figures were circling them. A face pressed against the passenger-side window. The guy sniffed at the opening and yelled:

'It smells like sex in there!'

Steph bent over, searching for her bra on the floor. More blows rained down on the roof and bonnet while the shapes kept disappearing and returning. It was impossible to say how many of them there were. The whole car was ringing. Anthony checked to be sure the doors were locked. The little Opel was now being rocked from side to side.

'Roll up the window!' he shouted, buttoning his flies.

But Steph was naked, exposed to all eyes. She huddled on the floor of the car, curled up in a ball.

'Hiiiiiiiii!' a voice yelled.

Fingers reached through the window opening. The attackers, somewhere between three and ten of them, were wailing, grunting like pigs, moaning. The car felt as it were about to lift off. You couldn't tell where to look any more.

'Stop it!' yelled Anthony.

Fingers reached through the window gap. They tried the door handles on both sides of the car. A face pressed against the window on Anthony's side. You would've sworn it was a big, pale fish stuck against the wall of an aquarium. The features were distorted but you could clearly see the ears sticking out on either side of the skull, giving this nightmare head a fantastic dimension. Anthony turned the key in the ignition and honked the horn.

The little car produced a long choking whine that echoed deep into the vast night. The chaos stopped immediately. Nothing remained of the attackers. Returned to itself, the darkness seemed to give the lie to what had happened.

'Get dressed,' said Anthony. 'Quick.'

Shivering, Steph did the best she could. Anthony switched on the headlights, then got out of the car. Outside, there was nothing left. Everything was empty, abandoned. Steph got out of the car in turn. She didn't take the time to put on her shoes, and could feel the rough texture of the road under her feet. The asphalt was still warm, whereas the air had become much cooler. You couldn't see three metres ahead and the surrounding forest had fallen silent. The landscape, which she guessed at without seeing, seemed to be waiting.

'I want you to take me home.'

He stared at a point in the distance.

'Right away.'

He went back to the Opel, opened the boot and took out a spanner, just in case. Then they got back in the car.

'Those were inbreds, definitely.'

369

'I'm freezing.'

She was in the passenger seat, shivering. He found a sweatshirt lying on the back seat and handed it to her. Steph didn't know exactly what Anthony meant by 'inbreds', though she knew the expression, of course. In her house, it meant those incestuous families out in the countryside and in makeshift camps, brutal, dazed-looking kids who rode around on motorbikes, necks shaved and noses running. They were the bottom, the lowest level, below weirdos even. Those people, the way they lived, their rustic isolation and their distorted features, seemed to emerge from a kind of state of nature. You imagined them shut in as recluses on farms, mixing like animals. Steph shivered again.

'Let's go, please.'

'I know. I'm taking you home now.'

They didn't exchange another word. Anthony looked at his watch at regular intervals. His bag was in the boot and his train was leaving in a few hours. Here he had finally managed to fuck Stéphanie Chaussoy, and all it left was bitterness and fatigue, and nobody he could boast about it to. Neither of them had come.

When they were a hundred metres from her house, Steph had him stop the car.

'This is fine. I'll walk the rest of the way.'

He stopped the car without bothering to park. The streets were deserted. He hadn't seen a soul during the whole drive.

'Do you live far away?'

'No.'

He didn't have time for more questions. Steph had already opened the door and put a foot down. She needed a shower and ten hours of sleep. She thought of her bedroom, the fresh sheets, her teenage decor. A Luke Perry poster was still pinned to the wall. And near the bed, a crucifix with some dried boxwood.

'Wait,' said Anthony.

'What?'

'I don't know. It feels lousy to say goodbye like this.'

'So what do you want? We're not going to make a big deal out of it.'

'I could write to you,' said Anthony.

'If you like.'

She was very close to him.

'I'm sorry,' he said.

'See you.'

She slammed the door, and he watched her walk away. She was bare-foot, carrying her trainers. She didn't even bother turning round. He had fucked her, at least. He consoled himself with that thought as he did a U-turn and headed home.

FOUR

1998
I Will
Survive

1

The Leclerc store had certainly grown. It now boasted a fabric section, an upgraded fish market and, especially, a hi-fi and electronics department worthy of the most beautiful shopping centres. In all, some 10,000 square metres of retail space. The store didn't even close during the refurbishment, which took place behind plywood partitions while customers went about their shopping.

Once the renovations were done, the whole valley was plastered with flyers promising exceptional discounts on everything from irons to DVD players. People showed up en masse. The police even had to be dispatched to direct traffic. Since then, two roundabouts had been built. Every Saturday, there were queues in the car park, queues at the cash registers, queues at the new McDonald's. This was heart-warming, at a time when naysayers were seeing the spectre of the crisis and the noxious effects of globalisation at every turn.

Not that it didn't cause some inconvenience. In the toiletries aisle, for example, Anthony found himself flummoxed. With such discounts, you couldn't even choose toothpaste without worrying that you might be missing out on something. He finally settled on a tube of Colgate and went on his way with his trolley fairly full. Around him, shoppers were cheerfully coming and going in large numbers, especially for a Wednesday. The entire store was decked out. For months, all of France was tricolour and the same words ricocheted around the whole country. He'd heard them on his clock radio at eight that morning: *France is in the semi-finals*.

This didn't keep Anthony from running his errands; he just did them as quickly as he could. Because around here you always ended up meeting someone you knew, and then you had to give them the news. 'How's your mother? What about you, what are you up to?' Anthony was twenty; he was young; he had his whole life ahead of him. That was the only thing people could ever think to tell him.

'What about work?'

'I'm looking.'

The baby boomers were understanding. It was a lot easier in their day.

'How's your mother doing? Say hello to her for me.'

She was doing okay. Yes, he'd pass on the hello. Have a nice day.

Since coming home, Anthony hadn't done anything worthwhile. It was true that he was young. At least that's what people kept telling him. He had to get moving. Just go to Canada. Or sign up for some training. Everybody had a piece of advice. People are very good at arranging other people's lives. Anthony didn't have the words to explain things for them.

He bought more tinned food, beans, peas, sardines. Aside from that, his shopping trolley contained the usual: ham, sausage, mince, pasta. Coca-Cola, some croissants for breakfast. Coffee, bananas, yogurt.

Finally he reached the alcohol section. There, he chose two bottles of red wine, a case of beer and a bottle of Label 5 whisky. He had a date with his cousin in the late afternoon to watch the game. He grabbed a box of rosé, so as not to arrive empty-handed. He would put it in the freezer until he left.

France is in the semi-finals. The loudspeakers reminded the customers of this and announced that, for the occasion, Leclerc was offering exceptional discounts on television sets. Anthony promptly recrossed the store to check this out.

In the electronics department, big Day-Glo signs announced bargain-basement prices. Shoppers were going from one screen to the next, anxious to find their happiness, and in growing numbers. Over the loud-speakers, the same voice repeated that France was in the semi-finals and warned that there wouldn't be enough televisions for everyone. Anthony made up his mind quickly. A forty-inch Samsung for twelve thousand francs, a bargain. It worked with a rear projector inside. When you watched the game, you felt you were actually on the field. The salesman had a little blue waistcoat and the soft face of a prelate. He didn't bother making a pitch. The TV sets were selling like hotcakes anyway and not just because of the discounts. Given what was happening, buying one was practically an act of patriotism. Anthony tried to bargain, out of habit, but the guy wasn't having any of it. At that price, it wasn't worth the trouble. While his invoice was being prepared, Anthony got absorbed in contemplating the wall of screens showing highlights of the game against Italy. Kids were sitting cross-legged on the floor, gazing wide-eyed. Even from a distance, each player was recognisable. Liza, Desailly, Zidane, Petit with his ponytail. Like fifty million other losers, Anthony was caught up in the game, his misfortune temporarily at bay, his yearning merging with the great national aspiration. From stock traders and kids in Bobigny to Patrick Bruel and José Bové, everyone was on the same page and it didn't matter whether you were in Paris or Heillange. From the top to the bottom of the pay scale, from the deepest countryside to La Défense, the country was cheering in unison. It was really simple. Just do like they do in America: think your country is the best in the world and revel in that forever.

Anthony made the down payment on the TV with a Crédit Mut cheque. He was already overdrawn, but the set could be paid for in six instalments with no interest and, at worst, his mother would bail him out. He passed through the checkout queue, stowed his purchases in the Clio's boot, and picked up his new TV from the warehouse behind the store. He drove home unhurriedly; it was a beautiful day, he wasn't working. On the radio, they were still talking about the semi-finals. Croatia was clearly beatable. But you had to stay focused and not get overconfident, otherwise you risked a nasty surprise. It was almost noon when he got home. He set up his new purchase and programmed the channels. To celebrate, he poured himself a small whisky. On Channel La Une, Jean-Pierre Pernaut kept talking excitedly. Croatia certainly had technical skills and some great players. Plus it was a brand-new country full of energy, with everything to prove. But France was a great football nation, playing at home and riding a totally unprecedented wave of popular fervour. All the commentators agreed on that and on the rest. Actually, everybody agreed on everything, so long as Zidane stayed on his feet. We'd had the baptism of Clovis, the Battle of Marignano, the Battle of the Somme. And now, France–Croatia. A people and its rendezvous with destiny. It was cool.

Anthony had another whisky, a somewhat bigger one this time. The alcohol began to affect him. He opened a bag of crisps, cut a few slices of saucisson and started to nibble in front of his new TV. He was pleased with his purchase. The image quality left something to be desired, but the set's format largely compensated for it. The Leclerc guy said that with gear like this, you'd think you were there. Meanwhile, the reports continued one after another and Anthony's excitement grew. It was going be a great game. Reporters fanned out to interview the French and found them all tricoloured, shouting and self-confident. Their kids could hardly keep still. People had appealing faces and accents from every part of the country. Then there was an ad break. Anthony switched off the set, thinking he ought to move a little, make something to eat. He could see his reflection in the black screen, legs spread, the glass on his knee. The smallest thing made him feel sad again. He turned the TV back on.

Anthony had injured himself in the army, playing football after class, in fact. The meniscus. It hadn't seemed serious, and he spent the first week in the infirmary with a bandage on his knee and taking paracetamol, bored out of his mind and in constant pain. A nurse once found him tangled in his sheets on the floor, unconscious. He was then prescribed codeine and was finally able to read magazines without feeling nauseous. When the chief doctor came back from leave, he examined him anyway. He was a well-groomed little man with a signet ring on his little finger who used words like 'shitheads' and 'fuckwits'. He pissed off his entire staff and had Anthony shipped back to France for immediate surgery at the Saint-Mandé military hospital. Six months of physical therapy followed, after which he was sent back to Germany. But after a series of physical tests to measure his fitness to serve, he was told there wasn't any point in trying any longer. Anthony found himself in an office three metres square where a guy in civvies gave him the news: he would receive his two years of pay and could go home. Sign here. At the time, it seemed like a good deal.

So that's how Anthony ended up on a train platform with a cheque for nearly twenty thousand francs in his pocket and his possessions in a duffel bag. A grey day, kind of chilly. It was a German train station, and none of the destinations – Dortmund, Munich, Poland – appealed to him. Should he go straight home to Heillange? Either way, he had to go through Paris. He would see when he got there. Maybe he'd stay for a day or two and enjoy himself.

Arriving at the Gare de l'Est, his heart sank. Here he was in Paris, for the first time in his life. Right away, his disliked the size of the place. A city full of black people, threats, shops, all those crowds and cars. He had the confused impression that every person there was determined to rip him off. He took refuge in the nearest bar, on rue d'Alsace and started playing pinball and drinking beers. There, at least, he felt at home. It was a sleazy little bar whose owner sported an old Elvis-style pompadour, played ska and served draught Belgian. Anthony bought a few rounds and made friends. At one in the morning the owner announced he was closing and Anthony found himself out on the pavement, drunk. He asked the owner if he needed a hand. The guy wore rings on each finger and had a fur collar on his denim jacket and he looked cool. He said, 'No thanks, I'm good.'

'So what we do now?'

'I'm going home, buddy. My day's over.'

'Do you know where I can sleep tonight?'

'At a hotel, of course.'

The guy had rolled down the metal shutter and padlocked it. Criss-crossed with quick shadows, boulevard Magenta descended towards the heart of the city with its colourful signs, its simmer of activity. Anthony didn't much like it. He needed someone to guide him. He felt scared.

'Please, man, I was in the army. I don' know nothin' about Paris.'

The owner studied him for a moment, vaguely amused. Clearly, he didn't quite see the connection.

'I can't do anything for you, mate. I've got a family. They're expecting me.'

Anthony rummaged in his pockets. He found his cheque and showed it to him, as if his being solvent settled everything.

'Yeah, great. So what?'

'Can't you put me up, just for one night?'

'Cut that out.'

'I'll pay you.'

Anthony put his hand on the man's shoulder, who jerked free.

'Look, mate, I don't know you. You keep on like that and I'll fix your face with a spanner.'

Anthony took a step backwards. The guy had seemed cool and Anthony had bought drinks for him, for everybody.

'Okay, goodnight.'

The guy's cowboy boots echoed on the pavement until he disappeared behind the station.

Anthony had found himself alone in Paris. Even from a distance, this city of theirs seemed complicated, with its ten thousand streets, its misleading lights, the mix of all sorts of people, the buildings, a church, money streaming over poverty, the feeling of being awake, of always being on your guard, immigrants at every turn, incredibly numerous and diverse, kinky hair, blacks, Chinese, millions of them. He walked down towards République. On either side, there was nothing but bar-bershops for Africans and shops selling luggage, narrow bars with neon lights and young men out front talking loudly and drinking cheap beer. Nobody looked at him. It was a week night and though the streets were never completely empty, they were still pretty quiet. Anthony wondered where all those people could be going. He found them different, without knowing why. The women were prettier than in other places, maybe. Some of the guys seemed a little swishy, but were out walking with their girlfriends. Overall, it was a place of mixing and menace. Gradually, Anthony's drunkenness faded. He walked some more. From time to time he made sure his cheque was still in his pocket. He wanted Paris. He wanted those women, wanted to drink in those cafes, wanted to live in one of those apartments whose chandeliers and mouldings he could glimpse from the pavement. It was tempting, promising. But unattainable. Which end were you supposed to start with? At one point he asked two young guys in leather jackets with highlights in their hair where the Eiffel Tower was.

'It's straight ahead.'

'And if you keep going, you'll see the ocean.'

Little pricks.

Afraid of getting lost, afraid of running into bad people, Anthony retraced his steps and waited outside the station. It was November. It was cold. Some homeless guys came over to bum a cigarette and started giving him a hard time because he didn't have any. He was in good physical shape and was tempted to punch one of them to set an example. The guys reeked and they could barely stand upright. It would be easy. But he decided to leave and walked around the area blowing on his hands, sitting down for a moment, then walking on. Hotels intimidated him. It was too late. Dawn wasn't that far away any more. What was the point of blowing a hundred francs? The first brasseries opened; he had a cup of coffee at the counter and watched the ballet of the bin lorries and the dustmen. The black army of cleanliness. As soon as he could, he bought a ticket for Heillange, via Nancy. He showed up at his mother's place in the early afternoon.

'What are you doing here?' she asked.

Truth be told, she didn't seem all that surprised. Anthony's bed was made. There was some cauliflower cheese and pasta left and she cooked him a cutlet in cream. He devoured the food, then went upstairs and slept for twenty hours straight.

Anthony took a series of temporary jobs after that, without touching the cheque the army had written him. He didn't dare. He had the feeling that once he cashed it, the money would disappear in seconds. Then it would be penury and misery, he would depend on his mother, be back to being poor, a child again. So he looked for work. Doing temp jobs was fine; all his friends did it. He cleaned the toilets at the Saint-Vincent clinic. Same thing for the abattoirs. Then he worked as a school caretaker. Soon he ended up on the kitchen crew at the prefecture. Problem was, the job wasn't right next door and nearly all his pay went on petrol. He mentioned this to the woman at Manpower who was handling his case. She advised him not to quit, it would give a bad impression. So for eight weeks Anthony got up at dawn every day to drive a hundred kilometres, work for four hours and drive home, all to earn barely four thousand francs a month. It wore you out and it drove you mad. But at least his mother didn't give him any grief when he got home. She believed in killing yourself working. In her family, this was considered normal. An idea that Anthony was almost starting to subscribe to. At least he had right on his side. It was now his turn to complain about taxes, immigrants and politicians. He didn't owe anyone anything, he was useful, he complained, he was exploited, he was dimly aware of being part of a vast majority, the mass of people who could do everything and were sure there was nothing to be done.

After that, he specialised in nursing homes, doing laundry and cleaning. He went through five of them in three months. Then it was the Vivarte warehouse, Liqui Moly, the Merax print shop and finally the Gordon factory, where he'd found a more or less permanent job in a workshop. The job consisted of stacking sheets of metal, rods and pieces of grillwork in a precise pattern. This produced a cubic, stainless-steel sarcophagus that was then raised by amazing forklifts and put in equally amazing ovens, where the temperature reached a thousand degrees and more. Which is apparently how you make an air conditioner. Gordon sold them all over Europe, though with more and more difficulty. Worried supervisors kept a watchful eye on the workers and an endless series of temps who were bounced at the slightest economic downturn. Above them were the bosses, the engineers, the executives. You saw them at the canteen. It was another world.

Anthony made a few good friends at work: Cyril, Krim, Dany, le Zouk and Martinet. In the morning, he was glad to see them. They ate at the canteen together and secretly smoked joints during breaks, sitting on pallets in the little courtyard behind workshop C. He saw them after work, too. They all had the same kind of hobbies, the same salary level, identical worries about their future and especially a reticence that kept them from bringing up their real problems, a life being frittered away almost in spite of them, day after day, in this backwater town they'd all wanted to leave, leading a life just like their fathers', a slow-motion malediction. They couldn't admit to having the congenital disease of daily routine. Confessing it would add to the shame of their submission. Because these guys were proud, and especially proud of not being wankers, profiteers, queer, unemployed. And, in Martinet's case, of being able to belch the alphabet.

After a while, Anthony was able to rent a little one-bedroom apartment. He furnished it from Confo and bought himself a car, a new Clio Williams that ate up his cheque. Since then, he ran up debts, but he still planned to buy himself a motorbike for the summer. His mother criticised his thoughtless spending, but as long as he was working, she had nothing to say. On the other hand, when it came to girls, times were pretty lean.

When Anthony went out with his mates on a Saturday night, he would sometimes pick up a woman at a party or at the Papagayo, of course. But those one-night stands didn't count. They were with cashiers, nursing assistants, nannies, or women who already had two kids and were treating themselves to a weekend break while the grandparents minded the little ones. He had a different ideal.

He didn't talk about it. But from time to time, when it was late and he'd drunk more than usual, he would grab a beer, go down the two flights of stairs from his apartment to the car park and climb into his Clio. He would find something good on the radio, light a cigarette and drive north. Towards Steph's neighbourhood.

For Anthony, the pleasure was driving drunk through Heillange at night, getting choked up listening to oldies on FM radio. He drove without pushing it, following the docks along the Henne, taking the too-familiar streets of his home town. The glow of street lights punctuated this smooth trajectory. Gradually he started to experience those deep feelings that sad songs bring up and yielded to them. Johnny Hallyday was his preference. He sang of disappointed hopes, failed love affairs, the city, loneliness. Of time passing. With one hand on the steering wheel and his beer in the other, Anthony criss-crossed the landscape. The gigantic steel mill caught in the spotlights. The bus shelters where he'd spent half his childhood waiting for the school bus. His old school, the busy kebab stands, the station he'd left from and to which he returned with his tail between his legs. The bridges where he used to spit into the river out of sheer boredom. The pari-mutuel betting shop, the McDonald's, the emptiness of the tennis courts, the darkened swimming pool, the slow cruise towards residential neighbourhoods, open country, nothingness. The lyrics of 'J'oublierai ton nom'. Soon he would find himself very close to Steph's house, almost without intending to. He would turn up the volume and take a sip of beer. From a distance, he would stare at the Chaussoys' beautiful house, with its grille and electronic gate lock. He wondered if she was in. Probably not. He lit a cigarette and smoked it while letting his thoughts wander. Then he would go home, like a fool.

But none of this mattered, because France was in the semi-finals. Around five, he took his box of rosé, got into his car and drove to his cousin's place.

Ever since Hacine and Coralie brought the baby home from the maternity ward, their life had become a never-ending series of chores. Getting up at night, making up bottles non-stop, changing nappies and taking walks, all while continuing to go to work. The days went by, all the same, all exhausting. He and Coralie couldn't even talk without getting into an argument. Mainly they passed by each other like zombies, partners in a business whose purpose was to keep this frail life going. The girl. Her name was Océane, an Aquarius. She would be six months old in early August.

As if that wasn't bad enough, Coralie was depressed about her weight gain. She still had eleven extra kilos she'd put on during her pregnancy and wasn't able to shed them. She would burst into tears at the drop of a hat, and when Hacine tried to put things in perspective, it was worse.

And this wasn't counting his in-laws, who had invented new rights over the couple's life since becoming Grandma and Grandpa. They now felt they were entitled to drop by unannounced whenever they felt like it, to see the baby and lend a hand. 'By the way, I made soup, I'll bring you some.' There seemed to be no way to resist this invasion of kindness.

Coralie's mother left an apron and some cleaning products at their place. She was helping to do the housework, so she may as well have the right tools. She had even reorganised their kitchen drawers; the kids didn't know how to do it right.

Sitting on the living-room sofa watching the news with his father-in-law, Hacine sometimes wondered how he ever ended up there. He felt like a stowaway in his own life. Nothing appealed to him; nothing looked like him; he behaved himself and waited. For her part, Coralie just took one nap after another. They had stopped fucking.

Hacine felt torn. On one hand he was grateful, of course. These people had adopted him. But he hated their little quirks and their way of living. Their absolutely rigid schedule of meals at noon and seven. Their habit of counting everything, rationing, breaking everything down, whether days or slices of pie. The dad's unbuttoning his trousers after meals. The simple, honest ideas they held about everything, being perennial losers. Their bland probity, which left them constantly aghast at the ways of the world. The three or four strong ideas they retained from primary school were useless in helping them understand current events, politics, the labour market, the rigged Eurovision votes or the Crédit Lyonnais affair. And even then, the most they could manage was to be mildly scandalised, saying it's not normal, it's not possible, it's not human. Those three dicta cut to the heart of all, or nearly all, questions for them. Even though life constantly contradicted their predictions, dashed their hopes and routinely deceived them, the in-laws clung valiantly to the principles they'd always held. They continued to respect their leaders, believed what the TV told them, were enthusiastic when appropriate and indignant on demand. They paid their taxes, wore slippers indoors, liked the chateaus of the Loire and the Tour de France, and bought French cars. Hacine's mother-in-law even read *Point de vue*. It made you want to shoot yourself.

What Hacine should have had was an ally, someone he could talk to about all this. He was now working on an open-ended contract at the Darty warehouse in Lameck. Whenever he dared tell his workmates that he couldn't stand it any more, someone always chimed in to say that having a kid was the most beautiful thing in the world. Conventional wisdom ruled at work as it did elsewhere, serving only to envelop and intoxicate you with happiness so the evidence of the facts wouldn't kill you.

Where Coralie was concerned, even mentioning any of this was out of the question. It was strange because, deep down, she had never really been who Hacine thought she was. Since Océane came into the world, he was discovering Coralie anew and couldn't believe it. He had always loved her cheerfulness, her strength of character, her ability to talk to anybody. Unlike Hacine, Coralie never said, 'No thanks, that's not for me.' Unlike him, she didn't feel that people prejudged her. Everything was worth doing, worth trying. You just had to want to. She was a woman who loved to have fun, to eat, to spend time with her friends. At Christmas she was completely out of control. This was her big moment, obligatory joy, running errands for weeks, thinking of thousands of details, little touches, getting tiny presents for everybody and wanting even more. And Hacine loved that, loved to see her blush, or dance, or have a third helping of roast beef. Her clumsiness, her somewhat leaden jokes, her unicorn-and-teddy-bear side, her multicoloured nail varnish. Coralie made the connection. Without her, he found life more than he could handle. He didn't dare. He would have stayed in his corner.

But since they'd had the baby, Hacine realised something else: that Coralie had always suffered from an emptiness. A place, deep inside, that had always been vacant. When Océane arrived, she was the first to take that place and fill it completely. From then on, everything operated from that starting point. The baby was the measure of all things and justified everything.

Hacine wasn't jealous of Océane. He didn't feel neglected, especially. He didn't resent her. He didn't say that he had better things to do than devote himself to a baby. But he himself had never had that emptiness, that available space. Océane came along as a bonus, on top of everything else: his neuroses, his unhappiness, the rage that never left him. Life wasn't enough for him and the baby didn't change anything. To the contrary. Well, it was more complicated than that. He couldn't have said how.

So when one of the salesmen at the warehouse where he worked placed an ad to sell his Suzuki DR, Hacine immediately went to see him. Without thinking, he wrote him a cheque. Coralie really yelled at him that evening. When it came to money, they were already in deep shit. They wouldn't be going on holiday this year. Besides, where would they put it? They didn't have a garage any more. And, finally, motorbikes killed their riders and everybody knew it, goddammit.

'When are you going to grow up?' she wanted to know.

Baby Océane was crouched in her cot, busily tearing the men's ready-to-wear pages in the La Redoute catalogue. Arms folded, Coralie seemed on the verge of tears. The circles under her eyes were scary. She had just dyed her hair for the third time this month. With the upheaval in her hormones, her nails, hair, skin, libido and everything had changed. She was trying to get a grip, but it wasn't easy.

'You don't even have a licence for it.'

'You don't need one. It's small.'

'How much did you pay for it?'

'It wasn't expensive.'

'How much?'

'A thousand francs.'

'What about insurance?'

'I'll manage.'

She closed her eyes, took a breath. Don't get angry in front of the kid, stay calm.

'My parents just asked me when we were going to repay the money we owe them. What do I tell them?'

The baby was now attacking the underwear pages. Hacine didn't have much to say. Coralie withdrew to their bedroom. He decided to go out for a spin on the bike. The sky was extremely pale. He trembled, shifting through the gears. He scared himself a few times, had wanted to flee. Unfortunately, the tank was almost empty and he hadn't brought his credit card. So he went home a little before ten.

'Are you happy?' Coralie asked.

The baby was asleep. Yes, he was happy.

From then on, Hacine made an effort. Coralie didn't understand, but she compromised. Their life as a couple gradually started to look like a war of attrition. She criticised him for doing whatever he felt like, for acting like a child. Hacine kept his reproaches to himself, in his gut. In the evenings, he would go out for a ride, without a helmet. It was reassuring. Overall, things seemed to have stabilised. But that wasn't reckoning with the World Cup.

His father-in-law had already started to tease him because Morocco had qualified and if by some mischance that pathetic nation ended up playing France, it would take a hammering like you never saw in your life. The arsehole laughed then, his belly and his double chins shaking like jelly. When Brazil scored three goals against Morocco, the sarcastic remarks redoubled. Fortunately, the Lions of the Atlas redeemed themselves by beating Scotland 3–0 a few days later. But the fact remained that Morocco had never made it to the finals.

Things really took a turn for the worse when, instead of coming straight home from work as usual, Hacine went to a bistro with his workmates to watch the France–Denmark game. He was dying to see it and he couldn't face going home to the same surroundings, the apartment, the in-laws, the crying. So he bunked off, had a beer like anyone else and watched the game with a mix of satisfaction and bad conscience. But it wasn't easy to enjoy it when he was already dreading the scene he would confront when he got home. He was so preoccupied that he didn't even see the first goal. It was only when he saw the others yelling that he realised what had happened. In the end, he wound up leaving at half-time, feeling both guilty and frustrated, the worst situation.

Coming home, he found the apartment empty. Coralie had left a note on the kitchen table: 'I'm at my parents' with the baby.' Hacine hated to admit it, but he felt relieved. He made himself a big plate of pasta and ate it in peace while he watched the end of the game. Since he was by himself for a change, he wanked off to a porno DVD before going to bed. He took his time and came so hard.

In the shower, he wondered what was really going on in his life. The water ran down his chest and his cock. He looked at the foam at his feet.

What was he going to do? He felt trapped. There was the baby. She didn't demand anything. He loved her like crazy. He couldn't stay. He took a Temesta and went to sleep.

Coralie came back the next morning and they didn't exchange three words the whole week. Then the French team began to drive the commentators crazy. After getting through the first round, they eliminated Paraguay in the first knockout round, then beat Italy in the quarter-finals. Everyone could see the team was on a roll. Once Italy, a perennial powerhouse, was out of the game, everything became possible. Only Coralie refused to join in the universal rapture. Hacine watched it all: the games, the highlights, the TV news, the commentaries, the replays, everything. He even bought the newspapers. It was exciting and at the same time, convenient. He was losing himself in the national epic, the better to forget his daily drama. And during this whole immersion in the blue wave, he could feel Coralie's dull disapproval. She didn't criticise him. But from the sound of her footsteps, the drawers she slammed, the way she closed the fridge, the way she ate yogurt, it was obvious that she was upset with him. And she wasn't even angry. She was sad, which was the worst.

Hacine bravely acted as if nothing was happening. The pressure increased. He expected an explosion. With the baby, he fulfilled the bare minimum requirements: every other nappy change, a bottle from time to time, beddy-byes in the evening, maybe a song, but quickly, with no encore. He slept on the sofa. A deserter.

The morning of the semi-finals, Coralie came into the living room and woke him with a cup of coffee.

'Here.'

He took the cup as she parted the curtains and opened the window wide. It was a nice day. Bright July sunshine reflected almost blindingly on the white tiled floor. The usual automotive hum from the nearby aqueduct. The good smell of coffee.

'Is she asleep?'

Coralie went to check, then came back and sat on the coffee table.

'What are you planning to do?' she asked.

'What do you mean?'

He was sitting up and rubbing his face. This looked very much like a set-up. He took a sip of his coffee.

'This evening. Your game. Where are you going?'

'I don't know.'

'You're not staying here.'

'What do you mean?'

He felt a little upset. This was his home, after all.

'I don't want to see you around here,' said Coralie.

'What is this bullshit? Why are you talking to me like this?'

'Hey . . .' She waved her open hand in front of his eyes, as if to make sure he was conscious. 'Have you had a stroke or something? What is it that you don't understand?'

'What I do understand is that you're busting my balls.'

She grabbed him by the ear and yanked it, nearly hard enough to tear it off. He yelped, a ridiculous shriek that echoed through the whole apartment. Even someone outside could have heard it. The two of them froze, worried about how the baby would react. It sometimes took more than half an hour to get her back to sleep. Hacine was about to say something, but Coralie stopped him with a look. The seconds ticked by one by one. The baby went on sleeping.

Then Coralie looked him right in the eye and very quietly said:

'Now listen to me, you little shit. Either you straighten up and sort yourself out or I'm packing my bags, taking my daughter and you'll never see us again in your life.'

She went out then, leaving Hacine with the baby just when he had to be at work in an hour. Fortunately his mother-in-law arrived. She didn't make a fuss, just took the baby from him.

'I'll take care of her, it'll be fine.'

As he hurried to get ready to go to work, he listened as the woman went coochie-coochie-coo and the baby burst out laughing. Océane was so little, so insignificant, but she had such a capacity for happiness. It took practically nothing to feed this tiny life. It also would take almost nothing to end it. A bad fall, a passing car, drowning in the bath; there was no end of ways the little wretches could find to die. A second's inattention, a moment's carelessness and you bought yourself a four-foot coffin. Shit. When Hacine was about to leave, he kissed her on the head and on her fist. Then he climbed onto his motorbike. Coralie had taken off with the car.

After that, he had the whole day to ruminate. The mood at work was so unusual, like the day before the holidays started, with everybody excited, and that phrase that kept going around: *France is in the semi-finals.* Customers and salesmen talked football. Warehousemen and drivers, ditto. Even the suppliers were delighted; flat-screen TVs were selling like hot cakes, as were beer dispensers, fridges and barbecues.

At knocking-off time, Hacine's workmates all went to watch the game on the big screen set up at the Renardière stadium. He didn't want to go with them. Instead, he rode his motorbike around town. The mood was completely insane. The bars were so crowded, people spilled out onto the pavements. Only one television channel existed, La Une and Thierry Roland and Jean-Michel Larqué were part of the family. By dint of riding around looking for a friendly place, one thing led to another, one bar led to another and Hacine wound up at L'Usine. He hadn't been there since his 'accident'. That was ages ago.

Davor Šuker took a long pass from Asanović and scored.

They never saw it coming. It was in the forty-sixth minute, fresh from the dressing rooms.

The country seemed to be hanging by a thread.

Davor Šuker was the guy with the sharp, bony face, jutting chin, hooded eyes. He looked like a mercenary, a brute from the maquis, a starving partisan. He looked like a bastard, his lipless mouth stretched around a cry of joy. He looked unpleasantly pale in his white jersey strewn with red squares as he ran, arms thrust out.

Davor Šuker. The very name brought up bad memories of the German air force, of speed against which you were helpless. In front of their TVs, millions sat stunned. Anthony set his beer on the counter and grabbed his head in both hands, like a lot of other people. The gesture was a dramatic one. You just didn't have that many opportunities for hope.

He had driven to his cousin's place around five o'clock, carrying the boxed wine. The cousin had just had a house built in a new development near the tennis courts. Things had changed fast for him. He'd met Nath about a year earlier, landed an open-ended contract with Kleinhoffer, the heating specialist, and secured a bank loan while he was at it. He'd put on a little weight, too. He and Nath were happy.

Anthony was treated to the owner's tour, which he got each time he came, to see how the work was progressing. The house was in good shape, standing in the middle of a small patch of ground that would soon be a lawn. Four walls, a roof, white tiled floors downstairs, a laminate floor in the bedrooms upstairs. Everything was new. Electrical wires still stuck out of walls that left white dust on your hands when you touched them. For the time being, they still needed a ladder to get upstairs. This was hard for Nath, so they were sleeping on a bed in the living room. The pine furniture looked ridiculously inadequate in this six-room house. The cousin had been thinking big. All that remained was to win the World Cup. And pay back the bank.

A pretty brunette with a hint of gold in her eyes, Nath was in the city police force. She was planning to go back to school or take a civil service exam. They would see about that later, when their kid started school. In the meantime the house was eating up all their time, money and energy. The cousin was feeling proud, but he was exhausted, and as worried as any homeowner.

'I just can't take it any more. I spend my time redoing everything. The shutters weren't the right size. There's not a bloody door in the house that closes properly. Those guys really are useless.'

After the tour, the three of them settled on the patio, or what stood in for a patio, namely a square of gravel with plastic garden furniture. Nath had her legs stretched out, feet propped on her man's knees. She was drinking water while the boys swigged cans of beer. Anthony was having a little trouble getting used to his cousin's new attitude, his worried, supervising, settled side. On the other hand, he was very fond of Nath. She was funny, a wit with a straight face. The two of them teamed up to make fun of the cousin. Anthony had found himself a family, in a way. He came often during the summer. They asked if he would consider being the child's godfather. He said yes.

The conversation mainly revolved around football. Nath absolutely refused to believe in the 'black-white-brown' business – so called because

394

Les Bleus had black, white and Arab players. It struck her as a passing fad, a funny distraction. As a cop, she'd seen it all and practised a protective, good-natured cynicism. The cousin didn't share her opinion.

'I don't think so,' he said. 'If we win, it'll leave something behind.'

'What will it leave?'

'Knowing that we can get along.'

'What are you talking about?' she scoffed. 'You yell about the Turkish mason and the Arab workers. You're always complaining about the racket that the Portuguese next door make.'

'Those guys, they're mental cases. They've been listening to "I Will Survive" non-stop since the start of the Cup. Honestly, it drives you out of your mind.'

'Yeah, so what is it that you say? "The Portagees are a pain in the arse."'

'That's not racism.'

'So what is it?'

'Simple observation.'

Anthony laughed. From time to time, you could hear firecrackers and cars honking in the distance. A rocket shot up from a house nearby. Kids raced around on quad bikes yelling, 'Les Bleus!' You sensed the same eagerness in every house in the development. After a while, the cousin put some pork ribs and sausages on the barbecue. People were eating outside. Television sets were on. Everything was calm and feverish. The two cousins poured themselves big glasses of rosé with lots of ice cubes, which made a nice tinkling sound in the evening. Nath was slowly beginning to fade. She was in her third month and she felt weary. The boys cleared the dishes quickly and left them in the sink, before going into the living room. It was about to begin. The whole country held its breath. The national anthems. It started.

The first half didn't go too badly, even though Les Bleus played cautiously, without much energy. After a while, the Croats started getting really threatening. They had nothing to lose, they were young, uninhibited and tough, and they had in mind the great game they'd played against Germany. The situation generated remarks from the cousins like, 'What the hell are they doing, for fuck's sake? Where's Guivarc'h – at a bar?' Karembeu was injured and was replaced by Thierry Henry. The boys watched the French centre being slowly picked apart, as the Croats stirred and stretched it like dough. Unbelievable blunders occurred at midfield. Anthony wasn't even able to drink. He was biting his nails while his cousin stood up, sat down, stood up again. Nath dozed off around the fortieth minute. She was done for.

At half-time the cousin suggested that they watch the rest of the game at a bar.

'She's out for twelve hours now,' he said. 'I'll put her to bed. Just wait for me outside. I'll be right there.'

'Step on it. We don't want to miss the start of the second half.'

'Okay, no problem.'

Sitting on the bonnet of his Clio, Anthony smoked a cigarette as the evening gathered. The houses around him shared a family resemblance, each with its little plot of land, red roof, new facade, spindly bushes and car parked out front. New streets named for trees meandered among them. A comfortable calm reigned over this little world. A thousand details revealed the care the inhabitants put into comfort, intimacy and respect for their property. A man stood watering his lawn with a hose, his shirt open, looking happy. From time to time you heard a burst of laughter in the distance, or the scraping of a chaise longue being dragged in for the night. Swallows streaked by overhead. The sky was vast and round, like a woman's belly. Just then, the cousin came out.

'Okay, let's head off.'

'Did Nath say anything?'

'She didn't even wake up.'

They got in the car and raced for the nearest bistro. There wasn't a free parking space in the whole town. The long, deserted streets were jammed with cars. Every bar and terrace overflowed with fans. You would've been hard-pressed to find a Croat anywhere. On the other hand, you saw some

pretty unusual-looking people, with shaved heads and unbelievable out-
fits. The surrounding countryside had emptied itself into the centre of
town. It was worse than during the sales. The cousin ended up leaving
his car double-parked. He was too drunk to parallel park, anyway. He and
Anthony went looking for a bar that still had some room. Every place was
full. They were running out of time. The half-time ad break was ending.
Finding themselves near the blast furnace, they sprinted into L'Usine and
made their way to the bar. Anthony spotted Rudi. Manu was there, too.
The boys had just enough time to order a beer.

Then Davor Šuker scored.

Everything fell silent, a whole country seized, disappointed.

'Fuck!' yelled Rudi.

At that very moment, a guy with kinky hair entered and sidled up to
the bar. He ordered a beer, then turned round to see if he knew anyone
there. He recognised Anthony. Anthony recognised him, too. Hacine
shifted his attention to the big TV screen mounted on the wall. It was the
forty-seventh minute of the game and Lilian Thuram, who never scored,
worked his way up the pitch and scored. At that, the bar exploded. A single shout rose from every mouth. A table was knocked over. Beer spilled
on the ground. The spectators started jumping in place, yelling and
hugging each other. Hacine raised two fists to the sky. He felt someone
shaking him. It was Anthony, who was out of his mind, amnesiac, terribly
French, as happy as a child.

The match continued in a completely frenzied atmosphere. Beer
flowed like water, people smoked like chimneys, yelling and calling to
each other from table to table. Anthony himself started drinking as
much as he could. He and the cousin were buying each other rounds, and
treating Rudi. He looked more haggard than ever, and screamed *Cock-a-
doodle-do!* at Les Bleus' every action. Hacine was drinking hard, too. He
had good reason to.

At the seventieth minute Thuram slotted in a second goal and it was
all over. People suddenly found themselves melded, wholly yielding to

their destiny as a horde, completely free of outliers and aberrations. Those who chose not to join in were incomprehensible. Everything caught inside tolled to the same bell. The entire country gathered in a mutual fantasy. It was a moment of sexual, serious unity. Nothing had ever existed before, neither history, nor the dead, nor debts, erased as if by enchantment. France was linked together, immensely fraternal.

At one point, unable to hold it any more, Anthony had to take a piss. There was a queue for the men's room. He decided to go outside.

'I'm stepping out for five minutes,' he warned his cousin.

The racket was so deafening, he had to mime his message with five fingers. His cousin pursed his lips, not understanding. Anthony would miss the end of the game, but it was either that or piss himself.

'I'll be back.'

Outside, the evening air helped him gather his wits a little. The street was calm. Shouts and waves of joy periodically erupted from the cafe. These were gusts of warmth in the twilight, bursts of steam from a pressure cooker. Anthony picked a spot off to the side and began to urinate against the fence around the Metalor mill. The formidable presence of the blast furnace weighed on him. He looked up and cursed its thousands of tons, while tracing arabesques on the bricks.

When Anthony entered the bar again, his cousin grabbed him and said:

'I've gotta go.'

'Really?'

'Yeah. I don' wanna wait for everybody to get going. It's gonna be the traffic jam of the century.'

'Aren't you going to celebrate this?'

'No, I'd rather go home.'

Anthony understood, of course. Nath and the baby, it was normal.

'We'll celebrate this the day of the final,' he said.

'That's right. C'mon...'

They hugged, pounding each other on the back. It was a special moment. They almost could've said that they loved each other. But they weren't like that.

'Go on,' said Anthony.

'Yeah, bye. See you soon. And don't do nothin' stupid.'

With his head, he gestured towards Hacine, who was sitting with an elbow on the bar, watching the television like everyone else.

'Nah, tonight's no time for us to get into a fight,' said Anthony.

The cousin ran off and Anthony went back to the bar and ordered a beer. France had won. France was in the final.

4

At the final whistle, Heillange erupted. An endless procession of cars immediately jammed the streets, hooting, randomly. Flags appeared at windows. People waved flags on long, flexible poles, creating an undulating curtain that suggested floor exercises in gymnastics. Faces were painted blue, white and red. Young people ran around whistling and lighting firecrackers. On the pavements, people toasted each other with big cans of beer. A few idiots hopped onto car bonnets and made their way through the traffic jam by jumping from one to the next. The police watched this with indulgent indifference, especially as passers-by kept stopping to hug and kiss them. The town hadn't realised it had so much strength and energy. It was rediscovering itself after three decades of bad luck, with victory sweeping away the crisis. At City Hall, they'd broken out the champagne. On the town square, a local reporter was gathering people's first impressions. The next day's newspaper would be full of soothing commentary. One pronoun was in every mouth. *We* won, *we* are in the final, *we* are the champions. A few Algerian flags ventured out into the streets as well. A local garage owner named Aubertin had even hung a banner a few days earlier that read 'Zidane for President'. The local National Front office had lowered its iron shutter for the time being.

Around midnight or one o'clock, Anthony and Hacine found themselves out on the pavement in front of L'Usine. By then, all you heard were sporadic explosions and a few car horns. The bars were closing, sending their cargoes of drunken meat home. Anthony was staggering so much, he had to lean against the wall to light a cigarette. All evening, he'd talked and drank with a lot of people, especially Rudi, who was so wasted he wound up stretched out under a table, where kids smeared his face with burnt cork. Anthony and Hacine had done their utmost to avoid each other. It took the late hour, alcohol, victory and the powerful mood of amnesty in the air for one of them to dare to say a word to the other. Hacine walked up, hands in his pockets. He was the one to speak.

'That was something, wasn't it?' he said.

'Yeah.'

The illuminated carcass of the blast furnace stood next to them. They didn't know quite what to say to each other. Hacine jumped in.

'You work around here?'

'Yeah. At Gordon.'

'Ah, that's good.'

'No, it isn't.'

The answer amused Hacine, who said:

'It's the same all over.'

'Where are you?'

'At Darty, in Lameck.'

'Funny, isn't it?'

'What is?'

'Us meeting like this.'

'Yeah.'

A few more seconds passed before Anthony spoke again.

'My dad died. Exactly two years ago.'

He looked to see if this had an effect on Hacine's face. He could've saved his breath. At least that settled a lot of things. It was finished. All that belonged to the past.

'What happened to him?'

'He drowned.'

'In the lake?'

'Yeah.'

Anthony puffed thoughtfully on his cigarette. Hacine remembered.

Truth to tell, his own father wasn't doing that great either. Pulmonary insufficiency. He refused to return to France to be treated and now went everywhere with an oxygen bottle on wheels. Hacine had gone to visit him and didn't like what he saw. The old man lived as if he were made of porcelain. He no longer went out, stayed in the shadows, counted his movements, isolated, forever sitting in front of his TV. For some reason, they were smearing his face and hands with a kind of lotion that made his pale skin shiny. He looked like some animal living deep in a cave, far from the sun, blind and soft. Not to mention the smell.

'I bought a motorbike.'

'No shit?' said Anthony, whose face suddenly lit up like a child's. 'That's pretty funny.'

'Yeah. It's funny.'

'So what is it?'

'A Suzuki DR 125.'

Anthony burst out laughing. All that stuff, just for this. Life was funny when you came right down to it. The thought cheered him.

'Will you let me try her out?'

'No, I don' think so.'

'I'll get on the back. We'll take a spin.'

'Nah, we're good.'

'Come on, don' be an arsehole.'

In an apartment overhead someone started singing 'La Marseillaise'. It was a woman's voice. She sang in tune but must not have known the lyrics well, because the song ended right after *Let an impure blood water our furrows!*

'C'mon, man,' Anthony insisted. 'Besides, my cousin bailed on me. I'm facin' a three-mile walk to get home.'

Hacine eventually gave in. And he was feeling pretty proud.

When they got to the bike, he asked:

'How old was your old man?'

'I don't know, actually.'

Anthony clung to the cargo rack as Hacine zigzagged around the debris left on the road. Heillange was a small city and the explosion of joy at eleven o'clock had quickly given way to a sinister after-party calm. Left in the streets were scraps of greasy paper, crushed cans, firecracker scorch marks and a few lurching stragglers. Hacine drove fast, nervously, jerkily: accelerator, brake, accelerator. Behind him Anthony was enjoying the night and his surroundings. The wind on his face felt like a caress. The smell of exhaust and the little motor's adolescent noise brought back old memories. He wanted to drive. When they stopped at a red light, he asked again.

'Seriously, let me try her. I'll be careful.'

'Sorry, man. No way.'

'We can stop in a car park. I'll just do one run, up and back. Quick and easy. Just to try her. I can drive with my eyes closed, man.'

'Sorry, but no.'

Anthony kept pestering him. So much so that they finally headed over to the new des Montets enterprise zone. The place was still a construction site, one of the city's big economic renewal projects. A few warehouses stood here and there, a Halle aux Vêtements department store, a Connexion outlet, and some recently built offices that looked like stacked containers. Each was a functional building, with walls erected in two days, raised passageways, stairs, and a general look of fragility, as if the first gust of wind could knock everything down. It would house an accounting office, doctors, all sorts of activities and open spaces, with computers, coffee makers and copy machines. The future. Already there were car parks, as vast as prairies, divided by concrete abutments and dotted with street lights. At night, it looked like the sea, an ocean of empty spaces.

Hacine put his foot down at the west entrance of the car park. From there, the scene was completely empty. Five hundred metres stretched straight in front of the boys. Anthony climbed down from the bike. Hacine switched it off, put it up on its stand. He hesitated. After all, they were in no hurry.

'Got any cigarettes?'

Anthony held his pack out to him. He was getting jumpy. He rode so much better than Hacine, it seemed unthinkable that he would refuse to lend him the Suzuki for a spin. More and more, he felt Hacine owed him this.

Hacine went to sit on the edge of a flower bed. He was very calm, smoking with his forearms draped over his knees. Still standing, Anthony looked at him. It was weird, having so little to say to each other. After all, they had grown up in the same town, been bored at the same jobs, gone to the same schools and dropped out of them too soon. Their fathers had both worked at Metalor. They had run into each other a hundred times. And yet those points in common meant nothing. A thickness hung between them. Anthony was starting to get impatient. The need to drive was burning in him, like the need to take a piss.

'C'mon, man,' he repeated.

Hacine looked up. The mood between them was changing fast. Anthony came over and stretched out his hand.

'C'mon...'

Hacine felt in his pockets, tossed him the key.

'You go to the end, then you come back.'

'Okay.'

'There and back, *basta*.'

Anthony pursed his lips. Hacine's insistence was annoying him.

'No problem,' he said, but with something mocking in his gaze.

'Seriously...' Hacine said.

This time, it was a threat.

Anthony turned his back to him, climbed on the Suzuki and pressed the starter. In the summer night's ideal calm, the motor chattered cruelly.

Anthony revved it and felt the 125's special vibration rise through his thighs and crotch to his chest. It felt good, a Cossack kind of pleasure. Broad-chested men like him, young and crude, had been riding and destroying since forever. Their heavy thighs gripping smelly mounts, they had come in waves, sometimes defeating empires. All it took was not caring about anything except moving forward. Anthony accelerated, and the bike leaped in response. He shot straight ahead, drinking it in, filling the night with the concentrated noise of metal driven by fire.

He slowed at the end of the car park, turned round, and put a foot down. At the other end, Hacine was on his feet. He waved his hand. Anthony started up again, faster this time, doing a wheelie, thundering along, still drunk, scarily skilful. When his front wheel came down to the asphalt, he sped up even more. It was frightening, roaring towards Hacine at nearly a hundred kilometres an hour. Hacine spun in place as Anthony circled him precisely, coming within an inch before roaring off again, full throttle, ripping the thin fabric of the night. Hacine started running after him.

'Come back, goddammit!'

Anthony defied him some more, for fun, roaring off only to come back faster. It was a kind of harrowing bullfight. Hacine ran around sweating, waving his arms, looking ridiculous. Anthony was becoming totally familiar with his machine. He easily dodged Hacine, in no danger.

Finally, he rode away. Without even thinking, he took the road to Steph's place. His heart was pounding harder than the motorbike's. He was going faster than its speed.

The bike slowed to a stop in front of the Chaussoy house with a graceful swaying of its shocks. It was a big, beautiful building, with an upper storey and gables and a balcony under the projecting eaves. Having never dared come so close before, Anthony looked it over. Hewn stones decorated the corners of the walls. Steps led to a heavy door bearing a cast-iron knocker. The lawn featured circular flower beds that looked very much like the ones on the roundabout in front of City Hall. There were also two willows, a silver birch and bougainvillea. A BMW Series 7 and an old Golf convertible were parked on the gravel driveway.

There was no light and not a sound. Anthony wiped his hands on his jeans. The neighbouring houses were likewise nestled in their settings of lawn and thuja trees. How could he tell if Steph was home? He shouldn't have come; it was obviously a stupid thing to do. Yet he couldn't bring himself to leave. It was a special night. A glance at the sky was all it took. The stars pricked your heart.

Anthony put the bike on its stand and walked towards the tall, imposing house. It wasn't one of those old-fashioned bourgeois homes he'd sometimes seen when he trimmed hedges with his father. This one had been built more recently. He tried to imagine the interior. When he was younger and dealing hashish, he'd visited a fair number of rich kids, and saw how those families lived. He had envied their American refrigerators, the deep carpets that muffled your footsteps, the heavy coffee tables with 500-franc art books, the paintings on the walls. The parents were never home. Often there wasn't even a TV in the living room. He imagined Steph's place to be more of a cocooning bric-a-brac, with a Stressless armchair next to the Roche Bobois sofa, and a sauna rigged up in the garage. He took another hesitant step, hands in his pockets. He was still drunk, but becoming less so. As he moved a little sideways, light suddenly blinded him.

'Shit…'

A row of fifty-watt spotlights mounted under the roof held him in their white glare. He raised a hand to shield his eyes, didn't dare move. Eventually the light went out.

He stood there for a few moments without budging. Then, as an experiment, he waved his hand. The light immediately came on again, as harsh as before. A prison pallor. He gave a small sigh of amusement. It was one of those motion-detection things that freaked out cats and burglars. Good to know. He thought he'd better go home. After a few seconds the light went out. When he turned back to the motorbike, it was like broad daylight again.

'Hey there!'

Someone was calling to him from the top of the steps.

'What are you doing here?'

It was Steph. Even backlit, he recognised her right away.

'Hi,' he said.

'Wait a minute.'

She fiddled with something inside, then closed the door and joined him. This time the light went out for good.

Barefoot in jeans and a blouse, she skipped down the stairs two at a time. Her hair wasn't as long as it used to be.

'You're lucky my parents aren't here.'

'Where are they?'

'Out.'

Anthony tried to see her face but couldn't. The only light available was the paleness of the sky and the dull glow of street lights from the road. It was very inadequate.

'So?'

'Nothin'. I was just passin' by.'

'Do you realise what time it is?'

'We're in the final.'

'Yeah, right...'

They were standing close, blue against the darkness. Around them, the patient summer was making its soft grass sound. He looked down. She began to get impatient.

'Is that all?'

'You feel like goin' for a spin?'

'What kind of spin?'

'Motorbike.'

'To go where?'

'Nowhere. Jus' for fun.'

'You stink of booze.'

He didn't have much of an answer for that. He would have liked to ask her a couple of questions. To know what she was doing, where she was living, if she had a boyfriend. But he didn't have the heart. Still, he tried again.

'You sure you don' wanna go for a spin? Ten minutes. I'll bring you right back.'

'No.'

He touched his left eyelid with his hand. An old reflex. He wouldn't have any more chances. The words bumped into each other.

'I'm sorry,' said Steph. 'That's all over.'

Anthony stuck his hands in his rear trouser pockets and took a deep breath. It was tomorrow already. The situation was slipping between his fingers. He would've liked to take her hand or something. He just said:

'I think about you all the time.'

In silhouette, Steph jerked, stiffening.

'You're dreaming,' she said. 'I'm going inside now. I have to get up early tomorrow.'

Steph turned her back on him and went into the house. In a few days, she would be taking a plane to Canada. Her boyfriend was waiting for her there. He had just finished his journalism degree and landed an internship with a local paper in Ottawa. She was supposed to stay only three weeks, but secretly planned to enrol at the university when she got there. She would work as a waitress on the side. People were said to be generous with tips and you could live just fine that way. A vast, brand-new country. She felt she was on her way, transatlantic; nothing to do with Heillange made any sense to her. She climbed the stairs two at a time. Anthony hadn't even seen her face.

'See you,' he said.

Steph raised her hand in farewell. It had lasted so long, been growing inside him. For a lifetime, pretty much. Once again, he saw her ponytail on a July day. He saw her silhouette one last time, framed by the door, which then closed. He would never touch her breasts again.

Before starting the motorbike, he carefully rolled it away from the house. Then he pressed the starter and the motor obeyed. Mechanisms were reliable, at least. Each element performed a precise function, of majestic simplicity. A spark lit the fuel–air mixture. The combustion powered the piston, which rose and fell, and in turn organised intake, combustion and exhaust. Fresh fuel drove out the burned ones. The movement repeated, faster, stronger, tireless. A perfect cycle. Provided the mechanism ran and the petrol flowed, you could produce non-stop energy this way and speed, and forgetfulness, to infinity.

Anthony rode around in the Heillange night for a while. Then he decided to stash the bike in the garage at his place. As he closed the metal door, he thought he should drop by his cousin's before going to work, to retrieve the Clio. A pain in the arse. Unless he went there by motorbike. He would see.

Then he went up to his apartment. He found the bottle of Label 5, poured himself a big glass, took two ice cubes from the freezer tray and swirled them around. Everything was quiet. The ice cubes tinkled. In the living room, light from the outside cast pale lozenges on the leather sofa. He looked out. Cars with a few years on them were parked in the comfort of the street lights. The building was full of its inhabitants' sleep. They were waiting for the alarm clock to ring. Anthony turned on the hi-fi. On the radio, a woman was wondering what her life would have been like if she had been a captain. The whisky was lousy, he poured himself another one. The pain had something delectable about it. He felt detached. In the middle of things. His mouth narrowed to a bitter slit. He looked at his watch. He would be starting work in three hours. He was due to have dinner with his mother. Gordon was closing completely between 14 July and 15 August. He had no plans for the holiday, nothing he wanted to do. 'It's over,' he told himself. He felt relieved of any obligation.

Anthony walked into the bathroom to have a shower. Once undressed, he looked at his reflection in the big mirror above the sink. Then he ran the water, very hot. He shook himself under the scalding jet, opening his mouth, running his fingers through his thick black hair. He stood there for a long time, until the water ran warm, then cool. Steph left a physical void. He could feel it in his chest, in his belly. Life would go on. That was the hardest part. Life would go on.

He went to bed still wet and immediately fell asleep.

5

The next day, Anthony decided to take the bus to work. He was late but probably wouldn't be the only one. Crossing the Gordon car park, he noticed that quite a few of the spaces were still empty. He walked over to his workshop without hurrying. He was feeling woolly, despite the two aspirins he'd taken when he got up. His legs were heavy and his head felt like it was caught in a vice. Yet it was a beautiful morning. The sky was the kind of blue you saw over Sicily. Birds were singing and it was warm. On the way, Anthony saw girls in skirts, mothers with pushchairs, street cleaners picking up the remains of the party. He expected to see Hacine pop up at any moment. He could practically sense his presence and was almost disappointed not to find him at the bus stop when he arrived. After all, Hacine knew where he worked.

At the stacking station Anthony found his workmates in a great mood. Their faces looked drawn, but radiant. They were all thinking of last night's game, which had sent France to the final. The kind of heaviness that usually weighed on the workshops had completely evaporated. Not that this energy made them work any faster, however. The trick at work is to maintain a steady pace without going overboard, because if you do, the targets will be raised the following month, and that way, bit by bit, a little pressure here and there, a production bonus after management tightens the screws, and you find yourself trapped in the machine, fleeced and devoured. Foremen were constantly prowling, looking casual, hunting for skiving and hidden sloth. They knew the strategy of minimal work, but couldn't prove anything. The workers' ruse was to work continuously, but with a studied slowness and economy, creating tiny pauses, a breath between two movements, little breaks, quietly getting ahead of schedule, the better to ease off later and always clandestinely. From this constant fiddling and the bosses' snooping around the workshops emerged a feeling of ongoing mistrust and seamless solidarity. And woe to the idiot who worked too hard.

At break time, the game was replayed around the coffee machine. Martinet was especially enthusiastic. He kept saying that he'd never seen anything like it, ever. Old Schlinger didn't agree and trotted out his expertise: Mexico, Kopa, Piantoni, Fontaine and so on, back to the Stone Age.

'You're la Fontaine, with those fables of yours,' said le Zouk.

That was vintage le Zouk, to come out with a laconic crack just when he seemed to be asleep on a bucket in his corner. His brows had been busted a couple of times, along with his nose. His face looked oddly chewed up and you could hardly see his eyes. Even at twenty-five, he looked forty. The fact that he smoked ten joints a day didn't much help his looks. Still, he was funny, in an inappropriate, unimaginative way.

The conversation continued. For once, the supervisors and foremen joined the workers. Everybody felt that Lilian Thuram deserved a medal and had entered French history, somewhere between Napoleon and Platini. They also discussed the game's prize money and Ronaldo's health problems. Brazil would be tough to beat, but South American teams rarely won a World Cup outside their hemisphere. Anyway, with Zinedine Zidane, France could do anything. You just had to believe. Karim wondered what could be in the big black notebook that manager Aimé Jacquet carried with him everywhere. Stats, for sure, but maybe also secret formulas and magic spells. Jacquet had once worked in a factory, too, a Saint-Chamond steel mill. Just goes to show, said Cyril, briefly melancholic. The bell rang, like at school, and it was time to go back to work. Anthony hadn't said a word. Martinet was concerned.

'You okay?'

'Leave me alone.'

'Oh, all right then.'

The men went back to work with a spring in their step. On that day, things felt easier, temporary. Only Anthony seemed in a bad mood. Nobody gave a damn.

In the canteen, they went at it again. To eat there, you had to buy tickets: red for food, blue for wine. Each person was entitled to ten blue tickets a month and you needed four to get a bottle of wine. This was the tactic management had found to limit the damage. At one point they tried to forbid the sale of alcohol, but that caused such an outcry they had to fall back on the ticket method.

On this day, the guys all pooled their wine tickets and snatched up every available bottle. An incredible din reigned all through lunch. People were laughing, talking, waving their arms. Sunday would be the big day. Predictions were flying. Nobody imagined France losing. It just wasn't possible any more. The age of miracles had begun. As proof, Karim stood on a chair and started singing 'La Marseillaise'. All the workers joined in, mainly for fun and the song made an unbearable, quasi-revolutionary racket. It was basically fooling around in the guise of patriotism, a good way to mess with the executives off eating in their corner.

Anthony didn't join in with the singing. He didn't touch his glass of wine and quickly ate his lunch: beef, carrots, potatoes. He had a chocolate Danette for dessert. It had the taste of childhood. When he was a kid, his mother always bought Danettes, chocolate for him and coffee for his father. Except that the old man ate his two at a time and when he went through his supply he fell back on the chocolate ones. Anthony remembered the three of them sharing those meals. Years of loving each other without saying anything, then hating each other, likewise. It all came down to the same thing in the end. His father was dead. As for his mother, she was remaking her life. She was seeing men. She had spiky auburn hair now. She would be able to retire in fifteen years, if the government didn't come up with some ruse before then. It was a long way off. She was counting the days. At the weekend, she saw her sister. She visited her friends.

Amazing, the number of single women who had finally decided to live a little. They went on outings, signed up for organised trips. Buses criss-crossing Alsace and the Black Forest were full of singles, widows and abandoned women. They did their laughing among their own kind now, stuffing themselves at inns with exposed beams and prix fixe menus, cheese and gourmet coffee included. They visited castles and typical villages, organised karaoke evenings, chipped in to kitties for trips to the Balearic Islands. Children and men had merely been an episode in their lives. These women were the first of their kind to break free of millennial servitudes. Amazons in Capri pants, they were modest, cheerful, careful about their looks, with dyed hair and bums they felt were too big and a desire to enjoy life, which after all was too short. They were daughters of proles, girls who grew up listening to yé-yé music and went out and got salaried jobs in huge numbers. They were now treating themselves to a good time after a life of worry and penny-pinching.

Nearly all of them had experienced multiple pregnancies and spouses who had been fired, depressed, violent, macho, unemployed or compulsively humiliated. With their lugubrious faces, big hands and crushed hearts, these men had been a burden for years, at the dinner table, at the bistro and in bed. They'd been inconsolable since their famous factories closed and the blast furnaces fell silent. Even the nice ones, the attentive fathers, the good guys, the quiet, obedient ones. All those men, or nearly all of them, were buried now. The sons had generally turned out badly, too, screwing up and causing no end of worry before finding a reason to settle down, very often a girl. During all this time the women had held on, enduring and mistreated. And things had finally started to turn round after the great chasm of the crisis. Except that the crisis wasn't just a moment any more. It was a position in the order of things. A destiny. Their destiny.

Anthony was actually due to see his mother that evening. She always did her shopping on Thursday, so they had a standing date to meet at the Leclerc cafeteria around seven o'clock. It was clean and steak with fries cost twenty francs. Anthony would have a carafe of Côtes du Rhône and *île flottante* for dessert. He and Hélène had settled on this arrangement to avoid their domestic arguments. The moment Anthony showed up at his mum's, she immediately reverted to mother-bear mode. She gave him advice, wanted to run his life, made scenes. Standing his ground, Anthony said no to everything and provoked her. At Leclerc, at least, they had to behave themselves. They took turns paying the bill. Smoking wasn't allowed at the table, so after coffee they had a cigarette out in the car park. Hélène talked a lot. Her voice was hoarse, her teeth yellowed. Withered circles under her eyes held the memory of past sorrows. Nowadays, she didn't worry so much. Her boy was settled, her husband in the grave. The men who went out with her now knew right away what to expect. She was calm.

After dessert, Anthony stood up and left the canteen without waiting for anyone. The other guys wondered what was up with him.

'He's never satisfied.'

'That's temps for you,' said old Schlinger.

'You're the temp,' said le Zouk, who himself was dispatched by Manpower.

Anthony smoked a cigarette in the car park between the canteen and his workshop. The heat had shot up during lunch and the air shimmered over the car bonnets. He looked at his watch. Twenty minutes to go. The tobacco had an acid taste. His hands were damp, his nails filthy. He was having trouble keeping it together. And there was that lurking anxiety: Hacine was coming; it was just a matter of time. Anthony was even surprised that he wasn't already there. He didn't have the slightest idea of what he would do then. All this had been going on for so long. He was tired, that's all.

Soon his workmates trooped out of the canteen, weighted down with alcohol, already distinctly less chipper than before. They dragged their feet across the gravel, sniffing. Two more hours to go. No air con in the workshops. But they buckled down to work anyway. The morning's joy was already unravelling. The three o'clock break was marked by yawns and silence. The coffee machine gurgled non-stop. People talked about holidays. Cyril was off that evening; he planned to take the kids to his in-laws' in the Jura. He had stuff to fix at home, wallpaper to hang. Then they'd all go to the seaside; it would do them good.

The two last hours of the day were the longest, stretching on in leaden silence. At last, the guys on the night shift showed up. When Anthony was about to clock off, he realised that he was two hours short, from being late so often. When you work three eight-hour days, it's impossible to catch up. He was in for a salary deduction and a stiff note from human resources. The temp agency would have a go. He felt his gut tighten. He was already living on the razor's edge as it was. He earned seven thousand francs a month. His rent took half of that, then he had the car, petrol, cigarettes groceries and various credit charges; four thousand francs, all told. So every month ended with him overdrawn by at least five hundred francs. And all it took was one mistake, a meal out or too many drinks at a bar and he was deeper in the red without any hope of getting out. On payday, he would settle up and promise himself to be careful, to tighten his belt. But the money disappeared very quickly and he was soon down to zero, then overdrawn again. He had worked things out with the bank to avoid charges, but his autonomy was still constantly at risk. For twenty days a month, he lived on his banker's generosity. So he kept going back to work, day after day. He had to pay for the car somehow, along with the fridge, the bed, the leather sofa and the new forty-inch Samsung TV.

Taking the bus home, Anthony had an odd feeling. There weren't any crowds. A lot of people had gone on holiday. Traffic was smooth, the air warm. Two old ladies right in front of him were chatting. Absent-mindedly, he listened to their talk. It was about tomatoes that didn't grow the way they used to, frosts that didn't come on schedule. The bus made its way across town one stop at a time: Pont-de-Lattre, Rue-Combes, Hôtel-de-Ville, Piscine-Debecker, Collège-Louis-Armand, Route-d'Étange. He got off at Trois-Épis. It was a bit far from his place, but he felt like walking. The light at day's end was restful, diffuse. He walked along carrying his backpack, not thinking of anything. He realised he was feeling good.

When he got home, he phoned his mother to tell her about an idea that had occurred to him.

'Do you remember the Déchetterie, the beach where my cousin and I used to go all the time?'

'Yes, so?'

'I was thinking we could eat there.'

'Have a picnic?'

'Yeah.'

His mother was undecided for a moment. This kind of initiative wasn't like him.

'Okay, why not?'

'Do you have anything to eat?' he asked.

'Sure. I have some leftover tabbouleh and chicken thighs.'

'I'll get us crisps and something to drink.'

'All right... There's nothing going on, is there?'

'No, no,' said Anthony. 'Don't worry.'

Hélène hung up first. Anthony was pleased by the effect he'd had on her. He put tumblers, a bottle of rosé, crisps and a chocolate bar in his backpack. Then he went to the garage and swung aboard Hacine's Suzuki. Starting it, he savoured the wonderful crackling sound of mechanical lace, as sharp as daggers. He let it warm up for a moment. He had come to a decision. Later that evening he would leave the motorbike in front of the Darty in Lameck where Hacine worked and drop the keys in the store's mailbox. Simplest thing in the world. He would walk home, or hitch. He set off.

Evening was falling on the valley as he raced through the woods, arms wide, legs spread. The trees zipped by in a changing, staccato parade.

July was a beatitude that he dived into head first, pained and safe, just barely twenty, deep in speed, where he belonged. He accelerated and the Suzuki's irritating whine slashed the light, opalescent air.

In spite of it all, Anthony felt free.

He found his mother waiting for him on the beach. She had set out paper plates on a checked cloth. A big bowl covered with tinfoil held the tabbouleh; the chicken thighs were in a Tupperware container. She had even thought to bring paper napkins. Anthony parked nearby. A little further down by the water, a small group of kids had gathered around a fire. They were what? Fifteen, sixteen years old? Three girls, five boys, some beers and a guitar.

'What's that motorbike?' asked Hélène.

Anthony kissed her, then took off his trainers and sat down.

'A friend lent it to me.'

'I see.'

One of the kids had started to play 'No Woman, No Cry'. Anthony uncorked the wine bottle. A little way below them, the lake spread its depths and its mystery.

'Cheers.'

'Cheers.'

They drank. Hélène looked at her son with an expression both affectionate and suspicious, as if she expected to be told secrets, an announcement – something important.

'So, then?'

'What?'

'You didn't bring me here just for the fun of it.'

Strange as it may seem, Anthony had never made the connection. He'd just wanted to do something different. The weather was nice. It had been a long time since he'd gone on a picnic. That was all.

'I thought you wanted to talk about your father.'

With the hand holding her glass, she gestured towards the lake. Mother and son contemplated its surface for a few moments. When evening fell you would've thought it was a layer of oil. On the other side, a shore and then the vague green of trees. Finally the sky, which covered everything.

After Patrick's death, they'd never really had a chance to talk about it. Anthony was serving in Germany. His mother chose to deliver the news in a letter. He came home for the funeral, but their time was taken up with formalities, paperwork and clearing out the apartment.

'What are we going to do with all his things?' Anthony had asked.

'What little there is.'

In fact, Patrick had been living in a tiny apartment, owned nothing, and had just two pairs of jeans, three shirts, a TV and a few pots and pans. He had been shortening his sails for a long time. His death was the logical conclusion of a slow process of erasure. Weeks had passed, then months. Neither Anthony nor his mother gave a thought to mourning or any of that American soap-opera stuff.

When Hélène talked about her husband now, she spoke neither well nor ill of him any more. Memories got scattered like loose change. She put the episodes in order and worked out a story that suited her. They'd had some good times, after all. It was a part of her life that she didn't regret. Nobody was responsible, certainly not the crisis. Not even the booze, really. It was destiny, their life, she wasn't ashamed. From time to time, when Anthony was being too hard or stubborn, she would say he was just like his father. It wasn't a compliment. He was proud.

'He's just as well off where he is.'

'Yeah,' Anthony agreed.

Then Hélène changed the subject. Her sister was due for tests of her thyroid. She had high hopes. According to her new doctor, it might explain quite a few things.

'She thinks her thyroid's been the cause of everything. Except that she's been a pain in the arse for long before that.'

They gossiped about people they knew while eating with gusto. It was a pleasant pastime. At least they found points of agreement there. The bottle of wine was soon polished off. The kids further down let out loud gales of laughter. Evening fell.

'I should have brought another bottle,' said Anthony.

'No, we're fine like this. Anyway, it's already late.'

It was time, the summer soap opera was about to start on La Une. Anthony felt like staying for a while longer. He helped Hélène pack up her things. She kept sneaking glances at him. He really did seem out of sorts.

'Okay then, kiss-kiss,' she said.

'Yeah, see you soon.'

She brushed his cheek. Barely touching.

'Are you sure you're all right?'

'Yeah, yeah, don't worry.'

'Okay. Tomorrow is another day.'

Hélène carried her heavy shopping bag to the car, a bit shaky in her platform sandals. She was still thin. Her elbows looked like dry fruits. Her jeans were a little loose around her hips.

Now alone, Anthony lit a cigarette. He thought of his old man. The life that was imposed on them. He was very sorry not to have anything more to drink. He rummaged in his pockets to see if he had money to buy a beer or two from the kids down below. But his pockets were empty. He watched the sun sliding towards the west. Soon the horizon was ablaze. The boy who had brought the guitar was now playing a complicated piece, probably Spanish. Two of the girls were clapping in time. Then two teens in the group decided to go for a swim. They got undressed while the others teased them good-naturedly. The boy had a very beautiful body, long and slim, sculpted by swimming. His girlfriend was heavier, big calves, not much chest, very pretty, the super-healthy hiker type, always smiling with a bright future ahead. Once in the water, they spent some time fooling around, diving and splashing each other. Then the boy with the guitar challenged them to swim across the lake.

'You're crazy, it'll be dark soon.'

'It's dead straight, it's easy.'

'Go on!'

'How much do you wanna bet?'

'A hundred francs,' said the guitar player.

They started swimming towards open water. All the others gathered on the shore to cheer and whistle and shout encouragement. They were enthusiastic, incredibly young and their two friends cut through the water with perfect grace, their strokes barely disturbing the lake's heavy repose.

Anthony preferred not to watch. He climbed on the Suzuki and quickly reached the departmental motorway. In his hands he experienced the motor's panicky vibration, the infernal noise, the delicious smell of the exhaust. And a certain unctuous quality of the light, when July in Heillange settled with a sigh and the sky took on that pink, feathery look at the end of the day. Those same impressions of summer evenings, the shadow of the woods, the wind on his face, the exact smell of the air, the texture of the road as familiar as a girl's skin. That imprint that the valley had left on his flesh. The terrible sweetness of belonging.

NICOLAS MATHIEU

Of Fangs and Talons

COMING FROM SCEPTRE IN AUGUST 2021

Nicolas Mathieu's gripping first novel is the
story of a world that has come to an end.
With a girl, a gun and acres of snow.

When a factory that employs most of a small town is
scheduled to close – to the despair of the workers and
disdain of the overlords – things start to fall apart. The
disenfranchised factory workers have nothing left to lose.
Martel, the trade union rep with innumerable tattoos
and Bruce, the body-builder addicted to steroids, resort to
desperate measures. A bungled kidnapping on the streets
of Strasbourg goes horribly wrong and they find themselves
falling prey to the machinations of the criminal underworld.

Nicolas Mathieu received universal praise for his second
novel, *And Their Children After Them*, which won the most
prestigious literary prize in France, the Prix Goncourt.
His first novel, *Of Fangs and Talons*, introduces the social
and political fresco which heralded comparisons to Balzac
and Zola, and is a vivid portrait of those left behind.

'Nicolas Mathieu has written one of the
best crime novels of the year.'
Le Monde magazine

'A first novel of rare power'
Le Figaro Littéraire

SCEPTRE

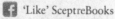
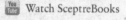